COOGAN'S BREAK

SIX PACK ONE : BOOKS 1-6

HOPE MALONE

Mandy is all about body positivity, refusing to hide her curves any longer. Logan is hiding from the world, his past, and especially his future.

ONE

LOGAN

After dumping my chainsaw in the back of the truck, I waste no time getting over to the fire pond. The sooner I can ditch my filthy uniform and wash away the sweat of the day, the better.

It's not until I'm standing naked on the side of the pond that I realize I forgot my towel. I guess I'm more tired than I realized. Still, it wouldn't be the first time I'd had to walk back to my truck bare-ass naked.

And anyway, my chances of running into anyone are slim, with no-one knowing about the boomerang-shaped pond that I'm aware of. Cheesy as it sounds; I consider it to be my special place, somewhere to come and unwind without the world constantly trying to interrupt.

Rather than wade slowly and painfully into the cold water, I walk out along a fallen tree and dive in where it's deeper. On hitting the water, every nerve ending in my body sparks; the electricity generated zinging through the top of my skull.

Damn, but that feels good.

In an instant, I'm no longer dirty or weary, and the water has restored my inner peace. You'd think after three years I'd have stopped giving Brooke Harrison head space, but I haven't. I can't.

At least when the upcoming fire season arrives, I'll be too busy to dwell on the past. It doesn't matter that I'm now employed as a forester rather than a firefighter. When I'm needed, I'm there.

I strike out for the elbow of the pond in an effortless crawl, deciding to make the most of my last days of self-imposed isolation. This has my thoughts drifting back to what should have been my wedding day.

I'm revisiting the scene from out front of the church when I swim straight into something, although a feminine shriek tells me it's a woman. Where the hell she's come from, I wouldn't have a clue. All I know is that my left hand is stuck firm in her long, dark hair.

When I try putting some distance between us, she shrieks again, this time in pain. Only then do I realize that it's my watch strap she's caught on. Unfortunately, the more she struggles, the worse the tangle gets.

"Calm down and stop moving, will you? You're caught on my watch."

My words must have been loud enough to cut through her panic, because she stops still. When she finally takes the time to look at me, there's a flash of recognition on her face.

Nope, never seen her before.

It isn't until she gasps I realize that in trying to stop myself from bumping into her, my free hand is all over one of her breasts. Well, mostly, because we're definitely talking more than a handful, here.

"Oh, sorry, sorry!"

The second I take my hand away, we bump together, telling me she's as naked as I am. Unable to stop myself, I peer beneath the water. I wonder if her nipples being pebbled are because of the cold water, or something else.

The water temperature, sure as hell, isn't affecting the erection I'm now working on. It only gets harder when I thump up against her sumptuous curves again.

Dammit, we're going to have to swim to the side and climb out if I'm to get us untangled. Once there, I won't have a hope in hell of hiding the state of my cock.

And knowing how she'll probably take that, I'm now extra pissed at having my solitude interrupted.

MANDY

Having to clear my throat for the third time in five minutes tells me I'm done for the day. Sure, it's easy enough to edit out all the extraneous noises, but I need to rest my voice. If I damage it, I can kiss goodbye to my career as a voice artist.

On moving back to Coogan's Break to help mom when my dad got sick, I'd been lucky I could work remotely. This helped financially and gave me a break from sitting at my dad's bedside as his life slipped away.

On shutting myself in the makeshift sound booth I'd set up in their basement, everything else faded into the background. No sick dad, no heartbroken mom, no foreboding of death.

After hanging up my headphones, I turn everything off in the small studio at the back of the cottage I now call home. It's been eighteen months since dad passed, and despite what mom says, she still enjoys having me near.

But not so near that we have to share a home.

I love my mom, but it was as if I was seventeen-years-old again. My bedroom hadn't changed since I'd gone off to college.

It was while studying economics and business at UCLA that I joined a local theater group. This led to voice-over work, something I was told I was a natural at. I'd been making enough freelancing to drop out, much to my parents' horror.

I've never regretted it, though; especially the freedom of working from home.

Despite a croaky voice, I've achieved more than I'd hoped for today. Usually a contract, like the one I'm working on for a home improvement vlog, would progress like molasses.

A quick check of the time says that if I'm to wash away the cares of the day, I'll need to hurry. I rarely work much past two o'clock, but when it's going well, I've learned to press on. It'll mean a lazy day tomorrow.

After locking the studio, I open the back gate onto the fire-break. This is all that's between my home and the forest, something that's both a blessing and a curse. While I love hearing the wind whistling through the trees, there's always the threat of fire.

I hold the gate open, waiting for Boston before I remember my Golden Retriever of ten years won't be joining me. Him having passed a month back, he's now keeping my dad company on the other side of the rainbow bridge.

I'm unable to stop a sniffle. But then I think of the two males who'd been such a big part of my life, enjoying zoomies together, and I break into a sad smile.

"Have fun, you two! Don't do anything I wouldn't."

My greeting is still ringing in my ears when I'm swallowed up by the trees. It's cooler in the shadow of these majestic monsters, but also louder. Bird song rings out as I zigzag my way through the trunks.

There isn't a trail and yet I know exactly where I'm going, and I have Boston to thank for this. It had been a year back that he'd slipped his leash when we were out for a walk. It wasn't long after I moved into the cottage, and so I'd freaked out in a big way.

On escaping, he'd gone from slow-old-dog to puppy in seconds, taking off as though his arthritis were a figment of the vet's imagination.

Thoughts of the damage he was doing, or him being lost in the woods, had me out of breath by the time I caught up with him.

He'd discovered an old fire pond and was frolicking in the shallows. As panicked and then annoyed as I'd been, I'd had to laugh as I watched him splashing about.

Of course, I'd also had to deal with his being a little slower on the way home. Despite this, it became a habit of ours at the end of my workday to hike to the pond for a swim. From what I could see, it hadn't made his arthritis any worse, and he loved it so.

On arriving at the pond, I have a quick check around before stripping off. Despite not having seen another soul since first finding it, I always check, especially with Boston no longer around, to act as my lookout.

The water is as cold as ever, but this doesn't stop me from floating on my back and gazing up at the old-growth redwoods. The other thing I love is the silence that descends when my ears are below the surface. All day I'm subjected to hearing my voice. A break from that and the constant chatter of the world is the perfect antidote.

I've been floating for five minutes at the most, when my shriek of surprise cuts through the quiet. When something yanks on the hair on the back of my head, I shriek even louder.

I'm freaking out until his, "Calm down!" breaks through my fear. He'd hardly do that if he was attacking me, would he?

It takes a second to get myself under control enough that I can even look at the guy. Then my biggest challenge isn't calming down, it's breathing. He's so familiar that it's as if I've run into an old friend or a celebrity, and yet I've never set eyes on him before.

It's also that this sense of familiarity is deeper than just how he looks. And, trust me; you don't forget a guy as drop-dead gorgeous as this one. At least, I wouldn't.

Transfixed as I am, it takes longer than it should to realize his free hand covers my left breast, and I gasp out. It's only when he removes it I see he wasn't fondling me as I'd thought. Our bodies bump together, and boom, he's hard up against me. And he's naked, too.

Now I'm curious, because, if his shoulders are anything to go by, the rest of him will be mighty fine, too. When we bump together again, I'm not as mad as I should be.

Actually, I'm not mad at all.

TWO

MANDY

I'm so busy wondering about what's hiding under the water that I have given no thought to how we'll actually untangle ourselves.

Especially not when all I want to do at this stage is *tangle* big time. Then I have to wonder how long it's been since I last *tangled*, certainly not since I got back to Coogan's Break.

"Come on, I've got a multi-tool in my shorts. I can use the scissors to cut us free."

He rolls onto his side and starts kicking, without waiting for me to agree to an emergency haircut. Instead, he drags me along in his wake thanks to his grip on the back of my neck.

It isn't until I've joined him in kicking that I realize this will see us both naked on the side of the pond. No water to hide under, just the two of us standing there with nothing on.

Okay, I can live with that. The question will be whether he can. Not all guys like curvy girls, and I'm definitely that. It's only on us awkwardly exiting the water together that I get a good look at the rest of the guy.

Seriously, he's got the body of a Greek god. And the cold water hasn't done him any harm in *that* department.

For me, hiding my arousal is as easy as crossing my arms over my breasts. He has no such chance with his erection. Instead, he simply ignores it.

I wish I could do the same. It's, ah, impressive. After we've both bent down so he can rummage through his short's pocket, I turn my back on him. This stops me from staring at his bits and makes it easier for him to separate us.

"Only cut what you have to."

"Right, I'm on it."

"I don't want a bald patch."

Rather than respond this time, he huffs out in what I'm thinking is annoyance. He follows this up by muttering as he works on the tangle, using what must be the world's smallest pair of scissors.

"Okay, we're done." He follows this up by holding a length of hair over my shoulder. "I only cut what I had to."

I take it off him and turn around, fighting to keep my eyes on his face. It's not exactly a chore, even if it is a challenge. Seriously, the guy is hot.

Despite us now being free to go our separate ways, he's not happy.

Actually, *not happy* is an understatement. The guy is furious. His brows knotted and his lips flat. The way his jawline is pulsing, says he's close to breaking a tooth.

"What the hell were you doing in there, anyway!?"

There's nothing polite about his question. Rather, it smacks of authority and has been loud enough that I take an involuntary step back.

"I would have thought it was obvious."

His uniform says he works for the forestry department, but does that give him the right to tell me to get lost? This is public land, not private.

"They'd blame us if anything were to happen to you while you were out here on your own." He reaches down and grabs his shorts off the ground. He drags them on without bothering with his underwear, which he stuffs in one pocket along with the multi-tool.

"You need to get out of here before I call headquarters."

His tone is brusque, his words clipped, and he hasn't let up on the grim looks he's been throwing in my direction. He's surely spouting BS. Unfortunately, there's no way I can prove it. My dad would have known if it was okay for me to be here.

"Now, go on, get out of here before I call this in."

I'm not sure what it is about his stance that sparks me off, but I'm flooded with memories of my dad. Either way, I'm mortified when tears prickle my eyes. Really, I'd been holding up so well until Boston passed away.

Rather than let Mr. Grumpy witness my tears, I throw the hank of hair in his face before rushing back into the pond. I then kick hard for the far end and my clothes.

On exiting the water again, I focus on holding myself tall, the water running down my back. I don't need to look back to know he's still looking at me, no doubt to make sure I leave as he's ordered.

And who the hell is he, anyway? Sure, he works for the forestry department, but other than that, I've not seen him around town. Coogan's Break is too darn small not to notice a man like that.

Even when consumed with grief at my dad's passing, I'd have noticed, if only cursorily. Still, he wouldn't be the first person to join the forestry service from out of town.

I then take my sweet time dressing in order to make a point. Like a striptease, but in reverse.

LOGAN

As I watch the stunning mystery woman dressing, I have to admire her resolve and her body. She's not hurrying. She's dragging it out, as if on purpose, and it's working with my erection, not going anywhere.

She's stacked, but in a good way, with those pearly orbs of hers matching an equally generous ass. On seeing her struggle to get into her clothes, it's apparent I'm not the only one who forgot to bring a towel. Would she have walked home naked if I hadn't been here?

It's a question that has my cock twitching in response and it's all I can do not to smile.

Only when she's disappeared into the surrounding redwoods, do I think back to the way I'd treated her. I hadn't meant to shout at her, but our collision had surprised me. The other surprise had been her voice. Deep and husky, it had been nothing like that breathy little girl voice Brooke had favored.

I can't believe I'd once found that attractive. Certainly all trace of it had been missing when she called me on the morning of our wedding to tell me she'd changed her mind.

So different, in fact, that for a moment I'd thought it was someone playing a trick on me, only it was no joke. She'd left it to me to show up at the church and tell everyone the wedding was off because my fiancé—ex-fiancé—was on her honeymoon at Lake Tahoe.

The one plus on that awful day had been that mom and dad weren't there to witness my ritual humiliation. Because Brooke changed the wedding date on no less than three occasions, my parents ended up being out of the country.

It was the same reason none of my friends from home were there to offer support, with it effectively a destination wedding for them. I'd truly been on my own that day, and if not for a few guys from work coming, I think I'd have done a runner, too.

Who knows why I've stayed at Coogan's Break. I'm not a local, originally being seconded here because of an out-of-control fire. I hadn't worked more than a couple of shifts when Brooke latched onto me, begging me to stay.

We were engaged in just shy of three months, and due to be married, two months, make that six weeks, nope, make it a month after that. Whirlwind was how Brooke described it to anyone who was interested, and even a few who weren't.

Disgraceful had been my mom's take on it when she eventually heard about it. She'd even asked me if Brooke was in the family way.

Now that I've lived here for as long as I have, the thought of returning to my hometown in Oregon has my gut in knots. Showing up still single after an engagement that had been the talk of the town would be hell.

Sure, the ribbing from old school friends and family would be good-natured, but it'd still hurt.

I'm back at my truck before I admit why it was I'd been so angry seeing that woman swimming in what I consider my piece of paradise. She'd invaded my space, a space I've worked hard to maintain. My unwanted reaction to her body only fueled my anger.

I don't seek company; I stick to myself, roughing it at any of the several look-out towers or cabins. And, if hikers have booked them, I've got a one-man tent I can use.

The most I see of my colleagues is at a weekly briefing meeting. I'll see more of them during the fire season, but then we're all too damned busy for chitchat and socializing.

It's been this way since I left the church on that fateful day. Being as I'd been living with Brooke at her apartment, staying on there wasn't an option.

It's a simple life, for sure, but one in which I can't get hurt, and with no chance of running into Brooke Harrison. Or worse, that loud-mouthed asshole she's married to.

THREE

I'm off to a slow start this morning, unlocking the door to my studio just after ten o'clock. My dreams being invaded as they had been by Mr. Grumpy Pants, sleep had been fleeting.

It would have been one thing if he was ugly, but how could so much nasty come in such a good-looking shell?

Sitting at my console, I take a fortifying sip of my coffee before opening my emails. I'd made it a rule from day one of working from my new home that I wouldn't have a computer in the house, and I've kept to it. When I leave the studio and walk back to my house, or to the pond, I want to leave work behind.

Can I even go to the pond again?

I am pretty sure I'm allowed to, but thoughts of having my private time interrupted by that man have me gritting my teeth. I'm busy seething when I open the first of a couple of emails from the day before. Annoyance turns to dismay in an instant.

"They're binning the home improvement vlog!?"

I've said this out loud, fully expecting Boston to come back with a growl of disapproval. He'd been able to pick up from my tone whether I was happy, sad, or annoyed, his response appropriate. He'd been such a clever pup.

I'm still reeling from the 'YOU'RE FIRED' email, when I open the next one, hoping for better news. I don't recognize who it's from, so that's potentially a good start.

After skimming over it, I lean forward in my chair to make sure I'm reading it correctly. Talk about a rollercoaster of emotions.

Sacked and hired in the space of two emails?

Okay, so it's only an interview at this stage, but as I continue reading, the knot of worry in my tummy unfurls with excitement. This could be a gigantic step up for me, and with the videos I'd be voicing part of an ongoing series, my income would be stable.

I could finally save up for those singing lessons my dad made me promise I'd get. Instead, I'd spent the money he gave me on vet bills for Boston. Something I've never regretted.

It's on reading the last line of the good news email that I squeak out in alarm. A quick look at my watch and I grab my coffee and drain it. I'll need that caffeine, and more, if I'm to make the appointment they've suggested.

Of all the mornings to sleep in.

A scant three hours later and I'm sitting in Chief Larson's office at fire headquarters, my chair tucked in behind the still open door. I'm on edge because of the interview when there's a loud knock on the door right next to me, and I'm momentarily off my seat.

Chief Larson looks up from flipping through my resume to address the new arrival. "Come on in, Logan, there's someone I'd like you to meet."

The ass that passes right in front of me at eye height is fine enough that my breath catches. I'm clearing my throat when the new arrival turns. On seeing who it is, I'm coughing hard enough my eyes water.

He—Logan—looks different with his clothes on, although his annoyance when he spots me is unchanged from the afternoon before.

LOGAN

I don't have a clue why Chief Larson has called me into the office. Until I walk in and hear someone spluttering behind me.

When I turn, anger flares in my chest. She made a complaint about my behavior yesterday? My reaction had been over-the-top, but to make an official complaint about it, really?

"Close the door and take a seat, Logan."

Yep, I'm about to get 'the talk'. Whether I'll lose my job over it, I wouldn't have a clue. I'm not going down without a fight, though. This alone has me sitting bolt upright in my seat, a posture that's being matched by the woman next to me.

It doesn't help that I've seen her buck naked, and liked it. This reminds me I'd been in a similar state. Sure, she'd seen I worked for the department because of my uniform, but I never told her my name.

"Mandy, I'd like you to meet Logan Young. He's one of our more qualified foresters. He's also got experience on the firefighting side of things. Logan, this is Mandy Gibson. You'll be working with her over the coming weeks."

Before I've responded, Mandy beats me to it.

"I, I've got the job?"

Not until I'm over my shock that we're to be working together, do I spit out, "You cannot be serious."

The thought of this woman trudging around weighed down by forty pounds of forest firefighting kit is laughable. She looks like she'd be more at home in my bed.

Damn it! Where the hell did that come from?

Chief Larson oscillates between Mandy and me, as if unsure whom he should address first. In the end, he answers her. "Yes, you coming in here was simply a formality. As soon as I heard you on that Tremaine Hardware 'How To' video, I knew you'd be perfect."

The old buzzard then winks at her, with even me surprised at my response. I know exactly what he's getting at about her voice, and I don't like it. That Mandy looks uncomfortable, adds to my ire.

It's just as well I've got questions, because I fire them at my boss. This soon stops him from looking at her like she's as bare as when I'd last seen her.

"Chief, you want to explain what this is all about? What job?"

I want to hear what his harebrained scheme is this time. Even if we're sadly lacking on the diversity front, we need to be realistic. To send this woman out to fight a fire would be foolhardy and potentially lift threatening.

It's a second before the Chief turns to face me. "Oh, yes, right?"

Rather than signing her on as a firefighter, he's investing in recruitment and induction videos to help boost numbers during the fire season. That's where her skills as a voice artist will come in.

Whether he'd decided on the expenditure before or after he'd heard her voice, he didn't say. But I've got my suspicions. Even after he's finished going through his ground-breaking plan, I'm still in the dark as to my involvement.

"But what do the videos have to do with me? Last time I checked, I was up-to-date with all my training."

Chief Larsen slaps his hands down on his desk. "Exactly, Logan. Extensive training is the key. And that makes you the perfect person to take Mandy here through her induction."

I stop staring at our newest recruit long enough to glare at the chief. "Her what?"

Mandy looks as confused as I am, with her, "My what?" coming out far squeakier than I would have thought her melodious voice would allow.

It appears neither of us is happy with the chief's plans.

FOUR

MANDY

The following day and I'm still reeling about the job offer. I'd said I'd think about it over the weekend, because why would I put myself through that?

The induction, as outlined in the interview, doesn't sound like a lot of fun. Logan, in particular, had been keen to stress what a challenge I'd find it. "Potentially impossible" had been his opinion of my chances of completing it.

If not for my bewilderment, I'd have enjoyed the chief trying to downplay things in response to Logan's up-scaling of them. As it was, I'd sat watching them back and forth like a tennis match.

Personally, I don't think it's necessary for me to undergo the full induction in order to produce an interesting voice-over. And then I think about spending days on end with Logan, undecided if this would be a plus or a minus.

Sure, he's easy on the eye, but do I really want to be around that much negative energy? The man has issues; around women is my suspicion. "It would be fun winding him up, though."

If Boston was here, he'd now be barking in delight. "You know what, Boston, you're right. I should take the job."

After all, it's not every day a girl gets to spend time with a hot guy AND get paid for it. I don't give myself a moment to think about it. I reply to the original email saying I'll take the job and look forward to hearing more, adding my phone number to speed things up.

Fifteen minutes later, I get a call from Logan, and he's not a happy camper. Clipped as they are, his words lack warmth. As soon as I hear what's up first in the induction, I know what he's got planned.

"I'll pick you up at six-thirty tomorrow morning. Be ready!"

I'm not given the opportunity to delay the trip until the Monday, or even negotiate a later start; he ends the call without giving me the chance.

I stare at my phone for a second before grinning. "Oh, and it is game on!"

Logan wants to show me one of their forest towers so he can go through what they're for, and some history around them. The early call time and that he's chosen the Bean Rock Tower let me know he plans on forcing me to quit.

And that is so not happening. I'm not my father's daughter for nothing.

The tower Logan has picked for our first outing is a good six hours from the nearest trailhead, meaning it'll be an overnighter. Something Logan has neglected to tell me.

My bet is that he'll rock up at my place tomorrow morning, say I'm woefully unprepared, and abort the trip.

I spend the rest of the day checking through all my gear, making sure I pack everything I'll need, and then some. Some might say I'm being petty, but he started it.

After getting to bed reasonably early, it takes a while to fall asleep. Every time I shut my eyes, I can see Logan as he'd been when we clambered out of the fire pond. Wet, naked, and smoking hot, if such a combination is technically possible.

That'd make him steamy, wouldn't it? Okay, that works, too.

Despite the man being annoying, there's no getting past the fact he's also good looking, with a body to die for, or even over.

The following morning, I'm up showered and waiting out front of my place when Logan pulls up in a forestry department truck.

On putting my backpack in the tray, I notice it's bigger than his. This only reinforces my suspicions that he expects to drop me home later today, and that he's packed accordingly.

I jump in next to him, greeting him with a cheery hello and a big smile. I wouldn't usually be so 'bubbly' in the morning, but he asked for it.

Once again, I'm subjected to his intense scrutiny, my body instantly heating in response. I need to get a grip; the guy hasn't even spoken yet.

I also register when he takes in my outfit. As tempting as it had been to dress in something inappropriate simply to irritate him, I've dressed for hiking and comfort.

The second my seat belt is secure, Logan stomps on the gas and I'm pressed back into my seat. Hah, it looks as if I've pushed a few buttons already. My smile only widens when he drives to the trailhead that's farthermost from the tower we're heading for.

He is in for one hell of a surprise. Curvy doesn't mean unfit or lazy.

LOGAN

On the drive over to Mandy's place, I'm still as angry as I'd been when I realized I couldn't get out of babysitting her.

I've done my best to avoid women, not to have one foisted on me for however long it will take to induct her. The last thing I need is to be stuck with one who affects me as much as she does.

I'd argued with the chief after she'd left, but the old guy wouldn't budge. He said I had the best all-round experience and my workload was the lightest of anyone at present. When he'd started hinting that my job could be on the line if I refused, I'd shut my mouth.

His last instruction as I'd stormed out of his office was to 'make it fun for her'.

Fine, if the boss wants her inducted, I'll induct her alright, and she'll have so much *fun*, she won't last the first day. Hell, I'm going to make it so much *fun* that she'll bail before lunch.

Even better will be if she's slept in, meaning I can wait a couple of minutes and then drive off. I'll tell the chief she'd been a no show, and that it wasn't appropriate to drag her out of bed. I then annoy myself more by visualizing that very thing, with her once again gloriously naked.

On turning into her street, I spot her standing on the sidewalk. My ire only increases when I see the size of her pack. She looks to be prepared for an overnighter, unlike me.

I stomp on any thoughts of us spending the night together, along with the brakes, pulling up next to her with a squeak of tires.

I'm about to get out to load her backpack into the tray of the truck when she lifts it in herself. It's an enormous pack, so given how easily she's handled it, it's more than likely full of a dollar-store sleeping bag. The cheaper the bag, the more space it takes up, or so it seems.

I give into an evil grin. If she thinks I'm sharing, she's in for a big surprise. That's if we'll need provisions. By my reckoning, I'll be dropping her back home in six hours, seven at the most.

All Machiavellian thoughts halt when she climbs in all smiles and sunshine. My body's reaction whenever she is near irritates me. I haven't so much as looked at a woman since Brooke decided my prospects didn't match the lifestyle she'd planned for herself.

I'm thinking I've got my body under control when Mandy sings along with the song on the radio. Her voice is sultry, the notes pure as they wind their way inside me, seeking all the dark spots. I reach over and wrench the radio off, the cab quiet but for the roar of the engine and rumble of the road under the tires.

It's not until we climb out of the truck at the trailhead that I see Mandy's boots. It's obvious they've seen a lot of miles. What I don't know is whether Mandy is the one responsible. Only adding to my suspicions is the weight of her pack when I remove it from the tray of the truck.

It mightn't be as easy to deter this woman as I've thought.

FIVE

MANDY

I wouldn't usually whistle and chatter, preferring the quiet of the woods. However, Logan's shoulders hunching up around his ears whenever I burst out, is satisfying me to no end.

Plus, it tells him I'm not out of breath, that I'm enjoying the hike, and that his plan to exhaust me is a bust. When we hit a fork in the track and he opts to go left, I decide to wind him up even further. Find another button to push.

"Oh, lovely, we're going the long way. It's so much prettier this way."

He stops so suddenly that I crash into him. It's only him spinning and grabbing hold of me that stops me from taking a tumble down the steep bank next to the trail.

And just like that, jammed up against his hard chest, my thoughts have me back at the pond, both of us naked, skin on skin. As I look up at him, I'm out of breath, my heart thundering, my body buzzing like never.

Of more interest is that Logan appears similarly affected. His moss green eyes are no longer as guarded, especially not as he drops his gaze to look at my breasts.

He's lowering his lips to mine when he catches himself.

Then his eyes dim, and he drops me like I'm hot, before edging around me on the uphill side of the trail and retracing his steps. I'm expecting him to head back to the truck, but he shoots off up the track that leads directly to the fire tower.

I have to dig deep to keep up with him, weighed down as I am by my backpack. It's a far cry from Logan's daypack. It's going to be an interesting night, that's for sure.

I reach the fire tower not long after him, although he does his best to ignore me, staring fixedly at the ridgeline opposite. I'm scrambling up the steps that wind their way around the outside of the tower when I see Logan shove his hands deep inside his trouser pockets.

Hmmm, someone looks to be making room for something. There's no stopping the image this evokes of me straddling him and taking my fill.

On reaching the window-lined viewing platform atop, my dirty thoughts have my arousal in full swing. My seeing there's only the one bed does nothing to cool it.

How on earth could I have forgotten that about this tower? Despite not having spent the night here, I've still seen pictures of it online.

What happens now? Are we meant to share? I doubt that's what Captain Serious has in mind. He's fought me every inch of the trip to remain distant, both physically and metaphorically.

One thing is for sure, though; I'm definitely not sleeping on the floor. This sees me dump my pack next to the bed and set about digging out my sleeping bag.

When Logan finally puts in an appearance, I've got it out of the compression sack and am fluffing it up.

He freezes inside the doorway. I guess he'd forgotten this tower only has the one bed, too.

Or maybe he thought we wouldn't make it this far.

Or that he'd arrive first and claim the bed for himself, leaving me to sleep on the floor. Hah, as if I'd let him get away with that. Either way, I have to keep my back to him to keep my thoughts to myself.

It's all I can do to keep a straight face when I then move onto a late lunch. On lifting the lid on a plastic container, I make a production out of sniffing the bacon and egg pie I'd picked up from Skye High Pies the day before.

Even a day old, it still smells wonderful enough that I can hear someone's tummy rumbling on the other side of the room.

LOGAN

As I watch Mandy taking in the view while eating her lunch, I'm angry, although mostly at myself for underestimating the woman.

It's a mistake I won't make again, even if all I can do as I stare at her back is wonder how soft her ass is. Probably not soft at all, given how quickly she'd made it up the steep part of the trail to the tower.

And strangely, I find I'm okay with the idea of tight muscles hiding under that cushiony softness. It's just another way in which Mandy is a polar opposite of Brooke. The only time I'd taken Brooke to visit one of the towers, it had been an unmitigated disaster.

First off, she'd refused to carry anything other than a stupid pink backpack only big enough to hold her make-up. Yep, my little princess managed the entire weekend with a full face of war paint. Apparently, her followers on social media would leave in droves if they saw what she really looked like.

The plan had been to spend a few nights at the tower. We'd lasted one. A night ruined by her constant sniping, about anything and everything. Strangely, none of this had shown in the Instagram posts about our *amaze-balls trip*.

On thinking back, I wonder if that weekend and the lead up to our wedding had been more about social media content than love.

Despite my trying to make the rest of the day arduous and boring, there have been no complaints from Mandy. Not even when I showed her how the Osborne Fire-Finder worked. Instead, she'd hung on my every word, and even asked intelligent questions.

She hadn't so much as peeped when I told her how to clean out the composting toilet in the small building at the base of the tower. In fact, after she'd finished, she'd said it wasn't as gross as she'd been expecting.

As I watch her preparing her dinner, I'm having difficulty swallowing the mouthful of protein bar I'm working on. I'm also struggling to stop comparing my protégé to my ex-fiancé. How can it be possible for two women to be more different from each other?

- Physique?
- Ethics?
- Human kindness?
- Not being a complete bitch?

The list is almost as long as the tightly wound plait running down the middle of Mandy's back. Thoughts of tugging her hair free and running my fingers through it swarm my brain, and I have to turn away. It doesn't help that I've been as good as living the life of a monk for years.

Only when she turns to face me do I see she's holding two battered titanium plates. She hands one to me, along with a set of matching cutlery. Our hands touch when I take it, and I could swear I've just received an electric shock.

It's enough of a shock that I immediately sit, hoping to hide my body's reaction.

On seeing what she pulls out of her pack next, I know she's suckered me on so many levels, and that I've only got myself to blame. My anger had blinded me to the obvious.

SIX

MANDY

I have to admit, I'm enjoying the trip for more than just an opportunity to annoy Logan. We'd spent the afternoon with him telling me all about the history of the fire towers, something he appears passionate about.

It was also something that saw us bumping into each other more than once in the confines of the viewing platform. While there'd been nothing sexual about this, that hadn't stopped my body from humming in response.

When going over many things I already knew, Logan had lost that haunted look, his eyes sparkling rather than dead. It would appear there's a heart underneath all that muscle, after all. Who knew?

Despite dad having worked for the forestry for a time, and me growing up in the area, it's the first time I've spent the night at one of the towers. My preference is to sleep in a tent among the trees where there's some protection from the strong winds you can encounter this high up.

By late afternoon, temperatures have fallen. It's something I've been expecting having checked the weather yesterday. This, as much as anything, had dictated what I'd packed.

Being February, sunset is just after six, with Logan closing all the windows and the door before flicking on the solar powered lights. It's this or we'll have more nightlife inside the tower than there is out.

As I set up my small camp stove and go about getting dinner ready, I'm conscious of his scrutiny. I can't help but reflect on whether he likes what he sees. These are thoughts I'd never have entertained when I'd first met him at the pond.

Dinner is of the dehydrated variety, with a few fresh ingredients and spices added to take things up a notch. Despite these meals having come a long way, they always taste better with some culinary help.

His face is a picture when I turn and hand him a plate of food. I know it'll be welcome, with him apparently only having granola bars and trail mix with him. I doubt very much he's got a sleeping bag.

When our hands touch, there's a belt of energy that shoots up my arm. That this then immediately heads south has me freezing for a second to process it.

Sheesh, I need to get a grip. We aren't going anywhere. There is no WE.

When I pull the bottle of 2019 California Syrah and a corkscrew out of my pack, there's no missing the muttering coming from behind me. On my handing Logan a titanium beaker of wine, I know I've taken him unawares, again.

This is yet more evidence of him thinking I wouldn't last the distance and us being back in town by now. Well, he won't be sleeping in his own bed tonight.

All that remains to be seen is whether he'll be sharing mine.

Time and a sharp drop in temperatures will soon tell. If the forecast is right, it's going to be a chilly one tonight. In the meantime, my temperature is heading in the other direction.

I'm putting it down to the warming effects of the wine when I see Logan looking at me, and I know alcohol has nothing to do with it.

LOGAN

As I take a sip of wine before tucking into a meal that wouldn't look out of place on a cooking show, I'm kicking myself. I'm also back to comparing Mandy to Brooke.

The meal is delicious and a far cry from the granola bars I'd been facing with my not having packed properly. It's for this reason I don't have a sleeping bag with me. I have to shake my head at my stupidity.

Wrapped up in flashbacks and anger, I hadn't prepared for the trip like I usually would. Such a rookie mistake and not one I should make with my years working in these woods.

As it is, I'm in for one rough night. There's not a chance I'm sharing that bed with Mandy. I'm only human and as it is, the blasted woman has had me sporting a semi most of the day.

There's something about her that appeals at a primal level, perhaps even borderline caveman. I've only got to glance in her direction to imagine her writhing under me on a bearskin rug, a fire blazing in the background.

At lights out, I'm still being bombarded by erotic images of Mandy. Unless I can clear my mind, I won't get any sleep.

I'm doing my best to get comfortable in my foil emergency bag on the drafty wooden floor when Mandy explodes.

"Oh, for goodness' sake, I can't sleep with you thrashing about in that thing. It's like sharing a room with a blasted baked potato." She flicks on the small camp light hanging on the head of the bed. "Get up off that floor and into this bed."

Her voice catches on the last word, as though realizing what she's telling me to do. She wipes her forehead with the heels of her hands, before adding, "I do not want to be dealing with you being hypothermic in the morning."

She then shimmies to the far side of the bed. Her invitation being pragmatic with an edge of annoyed, I'm quick to take her up on it, or as quickly as I can. It's only on standing that I realize exactly how stiff and cold I already am.

A squawk from Mandy confirms just how cold I am when I roll against her on the narrow bed. I'm doing my best to get back into the survival bag when she huffs out in annoyance.

"It's just as well this sleeping bag opens out."

After unzipping her bag completely, she throws it over the top of both of us before rolling onto her side, away from me.

I roll the other way, trying to keep as far from her as possible, with the temptation to turn my dreams into reality ever present. And there's no way I'm opening myself up to that sort of heartache again.

Ten minutes pass and despite having the sleeping bag over the top of me, I'm no warmer than I was when I got into bed. I must have chilled myself more than I thought. When a shiver wracks me, I hear a heavy sigh from the other side of the bed.

Mandy followed this up by rolling over and jamming herself hard up against my back. She even wraps an arm around my waist and shoves one of her thighs between my legs to get closer still.

Despite knowing she's only doing it to warm me up, my body has other ideas. Her leg is tight up against my balls. How the hell am I supposed to react? On slowing my breathing to kill off my growing erection, I notice Mandy's heart beating against my back.

Interesting. It would appear I'm not alone in being affected by our closeness. I'm even giving consideration to rolling over when I notice Mandy's heartbeat slowing. A change in her breathing then tells me she's nodded off.

That was close.

Eventually my erection eases and I'm warm enough that my lids get heavy and I close my eyes. This would usually have my mind full of images of Brooke in that ridiculously expensive wedding dress. The dress that I'd help pay for. The one she'd worn when marrying that mega rich asshole in my stead.

Her YouTube post chronicling the joyful event had been, in her words, 'epic'. It had also been borderline infomercial, given the amount of product placement.

Only that's not what I see tonight. Rather, I'm subjected to a series of snapshots of Mandy as she'd climbed regally out of the fire pond, water streaming down her luscious curves.

I like the new slide show better than the old one, and for the first time in years, I fall asleep smiling.

SEVEN

MANDY

Despite being fully clothed, I'm freezing when I wake in the morning, thanks to Logan hogging more than his half of the sleeping bag. I yank it back over myself and turn away from him, not surprised I can see my breath.

It's a lot colder than the weather forecast led me to believe. It looks as if I'll be wearing everything I brought with me back down to the trailhead.

The room, consisting mostly of single pane glass, means it'll likely be as cold inside as it is out. Until the sun puts in an appearance over the hills behind us, I'm staying exactly where I am.

As I lay waiting for sleep to reclaim me, I'm all too conscious of the heat rolling off Logan in waves. What is it about guys that they keep so warm? And yet he'd been icy when I made him get into bed last night.

What a fool he was to come so unprepared. It made a mockery of him showing me the ropes. Instead, it had been the other way around, and if not for me, he'd have spent a miserable night. He was just lucky I didn't let his animosity stop me from helping him out.

Not exactly a hardship sharing a bed with him, though. I'm close to falling back to sleep when Logan rolls over and jams himself tight against my back. I can tell by his breathing that he's still asleep, even if parts of him are up and raring to go.

When his arm snakes around my waist and cups one of my breasts, I'm torn. Do I wake him up and tell him to keep his hands to himself?

Or do I lie there and make the most of it?

In the end, I can't do it. If the circumstances were different, I'd be all over it. However, it wouldn't be fair to Logan, and would make today incredibly awkward.

I'm inching the sleeping bag to the side, in readiness to slide out from under his arm when he tweaks my nipple. It doesn't matter that I'm still wearing a bra, t-shirt, and even a hoodie, that zing goes straight to where it shouldn't, my gasp loud enough to wake Logan.

I know he's awake because his hand has stilled and he's lying next to me as if frozen.

Damn, this is going to be embarrassing for both of us.

LOGAN

I'm not sure what wakes me. Was it the loud gust of wind or was it realizing one of my hands is full of a deliciously plump breast? Add in the erection I'm currently jamming into Mandy's ass, and I doubt she's asleep either.

Her broken breathing, the tightness of her nipple and her moan when I unconsciously roll it between my fingers, say otherwise.

She rolls onto her back, allowing me to leave my hand right where it is. I gently squeeze her nipple again, all while observing her reaction, unsure of myself.

It's been too long since I was with a woman.

When thoughts of Brooke crowd my fevered brain, I studiously ignore them. Mandy is no substitute or an easy way to help me forget. As short as our acquaintance has been, I know she's worth more than that. There's nothing of Brooke about her.

I gently roll her nipple again, my eyes never leaving hers. "You like that?" I sure as hell know I do.

Mandy's nod is tentative; her gaze as she runs it over my face and chest is not. This has me looking more closely at her. "You're wearing far too many clothes."

She looks a little unsure of herself, so I decide to up the ante.

"I want to draw your right nipple into my mouth and suck on it until it's a bright cherry red." Her intake of breath has her close to coughing. "And then I'll move on to the other one. And then…"

Her breathing is now shallow as she waits for my next dirty promise.

"And then I'm going to run my tongue down your body until…"

Mandy's eyes are wide as she swallows deeply before whispering, "Until?"

"Until you're not cold anymore."

Despite our fumbling under the sleeping bag being akin to a couple of teenagers making out, Mandy is as womanly as they come. And if I have my way, she will, and soon.

For now, I take my time exploring her sweet curves, fulfilling my earlier promises. On lifting my head from where it's nestled between her rosy thighs, I'm met with the magnificent sight of her cherry red nipples.

She's so responsive that even pulling on her nipples with my teeth had her calling my name. She'd begged for the release we both knew was coming, but not just yet. Good things take time.

After pushing her knees up and to the sides, I spread her wide to feed on her swollen depths. I find I enjoy hearing her screaming my name, wanting her to drown out the wind howling around our haven.

I get my wish soon enough, with Mandy vibrating beneath my lips, my name on hers as the climax I've gifted her rips through her body.

Before it dies away completely, I plunge two fingers deep inside her, stretching her, all the while sucking hard on that little bundle of nerves. Yet again, I claim her as mine. Her cries of pleasure whipped away by the wind.

After crawling back up the bed, I drag her into my arms and hold her tight. I'm wondering what will happen now when I detect voices far below. It's something that has Mandy freeze, before struggling to get out of bed.

While I'm still fully clothed, she's naked. Wonderfully so in my mind, but I can see why she wouldn't want to get caught fooling around with me.

EIGHT

MANDY

I'm luxuriating in the afterglow of a double climax and being tucked up in Logan's arms when I notice voices, as in three or four of them. A quick flash of what they'd have seen if they'd turned up a couple of minutes back has me panicking.

I don't want to be caught like this. Coogan's Break is too small for that. I'm upright before my recently climaxed legs are ready for it, and I drop back to the mattress with a bounce. I don't let it slow me, though, dragging my clothes on as quickly as I can.

Whoever it is must have been camping nearby. If not, they'd have had to leave the nearest trailhead in the middle of the night. On listening to the inane chatter as they climb, I doubt they're that committed. Ill-prepared hikers would be my best guess.

The tower being as high as it was, I've got a head start on them. Time to throw on some clothes and be firing up the camp stove when they stumble into the relative warmth of the viewing platform.

It's slowly heating thanks to the sun, and Logan and my earlier antics. Even thinking back has my core body temperature jumping a degree or two.

I'd been right about them coming from a campsite nearby and to them being freezing and miserable. However, the little blonde who's last through the door perks up no end when she spots Logan dragging himself out of bed.

She then looks at me, and I know exactly what's on the checklist she's currently working through.

- He's with her?
- He's too good for her.
- He's perfect for me.
- This trip just got interesting.

And more than likely in that order, too.

The only plus is that Logan still has his clothes on from the day before, and when he sees he's being undressed, his defenses go up. Just as well I made the most of it while I could. Whatever had happened in Logan's past has done enough damage that he and I were only ever going to be an interlude.

I'm surprised at how much this saddens me.

On watching Blondie circling her prey, I have to agree the petite blonde looks better next to Logan than I do. Over breakfast, it's arranged that Logan and I will help them back to their vehicle by the quickest route possible.

So much for us spending another night up here, something I'd been entertaining.

The walk back to their car is painful. This isn't because I'm finding the going hard, but that Blondie is sticking to Logan like a hospital-strength plaster. Nor do I miss her passing her number over when we arrive at their vehicle.

Neither does the guy I suspect she had attached herself to for the overnight hike.

The thing that hurts most is that rather than hand it back, Logan stashes her number in the pocket of his shirt. I don't bother waiting to see their vehicle disappear down the gravel road; I turn back into the woods.

The sooner we're back at Logan's truck, the sooner I can get home and lick my wounds. It doesn't matter that I've only got myself to blame. Being rejected for a sleeker model still stings.

LOGAN

I'd call the hikers idiots but for them having entered the wilderness better prepared than I was. Instead, I turn to find Mandy is no longer behind me, although I can see her disappearing into the trees. This has me jogging to catch up, asking her what the hurry is.

"I need to get home. I've got projects I have to tidy up before I can start on the induction videos." Her response has been brief, polite, and not encouraging of a rejoinder.

I fall into step behind her; mesmerized by the bounce of her ass. After the chirpy blonde, Mandy is cool, with our walk back to my truck a somber affair compared to when we'd headed to the tower just the day before.

Mandy's ass is all action. Unfortunately, her shoulders are tight and her posture ramrod straight, and despite not having had a lot to do with women over the past three years, I know exactly what it means.

What I can't understand is why she's like this and why it annoys me as much as it does. Wasn't this exactly what I'd wanted to happen on setting out early the day before?

On reaching the truck, I grab the keys out of my backpack and open the doors. It's not until I'm doing up my seat belt I hear the crinkle of the scrappy piece of paper with the blonde's phone number on it.

To avoid it going through the wash, I take it out and stuff it in the center console. I don't know what to make of Mandy's 'humph'.

If I thought the walk back from the tower was awkward, it's nothing on the drive from the trailhead to Mandy's place. She doesn't say a word. Not one. I honestly didn't think things went that badly this morning.

I'm unaware of having said this aloud until her sharp intake of breath. The way she then crosses her arms tight across her chest, tells me to shut my mouth and keep it that way.

She needs time to cool down. Although again, wasn't this exactly what I wanted?

On pulling up at her place, she's got her seatbelt undone and is out of the cab before I've turned the engine off. When she makes quick work of grabbing her backpack out of the truck's tray and disappearing through the front gate, I take off.

My departure was as hasty as hers had been.

It's all good; I know when I've outstayed my welcome.

NINE

MANDY

I'm back at forest headquarters later in the week for a meeting with Chief Larsen. He wants to let me know what part of the induction I'll be undertaking next.

As bad as things had ended with Logan, the job pays too well for me to give up. Much as I want to tell the chief he needs to find someone else, I can't. Professional pride won't let me.

Even my pride is yelling 'NO!' I'll just have to have to suck it up and deal with Logan as best I can.

However, on being shown into Chief Larsen's office, it isn't Logan who's sitting in the second visitor's chair. Instead, it's an older man who reminds me of my late dad. Roger will take over from Logan after his resignation the day before.

"His what?" I only become aware I've shouted at the chief when he holds his hands up defensively. I have a magnificent set of lungs on me.

"Hey, I'm as surprised as anyone. I thought he was a career man. Just shows you what I know. Did anything happen on the trip that I should know about?"

Because of the amount of concealer I'd slathered on to hide the shadows beneath my eyes, I doubt my blush shows, although my stammer is telling, at least to me.

I go through everything, neglecting to tell the chief that Logan had been ill-prepared for an overnight trip. Just because he's resigned to avoid being with me, that's no need to tell tales about him to his old boss.

The chief nods after I've finished, giving nothing away. "It's a mystery. Anyway, Roger here has a wealth of experience at his fingertips, and he won't have you traipsing around like young Logan did." He shakes his head before continuing. "I still can't believe the boy dragged you all the way up to old Beanie."

On him checking me over, I know exactly what he's thinking, although I keep my thoughts on his assumptions to myself.

Bite your tongue. You've heard it all before.

When I become aware Roger is also scrutinizing me, I throw my hands up in despair. "Don't let appearances fool you. I've been hiking the back hills since I was seven and know my limitations. Bean Rock sure isn't it." I stare each man down until they're suitably chastised.

Never again will I have someone making me feel less because I'm a curvy girl. Never.

After making a time to meet up with Roger the next day, I'm back out in reception. I need to tidy the pile of paperwork he's given me if I'm to avoid dropping it on the way to my car.

It's while doing this that I overhear the receptionist talking to a forestry ranger. I'm still eavesdropping on their conversation when the double front doors swish open.

And who should swan in but the young blonde hiker who we'd met up at the tower, although she couldn't look more different? Make-up heavy, hair fluffed, skirt short, it's an outfit designed to attract male attention with the forest ranger's mouth dropping open and his eyes bulging.

Unlike her, I'm dressed in a dark brown trouser suit that has me blending into the wooden paneling. And because I've been head-down sorting through the papers, I'm invisible.

"Ah hi," says the young hiker to the receptionist, her voice as squeaky as I remember. "Has Logan left any messages for me?"

The pile of papers I'm riffling through forgotten, I look over, my breath held as I wait on the receptionist to respond.

"No honey, he hasn't." The receptionist then holds her hand up, "And before you ask, again, I have passed your number on to him, several times, in fact."

"Okay, I guess he's just busy." The girl leaves without once looking in my direction.

Perhaps it's because I've been as quiet as I have, that the receptionist speaks as freely as she does. "Honestly, she's phoned three or four times a day since Monday. Now she's fronting up. I told Logan, and he wants nothing to do with her. Wouldn't you think she'd have caught on by now?"

The ranger, distracted as he is by the young woman trotting across the parking lot, doesn't immediately answer. Only after she's roared off does he turn back to the receptionist.

"I doubt she'd be interested in visiting him at the old 473 hut, either. Not high-end enough for the likes of her."

Because of the 473 assigned to the hut, I've got a vague idea of where it is. I'm probably one of the few members of the public who would, with me having learned a lot about the forest from my dad. He hadn't always worked for the county and had spent many a year working as a firefighter during the season.

To actually find the darn thing, I'll need his old maps, resulting in an immediate visit to my mom. I'll also ask if she knows anything about Logan. Until bumping into him in the fire pond, I'd never seen him before. And despite the sense of familiarity I'd experienced, you don't forget someone like Logan in a hurry.

As it is, he's occupied my mind for the past three days, no matter how hard I tried to rid it of images of him and that little blonde. The sooner I catch up with him again, the better.

On leaving my mom's, I know the hut is close to the fire pond. I've also got a good idea of why Logan is as prickly as he is with women. And thanks to my high school memories of Brooke Harrison, I can't blame Logan for wanting to avoid town.

The woman was, and I should imagine still is, toxic. Her and her BFF, Sylvia Chamberlain, made life hell for more than a few girls in my year. Thankfully, I'd never attracted their attention.

LOGAN

Lying back on the lumpy cot at the hut, I'm doing my best to focus on what the future holds. If I take a job in town, my chances of running into Brooke and her ass of a husband regularly are greater than I'd like.

Nuts, but Mandy's rejection after we'd left the hikers at their vehicle had hurt almost as much as Brooke's dumping of me. I thought by now I'd be immune to that kind of pain.

In an instant, I'm back where I was after that phone call from Brooke on what was supposed to be my wedding day. Strange, but I can't see myself ever being married now, with thoughts of a full-blown church ceremony enough to give me heartburn.

I'm still lying there, staring at the rafters, when I hear movement outside. I'm on my feet in an instant, armed with a large can of bear spray. There's only one guy knows I'm staying out here, and he's told me he'll leave me to my own devices, that I can call him if I need anything.

The small hut isn't on any maps that I know of. This leaves a visit from something large and furry, my options being coyote, cougar, black bear, or deer. They're all easy enough to take care of, except for the bear.

And while it'd be a piece of cake to put a bullet between its eyes, I'd rather send it on its way than make a rug out of it.

A quick look around and I see nothing to interest a bear. I'd even been careful not to use any deodorant after my swim/bath this morning.

"Logan, are you in there?"

What the heck does she want? Damn it all to hell, I'd rather face down a bear.

On opening the rickety door, I'm scowling, with Mandy taking a step back. Her eyes widen when she spots the can of bear spray I'm still holding.

"I don't work for them anymore. We're done." I try shutting the door, but in a move perfected by door-to-door salespeople the world over, she jams her foot in the way.

"No, we're not done, Logan. Not by a long shot."

Her husky voice ripples right through me, again penetrating my defenses. It's been this way since that first time I heard her in the fire pond. Apparently, it doesn't matter whether one, or both of us, is naked, the result is still the same.

She takes a deep breath before she speaks again. "I heard about the number Brooke Harrison did on you." I'm close to turning her around and sending her on her way when she adds. "Hah, I'll bet she's regretting that now."

Mandy's grin is evil enough that I find myself curious.

"You'd better come in. It's not much, but ... it's not much."

TEN

MANDY

With Logan taking up most of the basic cot, I perch on the edge of the dodgy looking chair plonked at the end. I hope it doesn't give out on me, because it's in as rough a shape as the primitive cot that creaks every time Logan moves.

No wonder they don't list this dump on any of the modern maps. The only thing it's fit for is to be torched, although not recommended given its location.

After looking at dad's old map at mom's this morning, I'd known where to look for the hut. It hadn't been easy actually finding it, because of how well it's camouflaged.

Years of lichen and moss covered the rough wooden shelter, with it blending perfectly into the surrounding trees and ferns. If not for the map, I could just as easily have walked right by it.

I don't bother with niceties, instead rattling through everything I know about Brooke, not giving Logan a chance to interrupt. I suspect there are things about his ex-fiancé he doesn't know, but that he should.

When I finally fall silent, he runs his fingers through his hair, mussing it up. "Until she dumped me, I thought she was okay. I thought *we* were okay."

"Hey, you aren't the only one to be taken in by her. Word on the street is that her husband is miserable." I laugh with delight before adding. "So is she, since he confiscated her credit cards."

This is all news to Logan, but the more I tell him, the less haunted his eyes are. This is especially so when I drop the bomb that the new husband neglected to get Brooke to sign a pre-nup.

"Hah, more fool him. She's damned expensive to maintain." He quiets for a second. "Although it explains why the hell she was in such a hurry to drop me and marry him. I'll bet she put the pressure on big time."

When Logan's laughter rings out, it's rusty. A quality I'd love to see gone completely. Luckily, I have the perfect thing to hand.

When I'd picked up the bottle of bubbly and multi-pack of plastic flutes, I had given no thought to missing out on breakfast.

I hadn't been able to stomach anything that morning. My tummy had been in knots at the idea of facing Logan at that meeting. And after hearing what my mom had to say, I'd been too excited to eat.

Her local knowledge answered so many of the questions my subconscious had been firing at me over the preceding three days. With everything having gone down while I was still living in LA, I'd missed all the excitement. And with Logan having dropped off the map after the break-up, the gossip had soon died down.

Under Logan's watchful gaze, I have a quick rummage in my small

backpack. Then, like something out of a Vegas magic show, I lift the bubbly and plastic glasses out with a flamboyant "Voila!"

The surprise on Logan's face says I might just as well be holding up a rabbit, although he doesn't comment.

The glasses held gently between my knees, I set about loosening the cork while watching Logan carefully. I'm waiting for him to tell me to get lost, but he doesn't. He stays quiet.

Not until I've filled both glasses and put the bottle on the dirt floor, do I speak. "I propose we toast your lucky escape."

His brow wrinkles in confusion. "My what?"

"Lucky escape!" When he still looks confused, I add, "From getting yourself hitched to Brooke Harrison."

His reaction says I'm probably the first person to treat his being dumped on his wedding day as a good thing. It's perhaps this that has him taking the brimming glass and tentatively proposing a toast.

"Here's to, ah, lucky escapes."

I clink my glass dully against his before repeating his toast. "To lucky escapes."

After we've both taken a sip, we sit there grinning at each other like fools.

A few more sips—okay, most of the bottle—and we're looking at each other differently.

LOGAN

I'm feeling the bubbly in a big way, being more of a beer kinda guy. It might be different if I'd had more than granola bars for dinner last night and breakfast this morning.

I've been putting off a much-needed trip into town, unable to face it. If there was even a cupboard in the shanty, it'd be completely bare. But, if I'm driving south as I've been contemplating, I can eat junk food along the way.

Now, I'm not sure I'll be leaving. The gleam in Mandy's eye is familiar, with the last time I'd seen it being when I was tweaking her nipple experimentally up at the tower. A glance at the cot and I know full well it's not up to what I've got in mind.

"You fancy a trip to the pond?"

The question is simple. However, Mandy is quick to see the ramifications of me asking. It's a special place for both of us.

She answers with a broad grin before shoving the small backpack under her seat and standing with a slight sway. Okay, so I'm not alone in feeling the effects of the bubbly.

Before leaving the hut, I grab all the blankets off the bed, resulting in delighted laughter from Mandy.

Our timing is perfect, with the sun directly overhead. Lying around naked at any other time of day would be chilly. No such problems now, with the sun beating down on us as we stand face-to-face and slowly strip.

Neither of us is hiding anything from the other, which is a fresh experience for me. This amazing woman has obliterated three years of shying away from friendships, and females.

We reach for each other, my hands on her shoulders, hers at my waist. By mutual consent we draw close, my heart hammering in my chest.

It had never been this way with Brooke. With her, making love had been more like performance art, as though there were cameras

watching us all the time. It had always been more of an *Instagram moment* than actual love. With Mandy, everything is so damn real.

My finger under her chin, I tilt her face toward mine; the sun highlighting her features. I take a moment to admire her natural beauty before my lips touch hers. Her mouth opens, and I claim her fully in a poor imitation of what I'd really like to be doing to her right now.

We sink to the blankets I'd spread out earlier, and there isn't an inch of her I don't give special attention to. I want to hear her screaming my name out in passion as I worship her body.

She's not shy, this woman of mine. As I say this in my head, I smile. It sounds so right, so perfect, just like Mandy. As I sweep my hand down her body and between her legs, I'm pleased to find she's wet and ready for me.

I waste no time covering her body with mine and sinking into her until I can go no further. Even then I give it a little nudge, with her eyes widening in appreciation.

As I withdraw and leisurely plunge back in, the sun is hot on my back, while Mandy heats my front. She feels wonderful, and while my preference is to take my time, Mandy is having none of it.

"More, I want more than that," she whispers, before adding, "Faster, deeper, stronger!"

I burst out laughing with delight. "As you wish."

I then concentrate on doing exactly what she wants, the tension building for both of us until we light up as brightly as the sun.

Even then, I stay where I am, savoring our closeness, as we roll onto our sides and gaze at each other with fresh eyes. Right until the first mosquito attacks my bare ass.

"Come on, sweetheart, we need to move or we'll get eaten alive." I pull out before kissing her thoroughly. "Let's go get cleaned up."

The water is more invigorating than usual, or is it that my lightness of spirit makes it seem so? Either way, I've never splashed and played in the pond, as I'm doing with Mandy.

Gone is the serious man I've been hiding behind, replaced by someone I'll enjoy getting to know once more.

EPILOGUE

MANDY

After helping me arrange my hair into a messy up-do, my mom concentrates on pinning a crown of orange blossom in place. Once it's secure, I take a moment to breathe in the delicate scent.

Rather than being nervous, I'm excited. This is partly because of Logan and me already being married. The last thing I wanted on the day we celebrated our wedding was for him to be nervous that I wouldn't turn up.

This saw us getting married at the County Courthouse a couple of weeks back with only my mom and his parents in attendance. It had been a no-frills affair, something that made my dad not being there easier to bear. I know I'll miss his presence today, as Logan and I unofficially celebrate our marriage.

An hour later, and I'm ready to leave the house. Rather than using the front door, we leave through the back. Both mom and I are in sandals, better suited to the forest floor than heels.

Thanks to some work on Logan's part, there's now a straightforward path through to the fire pond, the place we've chosen to celebrate our marriage. It was where we'd first met.

On stepping out of the trees, I'm greeted by the incredible sight of Logan in a tuxedo, although not all is as it seems. When my gaze drops, I can see that rather than wearing designer shoes, he's wearing his work boots. Like me, he's smiling and happy, with no wedding day jitters in evidence.

We're not alone, with friends and family there to help us celebrate. As we stand facing each other, our hands linked, I'm reminded of the time we'd consummated our relationship on the other side of the pond.

On spotting Logan's cheeky grin, I can see he's doing the same, especially when he leans forward and whispers, "Soon enough, my darling, soon enough."

I'm more than a little aroused by the time Logan says his vows. Even though this isn't legally binding as the courthouse ceremony had been, to us it's more important. It's us declaring our love for each other publicly and without shame.

Logan squeezes my hands gently before he speaks. "Mandy, my darling. I love you with all my being. You make me the man I am today. You complete me, and I look forward to our long life together. You hold my heart in your hands." He follows this by kissing me reverently on the forehead.

Then it's my turn.

"Logan, my darling, I love you more than life itself. You complete me and support me. You make me more than I am on my own. You hold my heart in your hands." I reach up on tiptoe and kiss his forehead as reverently as he had mine.

We then turn to face our family and friends, and in unison declare. "We present to you, Mr. and Mrs. Young."

There's a second's silence before the group erupts in a loud cheer. A champagne cork popping follows this, confirming our celebratory picnic is underway.

I'm not sure what makes me turn, but on peering into the shadows cast by the trees, I spot my dad. He's smiling and, once again, the strong, rugged man of my youth. Boston sits patiently at his feet, sporting a wide doggie grin.

However, after I wipe my eyes, the pair is no longer there. While my seeing them was doubtless a dream, I prefer to think they're off enjoying zoomies rather than no longer a part of my life.

Have fun, you two. Have fun.

The picnic shows no signs of slowing when I hear the distinctive thump of a chopper. Surely there isn't a fire? I look around our friends, and in particular anyone employed by the forestry department, but they're all happy and relaxed.

Logan steps up behind me, wraps his arms around my waist, and places a kiss just behind my ear. "Your carriage awaits, milady."

A second later, he's got my hand in his and is leading me away from the picnic. That some of his forestry friends are in on the surprise is clear by their good-natured teasing.

Sure enough, on reaching a nearby clearing, there's a department helicopter festooned with a JUST MARRIED sign. There are also a multitude of tin cans tied to the landing skids by lengths of string.

"And just where are you taking me, Mr. Young?"

"You'll see soon enough, Mrs. Young."

LOGAN

I have to hand it to Chief Larsen; he's come through for me in a big way. Perhaps the biggest way had been him rehiring me. Even better is that he'd put me back with Mandy. There aren't many guys who get to woo their girl while they're on the clock.

After taking off, we fly over the small fire pond so we can wave goodbye to everyone below. The pilot then turns and heads inland.

It's taken weeks of work and the help of a lot of the forestry crew to get our final destination set up for tonight. I only hope Mandy is pleased with it.

"Where exactly are we going?"

Her words come through my headset loud and clear. However, I'm not giving up the surprise until I have to. "You'll see, soon enough." I'd kiss her but for the pilot and our headsets getting in the way.

It only takes five more minutes before the helicopter sets down on a patch of open ground near the tower. Mandy's grin tells me she's already worked out where we'll be spending the night.

What she doesn't know is that tonight we won't have to share a sleeping bag.

"Logan, I'll pick you up on Tuesday unless there's a fire."

"Okay Jerry. Yell if you need me."

I jump down before turning to help Mandy, making sure she doesn't catch her dress. It's billowing up in the downdraft from the rotors with her desperately trying to preserve her modesty in front of the pilot.

We're at the bottom of the stairs up to the tower when the helicopter takes off. Mandy turns to me. "So, Tuesday?" She holds her wedding dress out to the side and looks at my tux. "Not exactly dressed for it, are we?"

"Honey, with what I've got planned, we won't need clothes."

A second later, I'm chasing her up the tower, with her shrieking in delight.

On reaching the structure at the top, she stops in her tracks before turning to me, wonder in her eyes. "It's, it's beautiful." She then throws herself at me, kissing me soundly.

It's only as our kiss deepens that something becomes apparent. "You're naked under there, aren't you?"

"That's for me to know, and you to find out," she sings out, while squirming free of my arms and backing into the cabin.

"You're damned right, I will," I say, stalking after her.

Of the cabin we'd spent the night in all those months ago, there's no sign. A queen-size bed now takes pride of place in the middle of the room. It's draped with a mosquito net; the frame festooned with flowers, and the coverlet strewn with rose petals.

Pam, the receptionist at headquarters, hadn't been kidding when she'd said to leave it to her.

It will be magical when night falls, and the place is lit by all those solar twinkle lights. As always with the forestry department, it's safety first, and so no candles for us with summer just around the corner.

Mandy dances around the bed for a bit, her laughter ringing out. When she breaks into song, it's even better.

"You're an amazing singer. You should share it more."

She falls silent, and I'm bereft. She's not downhearted though, rather she's beaming when she grabs the sides of her flowing gown and lifts it free. A moment later, it drops to the floor, and she stands before me naked, but for a garland of pearls and a pale blue garter.

Next, she removes her halo of flowers and places it on the bedside table before loosening her gorgeous locks. They cascade over her breasts like water, with my groin tightening in response.

"Baby, it's you that makes me sing." She smiles before adding, "And you're wearing far too many clothes for that to happen."

While I don't strip as quickly as she has, I soon stand before her, wearing nothing but a broad grin. "Have I told you lately how much I love you?"

She nods. "Have I told you lately how much I love *you?*"

"You have, baby, you have." I reach out and pull her into my arms. "You want to show me?"

We land in a laughing tangle of arms and legs on the bed, falling silent when our lips meet and our tongues touch. Then her hands are everywhere, as are mine. I just can't get enough of this woman, and lucky for me, she feels the same way.

We take our time, our foreplay reverent, and then playful, but always leading us on, stoking the fire that burns between us. As easy as it would be to give Mandy what she's begging for, I want to be deep inside her when she finds her release.

As I ease myself into her core, an inch at a time, I whisper, "Mrs. Young, I'd like you to meet Mr. Young."

She's giggling and I can't help but smile back, her laughter infectious. Even though slow is good, I give into the desire to bury myself fully. When I thrust deeper still, she stares at me in wide-eyed wonder. A guy could get used to this. "You like that?"

She nods jerkily, unable to find the words.

I withdraw almost completely before burying myself back up to the hilt, with her lips parting on a moan of pleasure.

Not too fast.

Not too slow

Just right.

And repeat.

She bucks her hips to meet mine, matching me perfectly. It's only on listening carefully that I catch what it is she's whispering on repeat. "Faster, deeper, stronger."

As you wish, Mrs. Young. As you wish.

𝕸𝖀𝕾𝕴𝕮

Next time you're out on the town, make sure you pop into Maddies, the luxurious new cocktail bar at Maddigans Resort and Spa.

Headlining this month is local woman Mandy Young, treating us to a medley of jazz classics in her rich alto.

While new to the circuit, pundits are saying she's one to watch. There are even rumors of a recording contract.

Skye is a pastry chef with a sweet tooth. Seth is a veteran who's good with his hands, like really good. Can opposites attract when their worlds collide?

ONE

SETH

On driving around the headland, I spot a familiar sight. What the hell is Skye Fraser doing out here this time of night? I've just finished asking myself this when I provide the answer.

That heap of crap car of hers has died on her, again. There'd be no other reason she'd be parked up in the middle of nowhere like this. Hell, the only reason I'm out here is that I'm on the way back from a call out.

As I pull my tow truck in behind her pale pink hatchback, I flash my lights twice before turning them off. At the very least, this way she'll know it's me and not some random stranger. After flicking on the hazards, I kill the engine, open the door and jump out.

Rather than be caught with a dead battery, I slam the door shut, with the noise barely audible over the crash of the waves far below. It takes all my concentration to steady my breathing, to tell myself that it's just the waves: not heavy bombardment.

Even after all these years, the P.T.S.D. that saw me leave the military can come back to haunt me, and always at the worst imaginable times. Rather than give into the anxiety waiting for me in the wings, I focus on the car in front of me, illuminated by my hazards.

This along with some belly breathing, and I anchor myself as much as I can. I'm sure it'll be enough that I can behave reasonably normally. And if ever there was a woman who could take my mind off the horrors of war, it's Skye Fraser.

And who am I to keep a lady waiting?

Next to the car, I wait for her to roll the window down; instead, she opens her door, telling me the problem is with the car's electrics, but not the battery. I'd made sure she got a new one after saving her the last time.

I swing her door wide and hunker down so we're eye-to-eye. And damn if she isn't easy on the eye. Curves where curves should be and the occasional hollow just begging to be explored.

Thoughts of those fiery locks tumbling over my bare chest have my cock straining for release, leaving me glad it's dark out. There's no chance of my accidentally showing her what she does to me.

This has me thinking on mundane tasks so I can speak to her rather than give into my desires, and perhaps even hers. I'm sure I haven't imagined the way she looks at me when she thinks I won't notice.

Or am I simply deluding myself?

Who was I fooling? Of course she's not into me. A smart woman like her would hardly be interested in a damaged, dead-beat like me. Sure, she's got issues with maintaining her car, but other than that, she's as buttoned down as they come.

Oh man, I wouldn't mind making her co...

I shake my head to clear it enough that I'll be able to hear what the latest issue is with this junker of hers. Honestly, the custom paint job is all that's holding it together. Hell's teeth, the paint job is probably worth more than the car.

"So, Pie in the Skye, what's a nice girl like you doing in a place like this?"

SKYE

The lights behind me flashing twice, tell me who it is, with my ovaries immediately singing their approval. There are pluses to driving a rubbish car, with Seth Adams being the biggest plus of all. I've no need of jumper cables when that hottie is around.

He saunters up next to the car and stands there waiting, all while giving me a good view of his ah, package. My breathing hitches because even without fancy wrapping, it's the gift that keeps on giving.

I push the button to roll the window down, but nothing happens. This at least goes some way toward explaining why the engine died on me.

I was just lucky I hadn't been going fast, because the power steering had given up the ghost at the same time. I'd pumped the brakes twice before they'd died, too. Only by yanking on the parking brake had I been able to stop completely.

Without that, I'd have continued on over the cliff.

I inch my door open so I can speak to him and he grabs it, opening it wide. On his squatting down next to me, I get a whiff of his aftershave. I'm not sure what it is about that mix of citrus and sandalwood, but it does things to me it has no right doing.

Or could it be more down to the man himself? I should imagine he could douse himself in engine oil, and I'd still find him attractive.

Even if he was covered in oil as I'm currently picturing him, he's not your usual tow truck driver. There's no pot belly from hours spent behind the wheel. Rather, Seth's blessed with a six-pack solid enough that it shows through those tight t-shirts he favors.

Neither does he sport what appears to be the obligatory beard favored by most tow truck drivers. There's nothing to hide how gorgeous he is, nothing. Even that buzz cut he must have gotten used to when he was enlisted suits him.

On seeing his eyes glaze over, I suspect it must be the P.T.S.D. I've heard about. There's no hiding something like that in a place as small as Coogan's Break. One attack and half the town hear about it. A couple more and every man and his dog will know.

His voice when he asks me what's up is deep, rumbling through my body and filling it with longing. It takes all my concentration to remember what's wrong with the car. I'm not making sense, but there's nothing I can do about it.

Alpha males like Seth Adams do it for me. It's just a shame that little, okay, not so little, pie shop owners like me, don't do it for men like him. Never have, never will.

"I'm really not sure? I was driving along and then everything up and died."

I pull in a shuddering breath before continuing. "I had to use the parking brake..." I'm unable to finish the sentence, as the enormity of how close I'd come to going over the edge settles on me.

I stare straight ahead, even though the dark in front of the car reveals nothing. Mainly because there's nothing there other than fresh air. I've closed my eyes to block it out when Seth leans across in front of me so he can undo my seat belt.

I'm shocked on a couple of levels. First, if I hadn't yanked my parking brake on as violently as I had, I could have died. And second, that having Seth Adams this close to me has every hair on my body standing at attention.

Only adding to this overload to my system are my girly bits screaming they want in on the action. And for once, I'm tempted to listen to them.

TWO

SKYE

I'm still dealing with the effect of Seth's proximity to my body when he speaks again. "Come on Skye. Let's get you home. I'm not towing this hunk of junk right now. While I wouldn't mind sending it over the edge, I don't want to follow it down."

I take a second to realize what he's said. "But I can't leave Pinkie out here on her own. What if someone steals her?"

His raucous laughter at my suggestion immediately has my hackles up. "Hey, she's not that bad. She's always there for me." On seeing the incredulity on his face, I add a disclaimer. "Well, almost always."

He doesn't appear convinced. "Is she even insured?" The look on his face tells me he's already decided no insurer with a modicum of business sense would go near my darling car. I also can't help but notice he's acknowledged Pinkie Pie is a girl.

"Of course she's insured!"

He shrugs, as though the reality of him taking me home is now a done deal. "Well then, what's the problem? Even if someone is crazy enough to steal her, they won't get far." He laughs again, before adding, "Unless they disengage the parking brake, and then it'd serve 'em right."

Of course, he's right. I also know that thoughts of sitting in the cab next to him will have me wanting to help myself to his gorgeousness. And that is so not happening, at least not without major embarrassment when he turns me down flat, as I know he will.

He'll be polite, but his having manners won't lessen my chagrin at being rejected.

I take my time collecting my things, all while experiencing a curious mix of dread and anticipation. I hate it when someone invites me along out of pity, with this happening all too often in my life. I'm not socially inept. Rather, I'm an introvert, which, I'll admit, almost amounts to the same thing.

Even at Skye High Pies, my bakery, I stay out back, leaving my team to serve customers. Unfortunately, there's something about Seth that has me doubting he'll let me get away with it. That once we're safe inside that monster truck of his, he'll want to make conversation.

Just thinking about it has me breaking out in a cold sweat. On standing next to the passenger door of his truck, my cold sweat turns to terror as I remember something else. The first step of his truck is high enough that there isn't a chance I can climb up there on my own.

And short of Seth using the winch, he'll have to lift me. That's if he can. I don't bake all those yummy pies without occasionally trying them to see if they're up to standard.

Okay, more than occasionally. Suddenly, his knowing I have a thing for him is the least of my worries.

SETH

As I lean across to undo her seat belt, the need to turn and claim those plump lips of hers is overwhelming, but I resist. It'll be hell on earth having her next to me in the truck as it is.

On hearing her sharp intake of breath, I back out and stand as fast as I can. That my being close to her is as unpleasant as I've always imagined has been borne home. Why hadn't I simply asked her to undo the seat belt herself?

Because you wanted a chance to get close to her, that's why, you sad bastard.

It isn't until she's grabbed her things and inched her way out of her car to stand next to me I'm reminded of what a cutie she is. She only just reaches my shoulder. To be fair though, at six-four, most people are short where I'm concerned.

I stand back, giving her the space to lock the car, before walking over to the passenger side of my cab. It's only while standing there that I realize I've got a problem.

There isn't a chance Skye can get into the cab without help from me. And thoughts of having my hands all over her body have my cock readying itself for action. It never wastes time when Skye is around.

Damn it, what the hell had I been thinking when I said we couldn't tow her car tonight? Even though I said we'd have to leave it there, I knew otherwise. It would be easy enough for me to turn my truck around and hook up to the back of her car. No risk of going over the cliff that way.

Instead, I take her bags and stow them in the footwell before looking down at her. Part of me is all too eager for what's about to happen. "Ah, I'll need to help you up."

Only after a brief nod from her do I place my hands on either side of her waist in readiness. It's as if my body has a mind of its own. She's every bit as soft and yielding as I've always imagined, a real woman; one who fills my hands beautifully. It's as if that's where she belongs.

My thoughts out of control, I move on to dreaming about how other parts of her would feel under my hands, under my mouth. When she stiffens next to me, it's as if a bucket of cold water has been chucked over me. I'm lying to myself if I think I've got a chance with someone as beautiful as Skye.

She won't be interested in a damaged nobody like me. The only woman who'd be interested in me these days would be a psychologist writing a paper on P.T.S.D.

I'm a textbook case of how active duty can screw someone over for life.

THREE

SKYE

I've never been as embarrassed in all my life. Not even school field days could come close to my current humiliation. Not that Seth couldn't get me up into the cab. He did, and far more easily than I could ever have dreamed. It was as if I was at my goal weight, rather than...

No, it was the speed with which he'd completed the task that has me squirming. It's as if he couldn't wait to get his hands away from me, to be free of my weight. Dropped like a hot potato on the front seat.

"Um, thank you." I'm unable to add more thanks. He's slammed the door in my face and is stalking around the front of the truck as though the devil is after him.

Maybe I won't have to make conversation after all.

Sure enough, when he opens his door and climbs in as though the first step is at a normal height, he keeps quiet. When he turns the key in the ignition and the engine roars to life, conversation becomes impossible. Added to this cacophony is Seth singing along to the radio.

His voice is as smooth as the rest of him. Yet another quality I find attractive, blast it.

Okay, if we're not talking, then I can keep a lid on my desire to get up close and personal.

I even relax until I realize he'll need to help me out of the cab when we get to my place.

I'd jump, but I'm simply not that athletic. Nor do I want to risk twisting an ankle. I spend most of my day at the bakery on my feet. It's not the type of job you can do sitting down. Nope, as much as I'd like to avoid it, he'll have to help me.

There's no need for me to give him instructions back to my place. He's towed my car enough times to get there blindfolded. In an instant, my mind is crowded with images of him sitting, wearing one, and not a lot else.

I've got no control over where my mind goes after this. While my social life is about as active as any eighty-year-old, my imagination has the energy of a toddler. And like a toddler at the supermarket, it's currently running amok, not at thoughts of toys and chocolate bars, but about what I'd do to my savior.

So focused am I on my fantasies of a blindfolded and tied-up Seth, that when he turns the engine off, my moan of desire fills the cab. I do my best to turn it into a yawn and then a cough. I can only hope he's buying what I'm selling.

I've even thought I've gotten away with it when he twists in his seat to face me. He tilts his head to the side, a smile playing around his lips. "Anything you want to share with me?"

I open and close my mouth, but nothing comes out. As his smile broadens, my hopes of coming up with a credible lie flee, along with any other logical thoughts. All I'm capable of is staring at his lips illuminated by the streetlight outside my house.

They're currently all I can think about, to the point I'm not even aware of having spoken, until he does.

"My lips? What about them?" He follows this up by running his tongue over them and, boom, my body is no longer under my control.

SETH

The drive back to Skye's place is excruciating. While I'm glad there's no need to chat, with every mile covered, the P.S.I. in my balls climbs. The sooner I have her out of the cab and I'm on my way, the sooner I can deal with my not so slight problem.

On turning the engine off, rather than the usual sounds of it slowly cooling, I hear a sound that has my blood boiling. If that wasn't a moan of pleasure, then I'm not sure what is. Why on earth is she so fired up?

Could it be the engine vibrating through the cab that's set her off? Hell, it even gets to me some days.

On turning to take a proper look at her, my breath catches in my throat, and I have to swallow before I'm able to speak. If there's one thing that I'm sure of, it's what horny looks like. And man-oh-man, if the pocket rocket sitting next to me isn't ready to explode, then I'm not ex-military.

When I ask her if she wants to share, she doesn't appear capable of rational thought, although she eventually squeaks out, "Your lips." I deliberately run my tongue over them, watching her closely.

Sure enough, her eyes darken, and when she copies my action by licking her own, this confirms it. I undo my seat belt to slide across the bench seat in her direction. She watches my every move. Her lips are parted, and her gorgeous green eyes are wide.

Even as I undo her seat belt and lift her onto my lap, she says nothing. All she'd need to do was say no, and I'd stop it right there. But she doesn't. Add in her hands all over parts of me they shouldn't be, and I can tell she's as into this as I am.

I sweep in to taste her lips as I've wanted to since the first time I spotted her taking a break out back of her bakery. And damn, if she isn't every bit as sweet as those pies of hers, perhaps even sweeter.

FOUR

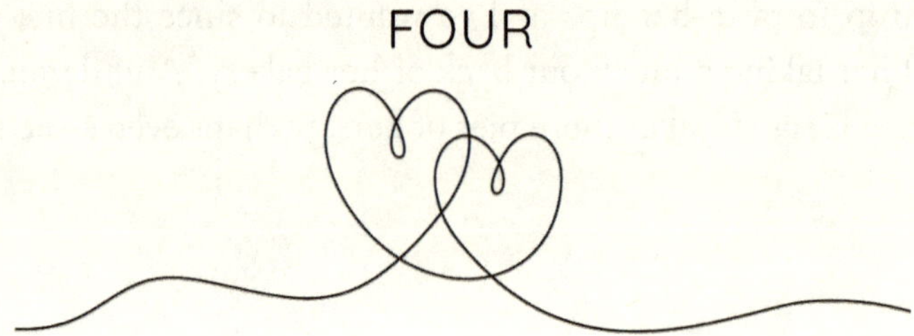

When Seth eventually takes his lips away from mine, I'm bereft. This only intensifies when he lifts me off his lap and puts me back on my side of the bench seat.

After sliding away from me, he opens his door. "Sit tight. I'll be around to help you down in a second."

To hide my embarrassment at our brief interlude being over, I busy myself collecting my things from the footwell. When he opens my door, I'm all ready to make my escape, to go inside and hide.

Well, I will be as soon as I'm back on terra firma and I'm not getting there on my own.

Deciding to make this as easy as possible, I turn in the seat and put my feet on the top step. I'm expecting him to lift me down, in the same way as he'd helped me up. He, however, has other ideas, reaching in so he can tuck one arm behind my back and the other under my knees.

Next thing, I'm out of the cab and he's using his shoulder to shut the truck door.

Rather than put me down as I've expected, he's soon crunching his way up the shell path to my front door.

Really? He's so keen to be rid of me he doesn't trust me to get there on my own?

To be fair, though, my legs are like jelly. If he had put me down, I suspect I'd have had to lean against the side of his truck to avoid collapsing in a puddle.

It's only when the front security light flares I catch his dirty grin. It's enough to have my lady parts squealing with delight. When he swings me around on the front porch while chuckling, this only intensifies.

He leans over, and I slide down his body to the welcome mat. When he straightens, I'm not sure what is supposed to happen next. I'm out of my depth here. It's one thing to read about guys like him in romances. It's completely different when that six-foot-four of gorgeousness is right in front of you.

Lucky for me, Seth knows exactly what he's about. His arm still behind my back, he bends and reclaims my lips. I'm only vaguely aware of all the bags dropping from my nerveless fingers.

It must be an hour later that we come up for air, although that's most likely wishful thinking. It's doubtless been a couple of minutes and nowhere near long enough so far as I'm concerned.

Lost as I am in a sensual haze, it takes a second for me to decipher what it is he's just said. "I'm sorry. What was that?" I'm hardly admitting I was so busy fantasizing about how he would look without a shirt that I hadn't been paying attention. Now was I?

"I'll swing by to take you to work in the morning. Would four-thirty be okay?"

I nod mutely while fumbling in my coat pocket for my keys. How could I have read the signals so badly? I could have sworn he was as into this as I was, ah, still am.

Just goes to show you how much I know about men.

SETH

It's all I can do to put some distance between Skye and me. There isn't a chance I want to rush this and screw it up. Sure, I want nothing more than to carry her inside and peel her clothes off her; to kiss every inch of her sumptuous body.

But I hold back. Skye isn't like the girls I've dated in the past. The major difference being that I want to see her again tomorrow.

And the day after. And the day after that.

There's nothing one-night-stand about the delectable woman next to me, nothing.

Not until she's in danger of dropping her house keys for the third time, do I step in. I've rattled her, that's for sure. The only thing I'm not sure of is whether it's because I kissed her, or because I stopped.

I could have sworn she was into those kisses as much as I was, but could that just have been a delusion? The door open, she's about to step inside, when I put my hand out to stop her.

I jerk my head toward the welcome mat. "Careful."

There isn't a chance I'm letting her get hurt by tripping over her pile of things.

When she bends to pick everything up, I'm a goner. Her ass is perfection. It's plump, and just begging to be touched. I'm not aware of having moved until I hear her moan.

It's a sound that cuts to my very core. Okay, and a few other parts as well. I want her so badly it hurts.

And it would appear this is reciprocated, judging by the speed with which Skye grabs all her belongings and tosses them into a small entryway. She then straightens, reaches up and grabs the front of my t-shirt, yanking on it.

Our lips are locked a second later, and stay this way as we stagger in through the front door, with it slamming with a little help from my foot. I briefly open my eyes and get a general layout of the room thanks to the security light.

I've only just lowered us to the sectional with Skye spread out beneath me when the light automatically turns off, plunging the room into darkness.

That'd be a 'hell no' from me. Pulling away from her briefly, I reach out and turn on the lamp next to us. I want to see her face when she calls out my name. Actually, if I have my way, she'll be screaming my name, over and over.

But before I've got started, she reaches out and flicks the lamp back off. I'm ready to argue my desire to see her pulling her O face when she runs her hands over the muscles of my chest. My cock wants in on the action, in a big way, in a VERY big way.

With me spread out on top, even with it being dark, there's no hiding my erection from her. It's a pain in the ass that the dark also hides her reaction to it. For all I know, it could be time for me to go home and take a freezing cold shower.

When she arches her hips and grinds her mons against my hard-on, it's the answer I've been hoping for. The one I've dreamed of every single time I've been there to rescue her.

FIVE

SKYE

I'm enjoying the dark of the lounge and Seth's proximity, when he reaches out and turns the lamp back on, again. I'm reaching out to flick it back off when he shakes his head.

"No, Skye, leave it on. When I make you come, I want to see your face. I want to see your body tremble with release. Please don't hide from me?"

There's something about this last part that stills my hand. I'm not sure what he means, but there's a hidden message there. I've not come to terms with what it might be when he speaks again.

"And don't you want to see my face when I come?"

OMG, if I was aroused before, it's nothing compared to how turned on I am now.

And damn it, why is he still wearing a shirt?

I grip the front of his t-shirt shyly for a start. Then the little devil in me has me dragging it up and over his head before I gaily toss it to one side.

Other than Seth's general magnificence, I'm struck by the crisscross of scars on his chest, a testament to his military career. Tentatively, I kiss my fingers before tracing a few of the larger ones. Even these, as hard won as they've likely been, are beautiful to me.

I'm running my finger along another, when I whisper out, "So brave."

Never in my life have I been this close to something as magnificent. However, it's Seth's stormy blue eyes that capture my soul. So much so that it takes a second to realize that while I've been transfixed by his battle scars, he's already unbuttoned the top button on my shirt.

One-by-one, he takes his time, kissing each newly exposed piece of flesh as it's brought into the light. I'm close to screaming with anticipation before he spreads the shirt wide.

"I like the pink. Let's see what's hiding here." Then, with an ease that hints at experience, he undoes the front closing on my bra with a mere flick of his wrist. As he'd done with my shirt, he sweeps the lace to the sides, before reverently kissing each breast.

He looks up, making sure he's got my attention before he speaks. "They're more perfect than I've dreamed of." He drops his head back down, with my right nipple soon jealous of the left, although thankfully, not for long.

He then trails kisses down my body until he reaches the buttons on my jeans. Again, he takes his time undoing the rest, ramping up my anticipation. That he deliberately brushes his knuckles against my heat while he's about it only builds on this.

Damn it, if he doesn't hurry, I'm gonna stand up and rip all my clothes off.

It's a thought that has a giggle breaking free, and him looking up to see what's funny. In answer to his raised eyebrow, all I can come up with is a breathy, "faster."

And Seth does not disappoint.

Thanks to his military training or good-looking guys always having the moves, I'm soon as naked as the day I was born. I'd feel exposed but for Seth's fiery gaze sweeping my body.

He's still taking too long, and so I arch my hips in silent invitation. He responds by sliding down my body, his lips, and tongue swiftly claiming that most sensitive of gems.

Hah, and my friends said I was crazy having such a large sectional in my tiny lounge. I have to be honest though, when I'd bought it, I was thinking more of movie nights. I'd never pictured myself lying here naked and being pleasured by a man like Seth.

Not even in my wildest dreams. And I've had plenty of those since the first time I saw Seth in town.

Thanks to the size of the sectional, there's plenty of room, with my body screaming out to make the most of it. I want to writhe against that gorgeous body of his, getting as close as humanly possible.

Seth's got other ideas. His hands on my thighs hold me right where he wants me. This leaves the very center of my being at the mercy of his mouth and tongue.

As he builds on the layers of my desire, my senses are close to being overwhelmed.

My very core sings its approval of this lavish attention with it only a matter of time before I'm also hitting the high notes.

Actually, only two minutes pass before I'm screaming Seth's name over and over, just as he'd promised. The orgasm rips through me and

I embrace it. After all, it's my first ever courtesy of a man. To say my love life to date had been underwhelming is an understatement.

I wonder briefly on how long it is since I've gone all the way with a guy. I hope I can cope physically, because Seth is in a whole different league from that last guy. We're talking Little League versus Major League, here.

Will it even be physically possible? My eyes meet Seth's and the knowledge I'm about to find out rushes through me. Strangely, though, I'm not scared, because my gut tells me he'd never hurt me. It also tells me he's still wearing a lot more clothes than I am.

Well, that needs to change.

SETH

Skye's so responsive, just as I've always dreamed of. Her release rippling under my mouth is enough to have me close to coming myself. And that's so not happening.

Nope, when I detonate I want to be buried up to the hilt in her wet and welcoming depths. I'm not hurrying though. I want to savor this.

As I slide back up her body, I suck on her nipples. Taking them into my mouth, I tug on them gently, and am rewarded when she arches her back. It's as though she can't get close enough to me, and it's a sentiment I share.

Hot damn, I'll be lucky to last at this rate.

I've reclaimed her lips when the lamp flashes bright. It's not until there's a rumble of thunder that I realize my mistake. That wasn't the lamp. Damn it to hell, the storm wasn't supposed to arrive until lunchtime tomorrow, at the earliest.

I need to get out of here, and fast.

Struggling to my feet, I search frantically for my keys, eventually spotting them on a small table in the entranceway. I make quick work of crossing the room and am relieved when my hand closes over them. A second later and I open the front door. "Ah, I'm sorry... Ah, I can't..." Then words fail me.

My sudden departure obviously takes Skye by surprise. The last thing I see before I close the front door is the poor woman still lying naked on the sofa, her face a mask of shock.

It wouldn't be as big a shock for her as watching me cowering in the room's corner, my hands stuffed over my ears.

I don't slow until I'm safely in the cab of my truck, only then realizing that I don't even have a shirt on. There's not a chance I'm going back for it. Instead, I hurry to start the engine, the noise it makes enough to drown out the thunder.

I just need to get home. I repeat this over and over, focusing on this rather than the anxiety attack that's threatening to overwhelm me. I've never disassociated while behind the wheel, and I sure as hell don't want to start now.

Screw it, that storm couldn't have arrived at a worse moment.

What must Skye think of me now?

I know what I'd be thinking if I was her, and it wouldn't be pretty. I never imagined I'd have a chance with someone like her, and after tonight, I doubt I ever will.

There'll be no coming back from abandoning her like I had. I'd wanted to stay, snuggling up to her, waking to find her ready to carry on from where we'd left off. Slow morning sex is a beautiful thing.

Then I think about what would have happened if we'd been in the throes of passion when that lightning and thunder struck.

And how would Skye have taken it when I was lost to memories of that land mine taking us out? Surely there's no bigger turnoff than a damaged man? We're the strong ones.

Even worse, is while I'm in that state, the real world ceases to exist. What if I hurt her because I mistook her for the enemy?

It's something that keeps circling until I'm flying up the outside stairs to my apartment over the garage after abandoning my truck out front. I've just made it inside when there's another clap of thunder and my world comes crashing down around me.

Yet again, I'm back on that dusty road in the desert.

SIX

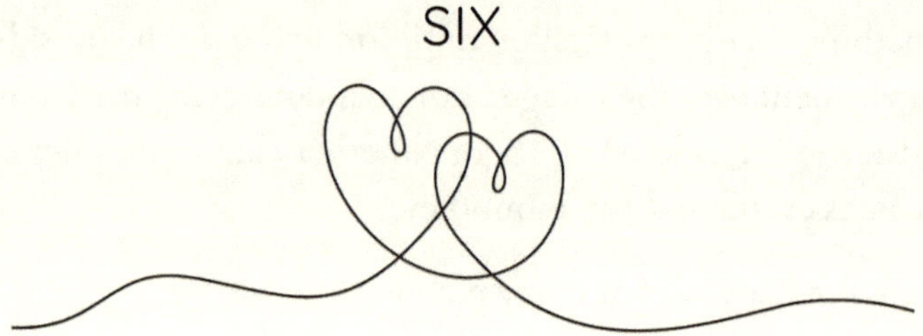

SKYE

I stand under the shower, the water blisteringly hot to wash away the shame that had been my companion throughout the night.

What on earth did I do wrong? Or was it I simply didn't live up to expectations?

I run out of hot water long before I run out of shame and humiliation.

Back in my room, I check the time on the bedside clock, to find three-fifty-five glaring back at me. I'm a little ahead of my usual schedule for week-days, although not as much as I'd like if I'm to avoid Seth. That's if he even turns up. It might be he's had a crappy night's sleep like me.

Over and over, I'd replayed the scene with Seth, to no avail. It hadn't mattered how much I'd analyzed it. I was still in the dark about what had gone so terribly wrong.

The only plus this morning is that I'm so used to getting ready for work in what equates to the middle-of-the-night for many, that I can do it on autopilot. After brushing my hair, I drag it back into a high ponytail.

Clothes are next, with white being my preferred color as it doesn't show the flour so much. Finally, I lace up my running shoes, ready for the walk to work. I'd deliberately set my alarm clock early as I wanted to be well away, just in case Seth turned up to take me to work as he'd promised.

Although after last night, I can't imagine why he would. Either way, there isn't a chance I want to risk being stuck in his truck with him this morning. It would be too much to bear. A walk might also go some way toward clearing the last of the cobwebs.

Morning hasn't deigned to get out of bed when I inch my front door open. However, a quick peek shows the road outside to be mercifully free of Seth's truck. Actually, the streets are as good as deserted, with no-one around this early on a Tuesday morning.

With the prime tourist season, well and truly over, the town is quieter.

After dropping my keys into my backpack, I shrug into it, tighten the straps and take off. It shouldn't take over ten minutes to walk to the bakery. That's plenty of time to work out where I'll go to from here. The first thing I need to organize is for someone, other than Seth, to collect my car from the headland.

If I can avoid facing him altogether, then I'm going for it.

This idea has barely crossed my mind when I hear the familiar rumble of a truck from back down the street. Despite the shortness of my legs, I lengthen my stride as much as I'm able. There isn't a chance I want to face him in the cold light of day.

Even the warm light of day doesn't hold much appeal.

All too soon, Seth catches up with me. I was dreaming if I thought I could outpace him. There aren't even any alleys I can cut through, and I am definitely not accepting a ride from the guy.

It's only good manners that have him trying to follow through on his promise to take me to work. The last thing I want from Seth is pity.

Ignoring him completely, I look straight ahead as I walk resolutely along, counting down the steps until I'm safely inside the bakery.

SETH

Last night had been hell from that first clap of thunder through until the sleeping tablets finally did their job of holding the nightmares at bay.

Actually, who am I kidding? It'd been crap after the alarm went off, too.

I'd usually give myself more time to get over an attack like that.

Often it took days.

This time was different. I couldn't leave Skye under the impression I'd found her to be anything other than desirable. The trick will be not revealing just how bad my P.T.S.D. is, because talking about it is a sure way to ruin a relationship.

Sad to say, this is something I know first-hand.

If only my guilt and shame at surviving were as easy to avoid. I wasn't the only one there that day. I was, however, the only one to make it out alive. Those guys were like brothers, their families like mine.

I still don't understand why I was spared. It wasn't as if I had a wife and kids waiting for me back home. They were the ones who should have returned, not me.

I'm fighting that last image of our world exploding in a flash of fire and surplus hardware when I spot a familiar figure.

I kinda knew that would be the case after I'd arrived at her place to find it in darkness. Despite this, I'd still knocked on the front door in case she'd slept through her alarm.

As I pull up next to her, I can tell she's angry. Her strides are longer than should be comfortable, her back ramrod straight, her hands fisted at her sides. Okay, so asking her if she wants a ride isn't as good an idea as I'd thought when I'd left home earlier. The best I can do is to make sure she gets to the bakery safely.

As with the night before, she drops her keys twice before she can get the door open. I'd jump out and go offer to help, but I'd probably end up with an oven tray wrapped around my head.

Not until the bakery lights flare into life, do I put my truck in gear and head on out to collect that rust bucket of hers. At least this way, I've got an excuse to see her again.

I'm working through various scenarios right until I round that last corner, only to discover that Pinkie Pie isn't where Skye had left her the night before.

I know damned well Skye hasn't had time to organize for one of the other towing companies in town to collect her car. I'd have heard about it on the radio if she had.

On pulling over to the side of the road enough that I can look down to the rocks below, my worst fears are imagined.

First, how am I supposed to recover the blasted car? And second, how on earth do I break the news to Skye that Pinkie Pie took a dive late last night?

So much for my promise that her hunk-of-junk car would be safe out here.

Well, buddy, you wanted a good excuse to talk to her...

I snort out. Yeah, not exactly what I had in mind.

SEVEN

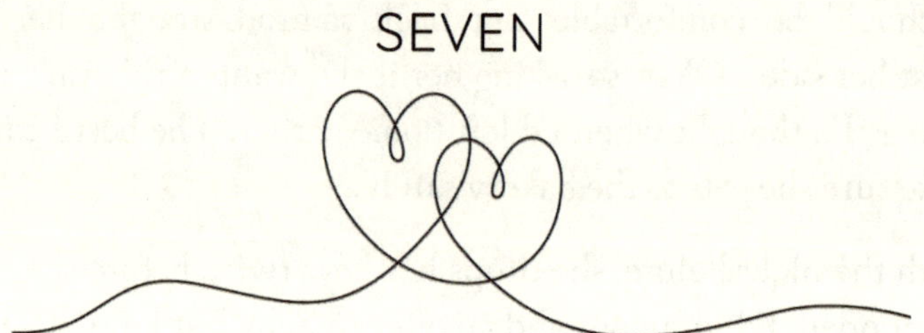

SKYE

Is he serious? Much as I'd hoped Seth would see I wasn't interested and drive off, he's keeping pace with me. I feel like an idiot walking along in the dark, a large tow truck shadowing my every move.

I try waving him away, but he ignores me, not driving off until I'm safely inside the bakery. As I'd done when getting up and dressed, I again switch to autopilot, turning on the ovens and getting everything ready for the team.

Usually I enjoy the solitude this time of the day. Not so today, with me greeting my team as though I haven't seen them in weeks rather than just the day before.

This morning, their presence is welcome, stopping my thoughts about what I'd done wrong last night from overwhelming me.

It isn't until three o'clock that things slow enough for me to once again worry about what had happened to Pinkie Pie. I'd called Bristol's Auto Repairs just after eight o'clock and arranged for them to tow Pinkie back to their shop.

Not even an hour had passed when they phoned back to say it wasn't where I'd said it was. They'd even driven up and down the road, in case I'd made a mistake about where I'd broken down. As if!

She must have been stolen, as I'd worried would happen. It's that, or Seth has her.

At this stage in proceedings, I'm actually hoping she's been stolen. Sure, there'd be a bucket-load of paperwork with the police and my insurance company, but I'd rather deal with all that than face Seth again.

It's something I dwell on when walking home. It takes three blocks before I realize that I'll have to speak to Seth whether or not I like it. I can't very well report Pinkie as stolen if he's got her back at his place, although it would serve him right.

He's just lucky I didn't act on that this morning.

I'm still having nefarious thoughts when I round the corner of my street and come to a grinding halt. The first thing to catch my eye is Seth's truck parked out front of my place.

The second is Pinkie Pie, sitting in the driveway.

What the heck did he do to her!?

I knew he didn't like my car, but to do this...

I'm walking again before I'm aware of having moved. Initially, I pretend Seth isn't there, my complete focus on Pinkie. On reaching my driveway, I complete a circuit of my precious vehicle.

There isn't a single panel that hasn't been dinged or scraped. As if this wasn't bad enough, the two front tires look to have exploded.

Aware that Seth has walked up behind me, I swing around. I'm so angry I'm not in my right mind.

"What on earth did you do? Take in a demolition derby on your way back here!?" I'm only aware I'm yelling when he takes a step back and holds his hands up.

"How on earth am I supposed to explain this to the insurance company?" I stomp up and down beside my car twice before stopping back in front of him. "Didn't you do enough damage last night?"

I stand and stare at him, rigid with anger, hands on my hips, waiting for a response. It's not the one I'm expecting, not by a long shot.

SETH

I knew when I was recovering Pinkie Pie from the rocks that Skye wouldn't be happy. In reality, the car is only fit to be totaled.

The last thing I expected was that she'd accuse me of inflicting all that damage. I'm still feeling guilty because I'd convinced her it would be safe leaving it there.

But how the heck was I supposed to know the parking brake was as suspect as everything else about that car? As I watch her storming back and forth, her eyes locked on mine, I conclude that I should have towed it to my shop.

No sooner has this crossed my mind than I notice smoke seeping out from under the hood. Not bothering to explain what I'm up to, I turn and yank open the storage box on my truck.

On turning back, I'm armed with a fire extinguisher.

By the time I've opened the driver's door and released the hood, there are flames shooting through all the gaps. It's this that stops me from lifting the hood so I can deal with the fire.

If I do that, I'll be losing my eyebrows, for sure. It's obviously something Skye hasn't thought through with her continuing to yell at me to 'put it out'. When something inside the engine explodes, it all becomes too much for me.

For all that my eyes are still open, the scene before me is half a world away. The Toyota is long gone, my damaged mind replacing it with the smoking remains of a Humvee. The other things that are as they were back on that fateful day are the crackle of flames, the smell of burning rubber, and the screaming.

I return from my hellish memories to find a fire truck on the scene. I'm sitting on the front porch of Skye's home and she's tucked in behind me, her arms wrapped tightly around my chest.

I place my hands over the top of hers to let her know she can let go, but she's not having any of it. Her arms tighten, her strength testament to a lot of kneading in her past.

I twist in her grip and address myself to her over one shoulder. "Skye, you can let go." And once she does, I'm out of here. Home to lick my wounds and give serious attention to that bottle of scotch I'd hidden from myself.

EIGHT

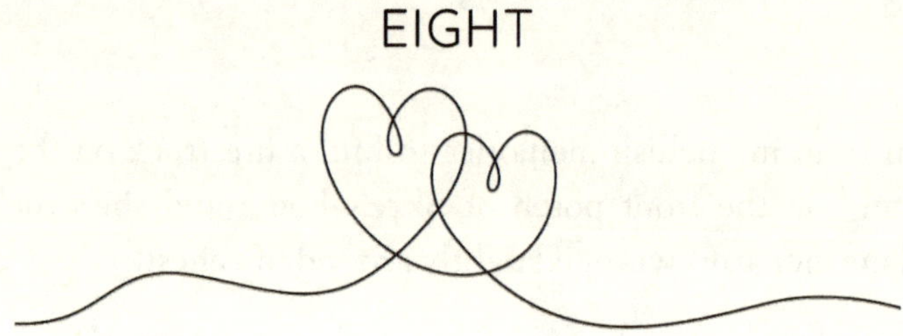

SKYE

I ignore Seth when he tells me to let go. There is not a chance I'm doing that. From the little I've read about P.T.S.D., his being on his own is probably the last thing he needs.

What was it that Facebook post said about sufferers self-medicating?

I can't believe I'd lost it like that, and over a stupid car, of all things. The other realization I've come to is why he might have abandoned me the night before. Personally, I love thunderstorms, but I can see how they could affect someone suffering as Seth does.

The problem was, I'd been too aroused to think straight. I also hadn't been aware of just how badly his flash-backs, or whatever they are, affect him.

I've got my cheek resting against his back when one fireman walks over. Rather than look at Seth, he looks at me.

"I'm taking it the car is yours?"

It's an educated guess with no-one like Seth ever owning a car of that hue. "Yes, it was, ah is."

"Yeah, well, can I have a word?"

That he wants this to be out of Seth's hearing is confirmed when he walks back to stand next to the smoldering wreck that was once Pinkie Pie. Only when I'm right next to him does he speak again.

"If this is for insurance, I don't fancy your chances."

I stare up at him, openmouthed. "My what?" I eventually splutter out before indignation takes over and I find my words. "Of course it's not. Seth can vouch for that. He was here when the blaze started. I'd just got home from work."

On looking over at the front porch, I find Seth is no longer sitting there. The engine on his truck roars to life a second later, and he's gone.

"Yeah, well, the fire is out, but you should get it moved as soon as you can. The city won't be happy if you leave it here." He's taken a couple of steps toward his truck when he stops. "Seth should be able to deal with it for you."

The fire truck has just left when I put in a request for an Uber. I'm not finished with Seth Adams. Not by a long shot. If he thinks he can sneak off like that, he doesn't know how hard it is to run a bakery.

The Uber arrives quickly, leading me to believe one of my neighbors must be moonlighting.

After I climb in the back, the soccer mum behind the wheel turns from looking at the steaming remains of Pinkie Pie to look at me. "What on earth happened?"

"I'll explain on the way, but can we hurry, please?"

The woman peels out of there as though she's got the oranges and is late for half time at her kid's game. I'm brief with my explanation of the vehicle fire, because the facts are definitely lacking. It's enough to satisfy her curiosity, though, and she falls silent.

On pulling up out front of Seth's place, I know he won't have been home for long. Although long enough for his truck to be parked inside and the enormous roller door, with its ADAMS TOWING logo, shut tight.

The driver turns, her concern at leaving me here on my own, clear. "Do you want me to wait?" She then waves her hand around, as if to draw my attention to the deserted industrial park. As if I haven't noticed this for myself.

I smile brightly to convince her I'll be fine, although I don't think it works for either of us. "No need to wait. I'm visiting a friend." When she still doesn't break into an answering smile, I open the door. "I'm expected. Have a great day." Any further arguments on her part are cut off when I close the door.

Conscious of my guardian angel still watching me, I hurry around the side of the gray block building. There I face the metal staircase that leads to Seth's apartment.

I take my time climbing the stairs. Why I'm being deliberately quiet, I wouldn't have a clue. Perhaps it's because I'm unsure of what sort of reception I'll get. If nothing else, I need to apologize that my awful behavior caused him to shut down.

Never in a million years when I'd woken this morning could I have imagined I'd be here now, apologizing. Every scenario had been quite the reverse.

SETH

I'm pouring my second drink when there's a gentle knock at the door of my apartment. "We don't want any!" I yell out. The only people who ever come calling here are after money, or trying to sell me cable.

Well, that sort, and my twin brother, and I avoid him as much as I can, these days.

I only half listen as I take another large mouthful of my bourbon. I don't bother savoring it, that's not what it's for. Dammit, whoever they are, they haven't left. Great, they'll be just the sort for me to take my frustrations out on.

The bourbon safely down on the coffee table in front of the leather sofa. I lurch to my feet. After crossing the open plan apartment in ground-devouring strides, I wrench the door open hard enough that it smashes into the wall.

It's just as well I own the blasted place.

Rather than face a collection bucket, or some creep selling cable, Skye stands there, her hand raised as if ready to knock again. I'm lost for words. Of all the people I've been expecting, she's not on the list.

"Ah jeez, just what I need, sympathy." I open my mouth to yell at her as she'd yelled at me earlier, but I can't. There's a fragility I've not noticed before. If I was to hazard a guess, I'd say she's close to tears.

Much as I want to be alone to lick my wounds, I don't have it in me to slam the door in her face. Instead, I move to the side and gesture for her to enter. "You'd better come in." The sooner she does, the sooner I can get rid of her.

She walks in, although her steps are as tentative as her knock had been earlier.

"Can I get you something to drink?" I've asked out of politeness, because in reality I don't want her here any longer than is necessary. She's already seen me at my lowest. The last thing I need is hand-wringing from her. I get enough of that from my brother.

"I'm good, thanks." Skye says nothing else until we're both seated at either end of the large sofa. And when she speaks, there's not an ounce of sympathy in the mix, rather she wants to understand my triggers so she can avoid them in the future.

"The future?"

She shrugs. "Hey even if we're only friends, I'd still rather know what's what."

I stare at her until she's out of focus. She'd seen how damaged I am and she still wants to... Actually, I'm not sure what's she's after. She'd mentioned friendship, but could there be more?

There's only one way to be sure. Fine, if she wants to know *what's what*, then I'll tell her. Let's see how keen she is to stick around after that.

So impersonal is my description of what happened in Afghanistan that it's as if I'm recounting the event to the Base Commander. That had been the only way I could get through it without breaking down.

Worried the scene will overwhelm me again, I dry wash my face and am horrified to find my hands wet when I take them away. I've never cried about that day; ever.

Before I've had time to hyperventilate, Skye is down my end of the sofa, dragging me into a tight hug. After a moment's hesitation, I hug her back, before explaining why I'd had to leave the night before.

"I didn't want you to see the damage three tours and that deadly ambush have done to me."

She pulls away enough that she can look me in the eye. "Are you serious? Of course, that sort of action will affect you. Why should you have to be stronger than anyone else?"

No-one's ever asked before, and I don't have an answer, but I suspect Skye will help me find it.

NINE

SKYE

It's been a few days since I last saw Seth. Time enough for me to research the heck out of P.T.S.D. While not a registered shrink, there are things I can apparently do to help.

As I tidy up after getting a final tray of apple pies into the oven, my mind is a muddled mess about how the afternoon will play out. While we're on civil terms, I don't have a clue how he'll react to my turning up out of the blue.

I'm wondering how much time I've got before I have to leave, when it's as if the bakery lights have been turned off. A look through the glass panel in the back door has me cussing quietly.

I honestly thought I had more time than this. After grabbing one of the cellophane-topped boxes we use for special orders, I waste no time folding it. My mom always says the way to a man's heart is through his stomach.

And while my apple pies are good, it's my cherry pies that will guarantee the fastest route. They always help me when I'm stressed. I collect half a dozen of them before helping myself to a seventh; purely medicinal, of course.

As the sugar floods my system, it goes some way toward calming my nerves. I've never been forthcoming about anything in my life, other than my business, that is.

This is uncharted territory for me on so many levels, and thoughts of what might happen have my heart thundering. Then another idea pops up, resulting in blood pumping through bits of me that aren't discussed in polite company.

"Paddy, I'm heading off for the day. Are you okay with taking the final tray of pies out of the oven and locking up?"

So unusual is this request that my employee stares at me open-mouthed, before assuring me he's more than capable of locking up. On seeing he's about to ask why, I hold my hand up before closing the lid on my box of cherry pies.

My nerves are such that I don't have a hope of explaining why I'm acting out of character. I'm so nervous, I risk telling him a lot more than I want to.

"I'll see you tomorrow." Color heats my cheeks before I stutter out, "I might be ah, a little, late."

I don't wait to see his reaction to this bombshell, and I'm out the back door before he has a chance. Despite Paddy having worked for me for over three years, I do not want to discuss my fledgling love life with him. I'm not sure I want to discuss it with myself.

Outside, I open the passenger door of my mom's car. I'm stuck with it until I sort my insurance claim out, with the company looking at me sideways after I'd listed the damage. In the meantime, it's her beige sedan or catching Ubers and I'd had enough from that soccer mom on Tuesday.

Pulling into the parking spot out front at Seth's place, I squint so I can see through one of the head-high skinny windows in that enormous roller door. Great, his truck's here. He's home for the evening.

The threatening sky tells me why he's not out and about tonight. I won't have been the only one checking the weather forecast.

Now comes the tricky part. After grabbing the box of pies off the passenger seat, I clamber out and put it on top of the car while I lock up. Soon after, I'm at the bottom of the stairs, ready to do one of the scariest things ever.

SETH

I'm staring at the bottle of bourbon on my coffee table, and the empty glass next to it, when there's a knock at the door. I'm about to yell out that I don't want any, when something occurs to me.

Surely she wouldn't be brave enough to visit me with a thunderstorm threatening? Especially with the weather report saying it'll be a big one and her knowing how loud noises affect me.

The last thing I need is company, with tonight all about self-medication and a weighted blanket.

Jeez, what woman would be interested in a man whose Friday night featured those two?

There's another knock, this one louder than the last. Damn it, she's not leaving me to it. I can't decide if I'm happy about this, or not.

One thing is for sure, though; I'll have to answer the door.

Sure enough, when I swing it wide, Skye stands there, surprising me on several levels.

First off is that she's holding a box of cherry pies, with their glistening filling visible through the cellophane top of the box.

The next thing I notice is that Skye is a mess. Her gorgeous hair is hidden under a battered paper hat, and there are smudges of flour on her face.

And yet, despite all this, she still does it for me.

Unable to speak, I stand to one side and gesture for her to enter. She's doing so when, out of nowhere, the rain arrives, hammering the windows of my apartment. I'm wondering how long I've got before the thunder hits town when it does, with a vengeance.

It's loud. Loud enough that I drop to the floor, my head cradled in my hands, my body curled in to protect my internal organs. I only become aware Skye is still there when she shoves me onto my back.

She then surprises me by climbing on top of me, draping that beautiful body of hers over mine as effectively as any weighted blanket.

She doesn't speak, rather she simply holds me tight, calming me by her very presence.

And she stays with me, not letting go until I'm again able to speak. Until I become conscious that I've never reacted to my weighted blanket the way I'm reacting to her right now.

What is it about near-death experiences that have you wanting to take hold of life? It's obvious my mind can't distinguish between real dangers, and imagined, because my body currently has a mind of its own.

It's only on tipping my head to the side that I see something sitting on the floor next to us, the perfect thing to break the tension in the room.

"Are those some of your famous cherry pies?"

TEN

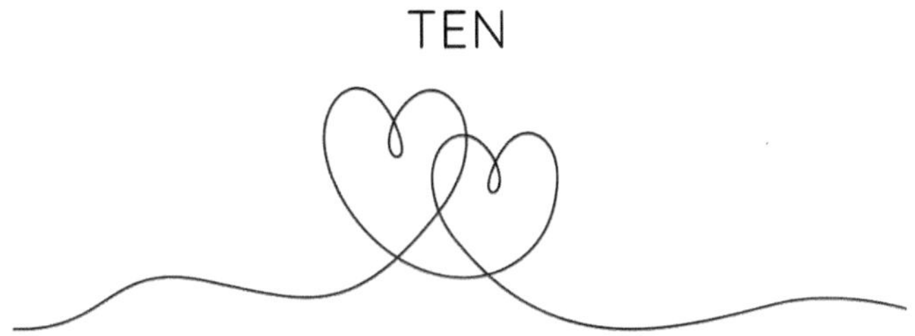

I'd felt silly when I'd turned Seth onto his back and climbed atop him. However, when he'd clung to me as though I was a lifeline, I knew it was the right thing to do.

It worked exactly like that article said it would, calming him, stopping his P.T.S.D. from claiming him fully. Apparently it's something companion dogs are trained to do.

But short of a dog, I figured my weight would work as well as that of any pooch. Perhaps even better thanks to my love of baked goods.

It isn't until Seth asks me about the cherry pies that I release my death grip on him. On looking down, I'm horrified by the state of him. "Oh, I'm sorry, I didn't think." I dust the flour off his chest as best as I can, but all that does is spread it farther.

I've gone from doing my best to clean him up, to stroking his chest differently altogether, when I become aware he's smiling. Forget that. He's not smiling, he's grinning, and his eyes are twinkling.

The article said nothing about this. Now what am I supposed to do?

I'm unaware of having spoken until he answers.

"You could start by kissing me, and we can go from there."

I'm both mortified and relieved. While mortified I've voiced my thoughts, I'm happy the assured, cocky man I lust after is back. OMG and he's spread out underneath me like the finest banquet.

I'm struggling to get off him, when it becomes obvious this isn't helping. Well, it is, but not how I'd imagined. A buck of his hips and I'm aware of exactly where we stand, or lie, or whatever.

He licks his lips, making sure I've seen before he speaks again. "So, what are you waiting for?"

Really? Why am I waiting? Isn't this what I've always wanted? It's something that has me dropping my lips to his.

What starts out cautiously soon has both our bodies involved. We're rolling around like a couple of horny teenagers when we take out the box of pies. I blindly push it away, my fingers coming back, covered in cherry filling.

Seth grabs my hand and sucks on one finger after another. He swirls his tongue around each fingertip, cleansing it, and doing wicked things to me.

I'm lying there boneless when he tugs at my paper hat and my hair tumbles free. His manhood soon straining even harder against the front of his jeans is telling.

Meanwhile, I'm berating myself for arriving in a glorified shower cap. Not my fault wearing them is second nature and I forget they're there.

My mind might also have been focusing more on what would happen at Seth's place than anything else.

Seth holds my face between his hands, and arches up for another kiss, dragging on my bottom lip with his teeth as he pulls away.

He allows his head to drop back down to the polished floor boards before giving my ass a no-nonsense pat. "Come on. Let's get cleaned up."

The accompanying words have been so matter-of-fact that I suspect I'm about to be dusted off and sent on my way. My heart sinks, although I take some comfort in having stopped Seth from disassociating because of the storm.

It's only when we're both standing that I realize I'm wrong. In fact, I couldn't be more wrong about what's happening.

SETH

Skye, ever the practical one, retrieves the squashed box of pies from the floor and puts it on the kitchen countertop before I've thought to do so.

Apparently, you don't mess around where cherries are concerned; although I can think of one cherry, I wouldn't mind messing around with. Thoughts of exactly how, and I'm grinning like a fool when I step in front of her.

Her gorgeous fiery locks tumble in waves around her shoulders, and there's still a bit of flour on one cheek. Despite my suggesting we should get cleaned up, things are about to get seriously dirty. Forget that. They're about to get deliciously dirty.

I've wiped the flour off her face and my hands are tangled in her hair when thunder once again fills the room. I freeze. I'm on the edge of shutting down, damn it. That is until Skye takes my hands away from her hair.

What? I'm expecting her to get me back on the floor and jump on me again, but she's got other ideas. And certainly nothing I'm expecting. Instead, she rips her t-shirt off and throws it in my face.

When her bra follows soon after, I'm jolted back to the here and now. In perfect synchronicity to a clap of thunder overhead, she liberally smears her breasts with cherry pie filling. The dark scarlet of the fruit is a perfect foil to her creamy white skin.

There now isn't a chance I'm disappearing inside my head. Not when it's as if my cock has been struck by lightning. Rather, my entire focus is on the decadent treat in front of me.

My hands rest gently on Skye's shoulders as I drop my head, first licking one breast clean, and then the other. "I think I missed a bit." I smile as I return to give the left nipple more attention. "Oh, and there's some more over there." Her right nipple is soon squeaky clean, and as hard as any cherry pit.

Damn if there was ever a better way to enjoy those cherry pies of hers. And yet she's nowhere near as naked as I'd like her to be. I'm undoing the button on her denim skirt when she slaps my hands away.

"Oh, no you don't. I want my slice of pie, too."

A second later my t-shirt is gone and I've had a handful of cherry pie filling spread all over my chest.

Once Skye gets started, it's not there for long.

After that, there's no holding either of us back, with both of us eating our fill.

ELEVEN

SKYE

While the solid oak floor is cool under my back, Seth's mouth is oh, so hot. I doubt there's any pie filling left on me, and yet he keeps licking. When he spreads me wide and runs his tongue slowly over my cherry, I arch my hips to get even closer to him.

I didn't think any filling had ended up there, but really, I'm past caring. "Ooooh, I think you missed some..." I arch my hips again, and dang if he doesn't suck at exactly the right time.

My keen of pleasure fills the room, my body trembling in release. Rather than allow it to fade, Seth continues tonguing that most sensitive part of me, to the point of pain. To the point when every nerve ending in my body explodes simultaneously.

When all that energy rushes back to the very spot still being revered by Seth's mouth, I burst into tears.

I never knew it could be like that. It's so much more than I could have imagined.

"Oh, baby." Seth moves up my body and drags me into a crushing embrace. "What is it? Are you okay?"

Unable to voice why I'm crying, I instead nod against his chest. How am I supposed to put into words what I'm unable to process internally? It doesn't matter that my body is currently like a half-set jelly. I've never experienced this level of vitality and freedom in my entire life.

I'd say it's like the rush of jumping off the high diving board, but that doesn't come close.

Only after my sobs have subsided does Seth pull himself free of my arms so he can stand. How is it he's still wearing jeans? It's something I'm dealing with as soon as I'm upright. That's pre-supposing I'm actually able to stand.

I have my doubts. It's something that has me burst out giggling with this confusing Seth as much as my tears had earlier. I wave away his concern before choking out that rather than me having a breakdown, I'm simply happy.

On him helping me to my feet, his grin is a match for mine. When he leads me toward a door at the back of the large open space, my smile only widens. As we walk through the master, I look at the super king bed that dominates the room, but Seth's steps don't slow.

We're in the bathroom and he's turned the shower on before he speaks.

"Sweetheart, I'm certain we both missed a few cherries."

When he drops his lips to mine, both of us are smiling into the kiss.

I don't bother taking my lips fully away from his when I answer. "I think you're right."

SETH

The thunderstorm is a distant memory as I run the soapy sponge over Skye's body. It helps that the bathroom doesn't have any windows.

After adding yet more citrus body wash to the large sponge, I continue cleaning every bit of her with reverence. If I'm being honest, it's now more about being dirty than getting clean.

My legs trembling as much as Skye's, I don't bother trying to stay standing. I drop to the built-in bench in the shower, for once glad of its presence. It doesn't matter that it was installed to allow me to take a break during a shower if I needed to. Now that I'm perched here, I can see other benefits.

The soapy sponge soon forgotten on the bench, I turn Skye to face me. I nudge first one knee and then the other between her legs, slowly spreading her wide.

For a start, she holds herself rigid, but the more attention I give to the curls at the apex of her thighs, the more compliant she becomes. After I've run my soapy hand through her cleft a half dozen times, her legs give out and she drops to my lap with a drawn-out whimper.

Even after I've hooked her knees up on the bench, she's still not as close as I'd like.

"Are you sure, sweetheart?" It's one thing for me to pleasure her with my tongue. My claiming her fully is another thing entirely.

Lost in a sensual haze, her nod is slow in coming. When I don't move, she nods again, and then leans forward to whisper, "Please. I want you so bad" against my forehead.

"I want you too, baby." One arm cradled under her ass, I lift her and position her, ready to bury myself slowly. But she's still slippery with soap and without warning, she drops, impaling herself fully on my length. Her moan of desire is as drawn-out as my own.

I grip her ass and ease her up before allowing her to lower again. "Oh god, that's so good."

It's even better when she moves on her own, lifting, before sliding back down and grinding into me for good measure. What starts out slowly soon speeds up, with both of us searching for something that's just out of reach.

This is killing me; I want to bury myself in her over and over, to touch her heart, to heal my own. "Hold tight, baby."

She's staring at me, her brow knotted, when I wrap my arms tight around her and surge to my feet. She's a quick study, hooking her ankles securely behind my back, and bringing us even closer together. But, still not as close as I want, and need.

It takes all my concentration to get us out of the shower and through to the master. After lowering us to the bed, I pull all the way out before plunging back in as far as I can.

"Oh god, that's, that's..."

Her response is inarticulate and breathy, but I get that she's enjoying this as much as I am. And yet it's still not enough. After running my hands down the backs of her legs, I gently uncouple her ankles and hook them over my shoulders.

Only then do I sink into her welcoming embrace until I can go no farther. A couple of quick thrusts, and then I pull fully out before sinking leisurely back in.

It's a pattern that starts out slowly but soon speeds up, with her meeting my every thrust. I don't last long after she discovers what tightening her muscles does for me. Her cries filling the room, and her pulsing around my length, tell me I haven't been alone.

It isn't until we're laying side by side, our heartbeats returning to normal that I realize the storm outside still rages. I drag Skye into my arms and hug her tight, secure, knowing that I've finally found my safe place.

EPILOGUE

On reading the weather forecast, I smile brightly. There's yet another storm brewing. Who'd have thought this unusual weather would benefit my love life as much as it has? The timing of the latest front is perfect for what I've got planned.

As I pack up early for the day, I yell out to Paddy that he's in charge. A couple of weeks back and I'd never have believed I could be this happy handing over the responsibility of running the bakery.

I'm also happier thanks to Seth and our blossoming relationship. Sure, I doubt his counselor had me in mind when she suggested diversion therapy, but who cares? Not Seth and definitely not me.

Soon after, I'm in my mom's car and on my way to Seth's place, although not straight there. I've got a pickup to make first, and a very important one. Luckily, he's ready and waiting, if a little sleepy.

With my new partner in the passenger seat, I can't help but wish I was driving Pinkie Pie. Despite being prone to breaking down; she'd also been instrumental in Seth and me getting together.

Pulling up outside the large roller door, I engage the parking brake just as I had that night above the cliff. I'm annoyed the insurance company is taking as long as they are to settle my claim. Even more annoying is that the insurance agent is an old school friend. Surely that should grease the wheels, and all that?

First, they'd put me through the hoops with all their questions, before finally admitting Pinkie Pie's demise *had* been an accident. Since then, they've been stalling, taking days to return my calls, and messing me about.

I've only just got the door open when Seth pops up next to me. While helping me out of the car, he glances at the gathering clouds, but rather than freeze, he breaks into a wide grin.

Has he seen my passenger? I was sure I was blocking his view.

"Oh, someone told you..." He doesn't let me finish, his lips effectively stopping my words where they are.

He eventually lifts his head and then closes the car door without taking his eyes off me. It says beyond doubt he hasn't seen my passenger. Before I rectify matters, he turns me around and pulls me hard up against his muscled chest.

He then covers my eyes with one of his hands.

It would appear I'm not the only one with a surprise.

On us stepping away from my mom's car, I worry that he's expecting me to climb the stairs with my eyes covered. However, on hearing the roller door rumbling into action, I know he's got other ideas.

Could it be he's got another location in mind? After all, we've christened every room in his apartment. I've not asked before the roller door rattles to a stop and Seth takes his hand away from my eyes.

I take a moment to make sense of what I'm seeing.

"But…" I step forward to better stare at the car sitting next to Seth's truck. "But how? The insurance company wrote her off."

"They did. There wasn't a chance I could resurrect your old car. But, it's the same model. It's even the same year. The color is a match, too."

As I walk around Pinkie Pie II, I'm in shock. My old car was never this gorgeous. I'd bought her second hand, but her replacement is like new.

I'm running my hand across the gleaming paintwork when Seth steps up next to me.

"Well, will she do?"

Unable to articulate how well she'll do, I turn and throw myself into his arms. Not until he squeaks do I pull back, and when I do, I'm even more lost for words. He's holding up a set of keys.

While I can see one key is for the car, I'm not sure about the second key. If I was a betting woman, I'd say that was a front door key.

"Is that…?"

His smile is hesitant as he awaits my response to him handing over a key to his apartment. Never that great with words, I instead show him with my lips what it means to me.

On pulling apart, I'm about to ask him to get the engine started on the truck when I remember my passenger. On my breaking into a wide grin, I get a responding smile from Seth. Unfortunately, it's one that's punctuated by a loud clap of thunder.

Blast, taken by surprise, again. We need to move it, and fast.

SETH

As I listen to the thunder rumbling away as if readying itself for the main event, I berate myself. Damn it, I'd lost track of time, but Skye had appreciated me replacing her Pinkie Pie. As romantic as it would have been to get her old car back on the road, there wasn't a chance after the fire.

And with Skye seemingly a constant in my life, I don't need the excuse of her car crapping out to see her. Her reaction to getting a key to my apartment has me confident of that. I also find that I quite like the idea of surprise visits from Skye.

She forcibly turns me around and marches me out of the garage before steering me around the side of the building. "Give me the remote! Get up those stairs! Get in the shower!"

These orders, having been shouted at a volume equal to that of any drill sergeant, my body responds accordingly. As when I was in the military, I don't question, I simply act. Once inside the internal bathroom, I strip off, turn on the shower, and climb in. Only now am I safe from the noise of the storm.

Thoughts of Skye soon joining me are also one hell of a distraction.

I'm perched on the shower's built-in seat when the door to the bathroom opens. Skye looks in briefly, smiles broadly and then disappears again. That's odd; she'd usually waste no time getting wet.

A second later, and she pops her head back inside the door.

"Is there room in there for two more?"

She disappears without giving me a chance to answer.

Two more? What the heck is she playing at?

I've come to no conclusions when the door opens wide, and Skye waltzes in buck-naked. Without bothering to close the door behind her, she saunters across the bathroom and into the stand-up shower next to me.

Meanwhile, I'm still staring at the doorway, waiting for whoever is to join us.

"Would you relax? You'll love him."

"Him? Um, sweetheart, I'm as adventurous as the next guy, but that's not my..."

The rest of my protest is lost when Skye gives a piercing whistle. It's one that's deafening in the confines of the shower, and I have to fight to stay calm.

Instead, I grit my teeth, ready to get rid of the guy. I'm not sharing Skye, no way. There's such a thing as taking diversion therapy too far, and this is it.

I'm on my feet, ready for action, when a puppy that's as dark as night races through the bathroom door. He then skates across the marble floor before tumbling into the shower stall with us.

He's a... Actually, I wouldn't have a clue what the hell breed he is, with at least a dozen bloodlines in on the action.

All I know by looking at the size of those feet is that when fully grown, he'll be the size of a small horse. A small horse that loves water, by the looks of things.

Skye smiles up at me. "He's only a foster for now, but if you like him..."

I take in Skye's beaming face before watching the puppy splashing around in the shower's bottom. "I hadn't planned on it, but I guess he'll be company in the truck."

Skye nods enthusiastically, before adding, "And with the proper training, he might even help you, with... You know, when I'm busy at work."

I know fellow veterans who have service dogs and swear by them. It would appear I'm to join their ranks. I shake my head in disbelief. Three weeks ago, I was in survival mode, blindly stumbling along in life, with no goals, and no dreams, only nightmares.

Now I've got a ready-made family, and my future shines bright.

"What's his name?"

Skye breaks into peals of laughter before spluttering out, "Storm!"

Soon our combined laughter fills the shower, with Storm joining in with delighted puppy barking.

𝔅 𝔍 ℜ 𝔗 ℌ 𝔖

Proud parents Seth and Skye Adams are delighted to announce the birth of their daughter Violet Iris Adams. Born on July 15 at home, Violet Iris, or Vie as she is fondly called, was 7 pounds 3 ounces and 18 inches long at birth. She is the first child for the couple and a beloved sister for their fur baby, Storm.

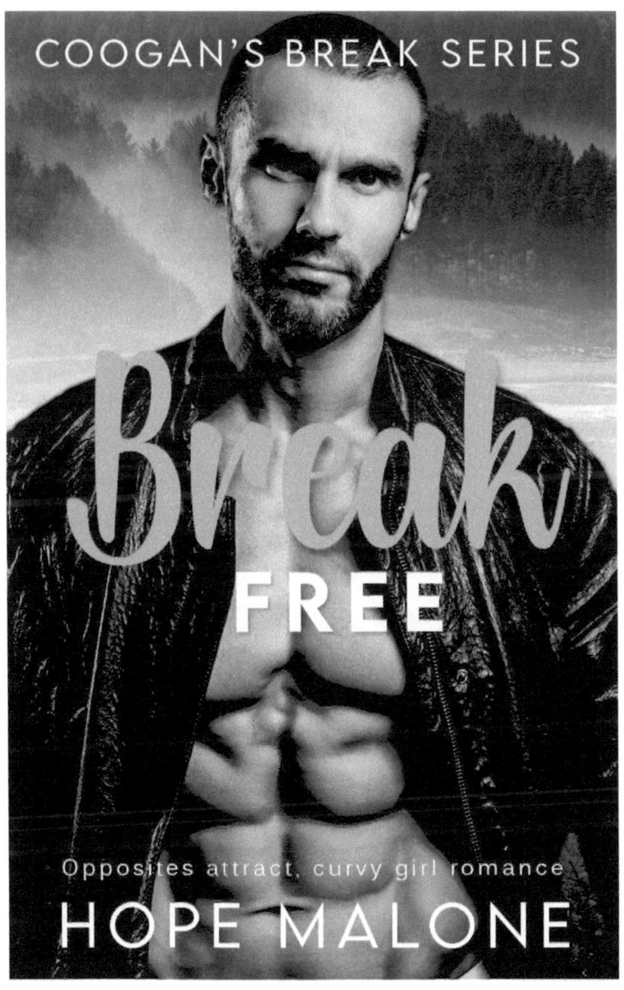

Josie is an accountant who likes order. Chase is a bounty hunter for whom life is chaotic and dangerous. Can opposites attract when his world comes knocking on her door?

ONE

CHASE

While I wait for my toast to look less anemic, I stir a pot of beans on the cooktop. It's not cordon bleu, but it'll have to do. Being a Bail Enforcement Agent means paydays can be few.

I've eaten this exact meal so often of late, there's no need to give it my full attention. Instead, I stare idly out the window of the rundown trailer I call home.

Perhaps *home* isn't the right term. Petri dish? Hovel? I'm also on the losing side in the ongoing war with the roaches. They must have one hell of a recruitment drive.

With a toaster that can go from bread to charcoal in sixty seconds, I check on my toast before going back to looking out the window. Soon, dinner is the last thing on my mind.

"Got you, you freaking asshole!" Well, not yet, but I've been tracking this guy for weeks after his failure to appear in court. FTAs are my bread and butter, or at least beans on toast, and here he is slithering past my trailer like the snake he is. There's not a chance he's getting away this time.

After ripping the toaster cord out of the wall and turning off the cooktop, I grab my leather jacket, with everything I need already stuffed in the pockets. There's no time for a shirt, and I'm thankful the tackiness of the floor sees me wearing my boots.

I don't bother locking the door behind me. The only thing of value I own is my motorbike, and that's chained to the large tree next to my trailer.

With Robert John Collings no longer in sight, I barrel down my narrow street to the crossroads in the middle of the trailer park. He's off to my right.

I haven't made a sound, and yet he immediately turns and spots me. And he's off, with his prowess running track in high school soon on full display.

But I'm no slouch, although I wish I was wearing running shoes like he is, rather than my boots. I'm not letting them slow me down, though, spurred on by thoughts of collecting my 10% of his seventy-five grand bail.

It's a good chunk of change and will put a stop to beans for a while. It's just a damned shame it won't be near enough to get me out of the financial hole I'm in. Something I have to thank my brother, Ethan, for.

Half an hour later and I'm no closer to taking him down, with the guy scaling backyard fences like they're nothing. The next fence is the tallest so far, and it's only the cross bars being on my side that allow me to lift myself up and over the top.

The delay has been enough that I'm in time to see the creep slowly opening the backdoor of the house whose yard we're in. There aren't any lights showing, so I hope to hell no-one's home because my FTA has a nasty reputation.

I'm sneaking across the yard when a crash comes from inside, followed by yelling and howling. The only thing I'm not sure of is who's responsible for the racket.

What the hell are you playing at, Bobby boy?

I'm close to the back door when lights flare inside the house. This shows Bobby standing in the doorway, cradling his right hand with his left. It's exactly the distraction I need.

I step up behind him, grab a handful of shirt and yank him backwards before shoving him to the ground. I have him cuffed and his ankles gaffer-taped, before light floods the backyard.

Only then do I notice the woman standing in the doorway, and suddenly Bobby is all but forgotten under the weight of my knee. I swallow hard because the woman is making my mouth water.

However much I want to, there's not a chance I'll be able to speak to her over the noise being kicked up by Bobby. My hand on the back of his head, I shove his face into the lush sod.

I'm about to introduce myself when I notice she's holding a rolling pin and I understand what's with all Bobby's cussing and moaning.

And hell if that isn't an even bigger turn-on.

JOSIE

On walking in the door Friday night, I'm tired after a full week thanks to one client putting their accounts in the too-hard basket. And I mean an actual basket, a cane dog bed that'd be big enough to hold a Golden Retriever or half a dozen Pugs.

While I'm tempted to drop my purse, kick off my shoes and collapse on the couch, I won't be able to relax in my work clothes. I'd also hate to damage the forest green vintage suit I'm wearing.

This sees me locking the front door and traipsing upstairs to the master. Later, when I sit down to watch one of my many classic movies, as I usually do on a Friday night, I want to be comfortable.

For many, this would involve sweats, but I'm not that girl. Not by a long shot. After hanging up the suit on its padded hanger, I drop my blouse down the laundry chute.

I'm soon dressed in a pair of three-quarter jeans, soft from frequent washing, and a baby-blue cashmere sweater. These, along with matching fluffy socks, will be perfect for a night on the couch.

Despite having worn the same outfit a hundred times, I glance in the mirror to check everything is as it should be. It doesn't matter that I'm spending my night alone. Appearance is important; with what I wear, a huge part of that.

As I turn to check out the rearview, my hand drops to explore the hole forming just below the back pocket. I'll need to buy another pair, and soon. Finding some that fit me as well as these won't be easy.

It's avoiding the dreaded gap at the back that's the challenge. Not everyone is straight up and down and I, for one, am anything but linear.

Back downstairs, I turn on the lamp in the living room and pull the drapes. Dinner will be a simple affair, being last night's lasagna. I set the table and pour myself a glass of wine while I wait for it to heat through in the oven. The vase of flowers in the middle of the table has me smiling.

As I take a sip of wine before tucking in, I think how nice it would be to share the meal with a special someone. Sadly, I'm plumb out of luck where men are concerned. A lot of them simply don't 'get' my obsession with all things vintage. Add in that I'm a curvy girl, and the pickings are slimmer still.

My dishes washed, dried and put away, I make myself a hot chocolate complete with whipped cream and those teeny tiny marshmallows. It's all part of my Friday night movie ritual.

This also has me turning off the kitchen light and the lamp next to the couch once I'm seated. I love the intimacy, plus it makes the black and white movies I favor easier to see.

Tonight's movie is an all-time favorite, with the heroine living the life I'd choose for myself right down to the picket fence. My lips move along with hers, professing my love for the dashing hero.

I know it's a pipe dream, with no-one living like they do in the classic movies. These days, everyone is in a hurry; more interested in staring at their phone than the person they're on a date with.

My last date had been a disaster. I still can't believe the guy parked outside and blasted his horn. It had taken him longer than it should to realize he should have come and knocked on my door.

It had tempted me to pull on my bathrobe and fake a headache, and I should have, with the date only going downhill from there.

On knowing what's coming up in the movie, I grab the cushion from next to me and hug it tight. It's time for the first kiss, and it's all I can do not to pucker up in readiness.

I'm lost in the kiss, when a noise from out back distracts me. More than this, it throws me out of the moment, my annoyance flaring in response.

It must be those blasted kids from over the back. If they want to smoke without their parents knowing, fine. But they're not trampling all over my flowers again.

The movie paused; I sneak through to the kitchen, the display panel on the range lighting my way. I'm right next to the back door when I see the handle turning. This tells me two things.

I hadn't locked the door after watering the garden this morning.

And whoever it is, it's not the kids from over the back.

TWO

Despite the dim light in the kitchen, I'm able to make out a hand and a gun inching through the gap. Stepping to the side so the door will hide me, I grab my marble rolling pin from the mint green cart next to me.

After a moment to get a sense of its weight, I grip the wooden handle tight. I've never knowingly hurt someone. But then I've never faced a situation like this either.

As the intruder inches forward, it took the luxury of hesitating from me. I'd rather face an unarmed intruder than an armed one.

I smash the rolling pin down, thwacking the out-stretched hand. This sends the gun clattering across the kitchen floor and under the freestanding range. There isn't a chance the intruder can get to it, not without serious burns.

What I'm supposed to do with him now, I wouldn't have the foggiest. I really hadn't thought things through. Whoever he is, he didn't give me that opportunity. Rather than stay standing in the dark, I flick a light on, all while staying behind the door.

I then hold the rolling pin up, ready to smack him again if I need to.

I knew it was a guy, the timber of the voice as he'd alternated between cussing and shouting, telling me that. It would appear I've broken his hand.

Well, that's just tough luck Mister, you interrupted my movie.

I'm readying myself for another go at him when he stumbles backward out the door. I can tell by his grunt of surprise that he's not moved on his own.

There's a scuffle taking place, but it's too dark outside for me to see who's involved. I turn on the outside lights, illuminating everything in my backyard to the point of daylight.

Of all the things I've expected to see, this isn't it. Or should I say, *he* isn't it. Transfixed as I am, I stand in the doorway, all thoughts of hiding gone.

There's no doubt in my mind the man on top in the fight is the good guy, him already having secured the man beneath him.

When he stands to face me, it's all I can do not to sink in a heap. I immediately recognize him from having seen him around town. Seen him and drooled over him, that is.

It doesn't matter that he's nothing like any of my movie crushes; he does it for me at some level. Okay, that level is six inches below my waist, if I'm being honest. This has me shaking my head to clear it of images you'd never find in a classic movie.

He has a haircut just the wrong side of brutal, and could do with a shave. However, that's not what catches my attention.

That would be the set of chiseled abs peeping out from under his distressed leather jacket. Why he's not wearing a shirt, who knows, but I'm not complaining. Add in jeans that skim all the good bits, and Kick-Ass boots, and he's quite the sight.

My gaze lands back on his face, and I spot his knowing smile. I've been well and truly sprung checking him out. Here's hoping the security lights shining in his eyes are enough to hide my scarlet face.

Only then do I notice I'm being assessed in return, with his eyes widening as he takes me in. Whether he likes what he sees, I'm not sure? I don't date enough to know.

CHASE

Even with the glare of the security lights, I like what I can see. I know she's tall simply by working out where she comes to on the doorjamb.

At six-three, I prefer women on the taller side. I would never date a shrimp.

Date? Steady on meat head, you've only just met the woman.

And not in ideal circumstances, either.

Hell, for all you know, she might be married.

I raise my hand both in greeting and to shield my eyes from the spotlights.

"Hey there, Chase Hunter, Bail Enforcement Agent. Are you okay?" She doesn't seem flustered, but you never can tell. Some people appear cool on the outside, while inside they're a quivering wreck.

Thoughts of this woman quivering make me wish I had a shirt on. Preferably one long enough to cover my reaction to her. There's no hiding under the glare of those lights.

"I'm. I'm, fine." There's a slight quaver in her reply.

"Was he armed?"

She lifts her rolling pin, smiling sheepishly. "Ah, not for long."

"That bitch smashed my hand. When I get her, I'm gonna..." The rest of Bobby's threat is for the worms, thanks to my foot on the back of his head. I can't allow a low-life like him to threaten a stunner like this.

"Where is it now?" I know Bobby is no longer armed, his hand apparently too damaged to hold a gun.

The woman frowns. "Um, it's under the range, but it'll be ages before it cools enough to reach the gun."

Confident my FTA isn't going anywhere, I step closer to her, all the while rummaging through the crap stuffed in my jacket pockets. The card I hand her is dog-eared, the dark blue ink on the front scratched. It'll do until I can afford to get more printed.

She peers at the card before a snort of nervous laughter escapes. I've been expecting it, amazed she hadn't reacted when I'd first told her my name.

Once she's got control of her mirth, she looks at my card again. "Chase Hunter? And you're a bounty hunter?" Her mouth tilts to the side. "I'll bet you get heaps about that."

This would usually annoy the hell out of me. Funny, but the teasing coming from her, I find I kinda like it. Rather than answer stiffly that I prefer Bail Enforcement Agent, I give her a wide grin.

She points the card in Bobby's direction. "Should I be calling the police?"

This has the creep spit out another threat, prompting me to step back and reintroduce his face to the lawn.

"I'll take care of the trash. You can report it tomorrow morning. They need to know he came onto your property with a gun, though. Will you be okay until your husband gets home?"

My question is clunky, but I want to know if she's single, although even if she did date me, she probably wouldn't stick around for long.

"I'm not married, but I've got this." She hefts her rolling pin and waves it about, coming close to whacking herself in the head.

"Show the police my card. They'll have a record of my taking him in tonight. And it might be best if they recover the firearm rather than you taking it in. Call me if they give you any grief about the rolling pin."

THREE

JOSIE

It takes a good long soak in my claw-foot tub the following morning before I'm ready to visit the police station. I hardly slept a wink last night, one ear constantly open for the slightest sound from downstairs.

Around one o'clock, I'd gotten up to double-check I'd locked the front and back doors. I had, but it hadn't been enough for peace of mind. In the end, I'd jammed kitchen chairs under the handles of both doors.

It didn't matter that I'd dealt with the intruder. And that I'd seen the county's hottest bounty hunter toss the guy into the back of a van that turned up as if on cue. Sleep had been elusive, perhaps because I'd spent as much time thinking about Chase as the intruder.

I'm still unsure why he was half-dressed, although you still won't hear me complaining. Which is strange, as the man of my dreams is nothing like Chase. That man would have a steady job at a bank, or insurance company. Like the men in my classic movies.

Chase is about as far from that as possible. My body doesn't seem to care, though. The idea of running my hands over his smooth chest has my blood pumping. And, that's NEVER happened before.

My experience at the police station hasn't been too bad. When he'd taken my intruder in the night before, Chase had filled them in on the capture.

This meant the officer on the front desk was expecting me when I arrived. All this resulted in it being a reasonably painless exercise, other than a hard plastic chair, and sub-par coffee.

After arranging for one of their officers to call at my place to retrieve the gun, I was free to go, armed with yet another tatty business card. This one was more official than the one I'd slipped carefully into the side pocket of my purse.

I'm opening the first of two glass doors required to leave the station when Chase opens the outer door. This sees us in our own private aquarium, neither inside the police station, nor out.

While the light hadn't been great last night, there are no such issues now, and he literally takes my breath away.

Perhaps it's his being properly clothed that draws my attention to his eyes. They're dark brown, bottomless pools in which I'd happily drown. They're the type often described as bedroom eyes, and it's all I can do not to raise my hand and yell, "Pick me!"

To temper their raw sexuality, they're framed by lines that tell me he can laugh with the best of them. It's an attractive feature in a man.

"I ... I... I..." Actually, I can't manage any more than this, despite fervently wanting to thank him again for coming to my rescue.

He grins, his eyes twinkling, before he says, "You're welcome," as though I've actually voiced my thanks. His hand on the inner door, he continues, "Are you okay to wait while I sort something out? Then we could maybe grab a coffee."

Still at a loss for words, I nod before mutely following him back inside the station.

I'm pleased when the officer manning the front desk greets Chase as an old friend and tells him to head on through the back. This gives me the space I need to get a handle on my libido. I've never had this reaction to a man before. I didn't think it was possible.

And especially not with a man who doesn't fit the one in my carefully curated dream future. I then spend my time waiting for Chase, wondering about a different future. It's one strangely devoid of picket fences, but full of lust and wanton behavior.

A future that has me squirming on that hard wooden bench.

CHASE

On opening the outer door at the police station, it's as though I've been sucker punched. Holy hell, if I thought she was a honey last night, it's nothing compared to when I'm at the mercy of her full impact.

Short, blonde curls held in place by a baby blue polka dot scarf, crystal blue eyes, and full lips painted a dark red. She'd look right at home on the cover of a magazine, although not a modern one, because she's definitely got a retro vibe going on.

I'd been right about her height, with this only amplified this morning by a pair of killer heels. Add in a dark blue dress that skims every curve on that stunning body and my cock is soon on its way to becoming a problem of epic proportions.

It's a relief when on entering the station that Josh tells me I can head straight on out the back. I'll only be able to get my big head straight when I'm safely away from this woman.

Damn it, I still don't know her name. This will be the first thing I'll get when I rejoin her. Hopefully, before my brain turns to mush again.

While I wait for Detective Farrow to finish his phone call, I'm reminded of other visits to the station, not all work-related. The most memorable was Ethan being arrested for investing in the type of pharmaceuticals not available at your local Walgreens.

I can still remember the shock on Gramps' face when Ethan called, although that was nothing compared to what happened next. Unable to face the consequences, Ethan did a runner stiffing my grandfather for the bail.

The bail being what it was, we'd come close to losing a home that had been in the family for generations. As it was, we'd had to put tenants in to cover the mortgage we'd had to take out.

This saw me move into the trailer park, while Gramps moved into what proved to be a rat-infested apartment. I'd soon dealt with the vermin, with each kill representative of what I'd like to do to my deadbeat brother. It was seeing the man who'd raised me, reduced to living in squalor, that led to me becoming a bounty hunter.

Back out front, I find the woman of last night's dreams standing staring out the grated front window of the station. If I thought she looked good from the front, that's got nothing on the vision I'm now faced with. That is one peach of an ass.

And bang, just like that, my cock is all 'well, hello there', taking any blood required for rational thought.

FOUR

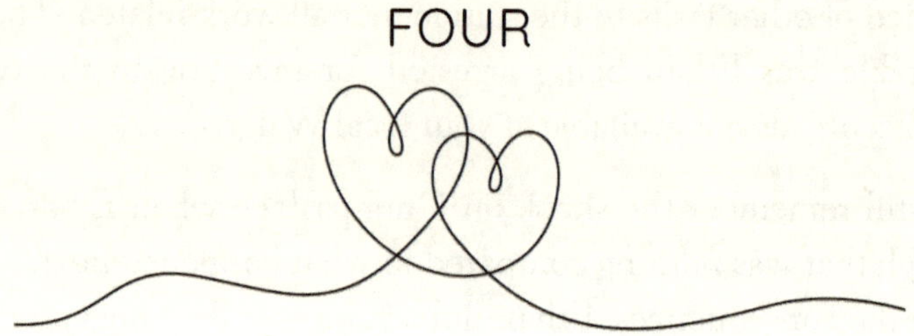

JOSIE

Unable to clear my head of thoughts of Chase and me doing the horizontal tango, and I can no longer sit still. And anyway, whoever designed that bench didn't have comfort in mind.

I'm on my feet, staring out the front window, when I hear footsteps behind me. Rather than being taken unawares, I spin around.

And yet, my heart still pitter patters in response to the guy. His impact on me reasserted, although not so much that I forget to introduce myself. "I'm Josie Robinson, by the way."

There's a flash of recognition from Chase, which comes as no surprise. Coogan's Break isn't that big, and my family has been here since the gold rush days.

Then, in a habit picked up by too many business meetings, I hold my hand out to shake.

Our fingers touch and any thoughts of business meetings flee in a sizzle of electricity that prickles my scalp, and other places. I'm only glad I've told him my name, because I'm now incapable of speech.

I then wonder if Chase isn't similarly affected. Rather than speak, he lets go of my hand and holds his out to the side, in an invitation to leave the station. I mentally shake my head to clear it of thoughts of him also being lost for words. Why would he be?

Out on the sidewalk, he pauses, taking a step first in one direction and then the other, before turning toward me. "What about that place down by the Surf Shack? They have excellent coffee."

Again, rather than speak, I smile and nod, falling into step beside him. We don't talk as we walk, thank goodness. If I had to concentrate on both, I knew I'd trip.

I'm glad about the walk. It gives me time to settle my nerves and cool my arousal. It helps when I go through the accounts I'll be working on come Monday. There's nothing like a balance sheet to take the edge off things.

On entering the deli, the aroma of espresso fills my senses. While I drink my hot chocolate with all the trimmings, I like my coffee strong and unadulterated, but for a little sugar. Lucky for me, the barista here knows this, with there being no need for me to state my order.

I'm already trying to locate my wallet when Chase settles his hand on mine. "I've got these. Why don't you find us a table?"

On him taking his hand away, I expect to find myself branded, but there's nothing to show. "Ah, thank you. I'll grab one down the back, overlooking the sea."

On sitting at a small table for two, I'm marveling at having spoken a full sentence when I check to see how Chase is getting on. He's rummaging through his pockets, dropping change on the counter as he goes. On receiving a nod from the barista, his shoulders drop, and I rush to look out the window.

That's odd; don't bounty hunters get paid thousands when they return a criminal? And yet, thanks to my years as a CPA, I'm able to spot financial desperation at thirty paces. It would have been all too easy to put the coffees on my tab, but I suspect that would never do with a man like Chase.

Even though our association is brief, there's an edge of pride that tells me he wouldn't appreciate my offer of help.

CHASE

When I'd first suggested a coffee, I hadn't given it as much thought as I should. Until I receive my fee for the capture of Bobby on Monday, I'm broke.

It's not until I've told Josie I'll cover the bill that I remember this. While I've got a reasonable amount of change on me, will I have enough? On hearing Josie is drinking an espresso; I think I might be okay, especially when I order the same for myself.

Despite this, I end up handing over every coin on my body, including a pathetic few for the tip jar. I can only hope Josie hasn't witnessed my desperate search because being broke is such a turnoff.

On joining her at the small table down the back of the deli, I'm pleased to see no reaction showing on her beautiful face. I hope to hell she doesn't want a second coffee, because if she does I'll have to come clean that until I get paid, she's outta luck.

Yet again, animosity toward my brother floods my system. If that bastard had stayed and faced the music, I wouldn't be at rock bottom, and Gramps and I would still live in the family home.

The latest tenants want to extend, and while that tempted my grandfather, I'm holding out, in case I get my hands on Ethan.

Settled in my seat, I take a moment to check out the woman opposite. "Did you sleep last night?"

I'm surprised that rather than answer straight off, color floods her face, and she stutters twice before she's able to speak properly.

"No, not really." She shakes her head, her face a picture of disbelief. "I can't believe I didn't lock the door. The neighborhood is usually so quiet and safe."

"Nowhere is completely safe when you've got men like Bobby Collings around. You might well have locked it."

Our coffees arrive with talk ceasing while we add sugar. She then takes a small sip before putting the cup carefully back down on its saucer. "So, where do we go from here?"

I'm thrown for a moment. *Is she talking about US?* Then reality bites and I realize she's talking about her intruder. More's the pity.

"Oh, ah, they'll set a date for the extra charges against him. I doubt they'll bail him out before that happens. We'll need to give evidence that he had a gun when he entered your house uninvited."

She stiffens, her earlier high color receding. "I didn't realize I'd have to. Is there any point in convicting him of further crimes? He was the only one who was hurt."

"I know it seems like that, but the longer he's away, the better." On seeing this hasn't settled her nerves, I press on. "I'll be there with you on the day, I promise."

I'd pat the back of her hand where it rests on the small table, except I don't want to come across as condescending. "Have you put my number into your phone?"

I get a brief shake in return.

"Would you like me to do that for you?"

In answer, she locates her phone, unlocks it, and passes it over.

"I'll be happier knowing you've got easy access to it, if you need it." I waste no time punching my number in. "Perhaps I should text myself, so I've got your number, too?" On receiving a small smile in answer, I get straight on it. You just never know when you'll want to phone someone to, say, ask them out on a date.

Although, to be fair, that wasn't happening until after I got my money on Monday.

FIVE

JOSIE

The weekend drags, with the minutes ticking by thanks to having Chase's number on my phone. The temptation to ring has been my constant companion.

Of course, I haven't given into it, but it has tempted me. The only thing holding me back is that I don't have a reason to call. I know when he answered that all I'd be capable of would be, "Uh ... uh... uh..." before I hung up. Like some thirteen-year-old schoolgirl with a crush.

One idea that's been circling like a buzzard is that he's having money troubles. The panic as he'd frantically searched through his pockets at the deli positively screamed it. Why, I wouldn't have a clue and it's not as if I can ask.

We're nothing more than passing acquaintances, no matter how much I'd wish it was otherwise. It's with this in mind that I drive to the grocery shop to stock up on food for the week.

I enjoy going shopping on a Sunday rather than during the week. Part of this is planning my meals, right down to what I'll take to work for lunch. There's a ritual around this that I find as calming as deciding on my outfits for the week.

I'll be the first to admit I might be a teensy bit OCD, but if I get enjoyment out of the process, does that make it a bad thing?

There's nothing spontaneous about my life, which is exactly how I like it.

And this makes my fixation with Chase even more mysterious. He's spontaneity personified from what I've seen.

I've nearly finished my shop, when I spot Chase at the checkout. Even from where I am toward the back of the store, I can see there's not much on the conveyor belt.

Certainly not enough to fuel a body like that.

I lick my lips before backing up behind some shelves. On stealing a glance around the corner, I see Chase hand a can of something over to the checkout girl.

Hmmm, he must be close to penniless to be passing a single item back.

What he needs is a good home-cooked meal. A quick scan of the groceries in my trolley and I break into a broad smile.

Usually, I'd empty my cart onto the conveyor belt in a logical sequence. Heavy items first, followed by fresh fruit and vegetables, with eggs last.

Today I dump everything on the conveyor belt and glare at the girl when she's not moving as quickly as I'd like. It has the desired effect, with me soon outside, and scouting around for Chase.

He's off to my left, stuffing his groceries into the pockets of his leather jacket.

I'm at his side soon after, with my sudden arrival obviously taking him by surprise. Before I lose my nerve, I blurt out, "Ah, would you like to come to dinner tonight?"

Such has my desire been to get the words out, that my invitation is totally lacking in niceties. "Ah, that is. I'd like to say thank you for all your help on Friday night. And you paid for our coffees yesterday. Making you dinner is the least I can do."

When he continues to hesitate, I pull out the big guns. "Do you like pot roast?"

CHASE

On seeing the total on the cash register, I know I've got problems. Hell, it's not even the good tuna. Ditto the noodles that have more to do with floor sweepings than Asian cuisine.

I pick up the second can of tuna and hand it to the checkout girl, and then wait on the updated total, not breathing properly until it pops up. It's taken me riffling through every pocket, under the bed, and behind cushions to come up with the paltry sum I have.

All I have to do is last until tomorrow; in the meantime, I'll just have to suck it up.

I'm outside the store, stuffing my measly rations into the inside pockets of my jacket, when a vision rolls up next to me.

Again, Josie is like a time traveler from the fifties, dressed in black fitted pants, a cherry red jacket, and matching sneakers. Once again, a polka dot scarf keeps her hair away from her face. This one matches her pants.

Retro it might be, but she owns it, even if the overall effect verges on goody two-shoes. Somehow, I doubt that's what I'd find if I was to peel it all off, layer by layer.

This image has me shoving my hands in the front pockets of my jeans to rearrange everything. Busy as I am, I take a second to catch up with what she's saying, although the words 'pot roast' soon have me back in the moment.

"Thank you. I'd really like that." I can't come up with anything more flowery. Not while I'm fighting my desire to take my hands out of my pockets and run them all over that voluptuous body.

"Would six o'clock be okay?" she squeaks out.

She's gripping the handle of her trolley hard enough that her knuckles have gone white. Her invitation hasn't come easily, because if there's one thing I've learned in this 'career', it's how to read people.

Despite knowing she's only asking me as a courtesy, I can't help wishing it was for real. And wishing is all it'll ever be. There wasn't a chance a classy girl like her would want anything to do with a penniless loser like me.

Sure, there'd been family money in the past, but that was gone now. The only thing of any value left is The Laurels. All it would take would be a downturn in the rental market, and we'd lose that, too.

There wasn't a chance I'd be acceptable to the Robinson family, even though I know my grandfather would welcome Josie with open arms.

On seeing she's looking at me as if frozen, I realize I haven't confirmed the time is suitable. To put her out of her misery, I nod jerkily before mumbling, "Perfect."

I can't manage any more than this. My mind crowded with images of her writhing under me and no sign of the fifties in sight. Okay, I might use that polka dot headscarf of hers as a blindfold.

SIX

JOSIE

Two o'clock arrives and I'm left wondering what on earth possessed me to invite Chase to dinner that very night? I'm back at the grocery store for the third time, having decided I wanted to make an apple pie for dessert.

At least I think this is what I'll go with. I've changed the menu so many times that I'm actually pleased I'd mentioned pot roast. Without that, I can't imagine how many menu changes there'd have been.

The pot roast underway and the pie ready to go into the oven, I collapse at my small kitchen table for a breather. It doesn't last long when I realize I don't have a clue what I'm going to wear.

I can't very well stay dressed as I am, with a few ingredients having slipped past my pink gingham apron. I'm a mess and hardly in a state to welcome visitors. With no time to waste, I head upstairs, considering and discarding potential outfits on the way.

It'll need to be something slimming. It doesn't matter that Chase is only coming over because of the home-cooked meal; I still want to look good. Actually, that's not true. I want to look amazing. How sad is that?

This sees me trying on every combination on offer thanks to an extensive selection, and I'm not happy with any of it. I'm even contemplating wearing control pants when I throw my hands up in defeat.

"What's the point? You don't have a hope in hell with a guy like him!" After shouting this at my reflection, I drop back on my bed and stare at the ceiling. Only part of my mind is now on what I'll wear. The rest focused on my dead-end life.

Strange though it is, until Chase crashed into it on Friday night, I'd never questioned it. Now I wonder if I'm not missing out on something. That in trying to find a guy like one out of my favorite movies, I'm setting myself up for failure.

Thoroughly demoralized, I give up on curating the perfect outfit, instead opting for my favorite jeans, a mint green sweater, and matching sneakers. I'm tying my curls back with one of my many scarves when I freeze.

"Come on, girl. Live on the edge for once."

The scarf is soon Kondo-folded and returned to its special box in my wardrobe. To add to this new natural air, my makeup is minimal, allowing the real me to shine through.

I can only hope I don't put Chase off his dinner.

Ten to six and everything is ready, right down to jazz music playing softly in the background. Only now do I consider he might not even turn up, because something had distracted him when he'd agreed to the time.

For all I know, he could be one of those people who arrives half an hour late acting as though nothing is wrong. While in reality, dinner is close to being incinerated, and the hostess is a sweating heap of worry.

I'm pacing back and forth across the living room pondering lunches to use up all that pot roast when there's a knock on the front door.

A glance at my watch and I give in to a relieved grin. He's one minute early. That's so unusual in this day and age.

Could Chase have more in common with my dream guy, after all?

CHASE

I make it to Josie's place bang on time, a miracle. I'd spent the rest of the day chasing down a couple of cheap-ass FTAs, a necessary evil when your finances are down the toilet.

It doesn't seem to matter how hard I work these days, I never get ahead. My accountant lays the blame on federal and state taxes, but there's got to be more to it than that, surely?

Either way, by the time I'd offloaded my FTAs and completed the paperwork, I'd only just had time for a shower at Gramps' place. Other than his shower being better than the upright coffin in my trailer, it means I can monitor him. Ideally, we'd have moved in somewhere together, but with the hours I kept, it wouldn't have been fair.

As always, Josie takes my breath away. It doesn't matter that her 'look' tonight is more in line with what she'd been wearing on Friday night than what I've seen her in since. To my mind, she's perfect.

I immediately have to squelch the image I'm working on of her with nothing on at all. Dinner will be hell on earth if I'm sitting there with a cock hard enough I could hammer in nails.

Josie's taken my jacket and left me on the couch while she prepares drinks, when I spot a display of old-school suitcases under the window. For a moment, I'm back on the day mom and dad dropped my brother Ethan and me at our grandfather's place.

When they'd dropped our suitcases next to us, I'd been excited, thinking we were staying at The Laurels as we had in the past.

As a five-year-old, I was fizzing about unlimited tree climbing and hide-and-seek, right up to the point mom and dad told Gramps they wouldn't be back. It turned out my folks had decided the whole parenting gig was harshing their buzz—their words, not mine—and it made better sense for us to be raised by Gramps.

My last view of them was their car disappearing down the long drive at The Laurels, and them waving gaily as if off on vacation. This left Ethan and me under the care of Gramps, with grandma having passed away when I was a baby. Were it not for this wonderful man, I think their abandonment would have destroyed me. It'd sure as hell done a number on Ethan.

Only on Josie handing me my drink do I escape my memories.

Dinner is wonderful, and the first decent meal I've had in weeks. After seconds of pot roast, and two slices of apple pie and ice cream, I'm fit to bust.

If I wasn't as keen as I am to impress this splendid creature, I'd undo my belt. Sad bastard that I am, this has my thoughts going in an entirely different direction. And that's so not happening tonight.

I'm on my feet a second later. "You cooked, I'll do the dishes." It had always been the routine when I was living with Gramps, and the familiarity has a nice feel to it.

Josie, however, has other plans and there's a bit of a tussle over control of the dishwashing liquid. It's one that sees me holding the bottle above my head and Josie jumping for it, and damn if her body jostling against mine doesn't do things for me.

All it takes is to see an answering glitter in her eyes, and I slam the bottle down next to the sink and drag her into my arms. Our lips touch. She wraps her arms tight around me, and my hand drops to explore the small hole in her jeans that I'd spotted earlier.

When I poke my finger through the gap and run it along the crease of her ass, she squeaks. Our kiss deepens; with any thoughts of the washing up a distant memory. Nope, I've got something altogether dirtier in mind.

This has me sweeping Josie up in my arms and backing through the swing door into the living room. We're soon spread out on the luxurious velvet sofa, desperately exploring each other's bodies with hands, lips, and tongues.

I've never had a woman inflame me as much as Josie does, and it looks as if I'm not alone. Her hands are all over me, the tip of her tongue playing with mine. I nudge a knee between her thighs, immediately able to feel her heat through two layers of denim.

This only intensifies when she rubs herself against my leg, her desperation to be closer still, a match for my own.

And there's only one way that's happening.

SEVEN

JOSIE

My world is a whirl of raw sexual hunger, unlike anything I've ever experienced. It's a kaleidoscope of hands, sounds, and passionate kisses playing in my head, like a movie.

Only this is no movie, it's so much better, and for once it's in glorious color and not black and white. It's something that has me giggling enough that Chase breaks contact, lifting his head to look at me.

A brief flash of hurt and my next chortle catches in my throat. "I wasn't laughing about us, ah you. I was just thinking this is nothing like in the movies." When he doesn't look convinced, I smile softly before adding, "This is so much better."

He dips his head until our foreheads touch, before whispering, "How could I make it better yet?"

Even though his jacket hangs on the coat stand next to the front door, he's wearing too many layers. I want to see if my recollection of his six-pack is on the money. I know from running my hands over them that his abs are rock hard. But that's not the same as actually seeing them in the flesh.

"You could take your shirt off."

He lifts his head, his eyes gleaming. "Are you asking?"

I try to respond, but the words stick in my throat. I'm not used to being this direct, to asking for what I want. But he waits, letting me know that until I ask properly, I won't get what I'm after.

I swallow deeply before rushing my words. "Yes, yes, I'd like you to take your shirt off."

His responding grin is one of the sexiest things I've ever seen. It's almost as sexy as when he gets slowly to his feet and makes a real production out of undoing the buttons on his shirt.

He starts with those at his wrists, before moving onto the ones running down the front, not once taking his eyes off me. He's taking his own sweet time, no doubt on purpose; to the point I'm close to jumping up and ripping the rest of them open.

As if sensing what's on my mind, he wags his finger at me to keep me where I am.

Finally, he shrugs out of his shirt, drops it on the coffee table, and then holds his arms out to the sides, all while licking his bottom lip. I'm lying there enjoying the view when he speaks, and my heart stutters in response.

"Now it's your turn, Betty Boop."

My horror must show, because his smile falters and his hands drop to his sides. How do I explain I can't remove my top because of the state of my underwear?

When I'd thrown my hands up in defeat earlier, not only had I chosen my clothes for comfort, I'd done the same with my bra and panties. They're not tattered and gray, but neither are they up to being seen by a good-looking man like this.

When he reaches for his shirt, I only have a second to decide. Either I leave him with the impression that I consider myself too good for him, or I flash him my everyday underwear.

He's already picked his shirt up when I jump to my feet and drag my sweater over my head and toss it on the couch. There's been nothing striptease about this, rather my actions have been utilitarian.

The moment is further ruined by my revealing I'm wearing a black sports bra. Never in a gazillion years could I have imagined Chase and I would end up like this tonight.

I stand there, exposed, waiting for his rejection of this badly wrapped package.

Unable to witness his revulsion, I drop my gaze, and in doing so, catch sight of the front of his jeans and realize I might just be wrong about that.

CHASE

As I take in Josie's generous curves, my cock twitches. Why she didn't want to take her sweater off, I'll never know. Sure, her bra is a basic black model, but to me, this only serves to emphasize her natural beauty.

My hands rest on the belt holding up my jeans, my recent weight loss meaning it's not there simply for show. "Shall I go next?" Again, I wait for her response.

"Yes, you should." She pauses before adding, "And soon." A smile dances on her lips as she taps her toe with mock impatience.

I doubt either of us is expecting things to move as rapidly as they do when I unbuckle my belt and yank it dramatically free of the belt loops. A second later, my jeans drop to my ankles, leaving me standing there in cartoon boxers.

I don't even bother with embarrassment, rather exploding with laughter as the absurdity of it all hits me. The sooner I get some money in my bank account, the better.

Helping to ease the sting of my embarrassment is Josie jumping to her feet. She's laughing as hard as I am, while struggling to undo the button fly on her jeans. A second later, her jeans are also around her ankles.

There are no silky boxers for her; rather, her panties are substantial enough she could wear them to the gym on their own without getting a second look. As we both kick our jeans to the side, I realize neither of us was ready for things to progress tonight, and I like that.

It tells me a lot about the woman standing vulnerably before me.

The moment we touch, her eyes darken with passion. Her moan as we sink back onto the couch is heartfelt, with her soon spread out under me invitingly.

It doesn't matter that we haven't known each other for long. There's a connection, a bond that goes way beyond physical attraction.

Wanting to savor the moment, I take my time sliding the bra straps down, kissing her shoulders reverently.

Her bra is of the sports variety, meaning it's supposed to stay in place, not be removed with the flick of a wrist. Thankfully, she struggles into a sitting position before ripping it up and over her head. Embarrassment mottles her face and chest.

"Ah, so that's the trick." My words have been automatic, transfixed as I am by her full breasts, the nipples tight puckered little buds.

I immediately give into the temptation to touch her breasts. More than this, I run my hands over them, rolling her nipples and am rewarded when she arches her back to be closer. She wants more, and I'm ready to give her whatever she wants.

Her breasts demand my attention, pebbled mounds just begging to be kissed. I run my tongue across her left nipple before blowing on it, with Josie's hiss telling me she likes the sensation. I get a similar reaction from the right.

"You like that, baby?"

Her response inarticulate, I check to see if she's okay. Her lips are parted, her eyes partially closed, her breath shallow. She's more than okay.

After hooking my finger under the elastic of her no-nonsense panties, I slide them down, although not as far as I need or she wants. Without prompting, she arches her hips off the couch, so I can remove them altogether.

I pull back, to take in her naked perfection, and caressing her body with my gaze before focusing on the object of my desire. I want to taste her, to suck on her jewel until she shudders under my mouth.

On parting her slick folds, I find the hidden gem I'm after, running my tongue roughly across it, again and again. Most of what Josie is now saying is gibberish, other than the word 'more' that is.

She'll get no arguments from me, and I get no resistance from her, with her laying herself open in silent invitation. I accept, to the point I'm sucking on her nub when an orgasm hurtles through her. So responsive, and so mine.

I'm drawing the last of the climax out of her when I hear a familiar tune. It's one that's as effective as a bucket of cold water in cooling my ardor. And it's not on the stereo.

It's coming from my leather jacket, with only calls from one individual programmed to play that tune. I need to answer before it goes to voicemail, because the person phoning doesn't leave messages, ever.

"Oh baby, I'm so sorry. I have to take this. It'll be important." I wrench myself away from her and shoot across the living room, desperately searching through the various pockets for my phone.

I open the call and put the phone up to my ear.

"I was thinking you wouldn't answer," says a voice, heavy with age and gravel. "Sunset Motor Lodge, Room 17."

EIGHT

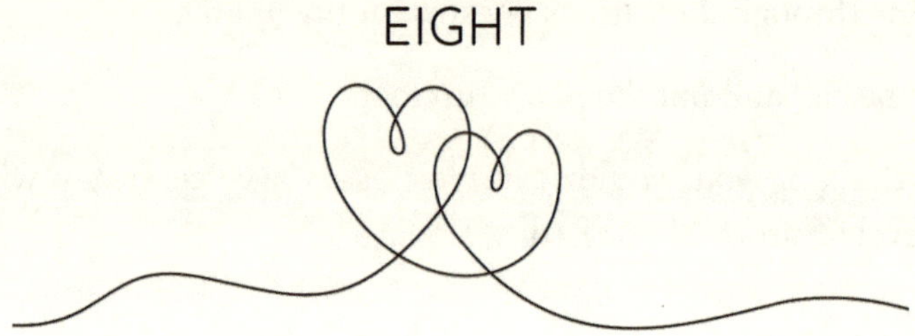

JOSIE

On flipping back the covers ready to get into bed, I'm at a loss. I didn't expect to be on my own after what had gone down earlier. And that had been Chase. I'm unable to stop an unladylike snort at my joke.

Even thinking about the climax that had ruled my body has me warming. How am I supposed to get to sleep when I'm on the verge of another one?

Why Chase had to leave was a mystery. It was something to do with an FTA, but that's all he'd say. If not for his reaction to the call and his reluctance to leave my side, I'd be worried it was an excuse.

Then I roll my eyes, the reason so obvious as to be laughable. I don't understand how his finances can be in such a mess when to my knowledge he's returned three criminals this weekend alone.

Until I'd met Chase, my experience with bounty hunters, sorry bail enforcement agents, was zip. It had me researching them online after our coffee yesterday, hoping to understand him better. He shouldn't be struggling financially, even if he's only getting the minimum 10% payout.

He'd be in better shape if I was in charge of his finances. *Whoa, steady on girl, it's not time for a joint checking account just yet.*

I'm sitting bleary-eyed at my desk on Monday morning when my mobile rings. On seeing who it is, my scalp and other bits are tingling before I've even answered his call.

Rather than state my name as I usually would, all I manage is a breathy, "Hey there."

"Hey yourself, sweetheart."

Wow, if his name on the screen did things for me, him calling me sweetheart does things that aren't appropriate for the office.

"I just wanted to say thank you for that amazing meal last night. Sorry I had to rush off."

On remembering what we'd been up to when he had to leave, I fan my face with my free hand. If anyone were to come into my office and see me, they'd ask if I was sick.

"That's okay, I understand. Did you catch them?"

It turns out he hadn't, disappointment clear in his tone.

"Don't worry, you'll get them." As a pep talk, it's pathetic, but I'm not sure what else to say. That these captures are important to him financially is obvious. However, I'm not going near that right now. Instead, I'm struggling to avoid saying something inane like, "isn't it a lovely day," when Chase speaks.

"I was wondering if I could repay you for last night's lovely meal by taking you out to dinner this week."

This floors me. Not that he's asking me out, but that he's done it so formally. It's more usual these days for a man to say, "You fancy grabbing a pizza some time?"

"That'd be lovely. What about Wednesday?" I'm being pushy suggesting that night, but tonight and Tuesday would be too early in the week, and there's something not quite right about Thursdays. Thursdays are blah, while Friday is too 'date night' for comfort. At least for now.

"Oh, right, Wednesday," rushes out Chase. "What about Maddigan's? Would that be okay?"

Okay? It'd be more than okay. The restaurant at Maddigan's Resort and Spa is one of my all-time favorites. It's also super expensive. While I can afford to eat there occasionally, I wouldn't have thought Chase's finances were up to that.

"Maddigan's? Are you sure?" I have to bite my lip to stop adding, "Isn't that pricey?"

"Hey, the food is out of this world, and I haven't been there in an age..."

Giving up on my subtle attempt to help him out financially, I simply say, "No, no, Maddigan's will be lovely. Let me know what time and I'll be there."

"No need. I'll pick you up at six thirty. Hey, I need to rush. I'll call you back."

On ending the call, the first thing to cross my mind is that he's taking me to the flashiest restaurant in town, on the back of a motorbike? I guess I'll be wearing my black satin cigarette pants and gold Lurex sweater.

CHASE

After shutting off the call, I have second thoughts. Not about asking Josie out, but what the hell made me suggest we go to Maddigans?

While I wasn't lying when I said the food was fantastic, the prices are just as mouth-watering. It's the main reason I haven't been there in years.

The last time I was there was with Gramps, and if anyone deserves a meal out, it's the old man. Great, now I'm feeling guilty that I'm taking Josie out for dinner, and not him.

It's thoughts of my last dinner out with my grandfather that have me facing another minor problem. What the hell am I supposed to wear? My body has undergone a drastic transformation from when I'd last dressed formally. I've bulked up across the shoulders, while my hips and waist are narrower, although not by choice.

There isn't a chance the suit hanging in the closet at Gramps' place will fit me.

A moment's pause and I know exactly where I'll be shopping that afternoon. I've not even kicked the engine of my motorcycle into action when it dawns that finding a suit will be the least of my worries. Whereas booking a table will be a nightmare.

It looks as if borrowing Gramps' car won't be the only thing I'll need his help on.

Three hours later, and my grandfather has somehow secured a decent table for me.

The last thing I want when I'm trying to chat up Josie is servers brushing by on their way to and from the kitchens. Or worse still, to have patrons barging past on their way to the restrooms.

I'm also in possession of decent clothes thanks to the ladies at the charity shop attached to the church the old man frequents. To complete the outfit, I'll be wearing my grandfather's *church shoes*.

Truth be told, the ladies at the charity shop had been as excited as Gramps when they'd found out I was taking a lady to dinner. They might have actually been more excited. One of them even ripped my t-shirt in her haste to remove it so I could try on the pale pink dress shirt she'd picked out for me.

It got out of hand enough that it was a wonder I didn't leave with dollar bills stuffed in my boxers. Either way, I'd left with a suit, shirt and tie that wouldn't have me mistaken for wait staff.

Wednesday afternoon, I grab my grandfather's car from the storage unit, before collecting my shirt, suit and tie from the dry cleaners. Last place to call into before I pick up Josie is my grandfather's so I can use the shower.

It's not until I'm standing under the stream of hot water that the nerves make themselves at home in my stomach. I haven't been out on a serious date since...

I stare at the flamingoes on the plastic shower curtain until they blur before I realize I've never been on a date like this.

Nothing this formal, this serious, this planned. Hah, if I was nervous before, that's got nothing on how I feel now!

NINE

JOSIE

Wednesday evening rolls around and I'm not so much suffering from butterflies as hosting a full-on tiger moth dog fight.

On shimmying into the form fitting dress and zipping it up at the side, I'm pleased to see it still fits me. I love this dress. A vintage designer number that probably cost me ten times the original price.

I'm looking in the mirror, turning this way and that, when there's a knock at the front door. Even though Chase told me earlier that he wasn't picking me up on his motorbike, I'd expected to hear his grandfather's car.

After grabbing my purse and coat off the end of my bed, I skip down the stairs as fast as my black suede pumps will allow. It's Chase as expected, but as I take in what he's wearing, my simple greeting jams in my throat.

I'm surprised he'd noticed my preference for all things retro. But I guess taking notice of the smaller details must be a prerequisite for a job like his. There's no other explanation for him standing looking like he's stepped straight out of a 1950s movie.

He's got a Dean Martin thing going on. It's one that suits him. But why would he bother going to all that trouble if this was just a thank you dinner?

And if it's just a thank you dinner, why are you bothering as much as you are?

I tamp this thought down immediately, knowing from experience what happens when I get my hopes up.

Chase steps inside the door and holds out his hand. I take a second to realize he wants to help me into my coat, again taking me by surprise.

Not until we're walking down the front path, do I catch sight of the car. The 1950s cherry-red Buick convertible parked out front of my house is amazing. And the paint color matches my dress perfectly.

Can tonight get any better?

Apparently it can. When we're shown to our table at the restaurant, I'm stunned. Chase must have dropped one doozy of a tip to get this table. Not even my parents have been able to book this table, and they eat here regularly.

"Ouch!"

Chase looks at me, his face a picture of concern. "What's wrong?" He runs his eyes over me as if to check for damage. "Are you okay?"

"Just pinching myself to make sure I'm not dreaming."

As we make ourselves comfortable at the table, I'm torn about what to look at. The amazing view out over Coogan's Break and the setting sun beyond, or my date? In the end, Chase wins hands-down. I can check the view out any time.

He looks so relaxed here, as though he's used to sitting at the best table on offer. I find this confidence to be as attractive as the man himself. When he takes control of ordering the wine, I wonder what else he's hiding from me.

There's a lot more to him than being a simple bounty hunter.

CHASE

The evening is perfect; too perfect. I keep waiting for something to go wrong. For Josie to realize she's with someone socially beneath her, to fake a trip to the ladies and then bail on me.

All evening I'm on edge, expecting something awful to happen. Sure enough, we're waiting for Josie's coat after dinner, when I get a text. With my finances long since putting paid to any social life, I know it'll be to do with work.

"Josie, are you okay if I check this message?"

"Of course."

I step away from her, not because I've got anything to hide, but because some texts sent to this phone, well, they aren't the nicest. And this one is no exception.

I shove my phone back into my pocket and take Josie's coat out of her hands. However, it's not so I can help her with it. "Ah, we've got a problem."

Josie stands frozen, her eyes darting around the hotel lobby. "He escaped?! But how?" Such is Josie's shock at hearing Bobby has done a runner that her voice is louder than I'd like.

"Shhhh! I'm not supposed to know. No-one is. Chief Sutton wants to keep it on the down-low."

Josie's eyes narrow as she struggles to steady her breathing. "Damn it, just because he's got the mayor breathing down his neck about crime, that doesn't give the old coot the right to keep this quiet." Her hand at her throat, she then whispers, "Can you drop me at my mom and dad's? I wouldn't feel safe at my place."

Rather than help her with her coat as she obviously wants, I keep a tight hold of it. "Ah, that's not a good idea." I pause, unsure how to proceed, although Josie, attempting to take her coat off me, prompts me soon enough. "He escaped this afternoon. There's a chance he followed us."

It doesn't take long for Josie to grasp the implications of this. I toss her coat over my shoulder and drag her into a tight embrace, doing my best to soothe her. All the while wondering, 'What the hell do we do now?'

With her place and her parents out of the question, the only other solution is to take her back to my trailer. Not happening in a million years. Bad enough I have to see the place. Never mind Josie seeing what a dump I live in.

After kissing the top of her head, I pull back so I can look her in the eye. "What about spending the night here?"

This gets her attention. "You mean us?"

"You'd be safe enough on your own. It's a big hotel and they're all over their security."

She bites her bottom lip before looking up at me. "I'd rather you stayed with me."

Because of a small mix-up on check in, we end up with the honeymoon suite. The old gal at reception must have thought we'd eloped given we had no baggage between us.

All the same, I'll make the most of the California King that dominates the room. There's no better way for me to take Josie's mind off tonight's bad news.

TEN

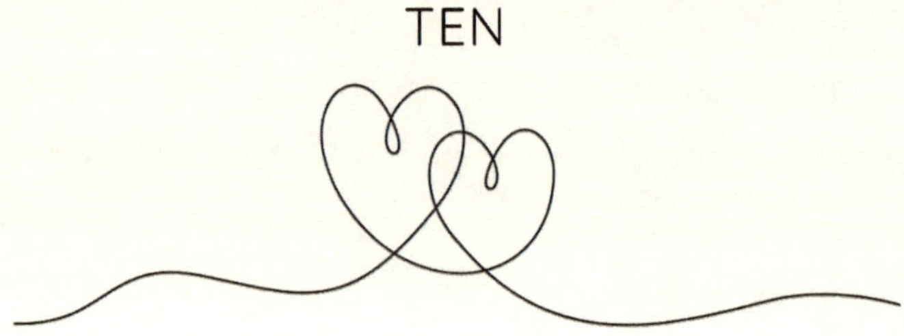

JOSIE

The following morning, on waking next to Chase in the honeymoon suite, for a moment, I'm confused, although this soon morphs into something else. It's something that works better than coffee at waking me up.

The glowing red numbers on the bedside-clock tell me it's still incredibly early and I steady my breathing to avoid waking him. With one thing, and another, he hadn't got a lot of sleep last night, something that has me grinning to myself.

He must sense the change in my breathing, because he rolls over and drags me into a tight embrace before kissing me softly on the cheek.

"Did you get any sleep, baby?"

I melt against him, taking comfort in his strength. "Not really." This is an understatement with my dreams of Chase constantly interrupted by Bobby Collins. The continual flip-flopping between arousal and fear had made sleep impossible.

He twists around to check the time on the clock. "We'd better get moving if we want to get over to your place before Bobby is out and about."

"My place?" I'm not sure why, but I thought I'd be avoiding home until Bobby was back behind bars. Chase, however, has other ideas.

This sees us at my place before seven, and early enough that I avoid the walk of shame in front of my neighbors, the elderly McKenzie sisters. It's also early enough that we avoid running into Bobby, with Chase declaring the felon isn't a morning person.

Only after I've parked in the basement at work and punched into a secure part of the building does Chase leave. According to him, he's got a better shot of re-taking Bobby than the police.

Work has been a waste of time today with me spending more time making paperclip chains than what I'm paid to do. A quick look at my watch and I sigh in relief. Not long to go now.

I'm not sure what is supposed to happen when it's time to go home. From what Chase said, my place and my folks are both off limits. I wouldn't be averse to another night in the hotel.

This has my mind crowded with memories of us in the throes of passion. Sadly, they're soon interrupted by thoughts of Bobby bursting in on us.

Every time my thoughts stray to the felon, I concentrate on remembering Chase's mouth covering my most intimate spot. As a distraction, it works beautifully, even if it leaves me damp and longing for more. I'm rocking back in my office chair, replaying the scene when the large, old-fashioned phone on my desk rings. I slam back into an upright position, doing my best not to look guilty.

On lifting the receiver, rather than it being a client as I've expected, the receptionist announces a gentleman is there to see me.

"You can go on through, sir. Third office on the right," she says, to my visitor.

Before I've asked who on earth it is, she hangs up on me. So much for my being safe here. I slam the phone down and jump to my feet, ready to defend myself. While I don't have a rolling pin handy, some files on my desk are hefty enough to do some damage.

I'm readying myself to hurl the heaviest when Chase appears in the doorway. Such is my relief that I drop into my seat and hug the folder to my chest before promptly bursting into tears.

He's across my office in a flash, uncurling my fingers from the file and gently putting it back on my desk. He then squats down next to me. "What's wrong, baby? Are you okay?" He's rubbing my back as you would a five-year-old who's had a nasty fall at the playground.

"I, I, I, thought you were Bobby," I stutter out, before swiping at my eyes.

He turns my office chair so I'm facing him, my fear replaced by an altogether different emotion. Thankfully, I come to my senses before I act on it.

"Please, if you'd just like to take a seat." My gesture as I point him toward the visitor's chair is flamboyant, deliberately so. On seeing Chase's confusion, I turn and look at the ceiling above my office door, tipping my head subtly.

This is enough to have Chase also looking in that direction. Without pause, he straightens, makes his way around my desk, and takes a seat.

Once settled, his scrutiny was intense. "Why didn't you answer your phone? I've rung half a dozen times. I was worrying."

The room falls quiet but for the hum of the ancient air-conditioning unit jammed in my office window.

"I'm so sorry." I grab my phone and check it, immediately seeing the problem. "Blast it, it's on silent." I stare at him for a second. "He's still on the loose, isn't he?"

He rubs his hand around the back of his neck, opens his mouth to speak, then changes his mind. Instead, he whispers. "Does that camera pick up sound?"

Unable to stop myself, I glance up before casually putting my hand over my mouth. "No, it doesn't, but I swear the receptionist can lip-read."

It's the only way to explain her knowing about anything and everything, seemingly before anyone else. Either that or she's bugged all the offices.

Chase looks up briefly before turning back to face me. So bewitched am I by his good looks, that it takes longer than it should to focus on what he's telling me?

"What? A semi-automatic?! But how did he get hold of one of those?"

"Shhhh! If Chief Sutton finds out I've got contacts at the station, heads will roll. And in answer to your question, he broke into the Mayor's place."

It turns out that while the mayor was big on crime, he's slack with his own security. I take a few calming breaths before leaning forward in my seat and again putting my hand up to my mouth.

"So, what happens now?" Even though I've got a few changes of clothes with me, I'm not prepared for anything beyond that. "I won't feel safe until Chief Sutton gets his A into G and catches that creep."

"I know, sweetheart, but trust me, I'll keep you safe. Let's grab your things. There's somewhere we can go that he'll never think to look for you."

CHASE

As I escort Josie out the back door of her office building, I'm on high alert. Word at the station is that Robert Collings didn't let up with his promises to get Josie back for breaking his hand.

I knew Josie was in danger the moment I got the text that Bobby had escaped. The guy has a vicious reputation for payback. Add in that it was my chasing the asshole that led him to her back door, and I consider her well and truly my responsibility.

Even if this wasn't the case, I'd still want to protect Josie from anything bad.

I waste no time bundling her into the back of the van waiting for us. There wasn't a chance I'd risk her driving her own car. Plus, the skirt she's wearing is way too tight to allow her to straddle my motorbike. She'd need to hitch it up, like right up.

Damn it, you can't be thinking about things like that right now. Later.

It's a short drive to what will serve as our safe house. But for the tenants moving out yesterday, I'd have had to take Josie back to her place and protect her as best I could. Here, we should have a better chance of avoiding Bobby altogether.

All we need to do is stay low until Chief Sutton gets off his fat ass and catches the creep. Hmmm, on second thoughts, I wouldn't mind if the Chief took his own sweet time as usual. The idea of hanging out with Josie for a few days appeals to me on many levels.

I've not broached the subject of us having to lie low for a while when the van grinds to a stop. Mike, the driver and my go-to transport man, thumps on the back of the bulkhead, and I open the side door before turning to help Josie clamber out.

Considering we'd had to sit on the floor to stay out of sight, she's looking remarkably unruffled. She runs her hands down her skirt to smooth it while I grab her small suitcase. Such a simple action and yet all I want to do is drop her case, flip her over one shoulder and head inside.

Instead, I drag my gaze away from her so I can talk to Mike briefly about bringing us some supplies. I hadn't exactly had time to plan for this. Add in that I don't have a clue what state the tenants left the place in, and I'm in uncharted territory.

This has me taking a deep breath while turning the key in the front door. It'll either be immaculate, or like the Clevelander South Beach after Spring Break.

I throw the door wide and step to the side, allowing Josie to go first.

ELEVEN

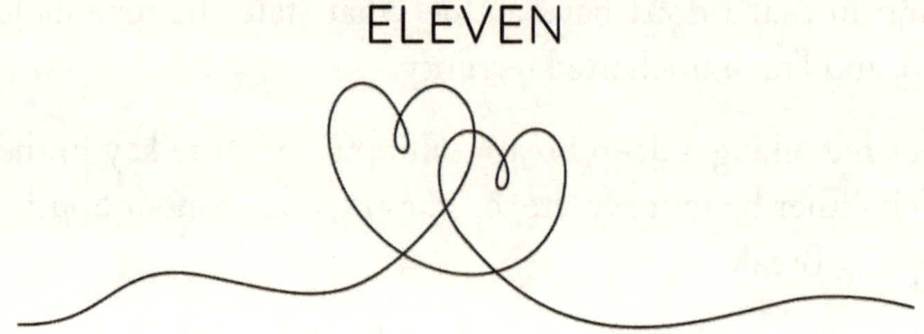

JOSIE

My mouth is now as wide open as the front door. The house is spectacular. Perhaps 'house' doesn't give the place credit, with the large home more akin to a mansion. The only thing I'm unsure of is whose house it is.

I doubt it belongs to Chase, although he looks at home next to me, and he had a front door key.

After closing the front door, he puts my case down. "Come on. Let me show you around the place."

"You've been here before?"

"Been here? This was my home from when I was five, through until a couple of years ago. These days it's tenanted, although not at the moment."

I open my mouth to fire questions at him, but hold back. How could he go from living in a home as stunning as this to subsisting in a trailer park in such a brief space of time? I still don't think he realizes he let slip about living in a trailer when we were out at dinner.

My brain scrambling, Chase takes hold of my hand and leads me down a wide hallway toward the back of the house. The tour of the first floor is perfunctory. Where things get really interesting is when we make our way up the sweeping staircase.

I guess I'm about to find out where I'll be sleeping tonight. I follow Chase along the hallway that spans the width of the house, with him walking into a room at the very end. "This used to be my room."

His description has been no frills, with him simply stating a fact, his words lacking in emotion. A peek at his shuttered eyes, and I know this can't be easy. A diversion is called for to avoid tonight being awkward on so many levels.

"It's a fabulous room. And check out the size of that bed." I run toward it, my gait severely limited thanks to the tightness of my skirt. At the last minute, I spin and throw myself backwards, landing with a bounce in the middle of the bed. I make sure I've caught his gaze before I lie back. "It is kinda lonely, though."

I don't need to say anything else.

CHASE

Josie's actions blast any remaining *what ifs* free. There isn't a chance I can remain maudlin when faced with the delectable pile in the middle of my old bed.

My leather jacket is the first to go, followed by my shirt, undone a button at a time. My reward is my cock getting harder with every second, and her eyes widening in appreciation.

Only when I'm standing naked at the end of the bed does Josie speak, although not until she's arched one of her delicate eyebrows. "Well, are you just going to stand there?"

Our laughter rings out around the room, although it dies away the second I drop to the bed and my lips touch hers. Rather than shy away from our physical contact, her hands are everywhere, and I mean everywhere. I didn't think it was possible to get harder. Looks like I was wrong.

I peck her before squeezing her ass. "You're wearing altogether too many clothes. Up you get. I stripped for you. Now it's your turn."

Wow, if I thought stripping for Josie was a turn-on, watching her peel out of that straitlaced office outfit is sex personified. There's also nothing serviceable about her bra and panties today. The froth of lace isn't up to concealing the outline of her pebbled nipples or the dampness of her sex.

She's about to kick out of her high heels when I hold my hand up. "No, leave them on."

A moment later, her lingerie lands atop our clothing on the floor and she crawls seductively over the end of the bed. She's naked but for her black suede pumps, with their little bows. I'm consumed with thoughts of those heels digging into my ass as I drive myself into her over and over.

Josie, however, has other ideas, straddling me a moment later, and rubbing her damp heat back and forth against my boner. I reach up to fondle her full breasts, but she slaps my hands away. "No, I've been working on this since you left me at the office this morning."

I lay back, my arms out to the sides in surrender. "And just what have you come up with in that pretty head of yours?"

She bites her bottom lip as if she's yet to decide. Again, she proves me wrong. "I want to ride you, to grind myself against you, for us to come so hard we both see stars."

What is it about this woman that she exudes prim and proper, and yet underneath she's a real firecracker? She might just be my ideal woman.

On her lifting herself up on her knees and guiding me into her warm depths, all rational thoughts flee. She then works away on that fantasy of hers to the point I could no longer tell you my name.

I'm on the brink of losing it when I give into a fantasy of my own. A quick thrust of my hips and I drive myself deeper, before rolling to the side and tucking her beneath me.

"Lock your ankles behind me. I want to feel those heels of yours while I enjoy every inch of you." And hell's bells, if Josie doesn't show herself to be a quick study, with this boding well for our sex life. I love a woman with a vivid imagination.

EPILOGUE

JOSIE

Sitting at the large desk in the second floor study at The Laurels, I shake my head in disbelief. It's hard to accept only six months have passed since I was reheating lasagna and whacking an armed intruder with a rolling pin.

However, it's not memories of that night that are making it difficult to concentrate right now. I lean to the side so I can glance under the oak desk. "What if your grandfather comes in?"

Chase runs his tongue slowly and deliberately over my pearl before looking up. "He never comes upstairs, but if you sit back and relax, you just might." He then returns to what he was doing.

There isn't a chance I can concentrate on his tax return now. Unable to stay upright, I slouch down in the large leather seat and open myself fully to him, my hands coming to rest atop his head.

I don't even realize I'm pushing down until I hear his muffled laughter. I love this about Chase. That he can laugh at life, and often at the most inappropriate times. It's a genuine gift, considering all he's been through over the years. I still can't fathom his parents just up and abandoning him and his brother.

Chase kept his place at the trailer park for a month after we got together, although he'd moved into my place when we left The Laurels. We couldn't stay there more than a few nights because there were new tenants ready to move in.

With him in my bed and a police cruiser parked out front, there wasn't a chance I'd feel vulnerable. Chase had also been vigilant about following me to and from work on his motorbike.

What Bobby had promised in the way of retribution didn't matter, with me never on my own.

It was then Chase finally let me check his accounts, and it hadn't taken more than a couple of hours to spot his accountants were incompetent or crooked. Either way, it explained why Chase had been having so much trouble getting ahead financially. Best of all was that rather than owing tax, he was actually due a refund.

Thanks to this, when the final lease expired, his grandfather moved out of that hideous apartment and back into The Laurels. This saw *Gramps* settled into the 'mother-in-law' suite over the three-car garage, with Chase given free rein of the house.

Chase had fought this, for all the good it did, with his grandfather saying he found the smaller space better suited to his needs. And that had been the end of any further discussion.

I suspect part of it was Gramps wanting to see Chase move things forward with me. This was something Chase had wasted no time on; making it official with a blinding solitaire that had belonged to his late grandmother.

. . .

I'm admiring the beautiful ring when Chase spreads me wide and adds his fingers to the mix. This has me in danger of sliding off the leather seat before my cries of release echo around the room.

I can only hope it hasn't been loud enough to be heard outside of what is now my new home, with my old place tenanted. Gramps loves nothing more than to wander around the gardens dead-heading roses.

CHASE

Smug doesn't describe my demeanor as I watch Josie tipped back in the leather office chair. Her cries of release fill the room, and me, with joy. I did that to her, although I'm not finished with my deliciously juicy fiancé.

Sure, our engagement had been quick, but right from the start, we'd slotted into each other's lives perfectly. She'd filled a gap in mine that had haunted me for most of my life.

Perhaps 'gap' is an understatement. With a great gaping void, a better descriptor of the hole left when my parents took off. It hadn't mattered that Gramps had taken Ethan and me in. Life was never the same again, with the sense of abandonment crushing to a five-year-old.

Only now, as I start on my family, am I experiencing a sense of completion that's long been missing. I also know Josie has more in common with my grandfather than either of my parents. She's steadfast, loyal, and above all else, reliable as the day is long.

Perhaps the biggest thing that's changed about my life is my finances. I know that sounds mundane, but worrying about where my next dollar was coming from had been slowly killing me.

It was also dreadful watching Gramps reduced to penury and forced to live in that awful apartment. He thinks he hid how bad things were, but his weight loss showed even more than my own. This had me worrying about losing the only constant in my life.

It's one reason I'm not giving up on tracking Ethan down. He did the crime, now he needs to do the time.

"No point being a bounty hunter otherwise," I mutter to myself.

Josie opens one eye and grins down at me. "Don't you mean Bail Enforcement Agent?"

"You're damn right I do." I push the leather chair back from the desk and climb out. On my feet, I grab my cuffs off the desk. "And I'm arresting you for being dazzling, young lady. Come with me!" I slap one half of my cuffs on her wrist before locking the other half around my own.

It doesn't take long to realize Josie is in no condition to stand. I pull her to her feet and scoop her up. It's a short walk to the master suite; where I lay her gently back on the Texas king that we'd chosen together.

Thank goodness I'd removed her panties and my clothes earlier, because I've waited too long already. Soon enough, I'm balls-deep and she's got her ankles locked tight behind my back. The way she's digging her heels into my ass guaranteed to have me over the edge.

I press my lips gently against hers. "Is it possible I could love you more than I already do?"

As I lift my head and I take in her soft smile, my heart is ready to explode out of my chest. It's kinda scary how much I love her. Trusting she won't leave me as my parents did has been the hardest thing of all.

"You couldn't possibly love me as much as I love you." She strokes my cheek gently, before adding. "I'll always be here for you." Her soft smile then turns into a broad grin. "Now get cracking!" She backs this demand up with a small kick of her heels.

It's all the encouragement I need.

CRIME

After being on the run for close to seven months, convicted felon Robert John Collings has been recaptured.

It was local Bail Enforcement Agent, Chase Hunter, who made the arrest, something Mayor Cooper was quick to commend him on.

As well as receiving the keys to the city, Mr Hunter also received the $10,000 reward put up by the Mayor.

Chole is a librarian who loves steamy romances. Blake is a surfer who likes it wet and wild. Will these two finally get it on when their long-held desires bubble to the surface?

Just a small trigger warning to let you know that this title contains bullying. And because bullying is never okay, I've made sure that with Blake's love, Chloe comes out on top. As one reviewer put it:

Just love a story where the girl not only gets her happily ever after, but her self worth too. Bravo Ms. Malone. 5 STARS - Zon Reviewer

---

ONE

BLAKE

After what feels like hours behind the wheel, I round the headland and Coogan's Break reveals itself. Force of habit has me checking out the surf, my practiced eye picking out the change in breaks with a cursory glance.

Despite not having lived here in years, and my folks having moved north to be near my grandparents, this place still feels like home. While it's increased in size over the years, the place still has a small-town vibe. One that the mayor apparently hates, much to the amusement of the locals who think he's got an over-inflated sense of self-importance.

Rather than continue into town, I pull off the road, allowing the cars banked up behind me to pass. The van isn't the fastest vehicle and overtaking on the narrow road south of town is never a good idea. If anyone tried, chances are they'd end up at the bottom of the cliff that skirts the seaward side of the road.

The engine eventually shudders to a ragged stop. While the van isn't the greatest thing on wheels, it is home. It's also all that I can afford on my current earnings. With my hip bothering me more and more of late, my winnings this season are down a worrying amount.

It takes a second for my ears to adjust to the relative quiet, with the engine a noisy beast at the best of times. Thanks to the long drive north from Baja, she's complaining more than ever. It's something I'll have to deal with when, and if, I can put enough money aside.

Damn it, the constant money worries are messing with my head. It's the last thing I need when facing the sort of competition I'll be up against later in the week.

"Hang in there, girl." I pat the engine cover before continuing. "Just another week and I'll get someone to look at you." Despite having learned a lot about engines over the years, whatever the hell it is that's making that noise is way beyond me.

After a couple of steadying breaths, I pick up on the waves crashing on the rocks below. This coupled with the ozone-laced air whipping in through the open window, and the sense of homecoming is overwhelming.

With my seatbelt flicked to one side, I grab the binoculars from the center console and clamber out. It takes a moment to get all the sensation back in my legs. While I can put some of this down to hours of sitting on an uncomfortable bench seat, that's not all of it.

My hip isn't only affecting my ability to win surf comps. If I catch my reflection in a shop window, I see my dad in how I walk. Despite loving my old man, I'm not in a hurry to become him, at least not in the next couple of years.

With the binoculars up to my eyes, I have a closer look at the surf. It's hardly recognizable from the last time I was here. That big storm must have really chewed up the ocean floor for the surf breaks to have changed as much as they have.

This is part of the reason I'm in town early. If I've got a hope in hell of taking out one of the major longboard prizes, I need to get to reacquaint myself with the waves.

The binoculars still up to my eyes, I sweep across the beach to check out the town. Hah, who am I fooling? I'm not just looking at the town; I'm looking at something in particular, one shop, and a reminder of a carefree youth.

Aside from that, my memories of the town are fairly tragic. I'd hated school, with my grades testimony to what appeared to be a sterling lack of effort.

In reality, it was all down to a little secret I'd kept well-hidden and that I still have to deal with every day. It's yet another reason the pain in my hip bothers me.

Thanks to the trouble I have filling in forms; the only work I can land in the off season is laboring on construction sites. Hard manual labor. The sort that'll be impossible if I'm hobbling around like an old man.

On spotting a familiar face through the large plate-glass window of the Surf Shack, I break into a wide grin. What's Chloe doing behind the counter? I thought she worked at the library, the perfect job for someone who loved reading as much as she used to. Despite no longer living here, I keep up-to-date with events through mates I'm still in touch with.

After putting the binoculars away, I haul myself into the driver's seat. I wonder if being next to her will have the same effect on me as it always did.

There's only one way to know for sure with the mere thought enough to have me grinning like a loon.

CHLOE

As I look around my parents' shop, I'm wondering what possessed me to agree to cover for them while they were away on a buying trip. We'd arranged it months ago, and it had rather taken me by surprise.

When they'd asked if I was okay managing the Surf Shack Thursday through Sunday, I hadn't given it much thought. Instead, I'd asked the head librarian if I could take annual leave for the two weekdays.

Mom and dad asked little of me, and it wasn't as if my social life was frantic enough that I'd be going out, or anything. More likely I'd be at home, sitting in my favorite chair, my nose buried in a book. Working in a library, there aren't enough hours in the day for me to read all the books I want to.

It wasn't until the week before I was due to babysit the shop that something dawned on me. The weekend after they were away, there was a big surf event.

That's not quite right. Big doesn't do the annual Coogan's Break Carnival justice. It's a major event on the surfing calendar, with the biggest draw, being the tens of thousands of dollars in prizes up for grabs. Thanks to this, there'll be surfers arriving in droves, be they amateur or professional.

Despite not having had a lot to do with the shop since I graduated and started working at the library, it was a given the shop would be manic. Thursday and Friday hadn't been too bad, despite Nina, the girl who usually works at the shop, failing to turn up for work.

However, today being Saturday, the shop is overrun. I knew it would be bad when I'd caught sight of the small crowd waiting for me to open up. Part of me had wanted to turn around and head back upstairs to my parent's apartment.

Unfortunately, it wasn't an option, especially not with Nina again missing in action. A quick peek at my phone sitting on the sales counter next to the cash register shows she hasn't replied to any of my many messages.

According to mom, Nina is reliable. With this so apparently out of character, my annoyance has now morphed into concern. I'd phone my folks, but there isn't much they can do about it, other than leave more messages.

The knowledge I'm flying solo coupled with the hubbub of voices around the shop, and I'm on edge. Every time there's a burst of laughter, it's all I can do not to tell the perpetrators to "Sssssh!"

Compared to the quiet of the library, the noise in the shop is threatening to overwhelm me. It would be one thing if Nina was here to help. On my own, I'm on the verge of slamming my hands over my ears and yelling at everyone to leave.

The next customer served and on their way, I grab my phone. As much as I want to know where Nina is, I also want to check if she's okay. My phone up against my ear, I ring up the next customer one-handed, but with a ready smile so they don't feel ignored.

So split is my attention that it takes a moment to realize my call has again gone through to voicemail. My message is therefore more abrupt than I'd like, reduced to a simple "Where the heck are you?" before I end the call.

I squeeze my phone into the back pocket of my denim shorts, so that if she calls back and I'm away from the register, I won't miss it.

On hearing the tinkle of the bell above the front door, I look up to see who's just walked in. When I see who it is, I'm glad I'm no longer holding my phone. If I had been, I'd have dropped it. As it is, I need to lean against the sales counter and lock my knees to stay upright.

Weirdly, his presence has the sounds of the shop fading into the background. The only thing I can hear now is the rapid beating of my heart and the resultant thrum of blood. I don't even need to touch my face to know it's flooded with color.

This is a shame, because to my mind, the only thing the color red looks good on is tomatoes and fire trucks. How can it be that Blake still affects me as he did all those years ago?

Let's see. Six-foot-two, tanned, shoulder-length dark curls, body honed from hours of surfing and deep blue eyes that draw me in? It's one hell of a list, so, of course, he still affects me as he did back in the day. I'd have to be clinically dead not to respond to the guy. As a teenager, he'd been impressive.

He's as out of my league now as he ever had been. As much as I'd love to act on the fantasies I've indulged in over the years, I daren't.

And why is that?

Because it would be one sure way of killing all those fantasies stone dead. The only thing I can't tell just by ogling him is whether he still has that sweet nature that set him apart from the other delinquents.

TWO

CHLOE

It takes all my self-control to close my mouth, to breathe properly and not pass out behind the sales counter. I also squeeze my thighs together to squelch my response to his nearness. It doesn't work.

It doesn't matter that I haven't seen Blake in years; my reaction this morning is what it always was. What had started out as a crush in high school has now developed into, I'm not sure what.

Whatever it is, my body responds at a cellular level and it takes all my nerve to speak to him, my words preferring to stay in my mouth.

"Hi, Blake. Ah, I guess you're in town for the, ah, carnival?"

I then kick myself for stumbling over my words as I did in high school. Then I kick myself again for asking such a stupid question. Of course he's in town for the carnival.

He answers for all the notice I take. *What a fool.* Guys like Blake aren't interested in girls like me. I'm altogether too shy and too fond of nibbling on chocolates when reading to appeal to men like him.

That's for statuesque blondes like the one currently plastered to his side. On recognizing who she is, it's all I can do not to be violently ill. Lost for words, I acknowledge her presence with a nod and a lackluster smile.

Sylvia Chamberlain is a former cheerleader who's lost none of her looks. Like Blake, the years have been kind to her. If it were possible, she's even more stunning than I remember, proving beyond doubt that life can be unfair. I suppose she must be in town with him, because it's the first time I've seen either of them since I left high school.

Sylvia, the quintessential mean girl, had made my life hell on earth. It was at lunch on the first day that she'd decided I made the perfect target. Taking in the venom in the woman's eyes, I suspect things have changed little on that front.

The other thing that hasn't changed is the woman doing whatever the heck she wants. She does nothing to hide her ice cream.

So much for the NO FOOD OR DRINK sign on the front door.

A flash of jealousy burns through my chest and up my throat. The only difference from when I was in high school is that I'm a homeowner, working in my dream job, and definitely more confident than I ever was.

Next to my old nemesis, Blake is every bit as good looking as I remember, with my heart fluttering in my chest like a caged bird. Topping that off, my mouth is dry, and my hands tingle.

"I'm sorry, Blake, what was it you were after again?"

"Fins for a longboard? I'm after something around eight inches."

He follows this up with a wink and a cheeky grin, and my body fizzes in response. My mind in my panties, he has to ask me the same question three times before I'm able to respond, at least verbally.

Even then, I have trouble. I open and close my mouth twice before I'm able to squeak out, "We might have eight and a half inches." I swallow deeply before continuing. "Will that do?"

His mouth quirks up at one side, and he licks his lips. "I guess we'll just have to see." I'm not used to this type of attention, my brain buzzing in response along with other parts.

Surely that isn't what he means?

Are you serious?

Of course, that's not what he means!

Whoa, desperate much?

Despite my internal chatter, I'm aware of Sylvia watching me like a hawk. No doubt she's waiting for the right moment to dig those hot pink, bejeweled talons of hers into me.

Without breaking eye contact with me, she leans closer to Blake, licking her ice cream in what I'd have to say is a carnal manner. Could it be my arousal is clouding my judgment?

Either way, when she holds the cone up to Blake's mouth, I'm as frozen as the sweet treat, transfixed by his full lips. So much so that it takes a moment to realize Sylvia has spoken to me. It requires all my willpower to drag my gaze away from Blake's mouth and stare at the woman. "Excuse me?"

"My mom said you'd been away to college. You didn't learn a thing while you were there, did you?" She jabs the ice cream in my direction, causing drips to fall onto the sales counter. She then looks me up and down. "You're still as stupid as ever. Still Doughy Chloe from what I can see."

On hearing the horrid nickname she'd saddled me with, my breathing hitches, my reaction as it always was to her bullying.

Despite no longer being the girl she used to bully, that awful name has me once again an awkward teenager. My response is such that if Pavlov was still alive, he'd be handing out the doggy treats.

However, I've changed a lot over the years and if the shop wasn't full of customers, I'd kick her out and laugh while I was about it. As it is, I have to keep quiet, to act professionally as my parents would expect, to swallow my retort. To once again, let her get away with it.

In the end, there's no need for me to defend myself, with Blake coming to my rescue.

He turns and glares at Sylvia. "Huh, and you accused Chloe of not learning anything while she was away. Didn't they teach you manners at that ivy league place your parents paid to get you into?"

BLAKE

On walking into the Surf Shack, the memories threaten to overwhelm me. So many hours spent hanging around the shop with my surfing buddies. Time spent drooling over the latest boards and the girls shopping for the latest bikini.

It doesn't matter that I haven't been in the shop in years; it's as if it was yesterday. A quick check around and apart from the stock being up to date, it doesn't appear as if Chloe's dad has changed the layout of the shop at all.

I know exactly where I'll find a new fin for my longboard. However, I don't bother heading in that direction, rather I make a beeline for the sales counter and the woman waiting there.

She's looking as sweet as ever, her light brown hair falling like silk to her shoulders. Soft pink lips and silvery gray eyes only adding to her air of innocence, and yet there's a mischievous edge I'd love to explore.

It's buried deep for sure, which is kinda how I'd like to be myself. Yep, balls-deep and loving every second would definitely be my first choice, although nowhere near my last. Could it be that I get to explore more than the waves over the coming week?

Short and curvy, Chloe is a complete opposite of the blonde all over me to the point I reckon I'll need a wax scraper to get rid of her. Much as I love surfing, I'm not keen on a woman who resembles one of my boards.

Despite having spotted her through the binoculars, I'm still surprised to find Chloe behind the sales counter, even if it is the weekend. With a full-time job, I'd thought she'd want those to herself. The other surprise is her parents not being around.

I always remember them working every hour God gave them, with this more a labor of love than a drive for profit. In his day, Chloe's dad had been a champion surfer, with his love of the waves not dying off over the years. Maybe this must be why she's running the shop?

Apart from being as cute as I remember, she also looks to be stunned and lost for words, her lips forming a perfect O. A perfect fit for...

I mentally slap myself to clear my mind of the filthy images I can't stop working on, although Sylvia shoving her ice cream in my face sure helps.

Even angling my head away doesn't help. "All good, thanks. Prefer surfing on an empty stomach." It's still not enough of a hint and it takes longer than it should for me to work out what the hell she's playing at.

It's that she's looking at Chloe while waiting for me to take a lick that tells me what she's up to. Sylvia always was a nasty piece of work. In the end, I push her hand away to avoid wearing the blasted ice cream. It's already enough of a challenge keeping on top of the laundry when I'm living in my van.

The other challenge I face is ditching the blonde leech.

Since running into her outside the ice cream parlor a couple of doors down, she's stuck to me like Velcro. When she started talking about great places for lunch and dinner, I resigned myself to being stuck with her for the duration.

Unless I do something drastic, and soon.

Ignoring her as best I can, I ask Chloe if they've got any of the Machado longboard fins in stock, for all the good it does. The cutie appears transfixed, as if in a daze. I'm opening my mouth to ask her again, when Sylvia talks over the top of me.

On hearing what the nasty piece of work said, I turn on her. Has the woman learned nothing since high school? I give her grief about it, for all the good it does. She always had an over-inflated sense of her own importance, and apparently still does.

"That's cool, Chloe, I can find them myself. Are they still down at the back of the shop?"

After receiving a mute nod in response, I move away from the sales counter and am pleased when Sylvia tags along. If she hadn't, I'd have dragged her away myself.

Not that I'm after her company, but that I don't want her attacking Chloe again. I also want to give Chloe some time to get over being called that awful name.

There's nothing doughy about Chloe, she's lush.

THREE

As much as I want to go home and drown my sorrows in a pint of Ben & Jerry's best, or a large box of chocolates, I can't. Nina's still missing in action, meaning it's up to me to keep the shop open and running.

With Blake and Sylvia safely down the back of the shop, I clean the sales counter. That done, I get on with serving the next customer in what's turning into a large crowd.

There's no letup, to the point they're three deep waiting to be served. Add in people yelling questions at me across the shop, and the place is chaos.

A quick peek at my phone is enough to see no missed calls or messages, meaning the chances of me getting a break soon are slim to nothing. Rather than get caught out, I put my coffee down on the shelf under the cash register. It's a thought that immediately has me wanting to use the bathroom.

Where on earth are you, Nina?

Despite rattling through the sales and telling customers where to find what they're after, I haven't made a dent in the crowd clamoring for my attention. And with half my attention firmly locked on Blake, there isn't much left to go around.

I've completed another sale when I look up to see Blake and Sylvia back waiting to be served. But Sylvia isn't in any mood to wait, barging through the assembled customers, dragging a patently embarrassed Blake behind her.

She's one person away from the sales counter when she reinforces her spiteful nature. "Huh, isn't it just typical you wouldn't have a clue when you're out of stock? We're off to Wright's Marine, aren't we Blake? They have a much better selection."

Her declaration has been cheerleader loud and I'm not at all surprised when a few customers at the back slink away. Their lack of eye contact leaves their destination in no doubt.

And there's nothing I can do about it, because Sylvia is right. I don't have a clue what is, or isn't, in stock. It would be different if my folks had invested in a modern system, but they preferred the old cash register and a personal touch. All good when you know your way around, a nightmare when you don't.

While I'd like to defend the Surf Shack, I can't. Not without looking pathetic. Wright's is good and all, but it's not a patch on the Shack for everything surfing. It also lacks the history and atmosphere of the Shack, something my parents have worked hard to preserve.

As if sensing I won't defend myself, Sylvia leans over the shorter man in front of her. She then takes delight in smashing the remains of her ice cream down on the sales counter. "Come on, Blake. Let's get out of this hole. Wright's isn't far."

As I watch Sylvia turn and barge back through the customers who've amassed behind her, I have to wonder if she's on commission. Given the number of times she's mentioned the opposition; surely she's getting a kick-back of some sort?

My gaze follows Blake as he trails Sylvia to the front door. I'm disappointed he's being so easily led, with his actions taking some of the shine off my memories of him.

Was I always this blinded by his good looks?

I'm not the only one, with one girl so intent on getting Blake's attention, that she walks into a mannequin. This sees both dummy and girl sprawled across the shop floor along with a pile of stock.

Great, just what I need. I'd say my day couldn't get worse, but I'm not about to tempt fate like that.

BLAKE

Despite being stuck with the dead weight that is Sylvia Chamberlain, I take my time walking around the shop, enjoying the memories as they reveal themselves.

Only now can I admit to myself that I'd spent all those hours at the Shack, not because of the latest boards, but a chance to catch sight of Chloe.

It wasn't anything I'd own back then, for fear of getting grief from my friends. Appearance is everything when you're fifteen, and cocky. I was also too damned scared to ask her out because girls like her didn't date stupid guys like me. College was never in my future, with even grade school a challenge.

Rather than walk straight to where I know I'll find an excellent selection of fins, I dwell, checking out anything and everything to do with surfing, no matter how tenuous. I hope Sylvia will get bored and leave.

I'm enjoying being back here, able to revisit my youth without strings attached. However, Sylvia is tenacious. She's also a slob with her leaving drips of ice cream everywhere.

"Hey can you be careful with that thing? Mess it up, and it's yours!"

At least that's what Chloe's dad always said if he caught us with food in the shop. And no one dared push it with Mr. Henderson. The guy meant business.

Unable to draw it out any longer, I walk over to where I'll find the fins. A quick check and I can see the one I'm after is out of stock. Blast it. I was hoping to try a few adjustments to its placement to see what worked best.

Preparation is crucial if I'm to have a shot at taking out the top prize. If I do, I can afford to take some time off and give my hip a rest down in Baja for the winter.

Miss out, and I'll be stuck looking for work again; odd jobs, laboring on building sites and general grunt work. All of which will take its toll on my body. The only plus will be a regular income helping me to sort out my finances.

I'll have to go ask Chloe if there are more board fins out back of the shop. Failing that, I'll get her to order one in for me. Not ideal, but better than nothing.

"Hey Sylvia, why don't you wait here? I'll ask Chloe when they'll be getting more stock in and we can be out of here." Anything is better than her attacking Chloe again.

Unfortunately, the woman isn't falling for it.

"I'm all good, surfer boy."

Surfer boy? Is she serious?

She slowly licks her ice cream while holding my gaze and it's all I can do not to laugh. Maybe this is the reason I'm still single?

We're not even close to the sales counter when Sylvia acts up again.

First she bad-mouths Chloe and the shop and then slams the remains of that blasted ice cream down on the counter. She then does her best to drag me out of the shop, declaring we're off to Wrights.

Like hell we are.

On seeing Chloe's disappointment and then disapproval, I make a snap decision. I remove Sylvia's fingers from around my wrist. "I'll catch you later." Once free, I back away, putting a few people between us.

Unable to return to my side without looking silly, she storms out of the shop. On her way, she sends a sunhat display stand flying. I'll deal with that later.

But before I can do that, I need to sort out some of these customers. First off is the guy next to me whose shirt is almost as loud as he is. "Right, you're after a new leash for your board, aren't you?" I put my hand on his shoulder and steer him toward the side of the shop.

There were pluses to Chloe's parents keeping the same layout over the years. I'll leave as soon as she has everything under control again.

FOUR

CHLOE

Eight hours later and my feet hurt and I'm wrung out. Add in my arousal thanks to Blake brushing against me whenever we're behind the sales counter, and my legs are ready to give out on me.

I've done my best to tamp down my feelings for him, knowing they're a dead end. He's far more interested in the likes of Sylvia. Well, maybe not Sylvia herself, but doubtless someone who looks exactly like her. Sleek, gorgeous, and confident.

There wasn't a chance he'd be interested in someone like me.

Too short, curvy and bookish for a yummy hunk of surfer, like him.

It doesn't matter that he's been teasing me all day long, joking and smiling whenever we caught sight of each other across the crowded shop. That's just him being friendly.

I can't wait to meet someone I'm as comfortable with, but who's actually in my league. There'd been a few close calls at college, but none that measured up to my memories of Blake.

It had been so natural working with him, of knowing exactly what he was thinking, and him being able to help. We'd made the perfect team, with him showing customers where everything was and answering their technical questions. Meanwhile, I was on the till and taking care of ordering anything in.

I've flipped the sign to CLOSED and then locked the door, when I remember what it was Blake came in for earlier. Yet again, cursing my parents' lack of up-to-date technology, I grab the stock book from under the cash register, nearly knocking my long-cold coffee over.

As I run my fingers down the columns, I'm conscious of Blake standing right next to me. So close, in fact, that I can feel the heat coming off his body in waves. As I straighten, I tap the middle column. "It says here we've got an eight-inch in stock. That's what you were after, wasn't it?"

He nods slowly before speaking. "Yeah, that'll do perfectly." His gaze locks with mine when he adds, "I want to try it out in a whole heap of positions. Forward, back, you know how it goes?"

I do, but I'm not so sure he's referring to where to mount the fin on his board. My mouth once more like cotton-candy, I have to run my tongue around to lubricate it before I can get the words out.

"If it's not on the shelf, it must be out the back. I'll go get it for you."

I'm working my way through the stock piled haphazardly on the back shelf of the storage room when Blake tucks a lock of hair back behind my ear. There's nothing I can do to stop my squeak of alarm. I didn't realize he was right behind me. Close on the heels of my surprise is a rush of longing that has me ready to go up in flames.

"I like it longer." He runs his fingers down the side of my neck. "It suits you."

He's just being friendly, that's all. I then say this inside my head twice more, hoping to convince my body to stand down.

There isn't a chance I'll risk misreading the signals as I have with other guys in the past. No way am I embarrassing myself by revealing my true feelings to him, of all people.

I'm not sure I want to acknowledge them to myself.

If I can ignore him and my attraction, he can't hurt me, even unintentionally.

Blake, however, has other ideas. His hands drop to my waist and he slowly turns me to face him. As I glance up, there's one thing I know for sure.

He's not just being friendly.

BLAKE

I've never enjoyed working as much as I have today, jammed in next to Chloe when she'd rung up purchases and brushing against her whenever I could.

Sure, my balls are blue as a result, but I can cope with that. With the signals she's sending out, there might even be a solution. Either way, I'm glad I'm wearing a baggy vintage Hawaiian shirt over my board shorts.

It isn't until Chloe says she'll grab a fin from out back I remember why I was there in the first place, although it wasn't the only reason.

As I follow her, I'm in no doubt what I'm after, and that's what's right in front of me. Damn, if those denim shorts of hers don't show off her ass to perfection, the sway of her hips is mesmerizing.

I'm as good as in a trance when she walks through the swinging bead curtain that separates the front of the shop from the back. It smacks me in the face, bringing me back to my senses, although not for long.

What is it about this woman that has me wanting to protect her, to go all Neanderthal? I want to toss her over one shoulder so I can have my way with her? Hell, if I give into these urges, I'll probably get a slap to the face.

Chloe isn't the sort of girl to settle for a quick fling with a guy like me.

If not a quickie, maybe she'd be interested in something slower. A lot slower. It's as if it's someone else reaching out to tuck that stray lock of hair behind her shell-like ear. However, it's definitely me who turns her and pulls her into a tight embrace.

The scent of her arousal has me giving into the temptation that's been there since I'd walked through the front door that morning.

Kissing Chloe is every bit as good as I'd imagined when I was sitting behind her in biology. My reactions are textbook, right down to the desire to bury myself in her until I can go no further.

As cheesy as it sounds, I want to brand her as mine.

As I listen to her mewing, it takes all my self-control to not lose it. I take my lips away from hers only long enough to whisper, "It feels good, doesn't it?"

She barely has time to murmur her agreement before I once more claim her lips.

Any doubts flee when she undoes a couple of buttons on my shirt so she can stroke my chest. My cock jumps in response, and I know if we don't slow down, I'll be taking her atop the rental wet-suits piled high in the corner.

As tempting as that is, I want my first time with Chloe to be special. There's nothing one-night stand about this girl. If I screw this up, I'll screw it up for good.

Reluctantly, I pull back from our kiss to stop myself from mimicking her actions. One thing is for sure, though, I'd be using my teeth on her nipples, not my hands.

"Slow down, baby. We've got all the time in the world."

I try to stand tall, to move away from her, to give us both some room to think rationally. She's having none of it, and who am I to argue with such a beautiful creature?

If she wants fast, then fast it is. My balls tighten at the very thought of burying myself in this gorgeous woman, again and again.

FIVE

My heart thunders in my chest in time with the blood pulsing through other parts of my body, all of them with a mind of their own. I've certainly got no control over what's happening to me. That's all down to Mother Nature.

On second thoughts, it's all down to Blake Mitchell.

As his lips move over mine, a logical part of me is asking what's what. A less logical part is telling it to shut the heck up and enjoy it. It's also this primal part that stops Blake from pulling away when he tries.

If he really wants out, I'll deal with it. However, if he's pulling back because he thinks I'm not into it, then I've just disabused him of that notion. I'll soon find out if I've misread all those signals throughout the day.

But I can't have. Whenever he was next to me behind the sales counter, the air was laced with electricity and arousal, at least on my part. I'd been damp from the moment he first scooted behind me. It'd also made me aware he was on edge, too.

I smile up at him shyly. "Are you sure we've got all the time in the world?"

For the first time in my life, I do something impulsive, something sinful, something I've wanted to do for a long time. I grab hold of the bottom of my Surf Shack t-shirt and lift it up and over the top of my head.

Despite the temptation to toss it to one side like a vaudeville performer to hide my embarrassment, I simply let it drop to the floor.

"Oh, Chloe, you've read my mind." This time, Blake's smile isn't cocky. Instead, it has a fragile quality to it, as though this is as new to him as it is to me.

Blake's lips once more claim mine, and when I press my breasts against his chest, our kiss deepens. There'll be no going back from here. This is what I want. This is what I've always wanted.

His hands drop to caress my ass and I can't help a peep of surprise when he lifts me. I also can't stop myself from wrapping my legs around his waist; my core closer to him now than it ever was in my dreams.

I'm only vaguely aware we're on the move, with an annoying part of my brain analyzing how easily he's been able to lift me. This same annoying voice comes up with the logic that I can't weigh much more than his vintage longboard. Okay, so I might have indulged in a little cyberstalking to see what he was up to.

After telling my internal dialog to shut up so I can enjoy myself, I focus on our kiss and where our bodies touch.

The relative cool of the polished boards of the workbench when Blake gently lowers me, tells me this is no dream, it's all too real.

He takes a step back, his gaze dropping from my face, to roam across my bare skin as gently as any caress. "I've waited so long for this, Chloe, so long."

Lost as I am in a carnal haze, it takes longer than it should for his words to register. "You have? I didn't think you..." There isn't a chance I'm putting my thoughts into words.

He slides his fingers under the straps of my bra and eases them down over my shoulders, before reaching around behind me to undo the clasp. He then kisses me deeply. So deeply that it's only the cool of the stock room biting at my nipples that tells me my bra has gone.

They're not cold for long, with Blake sucking first on one, and then the other. "You fit my mouth so perfectly. I wonder if..."

His unspoken thought leaves me with an aching need the likes of which I've only read about in books. Books I don't officially check out of the library.

As wondrous as his mouth is on my breasts, I need so much more of him than this.

I need all of him, deep inside me.

Pulsing... plunging... and completing me.

BLAKE

My balls must now be the color of the sea, screaming for release; screaming for Chloe. Gone is any trace of the shy girl I'd encountered when I'd walked into the shop that morning, replaced by a tiger. And one who wants me as much as I want her.

It's a pity about the surroundings because whenever I'd fantasized about burying myself in her, this wasn't what I'd pictured.

And yet I don't seem to slow myself down, and it doesn't look as if Chloe wants me to hold back either. It wasn't me who removed her t-shirt so she could squash those gorgeous breasts of hers against my chest.

I lean into the kiss and grip her ass, delighting in how much of a handful she is. She's as a real woman should be, not a bundle of ribs and muscles thanks to hours in the gym. She's so soft, so pliable, and all mine.

My tongue teases her lips wider still, and I slowly fill her mouth, in a poor imitation of what I'd really like to be doing.

When she trembles and sags in my arms, I scoop her up and cradle her against my chest. A quick peek around the stockroom and I spy the perfect spot to place this beauty of mine. The workbench runs the length of the room, and will be the perfect height for what I've got in mind.

As I move, she stiffens in my arms, as if scared I'll drop her. As if.

I pull my lips away enough that I can whisper, "Relax babe, I've got you," into the wet cave of her mouth. This has my thoughts spiraling out of control about other parts of her I suspect will be as wet.

Now I'm the one who's having trouble standing.

After placing her gently on the workbench, I take a moment to admire her sheer beauty. Then I make quick work of the lacy piece of nothing that is all that's between me and those stunning breasts.

Finally, faced with the objects of all those teenage dreams, I am not disappointed. Perfect, exactly like the woman herself. I lower my mouth first to one breast and then the other, sucking on the nipples, before gently biting them. Her whimpers tell me this is doing as much for her as it is for me.

When she progresses to moaning, any lingering doubts disappear. I undo the buttons of her denim shorts, one-by-one, deliberately taking my time, building on the desire and anticipation for both of us.

When I finally plunge my tongue into her very core, I want her to climax so hard that her hips lift free of the workbench. Hell, with the tension building in my balls, I won't be far behind her.

SIX

CHLOE

My entire world is now focused on that one point, the one where Blake's mouth worships me with a laser-like focus, burning me, branding me, making me his.

This is nothing like I've read about in my romance novels. No candles and soft music, instead the urge to scratch the most basic of urges. Hah, who am I kidding? There's nothing basic about the sensations threatening to overwhelm me.

I can't take any more.

Blake's hot breath, his mouth, his tongue, all working on that little piece of me that holds the key, a key he soon turns. A blinding climax of the sort I've only dreamed of burns through me, obliterating any trace of librarian.

Oh my god, oh my god, oh my god!

I grip the workbench to anchor myself, to stop myself from

splintering into a million pieces. It's pointless, with my very essence flying beyond the mere confines of my body.

I'm whole, taking up as much space as nature intended. Complete, replete, and satisfied as I've never been before.

My body is still tingling with the remains of the climax when I once again realize my surroundings, any lingering wantonness fading.

Okay, so it's not as if Blake is a stranger. I've known him for most of my life.

I also know he's not interested in anything long term. He'll be gone the moment the surf carnival is over, leaving me to deal with his departure. Focused as I am on preparing myself for heartache, it takes a moment to make sense of what he's saying.

I'm torn. I'm as keen to go upstairs as Blake is. But, and it's a big *but*, if I'm this vulnerable after what just happened, how will I be after I've given myself to him completely?

In my heart, I know it will be special, if only for me. No one has ever broken down my reserve like he just did. And just like that, the little voice inside my head reminds me of the last time I'd made out with a guy in my old room upstairs.

I try silencing it, but it refuses to shut up. Its chirpy reminders of what a debacle it had been in my final year of high school, when I'd dared to sneak Grady Simmons in.

Memories of all that sweat and unsuccessful fumbling, and there's nothing I can do about the shudder that wracks my body.

Next to me, Blake straightens. A quick peek and I see the smile that's been in place all day is gone. His emotions shuttered, he rushes to button his shirt.

On witnessing his eagerness to leave, it's all I can do to stop myself from bursting into tears. I need to hold it together, at least until he's gone, to preserve some of my self-worth.

Stupid, stupid, stupid.

Why would a guy as gorgeous as Blake, who can have any woman he wants, ever be interested in someone like me? Other than if I threw myself at him, that is.

BLAKE

There's no missing Chloe's unspoken HELL NO to my suggestion to move things along. There's also no missing the "Stupid, stupid, stupid," she's muttering under her breath on repeat.

Just shows how delusional I am. There was never a chance a brain box like Chloe Henderson would take things further with an illiterate, dumb surf rat. And damn if the rejection doesn't hurt, especially after she'd been so responsive.

If we took things further, I'm sure we'd be good together. What the hell is it about women that they want a guy with a corporate job and all the trappings that go with it? That anyone with a weak resume is just light entertainment.

Finding out Chloe is as shallow as the rest of them has me hurrying to button my shirt. It doesn't help that my mind is elsewhere and that I'm all fingers and thumbs.

While the gentleman in me is screaming to help her down off the workbench, the fifteen-year-old boy in me needs to get the hell out of there. I need to go find somewhere I can lick my wounds. There's also an erection that, despite my being turned down, still needs attention.

I'm even more cut up when I see her earlier revulsion replaced by what now looks to be regret. Regret that it happened on her dad's workbench. Regret that it happened at all. Or regret that it was me?

She sits up and swings her legs over the side of the workbench before lowering herself slowly to the ground. There's no doubt she's having trouble standing, but I can't bring myself to help her. I'm holding on by a thread as it is.

If she doesn't want me in her life, I'm gone. If I'm careful, I can stay out of her way for the rest of my time in town. Then I remember that blasted fin I need. I've got two choices. Ask her about it now, or go to Wrights.

Neither option sits well with me, but if I want to take out one of the top prizes, I can't do that with a smashed fin. And if I don't take out even a minor prize this weekend, I'm seriously screwed money-wise. I've never been so low in all my life.

Unable to face Chloe when I ask, I turn away, as if giving her some sense of privacy as she gets her clothes sorted out.

"So, about that fin for my board?"

The sharp intake of breath from behind me and I know I'm right royally screwed, both with Chloe and the surf comp. The last thing I see as I quietly shut the back door of the shop is Chloe swiping at her eyes.

Could it be I'd read things wrong with her? It wouldn't be the first time my comprehension sucked. A moment's hesitation and I try reopening the door to head back inside and talk things through with Chloe.

Only it's locked, and on checking through the back window, I can see she's gone. As tempting as it is to hammer on the door and demand entrance, I don't think it would help my cause.

It's also not my way.

SEVEN

CHLOE

Another hiccup of tears wracks my body as I sit at the kitchen island in my folk's apartment above the Surf Shack. The ready-meal I've microwaved sits on a plate in front of me. I'm not sure why I bothered.

After the earlier debacle with Blake, my appetite is as good as non-existent. If I tried to eat the lasagna, I'd be physically sick. Even looking at it has my tummy roiling in a nauseous mix of heartache and remorse.

If I hadn't undone the buttons on his shirt, things could have stayed as they were. But I'd wanted it so bad. No, not *IT*, him. Good old-fashioned lust had taken over my brain. Why on earth had I ever dreamed a guy like Blake would want to kiss me? I should have questioned it, but I didn't.

Stupid, stupid, stupid.

I bang my head on the marble top of the island, hoping to knock some sense into myself. Even a senseless kid would have known better than to think anything like that was going anywhere.

Much as I want to talk with one of my girlfriends, thoughts of going into the nitty gritty of what happened have me slapping my hand over my mouth. There isn't a chance I can share this with anyone.

If word were ever to get out that one of the senior librarians had stooped to being taken on a workbench, her reputation would be in tatters.

No, not *HER* reputation, *MY* reputation. Women like Sylvia Chamberlain are always on hand to make sure of that.

My forehead is still resting on the wonderfully cool marble when a text alert pings on my phone. I reach out to the side to grab it without lifting my head, all while crossing my fingers that it's Nina saying she'll be in tomorrow.

Without Blake's help today, I'd have been in big trouble, with Mom and Dad too far away to come to my rescue in time. Now, of course, I need rescuing from something else entirely, and my folks definitely can't help there.

My head still on the breakfast bar, I try reading the message sideways. Then I sit bolt upright so I can read it properly. It's not from Nina; it's not even from my parents.

I stare at the message until my eyes glaze over, and I'm still none the wiser. It's not an easy read thanks to enough text speech to break a librarian's heart. This coupled with atrocious spelling, and I have to read the jumbled mess three times to make sense of it.

How on earth does saying sorry make things better?

Sorry for what?

Sorry for his actions?

Or just sorry it was me?

Does he expect me to respond? Should I respond? I haven't felt this out of my depth in years. I'm still dithering over what I should do when I receive another almost unreadable text.

This is also from Blake, and now I'm more confused than ever.

BLAKE

Next to my van, I catch my reflection in the tinted windows. "You stupid, freaking idiot." Eventually, I lean in to avoid looking at myself any longer; bouncing my head on the panel above the window while repeating this to help it sink in.

I should never have moved that fast on Chloe. She isn't a Sylvia. She's also nothing like the women I usually hook up with. I should have taken my time. Then I wonder if I should have given into temptation in the first place?

Inside the back of the van, I put my foil-wrapped burger on the board that covers the mini sink.

Jeez, I can't leave things like this. The knowledge I'd left her in tears is killing me, and if my mom ever heard about what I'd done, she'd want to kill me, too. An apology is in order, and while I'd rather do that face-to-face, I'd doubtless get slapped for my trouble, and rightly so.

Damn it all to hell. I should never have asked about that blasted fin until I'd worked out why she was upset and made amends.

I'm still not sure what had her changing her mind. One minute she was into it, and the next she wasn't.

With the burger forgotten; I dig my phone out of the pocket of my shorts. A text when you're breaking up is unforgiveable, but an apology?

Surely that's okay?

My finger hovers over the keys, the letters swirling as always. Eventually, I get something sorted, although I then second-guess myself and delete it.

Another attempt follows. The right tone is everything, even though deep down I'm anything but sorry for what happened. Well, at least, up to the point she'd shut down on me. Hell, if I lick my lips, I can still taste her.

The burger has gone cold before I think the text is good enough to send. My stomach now in knots, I slide the door open and throw the burger into the trash can at the edge of the parking lot. I hate it when the van stinks of stale takeaways.

I check my phone again, confirming she's still not replied. This has me double checking I'd actually hit send on the message. Oh, I'd sent it alright, but after slowly rereading it, I'm soon cussing. Freaking hell, I checked it twice. How in the heck will she take that?

I can't leave it. If I do, I won't get any sleep and I've got to be up early to catch the turning tide. I'll be using one of my back-up fins, which, while not ideal, is better than not surfing at all.

Despite wanting to make things right with Chloe, I can't lose sight of the prize money on offer the following weekend. If I take out one of the major prizes, it will make an enormous difference in how comfortable my life is for the next six months.

I could even rest up in Coogan's Break for longer than I'd originally planned. As this thought takes hold, I have to admit to myself that I don't want to leave. If there's even an outside chance with Chloe, I want to take it.

On sending the second text, relief doesn't materialize. I'm more anxious than ever. Even worse is that I won't find out until the following morning if phase two of my apology has worked.

The idea of working through potential outcomes the entire night has me reaching for one of my smaller boards. If I can thrash myself enough with an evening session, I might just get some sleep.

EIGHT

CHLOE

I can't believe it. I'm never up and dressed by six in the morning, let alone on a Sunday. As I stare in the bathroom mirror, I grab the concealer out of my make-up bag, again.

A rubbish night's sleep with my mind whirring thanks to Blake's second text, and I need all the help I can get. Black circles are only cute on pandas.

The one worry Blake had removed was saying there was no need for me to respond to his text. He'd know what my decision was in the morning. That I'd either meet him down at the beach, or I wouldn't.

All I'd wanted to do on reading that was to text back, NO WAY!

Then my little voice got in on the act, and for once it wasn't beating me up, it was egging me on. I'd fought it for as long as I could before giving in.

And giving in meant panicking about what I'd wear the following morning. I only had a few clothes with me at my folks' place, and nothing that did me any favors.

Work clothes were fine for working, but not for looking your best at six-thirty on a Sunday morning. Add in a hot-looking guy, and desperate measures were called for.

This had seen me driving back to my place to ransack my wardrobe, looking for that elusive outfit. The last thing I wanted to do was turn up, looking ready to restock the library shelves.

A little powder over the top of the concealer and it's less obvious. I turn and walk through into my old bedroom to check myself out in the full-length mirror again. The one plus of not having had anything to eat since lunchtime yesterday is that my tummy is flatter than normal.

A cup of coffee in a go cup, and I'm as ready as I'll ever be. The fresh air on my walk to the beach does wonders for my foggy brain. On reaching the spot Blake mentioned in his text invite, I'm clear-headed and fully awake.

I'm also in time to see him walking up the beach, his board tucked under one arm, his wetsuit leaving nothing to the imagination. And I'd spent a lot of time imagining.

Then I spot who's running down the beach to meet him, and my cup of coffee freezes against my lips. I can't force myself to take a mouthful. If I did, I'd choke.

To add insult to injury, Sylvia looks gorgeous in her bikini. It doesn't matter that it's at odds with the freshness of the morning. There isn't a chance I want to find myself in a side-by-side comparison with that woman when she's as good as naked.

With unshed tears blurring my vision, I'm lucky to make it back to my parents' apartment without walking into something. How could I have been so delusional as to think he was actually interested in me?

And how could he have been so cruel as to invite me down to the beach at the same time as Sylvia? There's not a chance she was passing by at this hour in the morning.

BLAKE

I've enjoyed a good session. Even with my back-up fin, I've been able to handle everything the waves could throw at me. Things change when I get out of the water.

Rather than it be Chloe walking down the beach to meet me as I'd dreamed of the night before, it's blasted Sylvia. What the hell is she doing out here so early, and in a bikini, of all things? She's got the properties of superglue where I'm concerned.

I'd even moved the van to an industrial area for the night to avoid her popping up for a nightcap as she'd promised.

As I scan the boardwalk that runs the length of the beach, I spot Chloe. I know to the second when she sees Sylvia, her coffee up to her mouth, only to be taken away untouched. She'd then made quick work of getting away.

As much as I'd wanted to chase after her, there wasn't a chance I was showing my cards with Sylvia around. Better the vindictive blonde now running down the beach like a Bay Watch extra didn't know Chloe had been standing behind her.

I can't imagine what Chloe must think of me inviting her down here only for her to find Sylvia on the scene. All I know is that I need to fix this, and soon.

And by soon I mean as soon as the Surf Shack opens, if not before.

"Hi Blake." Sylvia reaches out and slicks back my hair. "I love your curls, and you're such an amazing surfer."

The enthusiasm in her words is about as fake as the woman herself.

Funny as hell is that she can't hide that she's freezing her ass off. She's a study in goosebumps.

Hah, serves her right for stalking me. It's no surprise she'd know I'd be down here with a heap of others. She's a local; she knows the best waves are just after high-tide, with it easy enough to check.

What is a surprise is that she'd rouse herself before ten in the morning. It was part of the reason I'd organized to meet Chloe when I did.

Sheesh, note to self, don't underestimate this bunny boiler.

I won't make the same mistake again.

Now all I need to do is ditch her so I can get over to the Surf Shack and make things right with Chloe. I try for a polite "I'll catch ya later," for all the good it does. Despite impressions, I know Sylvia isn't dense, and I'd know. Rather, she's deliberately missing the signals so she can hang around.

In the end, I chuck my board in the back of the van, jump in the driver's seat, still in my wetsuit. "I'm off to the gym for a shower. Catch ya later."

Although not if I can help it.

I zoom out of the carpark leaving her standing there. The only thing I haven't told her is which gym, because if I did, I suspect she'd be waiting outside for me after.

NINE

CHLOE

Back at my parents' apartment, I make quick work of ditching the outfit I'd spent so much time agonizing over. Next to go is the make-up. There isn't a chance I'm running the shop slathered in that many layers of concealer.

If, as I suspect, Nina pulls another no-show, I'll be frantic, leaving me a sweaty mess. While the shop is air-conditioned, the unit isn't really up to cooling such an enormous expanse.

On stepping down into the shop, I'm dismayed to see half a dozen customers already milling about outside. Some politely wait for me to get out of the way after I've opened the front door. But one guy rushes straight in and I come close to being taken out by the heavy glass-paneled door.

This jolts me out of auto-pilot and thoughts of why Blake bothered inviting me to the beach that morning. What was the point when he was already meeting up with Sylvia?

I didn't think he was that into her. Hah, but what did I know? I'd thought for a second he was into me. Looks like I was wrong on both counts.

By nine-thirty, I know Nina isn't coming in. The woman is regular as clock-work. She's never late without telling my parents, and in their absence, me. With her not having texted or phoned, I'm worrying about her. I hope she's okay. I'd ring Mom, but there's not much she can do while she's at the trade show.

My biggest concern right now is that today is even busier than yesterday. The only plus in being run off my feet is that it takes my mind off the past twenty-four-hours.

Smiling at customers is a step too far, to the point one obnoxious creep even suggests I try. The rictus smirk I give him in response has him questioning my sexuality before barging out of the shop. I'm not in the mood for that sort of behavior this morning.

Then I spot who has taken his place.

The only plus is that Sylvia's now wearing a coverall over her bikini. It's sheer enough I don't know why she bothered. The woman's other accessory is Blake, even if he doesn't appear anywhere near as comfortable as Sylvia.

And neither should he after his recent behavior.

The biggest shock of all is Blake's hair, or rather the lack of it. Why on earth would he shave his head? A number one cut, or whatever they call it. Those curls suited him.

Stuck behind the sales counter, I've never been as uncomfortable in my skin, knowing I'm a mess compared to the glamazon next to Blake. It's one thing to have your competition rubbed in your face; it's another when you know you're not looking your best.

When I tossed my more flattering outfit into my bag earlier that morning, I'd no clue I'd soon face Sylvia and, worse than that, Blake.

Instead, I'm decked out in a tank top emblazoned with the shop's logo, a denim skirt, and my favorite Chucks. While perfect for being run off my feet all day in the shop, it doesn't compare favorably with Sylvia's stylish outfit. On taking in the woman's sleek locks, my hand strays to my own messy bun, realizing that it's being held in place thanks to a pencil.

Well, there's nothing I can do about it right now. I'm trapped where I am for at least seven more hours. Thank goodness I hadn't finished my coffee earlier.

To take my mind off serving Sylvia and Blake, I concentrate on a young girl who's taking forever deciding which love bracelet she wants to buy.

She's still dithering when Sylvia puts her hands on the girl's shoulders and roughly moves her to the side. That is it. She can push me around, but she's not pushing my customers around. And she especially isn't picking on someone weaker than her.

I'd had enough of that back in high school.

And to hell with what my parents think about it when they hear of it, which they will. Coogan's Break is a hotbed of gossip.

BLAKE

Hell's teeth, the woman must have the scenting abilities of a flaming blood hound. There are at least half a dozen gyms in town, with Murphy's the least popular of all. Even better is that it's also the cheapest, with Mike, the owner, a mate of mine from high school.

I won't find it as easy to ditch her this time, with her leaning against the driver's door. The only way I can get behind the wheel, without going through her, is to use the passenger door, or climb in through the back. Thoughts of doing exactly that have me breaking into a broad grin, something Sylvia unfortunately takes as encouragement.

If only she knew my mom raised me better than to be rude to a woman. Looks like I'm stuck with her, at least for a while.

After I scan the parking lot, something becomes apparent. There are no other vehicles here. This wouldn't be unusual for a Sunday morning, except for me wondering how Sylvia got here.

"Oh, thank goodness you're here. My car broke down. Can you give me a ride back into town?"

This is a reasonable enough request. But while I never did well with exams, I'm not that stupid. If that woman hasn't got the latest iPhone in that monster handbag of hers, then I'll eat my sports socks. She could easily have called for help by now.

I'm not letting her get away with it. I take my time walking to the corner of the building and checking up and down the street. "Where's your car?"

By my reckoning, it's hidden around the corner. Either that or she caught an Uber here once she knew where I was.

She waves randomly toward the south. "A couple of blocks away. I'd keep walking, but I'm not comfortable dressed like this."

I'm not surprised she's uncomfortable. The woman is half-naked. The only difference between now and when she'd cornered me earlier is that she's wearing a brightly colored shirt over the top of her bikini.

There's nothing I can do but take her into town. At least then I can leave her to her own devices, knowing she won't come to any harm. The gym isn't in the best part of town.

"Sure I can. Jump in."

She races around the front of the van and is trying to open the door before I've even got my keys out. She's in the van waiting when I open my door.

When she strikes what she assumes is an attractive pose, I snort in laughter. Let's see how she likes my gym bag being stuck between us. Usually I'd throw it in the back to avoid the smell myself. Now, I even unzip it before I toss it into the middle of the bench seat.

I'd worked hard, sweating out my frustration at having my meeting with Chloe ruined by the woman on the other side of my smelly workout gear.

Let's see if she finds me as attractive after she's sat next to that for five minutes.

I'm hoping for the final nail in the coffin of her finding me attractive when I remove my cap to reveal the haircut from hell. If she liked my curls as much as she said, they're in the wastebasket in the men's changing rooms.

TEN

CHLOE

I've had enough of this, enough of being stepped on by the likes of Sylvia—Spiteful—Chamberlain. Enough of being looked over as unimportant.

Rather than ask Sylvia how I can help, I ignore her. Instead, I lock my gaze on the young girl who Sylvia has shoved to the side, and who's obviously upset.

"I'm sure we've got some more bracelets out the back. Would you like me to get them for you so you can have more to choose from?"

The young girl nods tentatively, and then the only thing louder than Sylvia grinding her teeth is Blake's muffled laughter. Eventually, he stops fighting it and gives into his mirth.

Sylvia is having none of it. Before I've been able to go check the storeroom, she slams her hands down on the glass-topped sales counter. There's no way I can ignore her any longer.

"Sylvia, I'm sorry, did Wright's not have what you were after?" I follow this up with a patently false smile. Despite this, I'm enjoying a grim delight at not giving into her as I always have in the past.

Sure, Mom and Dad will give me grief when they hear of it, but I no longer care. If I can hang on to a shred of self-esteem, then I'm going for it. And anyway, they can't fire me, because I'm not on the payroll.

Sylvia glares at me, her eyes awash with malice. "I told you the service at this place was as rubbish as the selection." She's said this loud enough that every customer in the shop can hear. "Come on, Blake. Let's get out of this dump. You'll be able to get what you want over at Wright's."

Even though Sylvia has supposedly addressed Blake, her actual target has been my customers. As with yesterday, a few of them slink away. The only difference today is that when she opens her mouth to continue her tirade, I decide I've had enough.

I round the sales counter and jam myself between Blake and Sylvia. Despite Sylvia being six inches taller than me; I'm all up in her face. "I want you out of here! Now!!" I follow this up by pointing dramatically at the door, leaving her in no doubt.

My actions have been every bit as blatant as hers, maybe even more so. I can't damage the store's reputation any more than the unpleasant woman in front of me. When Sylvia doesn't move, I grab her by the elbow and turn her to face the door. "Come on. You're wasting my time, and I've got real customers to attend to."

All those years of hefting books around in the library have me stronger than I appear, with Sylvia shocked at being moved so easily. Compared to a trolley full of books, the woman is a lightweight.

I don't slow until I've deposited her on the sidewalk, with this made easier by Blake opening the shop door for me. The biggest surprise is that when he shuts it, he's still inside with me.

While he's the first to bow and applaud my actions, other customers soon join in, the loudest of all being the young girl. The admiration she's giving me has me standing a lot taller than my five-foot-two.

Even Blake is looking at me admiringly. Closer inspection and I see that isn't all that's glinting in his eyes, with my body responding in a flash of heat and longing.

A smile dancing on his lips, he saunters over to stand next to me. He's so close his heat brushes against my exposed skin, doubly so when he leans over to whisper in my ear.

"Weren't you heading out back for some more bracelets? I can help if you like."

When he straightens, his friendly smile has gone. And that's okay, because I like his dirty grin a lot more. He runs his tongue over his bottom lip and steamy memories of yesterday hit me.

After this, it's all I can do to keep standing.

If only it was closing time and I could take him up on his offer.

Today is going to be endless.

BLAKE

Sylvia stands fuming out on the sidewalk. However, I've got no sympathy for the nasty piece of work. She asked for it and Chloe delivered.

I'm definitely looking at the curvy girl in front of me in a new light. What a little spitfire. As I imagine the response, if I was lucky enough to get her under the covers, I break into a lazy grin. A quick glance at Chloe, and the stockroom, and a plan emerges.

The shop's too busy for us to talk through everything, as had been my plan, when I asked her to join me down at the beach. Instead, any chance I get, I'll let her know how I feel about her, how I've always felt about her.

What she does to me, what I want, and what I need.

If things go according to my rough-and-ready plan, by the end of today, she'll be ready to blow. All I'll need to do is suggest touching her very core with the tip of my tongue and she'll implode. Now that'd be a wondrous sight.

I know from our brief interlude in the stock room yesterday that there's a lot more to this woman and her outwardly calm demeanor. The longer I dwell on what had taken place, the harder I get to the point I have to put some distance between us. She might not be the only one ready to blow after the day of whispered promises I've got in mind.

Despite my having trouble with the written word, I've no issues with anything oral, something I'd showed her yesterday.

Damn it, being this close to her and unable to do anything about it will be torture. Sure, I'm as adventurous as the next guy, but even I draw the line at a shop full of people.

And the number of people in the shop never gives up; it's like yesterday, but on steroids. At this rate, I'll be lucky to have enough energy left to take Chloe every which way I can think of.

Despite being rushed off our feet, every chance I get, I explain to Chloe what had happened down at the beach that morning and later at the gym.

By the time we're skin to skin, I want any doubts she might have had dealt with. The only thing I want between us when that happens is a slippery layer of sweat.

Hell dude, clear your head or you're gonna blow.

The longer I'm with Chloe, the less appealing the thought of leaving for Baja after the carnival the following weekend was.

Lunch is but a distant memory when Chloe's parents burst in through the back door of the shop. They then drop the bombshell that the girl who was supposed to be helping Chloe had actually quit. Mrs. Henderson is furious.

"I can't believe Nina would up and leave without notice. All we got was a text message. We'd have let you know, but there didn't seem any point. Craig from next door rang and told us you were handling things like a pro."

Craig? Ah, the guy from the deli. I vaguely remember his daughter had been the year ahead of me.

Chloe's dad then takes over. "We thought it was best to get on the road as soon as the trade show ended. She left for Vegas in pursuit of some man, apparently."

Two extra pairs of hands make all the difference, with the backlog of customers soon cleared. Chloe's mom is in charge of the register, while the rest of us are on the shop floor.

The rest of the afternoon is a blur, and it's not until I see Chloe locking the front door that I realize the time. All I want to do is walk across the shop, toss her over one shoulder and get outta there, but I can't. I'm stuck talking to her dad next to the row of surfboards that line one side of the shop.

"Thanks for helping, son. Chloe could never have managed alone, not with the carnival coming up. The shop is always like this, but trade shows don't change their dates to suit the likes of us. We didn't know Nina would up and leave."

He straightens a couple of boards before turning back to me. "I know you like to follow the surf, but would you be interested in helping us here until we can replace Nina?"

He pauses for a moment. "You know, I've been thinking about employing someone to help me with board repairs. Would that be something that interests you?"

ELEVEN

The afternoon is a challenge, even with my parents' help. I don't think I've ever seen the shop as busy. Looks as if Wright's hasn't cornered the market on everything surfing as Sylvia would have us believe.

In a brief lull, I bring my mom up to speed on having to escort a customer out of the shop. Better she hear about it from me than anyone else. Rather than blow up as I've been expecting, she responds with a slow handclap.

"I'm so pleased you finally stood up to her. It broke my heart hearing she'd bullied you in school. I only heard about it after you'd graduated and I'm still annoyed the school did nothing about it."

Mom busies herself counting the cash in the register while I lock the front door to stop anyone else coming in. If they're shopping this late in the day, they'll just have to deal with it. After flipping the sign to

CLOSED, I take a quick scan of the shop. I'm expecting Blake to be long gone, but he's still there.

He's with my dad. Unsure what it is the two men are talking about with their heads so close together; I inch my way ever closer under the guise of straightening stock. I'm in time to hear something that explains those messy text messages from Blake.

Like many people who have dyslexia, he hides it thanks to his basic intelligence and years of practice. Guess what, some of the brightest people I know have difficulties with reading. As a librarian, it is part of my job to help.

My dad grips Blake by the shoulder and squeezes. "Son, I'm sure we can work around that. If you're able to manage the shop floor during busy times, and assist with repairs, that'll be an enormous help."

I'm pleased Blake has his back to me and doesn't know I've heard his little secret, because I've got other plans for this evening. The sort of plans that have me packing faster than I have in my entire life.

Heck, I didn't pack this fast when it was time to leave summer camp for home. I don't bother folding anything; rather, I stuff everything into my hold-all, not caring how creased it will be when I unpack at home.

Following a quick goodbye to my folks, and a promise to come for dinner on the Monday, I head out the back door to grab my car. Blake is hot on my heels and every bit as eager to get back to my place as I am.

We can grab his van later.

I don't bother getting my bag out of the trunk when we arrive at my place. Instead, I race in through the mudroom, making quick work of kicking off my sneakers.

On turning, I find Blake is just as keen as I am, with his shirt already on the floor. The sight of his tanned six-pack is enough to have me sucking in air so hard I have a coughing fit.

Wow, and here I was thinking he looked good in a wetsuit. Unable to stop myself, I reach out and run my hands down his torso, resulting in a heart-felt groan.

"Darling, if you want me to last until we get upstairs, might be best if you stopped right there."

This is all the encouragement I need. However, I come to a crashing halt when I see the pile of clothes in the middle of my bed. Blast, I'd completely forgotten about last night's wardrobe dive.

On spotting a half-eaten box of chocolates on my bedside table, I open the top drawer and slide it in before Blake can witness my guilty pleasure.

I'm just as quick in removing the clothes that cover my bed. Sure, I'll be ironing for weeks, but I don't care. I want Blake. I want his body hard up against mine, our hearts touching, and him deep inside me.

Never have I been surer of anything in my life.

BLAKE

Chloe is a whirlwind, shoving all those clothes onto the floor beside the bed and whipping the covers back. I love a woman who knows her own mind. Stitch that. I've loved Chloe since as far back as I can remember.

There's no doubt she wants this as much as I do. I step over, and mimicking her actions of the day before, grab the bottom of her top and lift it up, and over her head. Next, I unzip the front of her denim skirt and slide it down her hips.

The scent of her arousal fills the air between us, nearly bringing me to my knees. Then I decide that's a great place to start, but not before she's as bare as nature intended. I'm fumbling with the hooks on her bra when I notice her ripping open the Velcro-closing on my shorts.

Two minutes later and we're both naked and unable to keep our hands off each other. Chloe is everything I'd imagined all these years. All those teenage dreams are finally being realized and they're every bit as wonderful as I'd hoped.

With her luscious body tight now against me, all thoughts of my usual seduction methods are out the window. I don't want to seduce Chloe; rather I want to make love to her. "You're perfect," I whisper into her flaxen hair.

After tumbling onto the bed, I nibble one pebbled nipple and then the other. Chloe mews in response, her back arching off the bed to be closer. It's nearly my undoing.

I move down her body, peppering her with passionate kisses, her body writhing under me in response. Hovering over her mons, I murmur, "I've dreamed of doing this all day long," my breath rippling the curls at the apex of her thighs.

With her soon spread wide, I suck hard, taking my fill. This woman of mine is as juicy as any peach. I slide first one finger, then two deep inside her and she responds as my dreams told me she would.

But I'm not giving her the release she begs for just yet. When that happens, I want to be deep inside her, our bodies moving in unison, our hearts beating in time.

I move up her body until I've poised the tip of my cock at the very entrance to her core, and there I wait for permission.

Chloe's light gray eyes have always been expressive, telling of pain, love, and a myriad of other emotions. Today, all I can see is a pure primal desire that's more than a match to my own.

As I drive into her heat, our eyes lock, and the sense of coming home is overwhelming, and every bit as good as I've fantasized about.

I pull out almost all the way and she whimpers for my return. I plunge back in, even deeper, with a burning need to make this woman mine for all eternity swamping rational thought.

When Chloe crosses her ankles behind my back, I sink balls-deep into her welcoming depths, with fulfillment soon arriving for both of us. It's been quicker than I could have imagined and I glory in her, trusting me like she does.

As I kiss the side of her mouth, I reach out and open the top drawer of her bedside cabinet. I then pop the chocolate I've grabbed between Chloe's lips.

It's only fair she should have something to nibble on while I'm doing the same. On sliding down her body, I know I'm finally home, and I couldn't be happier.

EPILOGUE

CHLOE

I can't believe Blake talked me into wearing a bikini and to the Coogan's Break Carnival, of all places. I'd feel naked but for the fire in his eyes whenever he looks at me.

What also helps is my having spent a lot of the past week in that exact state. The only thing that interrupted our exploration of each other's bodies was my having to work and him out surfing, or working at the Surf Shack.

Life is good. It's beyond my wildest dreams.

I roll onto my side and look at him. He's nervous, and with good reason. The surf is all over the place and proving a challenge, even for the pros. A couple of them have already wiped out in spectacular fashion in practice sessions.

I gently stroke his chest. "You know this beach better than any of that lot. You'll be brilliant out there."

I'd wish him luck, except that's not what he needs. He's an amazing surfer, and he grew up surfing these waves. His chances of taking out the big prize are as good as any of the sponsored surfers, if not better.

It doesn't hurt that he and my dad have been perfecting the settings of his longboard. Locked away like a couple of mad scientists in that workshop.

Blake actually blushed when he told me he'd had trouble concentrating when they were using 'our' part of the bench. "It was weird with your dad right next to me."

I'm about to continue my pep talk when a shadow falls across us, causing me to glance up. It's a second before I can make out who it is, and then my stomach drops. The hatred in Sylvia's eyes as she glares at me is enough to chill the hardiest of souls.

Already vulnerable in my new bikini, I take my hand away from Blake's chest to reach for my shirt. Only he's not having it. He takes hold of my hand, but rather than putting it back on his chest, he kisses, and then sucks on my fingers, one-by-one.

He's making such a production out of it, that I guess what he's up to.

"Ooooh, babe. Not with people watching. Remember what happened yesterday?" My words are breathy, dramatic, and totally false, but the woman glaring at me doesn't know that.

Sylvia's screech of anguish is loud enough to draw the attention of those around us, something I'd rather have avoided. It doesn't matter that Blake says I'm 'hot as hell' in my new bikini, it'll take a while for me to believe that.

With Blake continuing to suck on my fingers, there's nothing for Sylvia to do but storm off down the beach. That the spiteful woman takes vengeance on a sandcastle on her way makes what happens next even more delicious.

She was asking for it, and Mother Nature didn't let us down.

As a local, Sylvia knows you don't stomp through puddles on this beach, their hidden depths often a surprise. Sure enough, the next one she storms through proves far deeper than she's obviously expected.

As I watch her scrambling to get back to her feet, a snort of laughter escapes. It's one that's shared by Blake and the kid whose sandcastle Sylvia had just demolished.

That nasty piece of work has had it coming for a long time. And really, the only thing hurt when she face-planted the beach was her pride.

I'm still chuckling when Blake stills next to me.

"Blake, you're going to be amazing." I move closer before whispering, "And if you surf as well as you make love, you're a winner already."

I then kiss him soundly, only pulling away when the cheering from those around us becomes too hard to ignore.

"Now, go win this thing!"

BLAKE

Things couldn't be better. I'm in control of my board and dealing with the less than ideal conditions. Meanwhile, the unpredictability of the surf is giving my fellow competitors grief in a big way.

I guess Chloe was right about my years surfing this beach, making a difference. It doesn't matter that I'm up against seasoned professionals. As the day progresses, it takes on a dream-like quality as I take on wave after wave, consistently scoring eights and nines.

Add in my gorgeous Chloe waiting on the beach to celebrate each win, and life has never been better. Maybe it's that I'm happy, truly happy, for the first time in a long time.

. . .

I'm holding a big ass check under one arm and Chloe under the other when reality settles on me. A week ago, I'd have been happy simply holding the check, and yet I'd have been missing out on the best prize of all.

After a cheesy smile for the local paper, I swoop in and claim Chloe's lips in a searing kiss.

On finally pulling away, I find her mom and dad staring at us in surprise. It's one thing for Chloe's dad to be happy with me working at the shop; me dating his daughter is on a different level entirely. And it's not one I'm sure he'll be keen on. He knows my prospects aren't good thanks to my reading issues.

I'm nervous until Mr. Henderson pulls Chloe's mom against his side and squeezes her tight. The pair then beams at us and I sag in relief. Next to me, Chloe relaxes against my side, obviously having spotted this parental approval when I did.

For now, I can relax knowing the response I'll get when I ask for Chloe's hand in marriage. While it's still early days, when you know, you know.

SPORTS

Local boy takes out coveted top prize at Coogan's Break Surf Carnival for second year running.

Blake Mitchell says his knowledge of local conditions helped him win out against some of the biggest names in surfing, including 3x world champion, Brody Sinclair.

To celebrate his win, he proposed to girlfriend Chloe Henderson.

She said yes!

Bridget has never gotten over that first love, instead devoting herself to her business. Meanwhile, Jason's career is over, although not through any fault of his own.

ONE

JASON

After standing, I shake hands with Roscoe, my caseworker at the Coogan's Break Job Center. My hand engulfs his.

He's assessed my skills, aptitudes, and abilities. Some of the shadier talents I'd picked up during my time in the military had given him pause, despite him also being a veteran.

I'm officially on the job market after working for Uncle Sam for the past nine years. And I don't like it.

I didn't want to leave the army, but budgetary restraints said otherwise. Well, those and that asshat Mike Dawson, my commanding officer.

It didn't matter that I'd never openly challenged his authority, always doing exactly as he'd ordered. And hell, if that hadn't been asinine.

But when it came down to it, he knew. He knew I thought he was an idiot who shouldn't be in charge of running a bath.

While Roscoe is confident of finding me the right job, I'm not hoping. I doubt there's much call for military-grade thugs in the seaside community I'd grown up in.

His promise to call if anything comes up still ringing in my ears; I cross an expanse of sand colored carpet. This has me back in Afghanistan and still part of a team, still making a difference.

The odds of finding something like that locally are slim, and for the first time in my life, I feel adrift. I don't belong here. I don't belong anywhere anymore.

It's for this reason I've put the word out that I'd be interested in private contracts. There are plenty of jobs on the worldwide market where they're happy to pay good money to someone with my training.

There's also a feeling of being a sell-out if I did. I signed up and trained hard all those years to fight for *my* country, not someone else's. Here's hoping my desperation to belong to something—anything—doesn't cloud my judgement.

My emotions about Coogan's Break, a town I'd loved as a teenager, are also all over the place. It had been here that I'd enlisted at seventeen. The timing hadn't been great, but when Seth, my twin brother, informed me he had signed up, I had no option but to enlist.

We were a team. It was my job to protect my little brother. Okay, not so little at six-foot-four, and only younger by half-an-hour, but still shorter and younger than me.

I'd been wrong about him needing—or even wanting—my protection. His exact words at the time had been, "Sheesh, Jason, haven't you screwed my life up enough already?" Unfortunately, I knew exactly what he was talking about.

The other thing I'd screwed up was how I'd left town. Ten years later and memories of Bridget Myers' tears can still crush my heart like an empty soda can.

I never meant to hurt her. And even though I didn't feel like I had an option, leaving had come close to destroying me, too.

I wonder what she's up to these days.

Married with a couple of kids would be my guess. On this depressing thought, I march out onto the sidewalk and smash straight into a woman.

Only by wrapping my arms tight around her do I stop her from ending up in a heap on the sidewalk. On looking down into her upturned face, the years roll back. The woman I'm holding onto like my life depends on it is none other than Bridget.

It's as if my memories have somehow conjured her up. However, the woman in my arms differs from the teenager I'd left behind. My body doesn't care though, reacting as it always did.

Nope, that's not right. It's reacting way more than it ever did, because Bridget is way more than she ever was. Hell, if those womanly curves aren't doing it for me in a big way. I'd always wondered what sort of woman she'd become.

It's only when she gasps I become aware my hands are moving of their own volition. They're checking out places they really shouldn't. But hell, I'm only human and her new curves are out of this world.

The bright orange, figure-hugging dress brings attention to bits that would have been just fine on their own. Meanwhile, her full breasts squished tight against my chest have my cock twitching.

This has my head full of images of me caressing those gorgeous breasts to the point I'm close to drooling. Eventually I come to my senses, and drop my hands from where they've settled just beneath these magnificent orbs.

I then put a little distance between us despite my body screaming out that it wants me to do the exact opposite. I'll bet her nipples would be tight little buds with the merest brush of my thumb ... or my tongue...

I'm immediately racked by guilt at my dirty thoughts until I notice there's no ring on her left hand. Then the guilt is back because anything happening between us is a no-no. I'd left her once; I'm not going there again, all part of the new responsible me.

"Seth, I'm so sorry. I wasn't watching where I was going." There's no missing that she's giving me the side-eye thanks to my having manhandled her.

It would be so easy to pretend I was my twin, to have him taking the blame for my appalling behavior. Hell, I'd done it enough when we were younger. I'd thought it was hilarious, and I was stupid enough to think Seth agreed with me.

It was no wonder he'd been so angry when I enlisted. I had a lot to answer for with the way I'd treated my brother.

And that starts now.

No more running away.

Not today, never.

With the promises I'd made to Seth still ringing in my ears, this was my chance to follow through. I want to prove to him I've changed. Part of me might even want me to prove it to myself.

When I'd reached out after hearing he was suffering from PTSD, there'd been no response. While he could delete all those emails and texts, he'd had no option but to speak to me when I turned up unannounced at his garage yesterday afternoon.

Hell, putting things right with him was why I was back here. As my gaze sweeps over the woman in front of me, I'd be a fool to think it was the only reason.

That aside, to pretend I was Seth would simply delay the inevitable. Bridget will learn soon enough I'm back in town, even if briefly. I may as well get this over with.

I rub my hand around the back of my neck, not sure how I should break it to her. In the end, I go for utilitarian, as with everything else in my life.

"Not Seth, Jason."

There's a flash of recognition in her crystal-blue eyes, followed closely by crushing hurt. She involuntarily grabs a handful of her long ash blonde hair and twists it just like she used to.

Even more telling is when she takes a step back, and then another.

After the way I'd hurt her, I can't blame her for wanting to put some distance between us. She's also had no warning I would appear like this.

But if I'm sticking around, even if only for a couple of weeks, I need to make things right with her. And fast. The way I'd left her has been eating away at me for too long already. I want to rectify ALL the wrongs from my past.

"Have you got time for a coffee?"

BRIDGET

I'm walking aimlessly along Seaview Road when I come close to being laid out on the sidewalk by Seth Adams.

As surprising as the collision, is the way his hands are all over me. Wow, he's not even been married for three months. He'd better not do anything to hurt Skye.

A glance to my right and I see he must have walked out of the Job Center.

That's odd; I thought he owned Adam's Towing? It's also unusual to see him as tidy as he currently is, his preference being coveralls, usually with the odd spot of grease. It's something that's definitely improved since he got together with Skye.

And then my world comes crashing down. It's not Seth. It's Jason and I'm seventeen again. And distraught because my boyfriend has just told me he'll soon be leaving for basic training.

Saying his announcement was out of the blue would be an understatement. It was two days after prom and our future was looking bright. Heck, I was still trying to get rid of the last of the glitter from my Under the Sea costume.

His coming from a military family, it was almost a given he'd sign-up. But, for him to do so without at least discussing it with me first? That hurt so badly. The only plus at the time had been Seth enlisting, too.

It would have been torture having Jason's twin around. Seth, discharged for health reasons, came home as a shadow of his former self, and it had been bad enough.

Focused on the painful memories as I am, I only know Jason has asked me something by his expression.

"I'm sorry. What was that?"

He clears his throat before repeating himself. "Have you got time for a coffee?" He follows this up with a smile, no doubt designed to soften me up, as it always had in the past. Well, not any longer.

I'm working up the nerve to yell at him, "No, I don't have the time for a coffee," when he carries on as though the last ten years never happened.

"I should have explained ... I need to explain." His words falter as if he's searching for the right ones, without luck.

Oh, this should be good. A peek at my watch confirms I've got enough time.

I won't need to collect Steve, my foreman, from the chiropractors for at least another forty-five minutes. Plenty of time for Jason Adams to continue digging that hole he'd started ten years ago.

The hole he'd dropped my teenage heart in before covering it with dirt. The hole that meant I hadn't been able to commit to another guy since. That hole!

"Sure, I've got time for a coffee." There's nothing friendly with my acceptance, and given how much his abandonment still hurts, who can blame me?

That he then doesn't move tells me one of two things. He recently arrived back in town and isn't aware of what's good these days. Or he's waiting for me to decide.

Either way, I take charge, knowing that as soon as Steve calls, I'll have to go collect him. At least that's what I'm hoping will happen. When his back went into spasm after he'd picked up that bag of fertilizer, my heart had been in my throat. His being out of action is a nightmare, with my landscaping business finally taking off.

Steve's my right-hand man, and without him I'll be up the creek without a paddle. While I've also got casual laborers I can call on, I don't dare leave one of them in charge if I'm away from the site. And I can't be everywhere at once.

"I don't have a lot of time. Let's go to Magic Beans."

Without waiting for him to agree, I turn on my heel and walk off in ground-devouring strides. There are pluses to being five-foot-nine.

Jason doesn't take long to catch up and fall into step beside me, matching his pace to mine, as he always did. Part of me softens at the sense of familiarity, while another part of me is furious.

I'm furious at him for how he treated me. I'm also annoyed at myself for being taken in by a gorgeous smile and a body to die for. A glance to the side and I revise this to a body to die *under*.

Damn if the army hasn't turned him from a lanky teen into a solid hunk of muscle. It shouldn't come as any surprise, given how Seth turned out.

On arriving at the café, I do my best to ignore the images crossing my mind's eye. I'll need to concentrate if I'm to hear his excuses for why he'd treated me so badly all those years ago.

TWO

My mouth is hanging open, but I can't help it. Never in a million years did I expect to be sitting opposite Jason Adams this morning.

Nor did I expect the bombshell he's just dropped.

"But I thought you signed up before Seth?" My brow wrinkles as I think back on our last conversation, the words clear in my head. "Wasn't that what you said?"

Actually, he'd said far more than that, throwing information at me about family tradition, and wanting to serve his country.

On learning that he'd enlisted to monitor his younger brother, Seth, and not the other way around, my memories take on a different hue. It hadn't been me he'd been trying to convince that he'd had no choice but to sign on. It had been himself.

I'm about to ask him why he hadn't told me this. Then I remember how I'd exploded and ended our relationship on the spot. I'd been crying so hard, I wouldn't have heard him, anyway. So far as I was concerned, he'd dumped me.

And apparently, I wasn't the only one to explode when they'd discovered Jason had enlisted. Seth wasn't happy about it either, especially since he'd enlisted to escape from his brother's shadow.

How often had I heard *half-an-inch and half-an-hour* used to describe Seth in relation to Jason? I guess that must have gotten to him in the end. Well, that and him constantly taking the blame for Jason's wilder exploits.

Jason's gaze drops and he examines the table as if his life depends on it. "It got so bad in basic training the army separated us. I guess I blamed..."

Jason's mouth snaps shut, keeping the rest of his words where they are, although I'm dying to know who or what he blamed.

So even though Jason had signed on to keep an eye out for Seth, he'd then stayed on because I'd told him I never wanted to see him again. I might actually have screamed that last bit before slamming the door in his face.

As I play catch up with Jason, it's almost as if the past ten years never happened. He's surprised to find I'm still single. However, I keep it to myself that the reason I never had a successful relationship was my habit of comparing all men to him.

A glance in his direction and I can't altogether blame myself, even if this angers me deep down. Maybe part of me was aware he'd turn out like this?

Or was I just dreaming all those Friday and Saturday nights at home alone? On that depressing thought, I take a sip of coffee, and then another, as if stalling.

I want to ask him why he was at the Job Center, but refrain. His not having mentioned it says he doesn't want to talk about it. I do my best to keep my tone light when I instead ask, "How long are you back in town for?"

He puts his cup of coffee back on its saucer and straightens it slowly. "A couple of weeks? A couple of months? A couple of years?"

He follows his multi-choice response with a shrug.

"I guess if you told me, you'd have to kill me, right?" My laughter is as forced as my military joke.

Jason again fiddles with his coffee cup before he looks me dead in the eye. "I'm no longer in the military."

The hurt in his eyes says a lot more than his bald words, leaving me unsure of what to say next. I'm still dithering when he tells me. His words are succinct when he bullet-points the reasons for his leaving.

"Gosh, I didn't even realize the army could let people go."

"Hell yes they do. They've cut up to sixty thousand in the past." He snorts before continuing. "I guess all those peace-talks have to pay off, eventually."

We both fall silent, with each of us alone with our thoughts. It's something that isn't as unpleasant as you'd imagine. I've finished my coffee and even looked at my watch when my phone rings.

If it were any other day, I'd let it go to voicemail, but as I'm expecting a call from my foreman, I grab it immediately. A quick check of caller ID and I answer with, "Hey Steve, I'll be there in five minutes."

Sadly, he doesn't need a ride. He needs two weeks' bed rest and a course of horse-strength anti-inflammatories. His wife is already on her way to collect him from the chiropractors.

This is a disaster. I've got four projects on the go, and there isn't a chance I can handle all those on my own. The thought of messing up any of them has me fighting to calm my breathing.

When that doesn't work, my hand unconsciously strays to the pulse thundering in my throat. Throughout my mini meltdown, I'm aware of Jason watching me, his piercing blue eyes missing nothing.

JASON

There's no getting past Bridget's distress. Whatever it is she's just learned, it isn't good. I wait until she's put her phone away and done her best to calm down before I speak. "Anything I can help with?"

She gulps twice before she can answer. "I, I don't think..." She swallows before adding a simple, "No."

I tip my head to the side and wait. It was always this way with Bridget. She'll need time to process the news before I hear the full story.

Eventually, I'm rewarded when she blurts out, "It's my foreman. He's hurt his back."

I arch my eyebrows in a silent prompt for more information.

"And I've got four jobs on the go and no way of finishing them without him around," she rushes out.

It turns out her foreman isn't a simple guy to replace. When she goes through the jobs currently in progress, I can understand her distress.

"Hey, if there's one thing I know how to do, it's how to follow orders." When she opens her mouth to reject my offer, I keep talking. "Even when I don't know what the hell I'm doing, I can still get the job done. I can definitely manage those casual laborers for you."

She hesitates enough that I press on, with part of me surprised at just how eager I am to work with my ex-girlfriend. Then my mind wonders if I can even call her an ex after ten years?

The other thing the job will help with will be to ease the hours spent dwelling on what a mess my life is. It'll be good to have a purpose again. Anything is better than spending the day watching cable while waiting for job offers.

Eventually, she holds her hands up in surrender. "Okay, okay, but I can only offer a couple of weeks' work. Once Steve's back on board, I won't need your help."

Bridget's words are impersonal, and business-like, and I'm okay with that.

"You won't regret it. I can heft shi ... fertilizer with the best of them." I'm not sure what makes me do it, but I flex my guns while grinning broadly.

I'm unable to tell if it's influenced Bridget, but a woman at a nearby table showers her companion with cupcake crumbs.

Outside the café, Bridget and I go our separate ways, although I can't stop myself from looking back admiringly. Only when she sashays around a corner, do I stop and take a proper look at her business card. A quick check of the address tells me I'll be good and warm when I arrive at ten the following morning.

The mid-morning start is to allow her to get organized, and will also work well with my having to bike there. Until I decide whether I'm staying, there's no point getting a car.

While some would hire an Uber, I'm as happy borrowing my buddy Grady's mountain bike. I suspect Michelle, his wife, will also be happy to have me out of her way.

Well, not so much under her feet, as on the couch, something that's wearing thin for both of us. I'm used to more physical activity than my civilian life is offering; it'll be good to be active again.

Even with Seth and me now on speaking terms, we can't live together. And despite my mom wanting me to stay with her and dad, there wasn't a chance. Being back on base would be too painful by far, although I will visit at some stage.

It'll be good to see where Bridget is living. From what she's said, she runs the business out of her basement. The way she sees it, there's no point having a flash office when she only ever works at her clients' places.

With my new job organized, the next thing on my list was dinner at Seth's place. I still don't know if he's aware I'm coming, as it was Skye who'd rung and invited me.

I'm relieved that someone has lined up dinner. I'm doing everything I can not to treat the kitchen at Grady's like the mess hall, and this will help. All those years complaining about rations, and now I'd give anything for someone else to feed me.

THREE

I reach out and grope around until I locate the alarm clock, making quick work of turning it off. It takes a couple of minutes for me to wake enough to remember what's different about today.

That's right; Jason is about to turn up in ... I twist the alarm clock around so I can read the glowing red numbers. Four hours!

It's a thought that has me out of bed and through into the shower before I'm fully awake. I don't plan on primping and preening for him, rather, I've got a lot to do before he arrives.

If it was Steve, I could simply leave him to it, but because Jason doesn't know what's required, this means more work for me. Work I need to complete before my day kicks off for real.

After a quick shower I dress, glad I don't have to give thought to what to wear. As with every other morning, I pull on a uniform of khaki shorts and a dark-green company t-shirt; the logo printed small on the front.

As I lace up my boots, I'm still pleased that I hadn't run into Jason yesterday while dressed like this. I'd hate for his first impression of me after ten years to be based on how I'm dressed now.

Despite no longer being stick-thin as I was when a teenager, I love my extra curves and dress to show them off. I started off dressing that way, hoping to attract a man. These days I do it simply because it pleases me.

Thanks to a short commute, I'm soon sitting at my desk in the basement. I alternate between sipping my coffee and nibbling on a bagel with cream cheese while scrolling through the schedule.

The sheer amount of work is overwhelming, unless ... If I can leave Jason to manage the Wesley Park job, I'll be able to cover everything else.

While manageable, I'll be dead on my feet by the end of the day. Still, anything is better than missing deadlines, or worse, losing customers to the opposition.

I've raced around and checked on the teams and am back at my desk when there's a knock on the basement door. I'm taken by surprise because I didn't hear a car pulling up. There's only one person it can be, with my heart speeding up in concert with my annoyance at my reacting this way.

"Come on in, the door's open!"

Strange, but I thought I was ready to see Jason this morning. And yet when he opens the door and strides in, my ability to breathe abandons me. Damn it, I don't need this in my life. I don't need *him* in my life.

He's dressed in army fatigues that show years of wear and tear. His t-shirt, in particular, fits him like a second skin. The only incongruity is him gripping a fluoro-pink cartoon lunchbox.

When he sees me looking at it, he laughs self-consciously. "It was the only one on hand at my buddy Grady's place."

His simple statement tells me a lot of things. First, that he hasn't committed to a place of his own. And that his friend is married with kids, or at least a little girl.

From what he'd said over coffee yesterday, his preference was to stay with an old buddy rather than his brother. He'd said he didn't want to play third wheel to Seth and his new bride. I suspect more of it is to do with their falling out all those years ago.

Despite the color of that lunch box, there's nothing feminine about Jason. How on earth am I supposed to concentrate with that gorgeous body constantly crowding my field of vision?

And it's only going to get worse, as I need to take him through the scheduling software. This has him sitting right next to me, our shoulders mere inches from each other.

Blast it. He'd never affected me this much when we were teenagers.

Shouldn't you be over all your girly swooning by now?

It doesn't help that he smells of soap, testosterone, and remembered good times. In the end, I simply grit my teeth and get on with it.

The sooner he grasps the system, the sooner I can put him to work and put some distance between us. In my favor is him picking up the software easily.

I've relaxed and am even thinking we might just manage until Steve's return, when a couple of emails pop up. These prove to be both good and bad news, with Jason rolling his office chair back to give me some space. I'm close to hyperventilating in response to the emails.

Jason rolls his office chair back to give me some space. I'm close to hyperventilating in response to the emails.

"Bridget, you can do this. WE can do this. It's only two extra jobs. So long as you make a plan and follow it, you'll be golden."

Despite his confidence, I've got my doubts.

What happens when he gets offered what he considers a proper job?

What then? Will he up and leave me without warning, exactly as he did before? If he does, it won't be my heart that's damaged; it will be my bottom line.

JASON

Bridget sits hard up against her desk, her head in her hands. I'm unsure what distresses me the most. That she's worried about the workload, or that she doesn't think I can help her.

I mean, how hard can it be? I've dug trenches; a garden shouldn't be any different, should it? Just dig, toss the dirt over your shoulder. And repeat.

In my mind, I'm still digging when Bridget jumps up to grab something from the large filing cabinet behind her desk. I immediately forget about digging when I see how fantastic her peachy cheeks look in those shorts.

Hell, never mind digging. Holding a shovel will be a challenge if I'm fighting an erection the whole day. Damn it, I don't need a complication like this in my life right now.

Despite this, it takes all my concentration to drag my gaze away from the magnetic allure of her luscious ass. This has me reading the slogan printed across the back of her t-shirt, and I'm unable to stop a bark of laughter.

WE CUT YOUR GRASS
NOT CORNERS

She immediately stops riffling through the hanging files in the top drawer of the cabinet, turning slowly to stare at me. Damn it, she thinks I was laughing at her. As if.

I don't have time to think of anything clever to say, instead going for my usual brevity. "Your t-shirt." I wave my hand vaguely before pressing on. "I was laughing at the slogan. It's funny. It's clever."

It takes longer than it should for the haunted look to leave her eyes. It tells me two things. Someone has made fun of her body in the past. And if I ever find out who it was, they'll rue the day.

After dropping back into her seat, she searches through the bottom drawer of her desk. Damn, I wouldn't have minded her doing that while she was still standing.

"I didn't think I'd need a 3XL."

Muttered as her words have been, I doubt they were for my benefit. Before I've asked her what she's talking about, she slams the drawer shut with a loud thud.

Bridget once again sits up, only this time her hands aren't empty. She's holding a t-shirt out to me, with it obvious she expects me to wear it while I'm working for her.

"Even if you're only with us until you find something better, you need to look professional."

I open it out and hold it up. Aww, shoot me now. Despite the shirt being a 2XL, it'll still be a snug fit, if it fits at all. A quick flip of the shirt shows the slogan on the back is the same as hers.

I drop the company t-shirt on the desk, get to my feet and make quick work of ripping off my battered army surplus model.

Bridget's sharp intake of breath leaves me unsure if she likes what she sees, or is it she's shocked by the number of scars? If it's the latter, then I'll make no apologies. In the army, only desk jockeys escape unscathed.

Every one of those scars is hard-earned, and a lot easier to deal with than the mental scars Seth suffered. To be fair, Seth hadn't escaped physically, either.

It's a struggle to wriggle into the shirt. On smoothing it down, Bridget's stunned expression leaves me unsure if she approves or not. She wants me looking professional, whereas the 2XL is tight enough that it has a hint of stripper gram about it.

It's something that's confirmed when she subconsciously licks her bottom lip. Then it's all I can do not to rip the shirt off again. History tells me exactly what that mouth action means and I'm unable to stop myself from smiling.

This only results in her expression becoming shuttered and business-like, with any hint of her arousal firmly under wraps.

Good, I'm glad this is how she's playing it. It'll make it easier to ignore her succulent curves and get on with work. While not my dream job, it'll do until I hear about one of those contracts.

FOUR

Jason and I make it out to the Wesley Park project just after eleven. I'm not surprised when we arrive to see the casuals plodding away at the tasks I'd set them earlier.

As always, no sooner will Steve or I turn our backs than it's casual by name, casual by nature with these guys. And it's not like I don't pay them a decent hourly rate.

After giving Jason a quick rundown of the project and introducing him to the team, I stand back and watch with interest.

"Come on guys, we're not being paid to move at that pace." Jason's voice, while friendly, lets the crew know if they don't get a move on, they'll have him to deal with.

He reinforces this by yelling, "Move it, you lot!"

He then grabs a shovel and gets on with it, showing the team exactly what he expects from them. That rock-hard body of his in action is impressive. More than that, it's...

Yet again, I compare the new Jason to the boy I'd dated at high school. So far, the updated version is winning hands down, at least so far as his body goes. Sadly, I doubt he's changed in other ways, with part of me already preparing for his departure, sudden or otherwise.

It's also fascinating to watch how he manages the team, and more than a little annoying. If Steve or I had tried to encourage them like that, we'd never have gotten the results Jason is. Sure, they'd have sped up a bit, but this flurry of activity? That'd be a heck no.

Once I'm happy Jason has everything under control, I leave to go check on my other three projects. I'm relieved to find the teams there are doing okay, although again nowhere near as quickly as I'd like.

It's also a relief being away from Jason, with my hormones constantly clamoring for attention. Despite knowing he's only back in town briefly, I can't help but wonder what would happen if he was here to stay. And then I remember his contentment at once again being a part of a team.

The way he'd gotten the Wesley Park crew working was down to his time in charge of a platoon in the army. I can see why he'd want to belong to something like that again.

And with the US army no longer an option, apparently there are plenty of private organizations available to him. Whether they're legal, that's a different story.

Back at Wesley Park, I'm astounded to see how far along the project has moved. Jason must be really riding them hard to get this much work done.

And, bam, just like that, I'm wondering what it would be like to ride Jason that hard. A quick shake of my head to rid it of those very images and I check on the team.

Maybe he's working them too hard? They're only casual laborers. If they don't like it, they might not turn up the next day. This was something that happened all too often. Then I inspect the team. While they appear tired, they also appear proud of what they've achieved so far.

Even more impressive is that while I've been away, there's been a delivery of plants. Usually, someone would set them aside for me to arrange. Today there's no need with a good number already positioned.

My annoyance spikes before I check on where the plants have been placed, ready for planting. The plans back at the house, whoever positioned the plants, must have done so based on instinct.

On spotting Jason grabbing more plants, I realize it's not instinct, but what must be a photographic memory.

By the end of the day, Jason completely dispels any doubts I had about him running this team. On leaving the site, each one of them high-fives Jason and yells, "Oorah!"

This new ritual completed, Jason strolls over to join me. And isn't he satisfied with himself, although I can't altogether blame him?

He holds his arms out to the sides to encompass the site, although all this does is draw attention to his body. "Well, do you like what you see?"

Oh boy, do I ever.

The plants look good, too.

JASON

I can't believe how much I've enjoyed today. The physical work and the sense of belonging, and it was as if I was back in the army. I hadn't realized how much I'd missed that life. And all without having to answer to some idiot up the chain of command.

I don't think of Bridget in that light. Her instructions this morning had been clear, concise and practical. Mike Dawson, my old commanding officer, could learn a thing or two from Bridget.

The other surprise was the sense of achievement from positioning those plants. Some of this had been down to memory from when Bridget showed me the plans. More of it was down to imagining what would work well in the setting.

Luckily for a novice gardener like me, all the plants had tags showing what they looked like when mature.

These also listed heights and preferred growing positions. Without those, I'd have been as in the dark as a plant that enjoyed full sunshine.

With the team off home for the day, I turn to Bridget and hold my arms out to the side. I'm about to ask her if she's happy with the work completed, but change my mind, my words deliberately ambiguous.

"Well, do you like what you see?"

She gulps twice before nodding. While she hasn't actually said anything, she's spoken volumes so far as I'm concerned.

Three days of working with Bridget, and I'm caring less and less about hearing from any of the private armies I've applied to.

She pulls her truck to a stop outside my buddy's place and I decide it is time to test the waters. This has me undoing my seatbelt before stretching as if to straighten out any kinks in my spine.

What the move is really designed for is to pop my chest muscles and, when the t-shirt rides up, show off my abs. Some might call me vain, but I've worked hard for those. I may as well use them, and the undersized shirt, to my advantage.

Only when I'm sure I've got her full attention, do I speak.

"Damn, that hot tub is gonna be good tonight."

"Hot tub?" She whispers, a sense of longing in her brief response. "I've always wanted one of those."

"Grady has one." I jerk my head toward the house before adding. "The family is away for the next couple of days. You're welcome to join me."

I'm ready for why she couldn't possibly join me when she rattles it off.

"Come on, Bridget. It's not like we haven't seen each other naked before. Remember when we used to skinny dip up the far end of the beach?"

She does. Her pupils dilating like that is a sure sign.

Bridget showers first and is safely under the bubbles when I stroll out to join her. Well, she's mostly under the water. Her full breasts are being buffeted by the jets, the state of her nipples enough to have me swallowing deeply.

I'm naked but for a towel wrapped around my waist, and am holding a couple of cold beers. While I'm sure she's happier with a glass of wine these days, nothing beats a cold one after a long, hot day.

Sure enough, she takes one from me and taps it briefly against mine before taking a couple of mouthfuls. "Hmmm, I needed that. Today was a hot one."

She then puts the bottle on the deck next to the hot-tub before tipping her head back and closing her eyes. I know she's done this to avoid watching when I drop my towel and climb in.

I'd think she wasn't interested if not for her rapid breathing. She's physically fit; I know this from having worked side-by-side with her.

There's no way she should be this breathless after a shower and climbing into the hot tub.

Not by a long shot.

Sure enough, when I slide into the hot tub and deliberately sit closer than is necessary, she doesn't move. Rather, she opens her eyes and watches me, although she keeps her thoughts to herself.

Even a little encouragement would be good, with the water caressing us, as I long to caress her.

FIVE

BRIDGET

It takes all my concentration to talk about the day, and not be distracted by the bits of Jason I can see. "Thanks for today. We're well on track thanks to your efforts and the way you're running the team."

I pause, forming the words in my head before continuing. "You know, you could make a career out of this." To make clear what I'm talking about, I add, "of landscaping. You're a natural."

I say nothing further, not wanting to push it or come across as needy.

I can see he's thinking about what I've said, although when he speaks, his words surprise me. Of more interest is that they appear to surprise him, too.

"I'm really enjoying it, the physical work, the guys, being part of a team again." He falls silent for a beat before continuing, his words halting. "There were parts of the military I hated. Not the guys. I loved them like brothers. The red tape and desk monkeys I could have done without."

Even though his words have been brief, his expression speaks volumes. I suspect this is part guilt at dissing the army, part grief at no longer being a part of it.

"My biggest regret was what happened with Seth."

It takes time for the full story to come out, leaving him open and vulnerable, as I've never seen him before. Even when we were going steady, anything he'd said about his relationship with his brother had been superficial.

It hurts me to see him open and raw like this, and I scoot along the seat until I'm tight up against his side. While my move has been to comfort him, things don't stay that way for long.

Jason's body feels every bit as good as I've dreamed of over the preceding nights. It's also familiar, with this not the first time we've been so close.

It is, however, the first time we've been this close since he came back into my life. At least while naked.

Could this have been what I was looking for on all those disastrous dates I'd forced myself to go on? I'm unable to stop a shudder as some of those horrors flash through my mind.

"Are you okay?"

Jason reaches out under the water to take my hand. Instead, his fingers brush my leg, and there's nothing I can do to stop from gasping as desire swamps me.

It's all the encouragement he needs, with him gently squeezing my inner thigh. My body stills. Do I really need this in my life? It took me years to get over him last time.

There's nothing *casual* about my emotions where Jason is concerned.

Despite these rational thoughts, my body has a mind of its own. It's one that has me opening myself up to the gorgeous man at my side.

As if sensing my surrender, Jason runs his hand up my thigh to the curls at the apex. He then nudges my legs further apart, to dip his fingers into my depths.

Holy moly, that is so damned good.

My head drops back to the side of the hot tub as the sensations consuming my body leave me boneless. Jason has learned a thing or two in the ten years since we were last this close.

What else has he learned?

I'm still wondering when he shows me in agonizing detail.

His fingers working their magic, he nibbles the side of my mouth until my lips part with a sigh. With entrance gained, he plunges his tongue into my mouth and kisses me with an expertise that takes my breath away.

It's as if he's consuming me. He's everywhere at once; his hands and tongue have my body pleading for release. This happens sooner than I've expected, with him swallowing my cries of passion as if his life depends on it.

Along with my release comes a myriad of 'what ifs' as all the wasted years wash over me.

Am I making a huge mistake? Or will rejecting him hurt more than losing him again?

In my mind's eye, I see him leaving and can do nothing to stop the sob that bursts free. Jason's lips leave mine and he pulls back.

"Baby, what's wrong? What did I do? Are you okay?"

My tears choking me, I can't answer, but I don't resist when he draws me into a comforting embrace on his lap.

JASON

Bridget fills my lap; her lush ass jammed tight against my erection, causing pleasure and pain in equal amounts. I'm not sure what's upset her. All I know is her tears have me right back to the night I'd told her I was leaving all those years ago.

The memories and ache are as fresh now as they ever were. How many times when I was on watch had my thoughts returned to that night? To wonder if I could have handled it better.

I sure as hell couldn't have handled it any worse.

And should I be taking things further now if I plan on leaving as soon as the right contract comes along? It isn't until Bridget squeaks I realize how tight I'm holding her.

"Sorry, I didn't mean to squash you." I loosen my grip, although I don't let go completely. I don't want to. I like her being close like this, with some parts of me happier than others.

"Come on, Bee, let's get out of here before we both resemble prunes."

My use of the pet name I'd had for her back in the day surprises me as much as it obviously surprises her.

After easing her off my lap, I steady her while she stands. I'm standing in the pool next to her, my erection on full display, when I hear a car pulling into the driveway.

Damn it, Grady and the family weren't due home until tomorrow. Or maybe the family arriving early might be a good thing?

It's one thing to mess around with Bee in the hot tub. As soon as we take things further, that will add complications.

Complications, I'm not sure either of us is ready for.

Or is that just me? Hell knows what I want anymore. I don't even know who I am now that I'm no longer in the army, my purpose in life stolen from me.

All it takes is for someone to ask me what I do for a living, and I'm lost for words. No, more than that, I have to stop my automatic reply in its tracks. Without my rank, I'm nothing.

Then I take in Bee, now wrapped in a big fluffy towel, and some of that dissipates. My sense of well-being doesn't last long, though.

While wrapping the towel ever tighter around her wondrous curves, Bee looks nervously toward the house. "Is there a way I can sneak out?"

As much as I know why this is, it still hurts. I'd proudly introduce her to Grady, his wife, and even the kids. Bee, however, has other ideas.

This sees us back in the guest room thanks to its sliding doors out onto the patio. Bee then wastes no time in dragging on her dirty work clothes, ready to get out of there. I don't bother dressing, because I'll be under a cold shower soon enough.

After sneaking her down the side of the house, I stand next to the open window of her truck while she starts the engine. I don't give a damn that I'm naked but for a towel.

She's about to put the truck into gear when I shove my head through the open window and claim her lips.

On her pulling away from the curb, I'm confident I won't be the only one having trouble sleeping tonight.

SIX

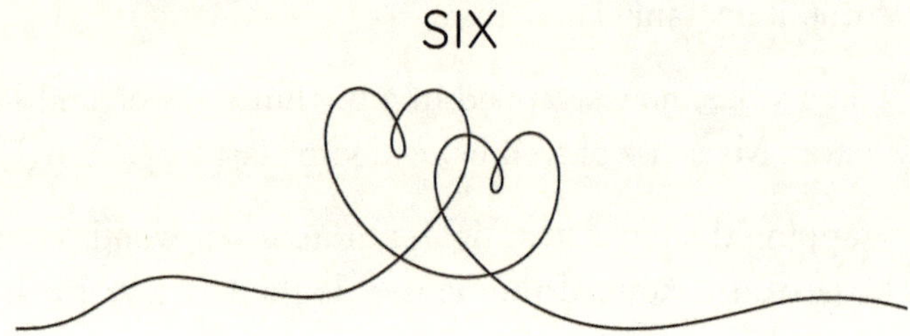

BRIDGET

I'm bleary-eyed the following morning. That kiss?! My lips still tingle at the memory, as do other bits of me. Damn it, that was a kiss designed for...

Actually, I don't have a clue what Jason had in mind.

The only thing I'm sure of is that sleep had been impossible as my fevered brain went over every scenario. Well that, and every position.

My mind is still awhirl with carnal images as I put in a load of washing. Tossing a pair of shorts into the machine, I hear a crinkle. On pulling a crumpled sheet of pale green paper out of the pocket, I'm confused.

Then I remember it had been on the front seat of the truck when I got home last night. I'd grabbed it rather than leave the cab messy.

It must be Jason's, because I know it's not mine. I don't leave paperwork lying around like that. After smoothing it out to check if it's okay to trash it, my heart is in my throat.

Rather than be a flyer, it's a printout of an email with a firm offer of work from some outfit in Colombia. A quick look at the date at the top and I fight the urge to be sick.

Jason had already received this when he told me to accept those extra contracts? How could he? Despite always knowing he'd up and leave me, seeing it in black and white is...

This is the last thing I need with my business finally taking off. It'll be bad enough losing Jason's man-power. The bigger challenge is that I'd been an emotional wreck when he left me last time.

The only thing going for me this time around is that I'm an adult and will hopefully deal with it better.

He'd made no secret of having applied for jobs that would take him out of state, or worse, out of the country. All he has to do is accept the offer in the email and he'll be off.

Down at my desk, I read the email again and see something I'd missed the first time. There's a firm cut-off date, the words in the last paragraph almost threatening. While not actually included, the words 'or else' are implicit.

Perhaps worse than this is that the cut-off date is today.

What if he's bowed to pressure, and said yes already?

It's this possibility that sees me screw up the email and fire it across the office to land in a corner. I need to get my head around how I'll cope without Jason, both personally and commercially.

This can't be happening. He's casting me aside, again? I'm close to bursting into tears when an email pings its arrival on my computer. My eyes watering from a lack of sleep, I swipe at them twice before I can focus enough to read it.

"What?! No! This can't be happening?!"

I'd applied for the Fielding contract months ago, and when I hadn't heard from the architectural firm, I'd written it off. "And they want to proceed now?"

I scroll down so I can read the rest of the email.

"Oh, of course it's urgent!"

I slam my hands down on either side of my keyboard and surge to my feet. My emotions are now a volatile mix of hurt at Jason leaving, and frustration and anger at the architectural firm.

The only plus to my gut being tied in knots is that Jason's arrival almost goes unnoticed. So much for my being embarrassed, or worse, retrieving that screwed up email and shoving it down his throat.

Rather than walk into my office, he stands in the doorway, holding the door open as if ready to escape. There isn't a chance I can take that huge landscaping job with his imminent departure hanging over my head.

"Damn it." I stop pacing back and forth behind my desk long enough to glare at the email on the screen. "I'm going to have to turn them down!"

It's only my fingernails digging into my palms that have me realizing my hands are fisted at my sides. I'm so freaking annoyed with the lot of them, but mostly Jason.

Eventually, curiosity must get the better of him because he walks into my office, closing the door behind him. Not content with that, he walks over and rounds my desk to stand next to me.

He's done so in order to stare at the computer screen as I am. And yet my body reacts as if he's done so to bend me over my desk and take me as I'd dreamed of last night.

Dammit, brain, I don't need this right now.

"Wow, that's huge."

It takes my cluttered mind a second to grasp what he means.

"You'd better believe it is. But I can't take it. Not with Steve away and you out of here any day."

Thanks to my emotions simmering just below the surface, my words have a hard edge to them. Much as I've said that he has a future in landscaping, he can't see past the military, or something akin to it. Surely he realizes he'll have to retire from combat postings at some stage? Or die trying.

As angry as I am, the thought of him dying alone in the jungles of South America has my heart thumping. It's only Jason tapping the top of my computer screen that has me back in the room.

"Bee, take it. You just have to. We can do this."

I turn and stare at him for a second before I'm able to find the right words. Well, in this case, word.

"We?"

JASON

I wake at zero six hundred the following morning, as always. However, I feel anything but rested thanks to my brain looping the same thoughts most of the night.

Could Bridget be onto something about me having a future with landscaping? After being a soldier for so many years, I find it difficult to see past the routine and requirements of active duty.

Can I really change to something else? Roscoe, my caseworker at the Job Center says it's possible. And yet, being a soldier is such a huge part of my life, and part of what makes me who I am today. I'm still furious that my old commanding officer made sure my name was at the top of the list of those being let go.

I'm lying there contemplating the loss of my old life when an email arrives on my phone. It's an offer of work from another outfit in Colombia. It wasn't a position I'd even applied for, but word got around.

While the pay is good and I'm keen to get back to active duty, I'm not working for people like that. Chances are these guys are in a turf war with the guys who'd offered me the last contract.

On arriving at the office, I needn't have worried about things being awkward between Bridget and me after last night. She's too keyed up for that.

More than that, she looks to be furious, although not because of me, thank goodness. At least, I don't think it's me, but what she's staring at on her computer.

Without bothering to look my way, she grits out, "I'm going to have to turn them down!"

This has curiosity getting the better of me, and I enter her office and wander over to stand next to her. I can read enough of the email to get the gist of it. The logo of the eminent architectural firm in town tells me, more than anything, that this is a big deal.

So why is she turning it down?

As if sensing my confusion, she grabs her mouse and highlights the last paragraph. How the hell did I miss that? Already my mind is awash with the logistics of the project, and how we can meet that horrifying deadline.

It isn't until Bee turns and says, "We?" that I know I've officially signed on for something. That it's something that doesn't involve guns, other than those in my arms, is the biggest surprise of all. And yet, it feels so right.

I stand tall, and hold my hand out to shake on it. "Yes, *we.*"

It's not until she finally takes my hand that I breathe properly. Her shake is tentative, as if she doesn't trust me. As if she expects me to abandon her again.

On looking into her eyes, I can see the doubt shining bright, and damned if that doesn't hurt. And yet, I can understand it. She's got cause not to trust me, after my past behavior.

But part of me is also happy to have committed as I have. It's something that has me dragging her into a tight embrace. This is partly to comfort her, but mostly because I can't help myself.

"We need to seal this with a kiss." She resists briefly, although her lips soon soften beneath mine. Meanwhile, parts of me are rock hard, ensuring today will be a torture on many levels.

SEVEN

BRIDGET

After sending Jason out to pack the truck for the day, I sit back down at my desk.

He's said he'll help me; we've even sealed the deal with a hand-shake and a kiss. A hand-shake from a soldier, okay ex-soldier, is surely sacrosanct? Jason wouldn't shake on something without meaning it, would he?

However, it's the kiss that has my mind muddled. There was nothing legally binding about that. Has he just committed to me, the contract, or both? I'm not jumping to conclusions. Safer for my heart if I simply think he's signed on for the contract and nothing else.

Once we're through with that, then I'll face any demons.

After a couple more sips of the coffee Jason had fixed for me, I'm ready to reply to the offer from the architects. Rather than let them rush me, I tell them I'll have a contract and completed plans through to them by the end of the week.

Far better to have everything in writing and signed off on before the first work is done. Okay, and part of me still can't quite believe Jason is sticking around. It's for this reason I want to check and see how Steve's back is healing.

Better safe than sorry has always worked for me in the past, at least where work is concerned.

The next few days are full-on, as we finish up two smaller projects, and find extra casuals. I've let Jason take care of this, through his contact at the Job Center.

It doesn't take long to see Jason's preference is to employ vets, which gets my tick of approval. I've seen firsthand how his military background has him working as part of a team. It's also a nice way of thanking the vets for their service.

The day before the Fielding Project is scheduled to start and I leave Jason to manage the two jobs still on the go. Safe in the knowledge he can cope, I spend the day double-checking my plans to see if I've missed anything.

To make a mistake on a project that's this important is not an option.

If it goes well, it'll lead to more work with the architectural firm, and perhaps even others. Of course, all of my grandiose plans hinge on Steve being back on board. I'm not factoring Jason into any of my long-term schemes.

I'm close to cross-eyed when he returns with my truck. He's hot and sweaty, his shirt clinging to every muscle. It's a combination that has me licking my lips, although I'm unaware of doing so until he laughs.

If we didn't know each other as well as we do, I'd be mortified and wanting to hide. As it is, I simply wave away his laughter and go back to looking at the final plans.

"Are they the plans for the Fielding job?"

I nod, and when he walks over to stand in front of my desk, I spin them around so he can read them. There isn't a chance I want him touching them with his hands as dirty as they are.

After scanning the plan of the front elevation, he nods slowly, likewise with the side elevation. It's only when I show him that plan for the backyard and service areas he frowns.

"What? What's wrong? I've double checked everything. What have I missed?"

When he points it out, I smack my forehead with the palm of my hand. How on earth could I have made such a rookie mistake? Even more astounding is that the architectural firm never picked up on it.

"Relax, would you? We've got time to fix this. I can come back after I've cleaned up and had dinner. We can go through everything then and flick through an update to the client. We can say we had to tweak the plans because of groundworks, or something."

I'm still checking over the plan for the backyard as if for the first time, when Jason opens the door to leave.

"Wait, wait. Don't leave. You can shower upstairs while I sort out dinner."

Two hours, two steaks and a half-a-bottle of wine later, and we've solved the service access issue. Only with that challenge sorted, do I take time to check on Jason properly. With his clothes in the wash, he's wearing one of my sarongs and not a lot else.

Despite his lack of clothing, he's grinning broadly and looking so damn pleased with himself. "We did it! I told you we could sort it out."

He grabs the half bottle of wine and holds it high in celebration before trying to top off my glass. However, I put my hand out to stop him. "Careful, we still need to do the actual work in the morning."

He reluctantly puts the bottle back down. "You're right." He pauses, while looking at me, before adding, "I guess I'd better get going, then."

I can hear the question in his voice; I can see it in his eyes. I know exactly what he's asking. The bigger question is, do I say yes or no?

In the end, I say what I've wanted to since we were in the hot tub together and to hell with the consequences. I know he'll likely leave once the contract is over, but I no longer care.

A little of *right now* with Jason is better than nothing at all.

JASON

I stand hard up against Bee, only a couple of layers of fabric between my erection and her delectable body. We're soon down to one after she tugs at the knot securing the sarong.

I briefly take in my naked form before my gaze slides to her womanly curves. They're being shown off to advantage by the slinky dress she'd put on after her shower.

"I'm rather underdressed now. That doesn't seem fair." I follow this up by reaching out and running a finger under the spaghetti strap of her dress.

I've hardly touched her, and yet she still hisses out as though in pain.

"You like that, do you?"

Her words catching in her throat, she instead nods jerkily.

"Think how much better it would be if you were naked, too."

From showering earlier, I know where the master is. But do I dare lead her there? There's something so fragile about our closeness. I don't want to shatter it.

In the end, I don't need to. Bee steps back, grabs the bottom of her dress, and drags it up and over her head. She's now down to her bra and panties and close to being as naked as I am.

She's reaching around behind to undo her bra when I come to my senses.

"No, my sweet Bee, if anyone is taking care of that, it's gonna be me."

With most of the blood in my body already pumping into my cock, my words sound sluggish, even to me.

Her hands drop to her sides and she waits, vulnerable and uncertain. Thankfully for both of us, I've never been more certain in my life. There's something so right about this that I don't hesitate.

I run my finger across the top of one cup, dipping just inside the lace edging. Close to her nipple, but not too close. Good things take time, and Bridget is one of the best things to happen to me.

Damned shame you didn't realize that all those years ago, you moron.

I run my finger lazily back and forth, enjoying the sight of her nipples straining against the sheer fabric of her bra. Somehow this is a bigger turn on than if she wasn't wearing the bra at all.

As I drop my gaze to her panties, I'm confronted by more of the same barely there fabric. Sheer enough that I can see she's damp, and as ready for me as I am for her.

On pulling her into my arms, our bodies are plastered together, my erection nudging her. As glorious as this is, it's still not enough, and so I reach behind her so I can undo her bra.

I drop it to the floor a moment later, loving the sensation of her bare breasts against my chest. I then make quick work of her panties, wanting nothing to come between us.

Again, I give thought to the master. A quick check of the chair I've just vacated and I've got a much better idea.

As I drop onto the oak seat, I drag Bridget with me. When she goes to sit sideways on my lap, I stop her. "No, sweet Bee. Why don't you face me instead? I want to see your beautiful face."

Her movements languid, she straddles me as I've suggested, her core ever closer to my cock. But not yet. I want her on the brink before I lower her slowly onto my length.

With her holding tight to my shoulders, I'm able to angle her back, to run my fingers through her cleft. On my squeezing the gorgeous little bud hidden by her curls, she moans, her head thrown back.

When I plunge two fingers into her swollen depths, her head tips forward, and she gazes at me in wonder. Her breathing tells me she can't hold out much longer. And when she comes, I want to be right there with her.

I pull my fingers free and slide my hands under her peach of an ass. Only then do I lift her high enough that I can slide my cock into her slick depths. Once she's fully seated, I concentrate on lifting her before allowing her to settle again.

Now I'm the one who's on the edge. She feels so good. Then I realize what I'm experiencing is way beyond the physical. Despite all the fooling around when we were teenagers, this is officially our first time making love.

And that's as big a deal to me as it obviously is to her. Do I really want to take one of those overseas jobs? Or do I want to stay where I obviously belong?

No sooner has this thought crossed my mind than it turns to putty. A climax the likes of which I've not experienced consumes me, with Bee along for the ride.

EIGHT

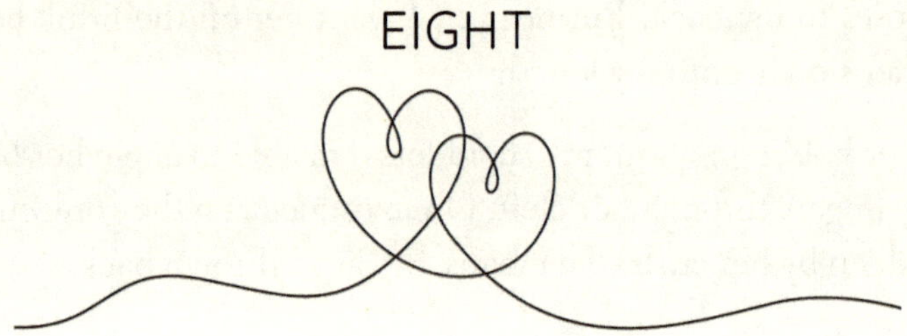

We're close to finishing our first week of the big contract, a week in which Jason has spent most nights at my place. While we're both suffering from a lack of sleep, neither of us is complaining.

I'm unable to stifle a wide yawn as I jump out of my truck after a visit to the bank. It doesn't take long to find Jason, with me reacting to his presence as always.

I love the way my body feels with him in my life; supple and alive as never. And the more we make love, the better it gets. I'd thought that the first time, on the hard-backed dining chair, was pretty damned amazing.

I didn't know the half of it, with Jason as adventurous as he is inventive in the hours after dark. Okay, and a few during the daytime, too. Heck, I'm still smiling about what we got up to yesterday afternoon.

Much as I want to grab him by the ass and lean in for a kiss, I can't.

Not while there are others around. As the business owner, I'm mindful of acting professionally.

I am, however, next to him, when an alert pings on his phone which sits atop his shirt dumped on the ground. If he's sticking around, I really need to get him some larger t-shirts. Sized so he can dig in without ripping the seams would be a good start.

When his phone pings again, he jams his shovel upright in the dirt, and grabs it. A quick check has his head snapping up. His expression speaks volumes, and yet I'm still in the dark.

"What is it? What's happened?"

He opens his mouth to speak, but nothing comes out. It's rare he's lost for words, and seeing him like this tugs at my heart. It must be terrible news for him to react like this. "What is it? Is it Seth?"

Surely only bad news concerning his twin would have him in this big a mess.

"No, it's..."

In the end, he simply hands his phone over so I can see for myself.

I have to read the email twice to grasp the implications. A quick scan initially convinced me the job offer was from the US Army.

There wasn't a chance Jason would turn them down. If they need him, he's there.

A second slower read-through and I see it's from an old army buddy, not the army itself. His friend has given the organization, a private security company in South Africa, the green light, saying they're 'legit'.

All Jason has to do is say yes, and the contract is his.

My heart in my stomach, I hold his phone out to him. I'm close to being sick. How could I have been so stupid as to commit to Jason again? I should have learned my lesson the first time around.

And yet, I hadn't been able to stop myself from hoping that this time it would be different.

What was that saying about a leopard not changing its spots?

Jason takes his phone and tosses it back atop his shirt. When he retrieves his shovel and digs, I'm left in the dark with what he plans on.

I can't worry about that, though. I need to focus on the business, not us, if there ever was an 'us'. If Jason leaves as soon as the sender of that email wants, I may as well resign the contract right now. This will leave the reputation of my company in tatters enough that I can give a kiss goodbye to anything more than cutting people's lawns.

While it's obvious he doesn't want to talk about it, I need confirmation both from a business and personal stand-point.

"So, are you going to take it?"

He stops digging long enough to answer me, although his keeping his gaze fixed on the ground doesn't bode well.

"I'm not sure, Bridget. I'll need to think about it." He then tosses a shovel of dirt to the side before adding. "I wouldn't leave until we've finished this contract though, if that's all you're worried about."

While his response removes some of the pressure, his even considering the position is a personal punch to my gut. "I'll, I'll, catch you later. I just need to..."

I don't bother completing my sentence, instead turning on my heel and making for the sanctuary of my truck.

JASON

After Bridget roars off, my mind is awhirl with the ramifications of that email. If Chuck Devon says the outfit is above-board, then that's the truth of it.

I'd hated the way Bee turned cold and professional when I said I'd have to think about it. There was no way in hell I was lying to her. I'd tried that once before and it hadn't worked out well at all.

While the temptation to be part of a tight-knit military group is alluring, don't I have that already? The only thing my new position doesn't offer is the ability to use the skills it's taken me years to hone.

Yet as I take in the site and my new team working like my old platoon used to, I'm filled with pride. By ensuring we only hire vets, we're making a difference to their lives.

Without this job and a sense of belonging, some of them could go down the route of drugs and even homelessness. It'd happened before, and it'll happen again. Hell, it could have happened to me if not for Grady letting me crash at his place.

At the end of the workday, Bridget wasn't there to pick me up. Part of me isn't altogether surprised. Thankfully, we've now had a small container delivered to the site, so I'm able to lock all our equipment in there.

Despite one of the team offering me a ride, I decide a walk will help center my thoughts. At least I hope it will.

I'm halfway back to Grady's place when I change direction. Much as Grady and his family are always welcoming, I need solitude. Luckily, I know exactly where to find it.

I don't need to think about where I'm headed. It had been a favorite of Seth and mine, and more recently, mine and Bee's. The overgrown state of the path tells me no-one comes here much these days.

With my mind a tangled mess, I'm not looking where I'm going, and come close to being tripped by the long grass. After this, I focus on where I'm putting my feet until the path crests the headland.

Coogan's Break is spread out before me, the dark blue sea rolling in to crash white on the beach. I'd forgotten how beautiful the place is.

I grab my phone out of my back pocket and sit down to take it all in.

I stare at the glorious vista until it blurs. My mind is elsewhere, Afghanistan, to be exact. Back when my future in the military was looking bright. Back when I had a purpose. Back when I belonged.

A quick swipe of my thumb and I re-read the email from Chuck about the South African contract. It's his last sentence that grabs me. "Jason, buddy, it's just like it was back in the day."

I'm aware of which 'day' he's talking about and the pull of belonging to something like that again is overwhelming.

Whether the desire to enlist again is as strong as my desire for Bee, that's what I have to decide.

I put my phone down next to me and lay back, exactly like I used to when Bee and I came up here together. But, on reaching out to the side, all I encounter is empty grass and not her lush form.

Not since enlisting all those years ago have I faced a decision as hard as this. On closing my eyes, to allow my thoughts to center, an image blazes to life.

And just like that, all doubt is gone, and I grab my phone. The sooner I reply to Chuck's email, the sooner I can get on with my new life.

NINE

BRIDGET

I'm at the site on daybreak the following morning, well before anyone else. I'm pleased to find the site tidy. Usually, I'd stick around to ensure everything was put away.

Sure, while it's obvious Jason took care of this yesterday, will he be around to do so today? Things hadn't ended well. That he even wants to consider the contract in South Africa says he hasn't committed to us. To me.

With our history, it isn't like we don't know each other. As much as lovers, we're old friends. Aren't we? Or is it more about the sex for him? On this depressing thought, I twist the tumblers on the combination lock on the container.

If I'm to stop my little spiral of doom, I need to move some dirt. While I dig, I think. I guess I can understand the pull of belonging to something like the position offered in that email.

He'll be able to use his training, and he'll be in charge of a team again. I look around the still-empty site. A real team and not a bunch of casual laborers like those who will soon turn up. They're all good reasons for him to accept that contract.

I try thinking of reasons for him to stay, but come up empty-handed. Life in Coogan's Break with someone like me doesn't cut it when compared to active duty in some far-flung, exotic location.

Or is he simply using the job offer as an excuse to escape again? To get away from me? Maybe the sex isn't as outstanding as I've thought?

Damn it, his leaving will hurt as much as it did when I was a teenager. It might even hurt more, with our relationship way beyond heavy petting.

An hour later and I'm unable to see what I'm digging because of my tears. I'm on autopilot, no longer sure if I'm even following the plans I'd worked so studiously on. My misery at how things have turned out, building as steadily as the pile of dirt next to me.

Only someone standing next to me and whistling brings me back to my surroundings.

Jason stands there, hands on hips, while he views the large hole. "I didn't realize we were putting in a pool." He steps closer, takes the shovel off me and jams it into the mound of fresh earth.

He gently turns my hands over and examines my palms. "Oh sweetheart, what have you done to yourself?"

His kind words are enough to set me off again, and I'm only vaguely aware of him leading me over to my truck. Rather than help me in behind the wheel, he puts me in the passenger seat, before getting behind the wheel himself.

I think he's taking me home until we pull up outside the medical center. Only then do I turn my hands palm-up.

So numb have I been at thoughts of Jason leaving that I hadn't even realized I'd rubbed my palms raw. I've done enough damage that they're seeping in places. And yet, I still can't feel a thing.

Numb, shutdown, protecting myself in the only way I know how.

JASON

As I wait while Bridget has her hands attended to, I contemplate my decision on the South African contract. I'm unsure if I've made the right choice, and it's eating me up inside. It wouldn't be the first time I'd screwed things up.

"Mr. Adams?"

I twist around in the hard plastic seat to find a nurse standing there. Bridget is next to her in a wheelchair. Despite Bee's legs not being damaged, she looks doped up enough that walking will be a challenge.

"There's no permanent damage to her hands." She eyeballs me to make sure she has my undivided attention. "She'll still need to avoid any more hard work for at least a week."

Seriously, she thinks I was the task-master who was responsible? I don't bother trying to explain. I need to get Bee home.

While I can carry her to where I've parked the truck, I borrow the wheelchair anyway. There's less chance of hurting her hands this way.

Back at her place, I've got no option but to carry her inside and up to her bedroom. On looking around the sumptuous room, my mind is flooded with images of our last night together.

Part of me is now wondering if that's what it had been..

Have I really screwed up that badly?

There's nothing sexual about me stripping her and tucking her up in bed. As heavily bandaged as her hands are, I position them carefully atop the blankets.

She's as secure as I can make her when she's as messy as this. Whatever they gave her at the medical center was hospital-grade.

"Just relax. I'll be right back."

Her head flops over on the pillow and she peers at me as if having trouble focusing. "Will you?"

Two simple little slurred words, and yet, it's as if she's punched me in the gut.

With her eyes having fluttered closed, I don't bother answering. Instead, I head out to the kitchen to grab a glass of water and the painkillers she'd been sent home with.

Back next to her bed, I put the glass down and check the instructions on the side of the bottle. I then open it and put two capsules next to the glass. Those child-proof lids can be enough of a challenge when you're fully conscious.

Heaven help you if you're not.

I've just smoothed her hair back from her forehead and kissed her gently when my phone vibrates in my pocket.

Rather than take the call next to her, I walk out into the hallway.

It's Dave, one of the casual workers. After giving him a rundown on the work they should get started with, I call Steve, Bridget's foreman. I can only hope he's capable of sitting, because I need his help.

That it's him, and not his wife, who answers my call is a promising sign.

"Hey Steve, it's Jason Adams. I'm hoping you can help. Are you able to take over management of the Fielding Project?"

While waiting for his response, I start down the stairs, worried I've left the guys on site alone for long enough already.

"Sorry, mate. I'm not up to being on the business end of a shovel, if that's what you're thinking."

"Nah. Just sitting there and telling the crew what they need to do."

My relief when he says yes to this is immediate. Rather than reluctant, he sounds eager, as if all that bed rest is getting to him. "Brilliant. If you could get over there as soon as you can, that'd be awesome."

It's one less thing for me to worry about when I'm not around.

TEN

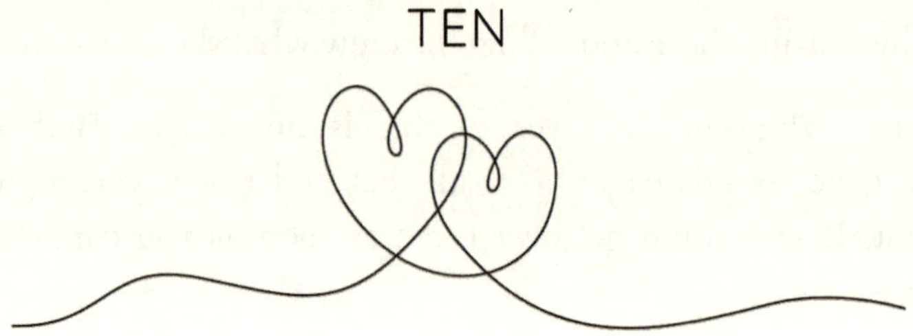

BRIDGET

I'm on site early the next morning. I shouldn't really be driving, but I don't have a choice. With Jason no longer around, the buck stops with me.

Even drugged up to the eyeballs as I had been, I'd still overheard Jason dumping his workload on Steve before he left my place. With no idea how my foreman's back is healing, I need to be on hand to ensure everything proceeds as planned.

If Steve comes back to work too early, he could risk permanent damage to his spine. The last thing I need right now is a lawsuit.

Part of me is still pissed that Jason has taken advantage of Steve's good nature. And all so he could leave town faster. So much for him staying on until the contract was over.

Being back on site is also better for my mental health than lying in bed crying. I'm no longer a teenager. I need to pull my big girl panties up and get on with my life. There is no way Jason Adams is derailing it again.

The first thing I notice is that the large hole I'd dug only the day before has been filled. It's as if my little meltdown never happened and yet I know it did. I'll even have the scars to prove it when the bandages come off.

It's because of these that my role today will be purely supervisory. The only concession I've made to working today is to replace the bandages put on by the nurse.

They were large to the point it had felt like I had my hands shoved in loaves of bread. Today my bandages are minimal, although I'm wearing a pair of leather work gloves to offer further protection.

I'm trudging through the mud, worrying about how on earth I'll finish the contract on time, when I hear footsteps behind me.

On turning, the first thing I notice is that Jason is wearing his company t-shirt. The second thing I notice is that rather than looking guilty, he's furious.

"What the hell are you doing here?"

I glare back at him. "What the hell am I doing here? I might ask you the same question?"

I've never been as angry as I am now, something that has me fisting my hands at my sides and immediately regretting it. There's nothing I can do to stop my yelp of pain.

Jason takes a step toward me, his face a picture of concern.

Hah, what a crock.

If he's so concerned about my welfare, how come he's okay ripping my heart out of my chest and stomping on it?

He jerks his head toward my hands, now cradled in front of my chest. "This right here. This is why you should be at home. I called around to fix you breakfast and help you in the shower and you weren't there."

He briefly looks skyward before continuing to berate me. "I didn't think you'd be stupid enough to come to work and possibly risk infection."

Wait, back up a second. Damn, those painkillers are doing a number on my brain. It takes longer than it should to process all he's just said.

"But. But I thought you were leaving town. Wasn't that why you asked Steve to take over your work?"

He takes another step toward me before placing his hands gently on my shoulders. "No Bee, I asked Steve to help, so I'd be free to take care of the smaller projects. And you."

Rather than relief, I'm flooded with guilt at the awful things I've been muttering about him all morning. Could he really have changed this much over the years?

"Bee, I've said no to the job in South Africa."

I'd cried so much overnight I didn't think I had any tears left, but my tears of happiness soon make themselves known.

JASON

On spotting the tears streaming down Bridget's face, my heart slams to a stop.

"Bee, what's wrong? I thought you wanted me to stay?"

My hands drop to my sides as I try to come to terms with her rejection.

When I'd called into her place this morning, my head had been of full of images of us having breakfast in bed. Okay, helping her in the shower after might also have been in the mix.

I didn't imagine her rejecting me like she was now. I guess it's not too late to get back to that place in South Africa about the contract.

I'm still processing my next steps when Bee slips forward and plasters herself against my chest. She then gently wraps her arms around my waist in a way that doesn't involve her hands.

"Of course I don't want you to leave, you big lump. I'm crying because I'm happy." Her watery laughter then ringing out around the site tells the truth of it.

I carefully return her hug before dipping my head and claiming her lips. So what if we've now got an audience? If I want to kiss Bee, then damn it, I'm gonna. I want the world to know how I feel about her.

When I'd seen her standing in the middle of that sea of mud, I knew I'd made the right choice. It didn't matter that I'd been furious with her for ignoring doctor's orders. Deep down, my love for her is true.

I lift my lips, but don't go far, keeping my forehead pressed against hers to keep my words between us. There are limits to what I want to share with my crew.

"Bee, I love you. Jobs like the South African one are a dime a dozen. Women like you are rare. Will you have me?"

She leans back in my arms, meeting my gaze. "Jason Adams, are you serious? Of course I'll have you. I love you. I always have. I always will."

It's all I can do not to squeeze the life out of her. I'm so damned happy. "I love you more than life itself. The number of times over the years that it was only thinking of you that got me through the dark times."

I drop my lips to hers again. At least this way I can show her how much I love her without risking further damage to her hands. It's only someone yelling out playfully that we should 'get a room', that has me realizing we need to leave.

After carefully disengaging from our embrace, I cross her hands in front of her chest. Only then do I scoop her up and stride across the site toward her truck.

"Let's get you home and into bed, where you belong."

To a background of cheering and whoops from the team, I gently ease her into the passenger seat. A quick buss of her lips and I close the door before racing around and getting in behind the wheel.

"I want to show you exactly how much I love you, and I sure as hell can't do that with an audience."

She bursts out laughing, her gaiety infectious. "I don't know about that, Jason Adams. You got pretty darned close just now." She backs this up by fanning her face with her bandaged hands.

I return her grin. "That's nothing compared to what I've got planned." Then I floor it, with neither of us keen on waiting any longer than we have to.

EPILOGUE

BRIDGET

I'm about to comment what a mess Jason is when I look down at myself. We're both filthy thanks to unseasonal rain and our latest project being more about earthworks than landscaping.

The site is a quagmire of epic proportions, with everyone to a man and woman, as filthy and miserable as I am. I can't help but notice a few of the team hadn't bothered to turn up at all. It's something we'll deal with tomorrow.

On trying to move to a drier spot, I find I'm stuck solid in the mud we've been battling for days. "Jason, a little help here."

He takes longer than he should to trudge over to me. Honestly, it's like walking in molasses, with even my man-mountain finding the going hard.

"Hell's teeth, this is bad, Bee. I've just checked the weather map, and it's looking like we've got a few more hours, at least."

He grabs me around the waist, lifts me clear of the mud, and kisses me briefly on the end of my nose. "I say we call it a day."

He's right, of course. These days, thanks to the success of the Fielding Project, we can pick our jobs. If we're running a little behind because of the weather, the client will understand. It also helps that we now go for fewer, but larger jobs, giving us more wriggle room on scheduling.

Another reason that sees me ready to head home is that Jason hasn't let go of me after lifting me free of the mud. As always, my body reacts to his, as he does to mine. What the crew can't see, because of his bright yellow wet weather gear, is that he's as ready for me as I am for him.

"You're right, let's call it a day."

I've barely got the words out when Jason's whistle nearly deafens me. Heads pop up all over the site, questioning looks all round. Jason lets go of me long enough to hold his hand high above his head and circle it around.

The crew doesn't question this, moving as one toward the on-site container to store their gear before heading off. No-one wants to work in weather like this.

It's miserable, and yet with Jason now a permanent fixture in my life, deep down, I couldn't be happier. That he's also bought into the business is a double plus, meaning I can share the pressure with an equal partner.

It was something I'd offered Steve in the past, but he'd never been in a financial position to take me up on it.

A quick call through to our foreman and I hear the other site isn't much better as regards mud. When I tell him he and the team can call it a day, his "Hallelujah" is heartfelt.

On arriving home, I'm chilled and waste no time in stripping out of my damp clothes in the mudroom. Jason matches my actions, with us soon both standing there naked but for our smiles.

Rather than join me in the shower as he usually would, he tells me to go ahead. Part of me is disappointed; part of me just wants to get under that hot water.

When he then tells me to get out that it's his turn, I know something is afoot. His buzzing with suppressed excitement is hard to miss, at least for me.

I'm still lounging around in a toweling robe when Jason finishes in the shower. It wasn't until I'd sat down that I realized how tired I was. I doubt there's a muscle in my body that's escaped unscathed today. Moving mud is hard work.

Jason appears unaffected. The man is a machine. And when he stalks into the lounge only dressed in a towel, I suspect I'm about to find out just how much of a machine he really is.

And just like that, some of my fatigue melts away.

JASON

I'm invigorated after the shower. And knowing what's coming up next is definitely helping my 'energy' levels.

Despite wanting to keep it a surprise until the last minute, I can't help but smile as I stroll across the lounge. "Come on, up you get. I've got something to show you."

Bee stays right where she is, instead patting the couch next to her. "Can't you show me here?" She follows this up with a sexy smile that has me close to sitting down.

"Nope, I can't show you here. Come on." I take both her hands in mine and drag her to her feet. Once upright, I scoop her up, deciding this will be quicker than her walking.

She's all smiles until I start down the stairs to the walkout basement and our shared office. "Where on earth are you taking me, Jason Adams? I'm too tired to work on anything now."

The only answer I give her is a burst of laughter. She really doesn't have a clue.

When she sees the sliding door to the garden is open, she looks up at me, her brow wrinkled in confusion. Despite her expression, I keep smiling, and I'm still smiling when I walk outside.

Thank goodness it'd stopped raining while she was in the shower. And thank goodness she hadn't spotted the pavers I'd had installed today while we were away on site.

This is the least of what the missing team members were up to.

"Jason, where on earth are you taking..." The rest of Bee's words die on her lips as we round the corner of the house. "What? When did you? But?"

I can't blame her confusion. What had until a few days ago been a bare patch of lawn now holds a top-of-the-line hot tub that's steaming and bubbling. To complete the set-up, there's a gazebo strung with strings of tiny white lights.

As I set her gently down on the decking next to the hot tub, Bridget looks up at me with wonder. "Jason ... I don't know what to say. Thank you, but..."

"Bee, you are everything to me. I want you to be as happy as I am." I drop my lips to hers, all while fumbling with the belt on her toweling robe.

A moment later, her luscious body is pressed tight against mine, with my towel in a heap at my feet. "Let's get in before it rains again."

The moment we're both being caressed by the bubbles, I pull her into an even tighter embrace. It's one that has her straddling my lap in such a way that if I move a little to the right, one jet...

Bee's squeal of delight has me stopping right where I am. If there's one thing the army taught me, it's that when you're in a prime position, you stay right where you are.

Well, not exactly right where I was, because with a slight change, I slide into Bee and we moan in unison. This would be spectacular enough on its own, but that jet action takes it to a whole new level.

"Damn, Bee. I love you so much." I lazily roll my hips, seating her more securely. "And I'm not just saying that because I'm about to blow."

"Jason. I love you more than life itself," she pants out in concert with the movement of my hips. On my plunging even deeper and grinding against her, she gasps out, "But don't you dare leave me hanging."

And I don't. Instead, I slide my hands under that peach of an ass and lift her almost free of my length, before letting her settle again. And repeat until both of us are in free-fall.

My lips claim hers, the cries of her climax filling my soul. After all those years of roaming the globe, I finally know I'm in exactly the right place.

And with exactly the right woman.

GARDEN

Bridget and Jason Adams, have done it again, taking out the top prize at this year's Home & Garden Show.

Judges said their winning design was a brilliant balance of both form and function.

As well as lush borders and hard landscaping, the design also included raised beds perfect for those facing mobility issues.

Donna needs a lucky break if she's making ends meet. Liam is stuck running one of the family's smaller hotel casinos. Could pretending to be engaged be a gamble that pays off for both of them?

ONE

LIAM

After casting my eye around the security office at Maddigan's Resort and Spa, I have to shake my head. First, that I'm stuck here, and second, why that is?

When my father said it was time for me to give up the playboy lifestyle and settle down, I had thought little of it. He'd said it often enough in the past for me to ignore him.

Little did I know what he'd lined up this time around? While I had nothing against Madeline Olsen, I didn't want to marry her, either.

Add in my father's track record of picking wives after mom died, and it was bound to fail. Even the idea of her taking my name is idiotic.

"I'd like to introduce Madeline Maddigan, my wife."

It was a nightmare of alliteration that would no doubt reflect on the marriage itself.

Heiress to the Olsen Empire, Madeline was a cold fish, more interested in turning a profit than a loving relationship.

Yep, my dad has me signed up for an arranged marriage of sorts. Anyone with half a brain can see it for what it is; a corporate merger that comes with grandchildren.

My refusal to bow to his wishes is why I'm stuck in Coogan's Break until I agree to his choice of daughter-in-law. A woman I find so unappealing, there'd be no chance of offspring.

I smile to myself. It's almost as if he's forgotten I'm as stubborn as he is.

My smile doesn't last long. Deep down, the thought of a loveless marriage and not having kids doesn't sit well with me.

Focused on my dad's plan and not the monitors, I almost miss a peach of a woman walking across the hotel foyer. Nope, walk is the wrong term. There is nothing pedestrian about the way this woman moves.

Carnal with a hint of amnesia, perhaps? Yep, that definitely fits, because if I was following her, I'd be lucky to remember my name.

I roll my chair to the side and stop in front of the next monitor. Thus, I follow her progress through the hotel.

Even though I'm mesmerized by her body, I don't miss her biting her bottom lip when she enters the casino. She's looked directly into the camera, and my soul, with my body reacting in accordance.

Was she nibbling her lip thanks to guilt or nerves? Neither is good when you're anywhere near a casino.

"Wyatt?" I turn to the guy sitting at the other end of the bank of monitors. "Are you okay with monitoring things while I check something out on the floor?"

Of course he says, "Yeah, sure." I'm the manager and a Maddigan, born and bred.

Before walking out the door, I straighten my dark red tie and shrug into the jacket of my gray suit. My reasons for wanting to appear sharp aren't all down to fitting in with our upmarket guests.

Two flights of stairs later and I slip through a security door at the back of the casino. After a quick scan of the casino, I spot the woman. I then waste no time exchanging a twenty out for coins, and making my way over to the slot machines.

I can't simply sit next to the woman and do nothing without it coming across as exceedingly weird. My plan goes out the window the moment I sit next to her. I thought she was gorgeous on the grainy security monitors.

Nothing could have prepared me for her impact on me when I'm this close. I'm still fumbling to get the first coin in the slot when she turns toward me. There's nothing I can do to stop myself from copying her action.

As I stare into her deep pansy eyes, the casino ceases to exist, and my breathing shallows. I'm in trouble, big trouble, and yet I couldn't be happier with a dirty smile to match.

As I watch her curl her fingers around the handle of the slot machine and pull slowly down, the joke is on me. She hasn't even touched me and yet I'm on my way to packing wood this suit was never designed for.

If I didn't know better, I'd think she'd handled my cock like that in the past, even though I've not met her before. Strange then, that there's a familiarity about her that baffles and excites.

Could it be what my mom always said is true?

DONNA

It's the first time I've been to Maddigan's since moving to Coogan's Break. The resort might have been in my price-range in my previous life, but that's no longer the case.

I'll bet I'm the only convenience store cashier here tonight. Thankfully, my last-minute decision to bring a nice dress and shoes when I escaped from San Francisco means no-one will have a clue.

As I wander through the hotel's reception area, I'm especially glad I'd opted to bring the dress I'm wearing. A dark purple, made-to-measure number that cost me a fortune. It may even fit me better now than when it was new.

Thanks to all those hours on my feet at work, I've lost a couple of pounds; although thankfully not the curves I love. While some girls long to be thin, I'm not one of them. I've tried that, and was miserable.

And why did I put myself through that? Because Bryan—my ex and the reason I left San Francisco—kept dropping hints I was putting on weight. I knew this wasn't the case, because I weighed myself every morning.

He'd kept saying I wasn't the girl who caught his eye until I gave in and started a diet. Along with losing weight, I'd lost my joy in life, my love of food, and my confidence.

Bryan had been thrilled with the results. And that folks was the nail in the coffin of our relationship. There wasn't a chance someone who professed they loved me as much as Bryan did would want to see me that miserable.

It took longer than it should for me to realize, but I got there eventually, moving back in with mom and dad. They'd been right about Bryan all along. It was also them who suggested I head north for a while to give that creep time to move on.

Of course, that was only after he started turning up at their place at all hours of the night, yelling for me and waking the neighbors. Thankfully, he'd left me alone at work.

The way he saw it, he should have ended our relationship, and not the other way around. I suspect if I'd taken him back, he'd have dumped me within a week just to prove his point.

I had thought about taking out a restraining order. However, with us both working for the same company, that couldn't happen. No way would MicroWorld choose to keep a lowly Marketing Manager over one of their star Vice Presidents.

The hardest part about resigning had been keeping it from Bryan, at least until I was on the bus heading north.

Coogan's Break had always held a special place in my heart, with happy memories of visiting there as a kid. Time spent frolicking in the waves and building epic sandcastles with my dad.

Nothing could be further from the truth these days. Whereas I'd felt welcomed as a child, now I'm viewed as an outsider. This was especially so with finding work, with it a case of not what you knew, but WHO you knew.

I knew that when I moved north that I'd have to downgrade my career, but not this far. The only plus is that I'm paid in cash, lessening my digital footprint. When your ex is a computer whiz, paranoia is by far the safest policy.

Unfortunately, the appalling hourly rate that goes along with being paid in cash sees me at the casino tonight. Even with the odds always favoring the house, I'm surely due some luck?

I've not long been settled at one of the slot machines, a container of coins in the cup-holder, when I'm on high alert.

Aftershave always had this effect on me, although this wouldn't be the case if it was the one Bryan doused himself in. Rather, this is a delicate citrus, with base notes of testosterone and good times.

Unable to stop myself, I turn to the left and my ability to breathe is taken from me, along with all reason.

We are talking about sex in a bespoke suit. Dark brown hair, beard, and a pair of go-to-bed eyes that have my heart missing beats. When he indulges in a knowing smile, I come close to sliding off my bar stool.

Of course I recognize him. However, those pictures in the society pages don't come close to showing how handsome he is in real life. It takes all my willpower to shut my mouth, smile briefly in response, and then turn back to face my slot machine.

Even then, I'm acutely aware he's watching when I put my next coin in the slot. I'm even more conscious when I wrap my fingers one-by-one around the knob on the end of the vintage machine's arm.

As I pull slowly down, my thoughts are no longer on a big payout. Oh no, they're not. Liam, struggling to clear his throat next to me, says I might not be alone on that front.

TWO

DONNA

As I watch the tumblers whirring on the machine, I cross the fingers of the hand resting in my lap. It doesn't matter that Liam Maddigan is still watching my every move. A bit of extra luck can't hurt.

First one banana pops up and then another. I stop breathing, waiting for the final tumbler to stop. Three bananas! I'm unable to squelch my excitement.

The edge is taken off when, rather than the machine light up like Vegas, several dozen coins drop into the tray in front of me.

It's better than nothing, but not by much. After scooping them up, I grab another coin, ready to try my luck again. The chances of me winning again are slim, but now that I'm ahead, I have a few coins to spare.

Liam still watches me like a hawk, even with him randomly plugging coins into his own machine. I can't help but admire his long, tapered fingers and come close to dropping my next coin. After sliding it carefully into the slot, I take hold of the stick rather than the knob on the end.

My ovaries can only take so much action.

I pull down and am rewarded with a trio of apples. While the pay-out is better than for bananas, it's nothing to scream and shout about. Of interest is Liam sitting up straighter in his seat.

He's no longer plugging those coins in as fast as he was, his attention firmly hooked on me rather than his machine.

So focused have I been on my two small wins, that I've forgotten gambling is only part of the reason I'm out tonight. There's only so much a girl can take from the scurrying of her *roommates* in the ceiling above her bed.

Sure, I could call on mom and dad to help me out financially, but the less I have to do with them, the better. I simply don't trust Bryan not to pull some dodgy crap and hack their phone records.

I'll do it if I have to, but I'm not yet that short of funds. The longer I can hold out, the better my chances of reclaiming my life back in the city.

I've taken a couple of sips of my local white wine when I stop. If I have to visit the ladies, I might lose my lucky machine. I put my glass down on the ledge in front of me and take another coin from my growing collection.

If this doesn't pay out, I'll call it a day and quit while I'm ahead. Regardless of not having counted my winnings, they'll definitely go some way to covering next week's rent. It'll be one less thing to worry about.

I slide the coin into the slot, already wondering when the next complimentary shuttle to town will be. I've pulled the handle and picked up my cup of coins before the tumblers have stopped spinning.

My evening bag is over my shoulder and I'm ready to stand when the machine lights up. I stare in disbelief at the row of cherries, before my gaze drops to the overflowing tray beneath. Even a gambling newbie like me knows the odds of winning three-in-a-row are slim.

It must be a concept Liam agrees with, him having completely abandoned any pretense of playing the machine next to me. "You're one lucky lady. There aren't many who could pop the cherry on their third go."

His deep baritone cuts me to the core before I focus on the words themselves. Actually, it's my ovaries that latch onto his innuendo, singing their approval at such a volume that they're hard to ignore.

I haven't come up with a response when my evening bag vibrates violently with this, followed up by a loud BING.

What? I'm darn sure I turned that off.

Any thoughts at the ambiguity of Liam's words flee in my haste to get out of the casino before I'm busted for having my phone turned on. Even a stranger to casinos like myself is aware this is against the rules.

I can only hope he didn't hear the text alert over the dinging and bells from my slot machine.

Such is my haste to distance myself; I almost forget to collect my latest pay out. It's only Liam putting his hand on my forearm and pointing at the overflowing tray that stops me.

Actually, my body's response to him touching me what it is, I doubt I could move if the place was on fire. Only by squeezing my thighs together and gritting my teeth do I dampen the resulting zing.

My unwanted—make that mostly—arousal aside; only two people have this phone number. I need to check the message if I'm to see how the rest of my evening will play out.

After scooping my winnings into my purse, I hustle out of the casino, all too aware Liam is right behind me. When I suddenly veer toward one of the squishy couches dotted around reception, his steps match mine.

I doubt this is a coincidence.

LIAM

Damn, if I thought she was hot when I was sitting next to her, following her out of the casino is the next level. As I trail behind her, I button my suit jacket to hide my burgeoning erection.

As the manager of the hotel, I can hardly stroll through reception like something out of an adult movie. I'd cop heaps from the old man if word ever got out.

Focused as I am on the swaying of her ass, I take a second to catch up when she shoots off to the left. When she perches herself on the edge of a couch, I drop into its plush depths right next to her.

We're way beyond pretending nothing happened in the casino and the fewer people who hear what I have to say, the better.

"It's against house rules for you to have your phone on when you're in there."

Even though I'm staring straight ahead, I'm well aware when her gaze darts in my direction.

"I know. I didn't mean to. I thought I'd turned it off."

She takes her phone out of her purse, but doesn't hand it over as I've been expecting. All the while she's nibbling on her bottom lip in a manner that has me back to fighting my reaction to her.

Damn it, she could just as well be nibbling on ... To rid my brain of this errant thought, I visualize Madeline Olsen. The woman dad wants me to marry could chew both her lips off and I wouldn't react as I am now.

"I'm afraid I have to ask you a few questions, and I can't do that sitting out here."

After flashing my hotel ID pass, I get awkwardly to my feet and gesture toward the main reception desk.

"But, but, I did nothing wrong. You were next to me." She narrows her gaze and stares up at me. "You watched my every move. You're well aware I wasn't on my phone."

"In that case, you won't mind answering a few questions, will you?" I again gesture toward reception, or rather to the door next to it. The one marked PRIVATE.

After putting her phone back in her purse, she surges to her feet. "Fine, but can we please make this quick? I've got places I need to be?!"

She's then off across reception at a speed that has her waiting next to the door, tapping her toe when I join her.

Hmmm, someone is in a hurry, and now I'm wondering why. I hold my pass key in front of the security panel on the door and it clicks open. After I swing it wide, I stand to the side and allow her to enter ahead of me.

However, this time, I keep my gaze firmly locked on the back of her head. For all it helps. The woman's hair falls in molten waves to the middle of her back. It's just asking to be messed up.

"Please take a seat. If you co-operate, this shouldn't take long."

She drops into the visitor seat, all the while mumbling about something being *absolutely ridiculous*. She then makes a production out of checking her watch and holding her purse tight in her lap.

Only once I'm seated do I hold my hand out and beckon with my fingers.

Confusion crosses her face briefly before this is replaced by realization.

"Fine!" She grabs her phone out of her purse, unlocks it, and as good as throws it across the desk. This surprises me until I see what a basic model it is, possibly too basic to interfere with the casino's electronics.

After taking a note of her number, I trawl through her phone. "I'll also need ID."

The response is another terse, "Fine!" A second later, her driver's license is slammed down on the desk in front of me.

"Thank you for your cooperation."

My thanks have been automatic, my attention firmly on her phone. There are no photos of pets or family. In fact, no photos at all, which is strange? Not even a selfie.

Usually women as good-looking at this one are snapping pics of themselves at every opportunity. With her skin as flawless as it is, she wouldn't even need to bother with filters.

The other oddity is that apart from a couple of basic apps, there are only two numbers programmed into the phone. One is marked Mom and Dad, the other is simply marked 'B'.

It's when I check the text messages that things get messy. There's only one, and it's the one she'd received not five minutes earlier.

DELIVERY COMPLETE!!
WHY AREN'T YOU HERE?!!

I turn the phone around so she can read it, a simple task with it being all in shouty capitals.

She puffs out through pursed lips in what appears to be a strange mix of relief and annoyance.

"I need to get going." She pauses before gazing at me, as if to gauge how much she's willing to tell me. "It's from my boss." Her shoulders slump before she continues. "If I'm not there within half-an-hour, I can kiss my job goodbye."

I stop trying to make sense of the text message and look at her again. "Work? At ten at night?"

Rather than answer me, she holds her hand out. "I'd like my phone back, please." When I don't move to hand it over, she continues. "Fine, let's get the cops involved. I can call my key witness to prove I did nothing illegal."

"Key witness?"

In answer, she raises a carefully sculpted eyebrow, before again beckoning for the return of her phone. She's right though. I was sitting next to her, and she didn't receive that weird text until after her third win.

If I factor in the slots being mechanical and not electronic, I have nothing I can hold her on. The cops would give me grief if I called them in on such flimsy evidence.

After taking a photo of her license, I hand it back to her along with her phone. She wastes no time putting them away and standing.

I also get to my feet and stare at her, glad there's a desk between us. If there wasn't, I'd be doing my best to seduce her. "Next time you visit the casino, turn your phone off, or even better, leave it in your car."

She snorts at my suggestion. "Car? Yeah, right?"

She's already opened the office door when she adds, "And trust me, there won't be a next time." Then, without bothering to say goodbye, she storms off.

By the time I'm back in reception, she's out front, waving frantically, to stop the hotel shuttle that's just pulling away. The driver either doesn't see her, or chooses not to.

Either way, it'll be at least half an hour until the next one. Then she does something that surprises me. Instead of taking one of the taxis parked out front, she starts walking.

It's only when she's halfway to the ornate front gates that I come to my senses.

THREE

DONNA

As frustrated as I am at having just missed the shuttle, I embrace the night air. It's welcome after the near constant arousal I've experienced since Liam Maddigan first sat next to me at the slot machines.

It makes no sense. He's not the sort of man I'd ever date, and especially not when I was trying to keep a low profile. One date with an entitled player like him and my image would be plastered all over social media.

And because I'm a complete opposite of the women usually found hanging off his arm, the comments would be brutal. There'd be no keeping my location quiet after that.

As I march down the long driveway of the resort, I'm now regretting having worn heels. While they suit the dress, they're the last thing I need for the walk to work.

It won't matter how fast I walk, I'll still be late. At most, it's a twenty-minute walk from my apartment, so that's what Bernie will be expecting. Who knows how he'll respond to my tardiness? He's volatile at the best of times.

With my job as a cashier at Montrose Day 'N' Night my only source of income, I can't afford to lose it. Honestly, the place sounds fancier than it is, with the windows not having been cleaned in decades.

Bernie Montrose calls it 'security frosting'. I call it laziness. I'd offer to clean them, but he'd just say it wasn't in my contract—I don't have a contract—and so he couldn't pay me for it.

Make that WOULDN'T pay me for it. Heck, he hardly pays me as it is, but beggars can't be choosers, and all that. Even if my purse is heavy with my winnings, it won't go far if I'm laid off.

I'm outside the gates when I stop. Surely it's better to at least let Bernie know I'm on my way?

I'm laboring over my text when a late model sedan with the hotel logo on the door pulls up next to me. The tinted window rolls down and Liam leans across the center console to talk to me.

I don't give him the chance. I look at him only as long as I have to, before blurting out. "What now? I'm not even on the property." I then go back to my text in hopes he'll drive on and leave me alone.

He has other ideas.

"Hop in, and I can drop you somewhere. I saw you missed the shuttle."

He opens his mouth to say something else, but then thinks better of it. Part of me knows what he was going to say, anyway. And that was why, after winning three times in a row, was I choosing to walk rather than take a taxi.

Part of me wants to reply that I don't want to accept a ride from someone who thinks I'm dishonest, but I'm no-one's fool. I've opened the door and settled in before he's even thought to get out and come open it for me.

I then pretend I'm still working on the text to avoid speaking to the insufferable man. The only time I pay attention to the road is when I say, "Right, left, or straight ahead."

After I direct him to pull up outside the convenience store, he does so. He checks out the front of the place and then twists in his seat to stare at me. "You want me to drop you here?"

"This will do fine." I've got my seatbelt undone and have opened the door before he's so much as moved. I then shut the car door on anything else he's got to say. It's no secret the place is a dump. I don't need to hear his opinions on it.

Because I'm still annoyed that he'd questioned my honesty, I haven't thanked him for the ride. This goes against everything my parents taught me, but I am not giving in. Without a backward glance, I walk through the front doors of Montrose Day 'N' Night, making for my locker out the back.

I can hardly serve customers dressed in my designer number, and I sure as heck can't last a full shift in heels. Lucky for me, Bernie won't let me take the uniform home, and I always keep a pair of flats in my locker.

As I hang my dress up, I'm annoyed with both Liam and myself. Him for questioning my honesty, and me for still wondering what his body is like underneath that sharp suit?

Despite this, if I ever see Liam Maddigan again, it will be too soon.

LIAM

I don't follow Donna into the cruddy convenience store. The ease with which she'd entered the establishment tells me she's familiar with it. There isn't a chance a woman of her class would walk in there, otherwise.

Just how familiar that is, becomes apparent when she reappears from down the back of the shop. Gone is the gorgeous dress. She's now dressed in pants and a tunic of a hideous shade of brown.

The uniform does her body no favors, although to be fair, a supermodel wouldn't be able to pull off that miracle.

When I see the sleazy creep following in her wake, part of me is pleased she isn't looking as sexy as earlier. The guy's vest is as filthy as the front windows, a cigarette hangs out of his mouth, and a beer gut hides his belt.

A glance at the name above the front doors and I have to assume this is Bernie Montrose Proprietor. He has to be, because no employer would let an employee run around in that state.

I don't like the way he's undressing Donna with his eyes and only become aware I'm fisting my hands when my knuckles crack. I'm not usually drawn to violence, but for this guy, I'd make an exception.

As if sensing his ogling, Donna hastens behind the counter just inside the front doors. She then spins, eyeballing the guy enough that he backs away, hands up in surrender.

With the show now over, he yells at her briefly, steps close enough to the front doors to activate them, and flicks his cigarette butt out onto the sidewalk.

The filthy glass is out of the way long enough for Donna and me to make eye contact. She doesn't hold it though, rather tilting her head proudly and looking away.

As I drive back to the resort, my mind is whirring. It wouldn't be the first time someone in financial difficulties was taken advantage of by the sorts who scam casinos.

Could it be Donna is involved in some sort of racket, or is she simply a problem gambler? Neither option sits comfortably.

This has me thinking back to her elation at her small wins. Was this down to an addiction, or is she really that short of funds? From the little I'd seen of her workplace, I can't imagine she's being paid a living wage.

A flashback to her employer, and I have to wonder if she's even being paid the minimum. And yet she'd been worried about losing that job. It made no sense.

From my brief time with her, I got she was educated and capable of a much better job than working in a place like that. If I didn't know better, I'd think she was hiding from something.

Or is that someone?

I'm almost back at the resort when I get a call from Wyatt in the security office. He needs me there, and the sooner, the better.

"Be with you in five minutes." I end the call and put my foot down, racing through the front gates. Rather than park around back, I drive up to the front entrance, leaving the car door open for the valet.

In the three months I've been managing the hotel, Wyatt has never spoken to me with that level of urgency. The guy is so laid back as to be almost horizontal. It's strange in someone with his background in security.

Not bothering with the elevator, I sprint up the stairs to the office. Wyatt is ready and waiting and no sooner have I sat down than he hits play on the recorder.

He has to play the footage twice for me to spot what the cashier is up to. His con is based on the premise that no-one ever counts the contents of their Bucket-o-Coins.

They simply hand their notes over, expecting to get the exact change in return. However, the cashier we're watching will often slip one or two notes under the overhang of the counter.

This is most often when the guest is distracted by someone winning big, or the like. He then hands back coins to match the notes that've actually made it as far as the cash drawer.

By doing so, the coins and notes will match up. It's another reason I think my father is an idiot for sticking with coin-machines. I don't care what a *steal* they were; there was a reason the Vegas casinos ditched them.

"Wyatt, I'm going downstairs to take a closer look. Have you got an earpiece I can use?"

It's unusual for me to be wired for sound, but I want to know the cashier's movements before I pay him a visit. Only by taking the guy by surprise will I have a chance of working out what's happening to those notes.

The plan works, because I'm in time to see the guy slide a pile of notes down a gap at the back of the desk. I don't care where they've gone; all I know is that this guy needs to go. He does shortly afterwards, in handcuffs.

This leaves me with two problems. I'm down a cashier, and all I can think of is Donna in handcuffs. *You sick bastard.*

It gives me an idea, though. "Wyatt, can you check someone out for me?"

I don't go into any more detail than this, simply emailing him the photo I'd taken of her driver's license.

If anyone can dig up anything on this woman, it's Wyatt. Whether it's legal, the less we say about that, the better.

FOUR

DONNA

It's six the following morning, and I'm so tired, I can't think straight. "Hey, Bernie!" I listen out for a response, without luck. No doubt the lazy good-for-nothing is asleep on the sagging twin bed in his office, as usual.

I yell again, louder this time, and finally get a grunt in response. He appears shortly after, busy tightening his belt.

"What the hell do you want? I was busy."

There's nothing polite, or even truthful, about his words. This had shocked me when I first started. I was used to being spoken to with respect, or at least a semblance of that. It was hard to tell with some marketing types.

"I'm due to clock off. Where's Tegan?"

There's nothing nice about his smile as he stares at me. When he licks his lips, I want to grab the spray bottle of disinfectant from below the counter and let him have it.

"Didn't I tell you? She can't make it in this morning."

He laughs again before turning back to his office.

"But, I've been..." I don't bother with anything else. He knows as well as I do how long I've been working. And how many more hours I'll have to clock until the afternoon shift arrives.

The only plus is the extra ten hours' pay. While it might be peanuts to some, for me it's a lifesaver. So, despite sore feet and a sore back, I grit my teeth and settle in.

It's just after eleven when I spot a sedan with the Maddigan's Resort livery pulling up outside. Even though it's a different model to that Liam had been driving the night before, there's no doubt in my mind that it'll be him.

I thought I'd seen the last of him. He's got nothing on me, because I wasn't doing anything illegal. It's for this reason my greeting is anything but cordial. I'm hot, I'm tired, and I don't need the grief.

"What the hell are you doing here?" There isn't a chance he's simply here to pick up a few bits and pieces. Men of his ilk didn't shop. There were people for tasks like that.

"Well, hello to you, too."

He then leans his hip against my counter and crosses his arms, telling me he isn't leaving soon.

"What? I told you I wouldn't step foot in the resort again. Perhaps you'd be good enough to return the favor and leave my place of work?"

He straightens. "Yeah, about that. Sorry I gave you grief last night." He then takes his time looking around the store. The slight curl of his lip says his opinion of the place matches mine. His gaze once again on me, he clears his throat. "So, here's the thing. I've got a proposition for you."

I can't believe this is happening, and no amount of air being sucked in through flared nostrils will calm me down. How dare he? What does he take me for? Just because I'm in a dead-end job doesn't mean I'm desperate.

Well, I am, but I'm not THAT desperate. Then I'm annoyed at my subconscious calling out that there are worse ways to spend a night and that he is easy on the eye.

Oh, who am I kidding? He's way more than that.

It's a shame he's also an entitled player more interested in publicity than his date. Not once in all those photos I'd seen of him online did he appear vaguely enamored of whatever woman was glued to his side.

And yet the way he's checking me out says he's definitely into women. A quick look down at my uniform and I'm at a loss. There is nothing sexy about the tunic and pants, although I welcome this given the state of some customers, but especially Bernie.

Comprehension finally makes itself at home on his face. "No! Not that." He shakes his head before continuing. "No, we've got an opening for a cashier in the casino. Am I right in thinking you know how to make change?"

I stare at him, aghast. "Didn't you just hear me? I said I'd never set foot in that place again, and I meant it."

My words are as water off a duck's back as he outlines what the job entails. When he moves onto the urgency of filling the position, my internal lie detector is off the charts.

Wasn't this the guy who only last night accused me of casino fraud? For him to offer me a job handling money makes little sense, shape, or form.

And what if this is all a game to him? Sure, my current job is awful, but it still took me a month to land. I'm not jeopardizing it simply to amuse him.

He doesn't have time to say anything else. The unmistakable sound of a whole pile of coins hitting a grimy tiled floor interrupts him.

That didn't come from Bernie's office, it came from the staffroom.

"Why, you little creep." I'm out from behind my counter and striding down the main aisle before giving thought to what I'll do if my suspicions are correct.

Even stranger is that Liam is hot on my heels, something I actually take comfort in. Bernie can turn feral when he's cornered.

LIAM

My having been brought up around casinos, the sound is familiar. Donna's reaction gives me everything else I need to know.

It's for this reason I stick close to her as she races down to the back of the store. There isn't a chance I want her confronting a thief on her own.

Her cry of anguish when she takes in the scene cuts right through me. There's no need for CSI to see what's happening. Her boss is on his hands and knees, with coins everywhere. The most damning piece of evidence is Donna's purse lying on the floor next to him.

Her basic phone is also on the ground, explaining why she didn't answer my calls. Now I'm glad of it, because otherwise, I wouldn't have been here to help her.

The way her boss sneers at her, says he's not giving up *his* winnings without a fight. That he hasn't seen me is obvious by this behavior.

As angry as I am, my voice comes out deeper and with more authority than it usually would. "Pick them up, now!"

Before I know what's happening, Donna has dropped to her hands and knees, and is scooping up coins and trying to put them back in her purse.

"Not you, darling." I step into the small room, pull myself up to my full six-foot-three, and then scowl at her boss. "This low life!"

I help Donna regain her feet with difficulty, confirming she's been working without a break since I dropped her off last night.

Meanwhile, I glare at the odious little man in front of us with him scrambling to stand. Like hell he is. I put my hand on one of his shoulders and apply pressure. "You dropped them, you pick them up."

For a slovenly dude, he sure can move fast, with all the coins retrieved and back in Donna's purse with surprising speed.

"Grab the rest of your things and we can get going."

She turns and stares at me, clutching her purse protectively against her chest. "I can't leave. My shift isn't over."

I'm momentarily speechless. "What? You can't be serious. You'd stay working for this creep after we caught him stealing from you?"

Out of the corner of my eye, I can see her boss indulging in a smug smile. Like hell I'm giving up that easily, and especially not to someone like him.

"Whatever he's paying you, I'll double it."

Now who's acting smug?

When Donna doesn't make to clear out her locker, I up the ante. "Okay!" I jerk my head in Bernie's direction. "I'll triple what he's paying you."

I feel safe in making this offer. From what I've seen of her erstwhile employer, I could probably quadruple it and come out on top. But I only know she's accepted my offer when she steps over to her locker and empties it of her belongings.

We're nearly out the automatic front doors when Bernie calls out. "Hey you can't leave. That's stealing."

After a moment's hesitation, Donna appears to work out what he's talking about. I'm ready to go back and deal to the guy. She, however, has other ideas. "This?" She jerks on the front of her tunic with her free hand, the action having an edge of hysteria to it.

He nods, crossing his arms over his beer gut. I'm expecting Donna to return to the staffroom so she can change. Or at least promise to drop the uniform back the following day. She does neither.

After shoving her belongings at me to hold, she rips open her top, causing buttons to fly in all directions. "I was going to wash them, you odious little creep!"

She throws the top in his face before moving onto the ugly brown pants. Soon enough, these sit in a heap on the ground, leaving her standing there in her bra and panties.

Her magnificent body, the barely there lingerie skimming every dip and hollow, is mesmerizing. Bernie's made the most of it before I think to shrug out of my jacket and drape it over her shoulders.

The jacket doesn't come close to covering her lush curves, and I have to fight the urge to get a better look at her ass cheeks in those panties.

After leaving the store, I rush to open the car door for Donna and settle her in as my mother always insisted. Part of me also isn't keen on her waltzing around as good as naked. You never knew who was about.

As I walk around to the driver's side, I'm all too aware of Bernie Montrose watching my every move. If I didn't have a better sense of my ability to take care of myself, I might find it intimidating.

Instead, I beam; making sure none of my amusement makes it to my eyes. I've been told the effect is deadly in its intensity. Sure enough,

Bernie backs up sharpish, allowing the front doors to close in front of him.

After doing up my seatbelt and starting the engine, I turn to Donna. She's staring straight ahead, although I doubt she's seeing anything. She appears stunned, as if she can't quite believe what just happened. I must admit I'm having trouble myself.

Even though I hate to intrude, we can't sit here all day, especially not with her in her current state. "Where are we off to?"

Her eyes flicker and she turns to look at me. "I thought we'd be going to the resort. Didn't you say you needed to fill the post urgently?"

"We do, but it's not so urgent that we want you fainting because you haven't slept in a couple of days. Now let's get you home and into bed."

I've said the words without thought, and then all I can think of is exactly that. Not to sleep, though. That'd be the last thing I'd be interested in.

FIVE

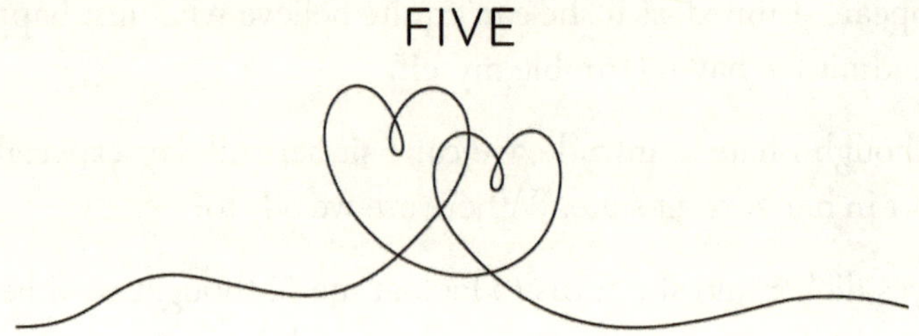

DONNA

Unlike other staff turning up at Maddigan's late that same afternoon, I'm the only one being chauffeur driven. Well, not exactly, but after hearing I didn't own a car, Liam had offered to collect me.

Tired as I'd been, I hadn't argued. Instead, after he'd opened the car door and helped me out, I'd left him without as much as a thank you. I'd been too busy Zombie-walking up to my apartment. By the time I realized I was still wearing his suit jacket, he'd already left.

Rather than pulling up out front of the hotel, Liam drives around the back and into a basement carpark. After parking, he turns to me. "I only use the front entrance if I'm in a hurry. Don't want people to think I'm full of myself."

With everyone in HR already having left for the day, Liam, and a guy called Wyatt, will take me through everything. This strikes me as unusual, and then things only get weirder.

When I hand my W-4 form over, Wyatt hands it straight back. He doesn't even bother looking at it, merely saying there's, "No need."

That's not right. Without that, Maddigan's won't know how much tax to deduct. Even Bernie Montrose wanted to see my W-4, for all the good it did in how much *tax* he helped himself to.

The final straw is when instead of the standard I-9 form, I'm handed a basic typed version to complete.

Something is up, for sure. Something really dodgy.

My pen poised over the first blank space on the no-frills version, I stare at Wyatt and wait. However, it's Liam who answers my unspoken question.

"When Wyatt did a security check on you, he picked up on a few things."

He doesn't have to say what they've picked up on. *Bryan.* While my heart stutters in my chest to hear they've been snooping, it's standard practice for a position like this.

Well, any position except for that of a cashier at Montrose Day 'N' Night, with that part of the appeal.

Wyatt taps the top of the basic details sheet. "We'll keep track of everything we pay you, but for now, it's off the books."

I'm unsure if the wave of giddiness that strikes me is down to relief or a distinct lack of sleep. Either way, after a brief shake of my head, I set about completing the form.

I'm then given a uniform and told to change, following which I'm expecting to be handed off to someone for training. However, it's Liam who accompanies me to the cashier's booth I'll be manning that evening.

When he rolls another tall chair into the cramped space, I relax, knowing my trainer will arrive soon. Instead, it's Liam who sits next to me, and there's nothing I can do to hide my surprise.

"Hah, you don't need to be so shocked. Dad said I needed to understand the operation from the ground up. This won't be the first time I've worked as a cashier."

How on earth am I supposed to concentrate with him right next to me? While I'm not his type, and he's not mine, I'd be fooling myself to say I didn't find him attractive. And if that was the case, what did I find him?

Desirable?

Yummy?

Lickable?

Okay, subconscious, you can shut up now.

If only it were that easy. There's no ignoring Liam's muscled thigh hard up against my less defined one. It's going to be a long shift.

And it is. Four hours of keeping my constant arousal under wraps and I'm exhausted. To say my panties are damp would be like saying the North Pole is a little chilly.

After turning the sign to CLOSED, Liam rolls his seat back and stands. "Come on, you did well tonight. I'll drop you home."

His words, being as casual as they are, tell me he's been unaffected by our closeness. I'm part relieved, and part disappointed. Chatting between customers, I know he's not entitled at all. He's anything but.

Those women's magazines also have a lot to answer for with his reputation. Something he's tried convincing his father of, without success.

On the drive back to my place, I can't help thinking about his situation. "I still can't believe your dad is trying to force you into marriage." This is such a foreign concept that I'm having trouble grasping it. There isn't a chance my folks would pull that crap with me.

On seeing who's out front of my apartment complex when Liam pulls up, I can't help but give into a heartfelt sigh. The rats in the ceiling above my bed aren't the only vermin I have to contend with.

He turns to face me. "What?"

"It's nothing, just what I'll have to put up with between here and my front door."

I don't have time to say anything else before Liam turns the engine off and climbs out. Next thing, he's opened my door and is helping me out. Him then setting the alarm on the car tells me it's a door-to-door service tonight.

We've not taken a couple of steps when my neighbor makes one of his usual nasty remarks. They're always personal, and always about my curves. Liam slows while I do my best to keep walking. I've found ignoring the guy is the best option.

I don't hear Liam say anything, but whatever he does has my neighbor falling silent immediately. Even the usual cat calls when I walk up the stairs to the upper level are missing. I wish I could silence the creep simply by staring at him.

After opening the door and switching on the lights, I turn to face Liam. "Thank you for dropping me home. I really appreciate it."

Liam's top lip curls as he takes in my luxurious domicile. "Donna, you cannot stay here. I didn't realize..."

He doesn't say what he didn't realize. There's no need. The place is a dump, with awful neighbors and vermin. "It's not that bad. The door's solid, and the locks are good."

I've just finished this up-sell, when one of the resident roaches scuttles across the front door, and my shoulders drop.

"How long would it take you to pack?"

So out of left field is Liam's question that it takes a second to process it. Even then, I'm not sure what he means by it, although I soon find out.

LIAM

There isn't a chance I'm leaving Donna in this awful place. The cockroach had been the final straw. While I'm taking one hell of a risk, sometimes you just have to.

"Grab your things. One perk of being a Maddigan is that there's an owner's suite at the hotel." On spotting her shocked expression, I'm quick to add. "You'd have your own room, with an attached bath."

With her still standing stock still, I hold my hands up, confirming there will be none of *that* on offer. Perhaps as surprising as her reluctance to come home with me, is the disappointment this sparks. I shouldn't take it personally, but I do.

"It will just be until you can get on your feet financially. You can even pay me the same as you're paying here, if it'll make you feel better."

Apparently it will, with the woman a whirl of efficiency at how quickly she packs. The only thing she leaves is her bedding, worried about freeloaders. "Best I leave it behind. Anything worth a dime is at my folks' place."

The last thing she does after I've put her two small suitcases in the trunk is to chuck the front door key at her neighbor. I can't help but join her in smiling after the large plastic tag smacks him on the nose.

"Did that feel good?"

She laughs victoriously while nodding, her delight infectious.

She's still indulging in the occasional giggle when we drive through the front gates of the resort. However, on driving around the back, she falls silent, although not for long.

"Will it be okay with management that I'm staying here?"

While waiting for me to answer, she chews on her bottom lip, and damned if my cock isn't all, 'Well, hello there!'

"Ah, Donna, I am management, and I say it's fine."

A glance to the side shows me Donna isn't like any of the women I've dated. And yet, there's something about her, something I need to ignore with her effectively being an employee.

Even if she's not officially on the books, the premise is the same. What did they say about it at Maddigan's London? That's right, 'Don't screw the crew!'

I run this mantra on repeat after I get her bags out of the trunk and we walk over to the service elevator. I continue on our ride up to the second-to-top floor.

The elevator doors open, and Donna turns to me, surprise clear in her eyes. "But I thought ... the owner's suite..."

"Hah, there isn't a chance my father is losing out on potential income by us taking an entire floor, and especially not the top one. It's the same reason we don't have sea views."

Once inside the suite, I take her bags and drop them in what will be her room while she's staying here. On turning to leave, I find she's right behind me, looking up at me with those big blue eyes of hers.

And just like that, my mantra to leave her alone is out the window. My hand gently under her chin, I lift it so I can see her beautiful face. I lower my lips to hers slowly, giving her plenty of time to tell me no.

She does nothing of the sort, instead reaching up on her toes. When our lips meet, the room ceases to exist. More than that, my world ceases to exist. No being stuck in a backwater, no being forced into a loveless marriage, no lack of family.

All burned to a crisp by a kiss that strikes at my very core. No longer am I the millionaire playboy beloved by the gossips. I'm just a man, and she's just a woman, one who fits my embrace perfectly, when really she shouldn't.

We pull back simultaneously, apologies tumbling over each other in our haste to get the words out. 'Sorry' features almost as often as 'I forgot myself' and then finally the death knell of 'Let's forget this ever happened'.

It's this last remark from Donna that hurts the most, and yet she's right.

It could never work between us.

We're from different worlds.

We're total opposites.

And yet it had felt so right.

And so damned good.

SIX

DONNA

I stare at the door a full minute after Liam closes it on leaving. My mind is now full of a kaleidoscope of erotic images that has no right being there.

What the heck just happened? Sure, we kissed, but there was so much more to it than that. And it was freaking amazing. No, make that stupendous.

He's nothing like the guys I'm usually attracted to. Bryan was a case in point, even if his beauty had proven to only be skin-deep.

As I unpack my bags, the images flickering in my mind don't show any sign of slowing. It's a distraction that sees me shoving things in random drawers.

A quick trip to the bathroom to brush my teeth shows it to be identical to that found in hotels the world over. Surplus of white subway tiles, lovely fluffy white towels, small soaps in a bowl next to the sink.

The only thing missing is a robe on the back of the bathroom door.

I close my eyes, and I can see mine hanging just like that. The only problem is that it's back at my old apartment. So it's gone for good.

After turning on the lamp on the bedside table, I flick the covers back, strip down to my camisole and panties, and dive in.

The sheets are wonderfully cool. Their smoothness when I indulge in a 'clean sheets angel', testament to the thread count being well over 500. Because I'm scheduled to work in the morning, I immediately lean over and turn the light off, determined to get enough sleep tonight.

For all the good it does. Half an hour later, and my brain is still spinning and I've examined every inch of the ceiling thanks to the bright moonlight and my having left the drapes open.

The tickle in my throat starts off innocuously enough, but soon builds. I need a glass of water if I'm to avoid waking the entire floor with my coughing. Surely Liam is asleep by now?

A moment later, I open my bedroom door without so much as a squeak, with the lush carpet in the hallway muffling my footfalls.

On reaching the marble tiles in the kitchen, I'm glad I'm barefoot with my steps barely registering, even to me. There isn't a chance I'll wake him.

The moonlight streaming in through the floor-to-ceiling windows makes finding a glass easy enough. As does filling it using the filter tap next to the sink.

It's only on spinning around to return to my bedroom that I run into trouble.

Trouble of the six-foot-three and muscled kind.

There's nothing I can do to stop sloshing my water all over him, his sharp intake of breath testimony to it being chilled.

"Oh, I'm so sorry." I put my glass on the countertop next to me, furiously searching for a hand towel.

I still haven't found one when the room erupts in light.

This reveals two things.

That I'm as wet as Liam, with my camisole and panties stuck to me like a second skin. And, more interesting to my mind, is that Liam's boxers are doing nothing to hide his current state of arousal.

I need another glass of water, stat.

LIAM

On returning to my room after saying goodnight to Donna, I'm giving serious thought to having a cold shower.

The only problem is that I'm quite enjoying the state of my cock. It's a perfect match to my memories of how Donna had felt under my lips. And yet, this shouldn't be the case at all.

The gossip mags would salivate with glee if we were ever to go out on a date. "Date? Seriously?" I can't believe I'm even thinking that way, with my love life complicated enough as it is.

It's been on hold since I moved to Coogan's Break. I'm worried dad will see this as a sign that I'm ready to settle down.

And that is so not happening, old man.

As soon as I get this resort turning a decent profit, I'm out of here, back to the east coast. Back to a life of parties and beautiful women hanging off me. Yet when I try to recall the many women I've dated over the years, all I can see is Donna's sweet face.

Perhaps it's because I'm focused on her I hear movement out in the kitchen. If I'd been asleep, it wouldn't have been loud enough to wake me.

I'm wondering what she's up to when the thought explodes that maybe she's changed her mind about staying here. The bedside clock shows me it's too late for her to be disappearing into the night.

Such is my desire to keep her safe that I immediately leap out of bed and stride through to the kitchen. I don't get far before it's as if I'm having that cold shower after all.

The semi I'd been sporting courtesy of that kiss is immediately shocked into submission, although it doesn't last long.

Rather than stumble around in the dark, I reach out and turn on the row of lights that hang above the marbled-topped kitchen island.

And, boom, just like that, I'm well on the way to being rock hard again. I wasn't the only one who got wet when we collided. She's worn more of it, with her slinky top and panties plastered to her.

This leaves nothing to my imagination, and believe me, there's nothing wrong with that where this woman is concerned. As focused as I am on her pebbled nipples, it takes longer than it should to make sense of her string of apologies.

The temptation to reach out and stroke her magnificent breasts almost overrides everything else. It takes more willpower than I knew I possessed to drop my hands to my sides.

I then do my best to keep eye contact, but my gaze drops again of its own volition. "No, I'm the one who's sorry. You should never have seen me in this state." A quick peek at her face and I see she's checking me out, her breathing rapid.

I'm not sure who steps forward. Maybe we both do. Either way, we're soon smooched up against each other, my chest plastered to her breasts. And damned if they don't feel every bit as good as I've been imagining.

As I drop my head, she lifts herself on tiptoes and our lips clash. There's nothing gentle about the kiss. It's primal, urgent, and wonderful. None of the models or influencers I've dated over the years have had me as close to losing it as Donna does now.

There's something about this woman that does me in, but in a good way, a wonderful way. Her lips part on a sigh, and I plunge my tongue into her sweet mouth. If I could inhale her, I would.

Her tongue tangling with mine and her hands all over my body, says the desire is returned, and then some. This can't be happening? This can't happen? There's a rational corner of my mind that tells me this is all-sorts of wrong.

I wrench my lips free of hers, hoping for sanity to return. It's a long shot with me still busy caressing her full breasts. How the hell did I miss that? Oh, that's right, my entire world was focused on her mouth, her lips.

I stop tugging her nipples like they're hot, which they are, and take a big step back to give us both some distance. "Right, ah hem, I'll leave you to it."

I'm not apologizing, because I'm not sorry. Also, I wasn't alone in moving things along.

However, I've already been too familiar with this woman. It can't go further, not without screwing things up right royally. Donna is not like the women I date back east.

I shut my bedroom door with a loud bang, signaling to myself, as much as her, that this is over. I'm about to climb back into bed when I remember the state of my boxers and my cock.

Looks like I need that cold shower, after all.

SEVEN

DONNA

Awkward doesn't describe the following morning, and it takes every bit of my self-control not to give Liam the once over.

Aware of what's under that sharp suit, and how good his lips and hands had felt last night, I can think of nothing else. He doesn't appear to be having any trouble acting like nothing happened.

Perhaps to him it was nothing. Maybe I should follow his lead on that, because by rights nothing should happen. Bryan will move on. I'll head back to San Francisco and get myself a decent job, and life will continue.

It's something that plays on repeat at the back of my mind as I start my morning shift. Rather than have Liam overseeing my training, I'm joined by Vera, an older woman, who's as thin as she is cold.

However, she's a model of efficiency, and I appreciate her forthright manner with the ins and outs of the position. I'm also retaining more information now that I'm no longer in a constant state of arousal.

It's getting close to the end of my shift when Vera spots Liam on the other side of the casino. "He's a smooth one, he is, but you'd know all about that, wouldn't you?" Her sideways glance and sly grin have alarm bells ringing.

"What do you mean?"

So far as I'm aware, no-one knows I'm staying upstairs. Liam and Wyatt had made sure of that. I've even got a key card, and it's not like there aren't other suites on the same floor. I could just as well be staying in one of them.

Eventually Vera takes pity on me. "You haven't seen them, have you?"

"Seen what?"

After a furtive look around, she reaches into the pocket of her uniform and slides her phone out. We both know this is against casino rules, but there isn't a chance I'm saying anything.

I'm equally surprised when she opens Facebook. A bit of scrolling and she finds the post she's after on a local community page. When she opens it, I'm glad I'm sitting down.

There are a series of photos of me and Liam outside my apartment, a few from during the day, then a flurry after dark.

While the photos are poor quality, it's easy enough to see I'm as good as naked but for a man's suit jacket. With Liam next to me in his shirt sleeves, you don't need to be a rocket scientist to deduce the jacket is his.

More damning are the photos taken after dark, when Liam had helped me move out of that awful apartment. I think back, but can't recall anyone being around.

I'm wondering who, how or what, when Vera opens the profile of the person who'd originally posted the images. I instantly recognize my sleazy neighbor. Damn it.

If those shots go viral not only will Liam's dad be furious with him, there's a chance Bryan might see them. "Oh, crap."

A raised eyebrow from Vera, and I blurt out. "It's not what it looks like, honestly."

I then ramble on about what lead up to my being in a state of undress. Liam carrying my suitcases as we'd left later in the day isn't as easy to explain. In the end, I out-and-out lie, saying he'd helped me move into another apartment.

While I hate lying, Liam had stressed the importance of keeping quiet about my staying upstairs. It was something I'd crossed my heart over, and so I wasn't going back on my word, especially not after all his help.

After my shift ends, I race upstairs via an indirect route, hoping to find him in the suite. The sooner he knows about those photos, the quicker he can start damage control. Unfortunately, he's not there, and my calls to him go unanswered.

I'm pacing back and forth in the living area when he enters the suite. He's not wearing his suit, but he is dressed. Well, kind of, with his track pants sitting low on his hips, a sweaty t-shirt clinging to his chiseled torso.

Damn it, his six-pack looks even better than it had felt last night. Overawed by how gorgeous he is, I don't initially spot that he appears on edge.

Could it be he's already seen those photos online, and he thinks I haven't?

After running his hands through his hair, he leans against the kitchen island, his arms folded tight. His posture alone says the news isn't good, so I drop into the depths of a couch. A moment later, I'm hugging one of the many cushions to my chest.

The images have indeed gone viral, with his father having already left messages berating him for being an idiot.

And if that wasn't bad enough, Wyatt has reported a man had already called asking to be put through to Donna Wilder's room. Thankfully, the operator didn't have anyone checked in under that name.

After hearing this snippet, there isn't a chance I can remain seated. While I'm outwardly quiet, inside I'm screaming.

"Ah, Donna, move away from the windows."

I stop and look across the room at him? "What? Why?"

He stares at the ceiling fixedly for a second or two, before giving me the same level of scrutiny. His expression is a mix of exasperation and guilt.

"Now that those photos are out there, it's only a matter of time before..."

He doesn't need to say anything else. I'm familiar enough with the gossip sites to know how these things go.

"Oh, hecking heck!" I drop to my hands and knees before scrambling to get away from the windows. "What if I'm too late? What if they've got a photo of me up here in your suite? What will people think?"

Liam helps me to my feet, leaving his hands on my upper arms after doing so. "If we want to manage how people perceive us, then we need to take control."

He guides onto a barstool before skewering me with his piercing gaze. When he tells me his plan, I'm lost for words, unless, "uh, uh, uh," counts.

LIAM

Donna stares agape at my suggestion. I've sprung it on her, but to me it makes sense. At least it had when I was running myself into the ground on the treadmill.

I stop my back and forth of the kitchen, long enough to eyeball her.

"Donna, admit that it makes sense. It'll get dad and Madeline off my back and Bryan off yours."

"But what about my folks? They'll think I'm out of my mind if I suddenly tell them I'm engaged. Especially when it's to someone they don't even know."

"I'll admit that's not great. But for it to work, people need to believe it's for real, if unexpected."

On seeing she's starting to waiver, I pull out the big guns.

"Would you rather Bryan heard you were engaged to me? Or would you rather he knew you were still single, and where to find you? Even if he doesn't know you're staying at the hotel, he still knows you're in Coogan's Break."

I make sure our eyes have locked before continuing. "What if he comes after you? You can't hide forever."

The following morning, I find Donna at the breakfast bar, in her staff uniform, a large cup of coffee, all that sits in front of her. It's hardly the right sort of breakfast for the day I've got planned. That's if she's going full-in, although her being dressed for work says otherwise.

"Did you think about my proposal?" Hell, I'm making it sound more like a business deal than ever. Even though that's what it is, it still doesn't feel right.

Instead of answering me, she continues staring into her coffee as though it's a crystal ball, and the answers lie there.

"Trust me on this, Donna. We're better using the gossip sites to our advantage, and not the other way around."

She gets to her feet and starts toward the floor-to-ceiling windows. Then, on realizing what she's doing, she comes to an abrupt stop.

"Can I at least think about it?"

I nod my acceptance. "You can, but don't take too long. If they're out there, it's only a matter of time until they catch up with us."

"But surely we're safe in the hotel, aren't we?"

I blink rapidly before tipping my head to the side in acknowledgement. "By rights we should be, but those guys will go to any lengths to get an exclusive. False IDs, disguises, telephoto lenses, the list goes on. Hell, they've even smashed windows to catch up with me in the past."

The haunted look in her eyes has me longing to drag her into my arms and hold her tight until the trembles subside. But I don't, knowing full-well I won't be able to stop at that level of comfort.

"Donna, I've spoken to Wyatt, and he's said you can help with the monitors this morning. It'll be safer than you working a cashier shift. We can use the service elevator."

"Okay. I'll just grab my purse and key card. Can you show me where I'll be working?"

"Absolutely. I'll let Wyatt know we're on our way."

She's soon back at my side, her purse hanging from her shoulder. The moment I swing the door wide and stand back so Donna can lead the way, I know we've got problems.

We're welcomed by dozens of bright flashes, which are closely followed by the thunder of feet. Blinded as I've been, I can't even see which direction the photographer—or was that photographers—went in.

Next to me, Donna is likewise stunned, leaving it to me to pull her back into the room and slam the door shut using one of my feet.

It's too late, of course, far too late.

We've no longer got the luxury of her taking her time to decide about us faking a relationship. We need to act, and fast.

EIGHT

DONNA

Liam and I stand rooted to the spot, although not for long. I've even managed to re-open the door when he steps forward and puts his full weight against it, slamming it shut.

"I wouldn't be in a hurry to go out there if I were you."

His comment has me peering through the peephole in the door. I can't see any photographers, although they could stand out of sight further along.

I give up trying and instead spin to face him. "We're trapped in here? What about my job?"

"No, we're not trapped here! Well, not exactly. Hang on, just give me a second." He's soon got his phone and hits a pre-programmed number. "Wyatt, we've got a situation."

Liam then wanders off down the hall to his bedroom, and I miss the rest of what he says to his head of security. It hadn't helped that he'd dropped his voice to be not much above a whisper while still within hearing distance.

If I wasn't nervous before, I am now. I was so close to being able to move back to San Francisco, and be mercifully free of Bryan. Who knows where I'll be safe after this?

Seattle or even Chicago could work, with both cities big enough to allow me to hide from my narcissistic ex.

At least until he moves on. Hadn't he talked about how cute he'd found the accountant who started a few months before I left? I hope he doesn't end up dating the poor woman.

She's curvy like I am, meaning it will only be a matter of time before Bryan starts in on her self-esteem, exactly as he had with me.

No-one deserves to be shamed like that.

I'm close to walking to my bedroom and packing when there's a discreet knock on the door. I don't so much as have time to get my eye up to the peephole before Liam is at my side.

After a quick spy to see who's out there, he opens the door, although only enough for Wyatt to slip inside the suite. He also makes sure I stay hidden behind the slab of wood.

It's Wyatt who suggests we move to the home cinema, a room I didn't even know existed. The main thing in its favor being that there are no windows.

In the past, we'd have been safe simply being on one of the upper floors. However, the advances in drone technology had taken care of that.

"It's not good news. I'm sorry." Wyatt holds his fist out before opening his fingers so Liam and I can see the contents.

It used to be a camera, a tiny camera. It's no longer operable, thanks to apparently being introduced to the heel of Wyatt's boot. He drops the remnants of the small device on a nearby table before looking at me.

"That's how they knew you were staying with Liam." He then looks at Liam, his face a picture of apology. "Sorry, they've probably been in place since you took up residence."

I drop onto the nearest squishy couch to digest the information. Then I sit upright. "Can't we just tell them I'm the housekeeper and that's why Liam was helping me the other night?"

I wave in Liam's general direction before gesturing at my curves like some game show hostess. "Liam would never be romantically involved with someone like me. Not in a million years."

Liam has already shaken his head when Wyatt speaks. "That's true. No offense, Donna, but you're different to..."

He doesn't get any further, with Liam slamming his hand down on Wyatt's shoulder. "Wyatt, can you get a team up here to sweep the rest of the floor? Make it government level to ensure we pick up on anything, no matter how small."

LIAM

Back out in the living area, I can tell my words have shocked Donna. She's not used to being in the public eye as I am.

I've learned the hard way that you can't be too careful. And yet I've dropped my guard since moving here. Grown soft, and made myself an easy target.

And that might cost both of us. Unless...

"Donna, there's still plan A." I retrieve the small gift bag Wyatt had dropped on the kitchen island when he'd first arrived. Opening the top wide, I can see he's done as I asked.

As I delve inside the bag and take hold of the small box nestled in the bottom, I've got mixed emotions. I always thought when I asked a woman to marry me, it would be for real.

A second later, I've retrieved the box and opened it. I then hold it out for Donna to see. "You wouldn't be stuck with me forever, only as long as it takes for things to cool down."

She stares wide-eyed at the enormous solitaire. "Goodness, didn't they have anything bigger?"

"Hey, I'm with you on this, but the bigger and shinier it is, the more likely it'll show up in photographs. We don't want anyone mistaking it for a friendship ring."

Donna plucks the monster solitaire from the padded box and slides it on her ring finger, showing it to be a perfect fit. Finally, something is in our favor.

"It's not what I would usually wear, but I can see why you chose it. Well, you didn't choose it, that is Wyatt did, but you know what I mean..."

After this nervous chatter, I'm expecting her to remove the solitaire and put it back in the box, but she does neither. Instead, she smiles at me, although even I can see it's forced.

"Okay, let's do this." She then holds her hand out and makes a show of admiring the ostentatious ring. "If there's one thing I know from working in marketing, it's that we need to advertise the heck out of this!"

She then carefully examines her nails. "But before that can happen, I'll need a manicure." A quick glance at her uniform and she adds, "Plus, I'll need some of my clothes from San Francisco."

In the end, I allow Donna to call her mom and explain the situation. She's vouched for her parent's ability to remain tight-lipped, with them as keen to see the back of Bryan as Donna herself.

It also means her mom can grab everything Donna needs from her wardrobe and put it in a suitcase to be collected by a courier. With the suitcase not due to be delivered until the following morning, we'll be spending the evening hunkered down in the suite.

Strange, but at one time I'd have dreaded the idea of a night in, whereas I now look forward to it. Hah, who am I kidding? It's who I'll be spending it with that I'm looking forward to.

After a room-service dinner, I find myself next to Donna on one of the large couches that forms the front row of the home cinema. Because it mostly comprises large poufs, it's perfect for lounging on, and other horizontal activities, if the fancy takes you.

On peeking sideways at Donna in her skin-tight jeans and tank top, the fancy takes me in a big way. Right from the get-go, this woman's curves have called to me. It's something that has me struggling to get comfortable.

Strange, because as Wyatt had been about to point out when I shut him up, she's not my usual model and perhaps this is part of the appeal.

Despite giving it my best shot, my mind is soon crammed with images of Donna naked, and spread out on the cushions that we're leaning back on.

Movie, what movie? I doubt I could tell you what it's about if I tried.

She's pushing herself upright to grab more popcorn when her hand slips between the cushions and she tumbles sideways. With her now plastered all over my chest, it's as if she's read my mind. The only thing different from my fevered imaginings is that we're still clothed.

It's when she tips her head back and flashes those deep, pansy eyes of hers at me. I stop fighting it. Thankfully, I'm not alone in feeling this way.

"Come here, you." I drag her up my chest until her breath tickles my lips. A moment later, our breath mingles as I ravage her lips with mine. Sanity rears its ugly head sooner than I'd have liked, and I pull back.

However, Donna is having none of it. "For us to pull off this deception, we need to be comfortable in each other's presence."

She makes a good point, but after kissing her again, I lift my head so I can gauge her reaction to my words. "Just how comfortable are we talking here?"

Rather than answer, she reaches across me and grabs the room's remote. A moment later, she kills the movie. The last thing I see before darkness descends on the room is her smile.

It's full of enough promise that my cock is screaming for release. To my mind, the more I'm buried in her lush depths when that happens, the better.

NINE

DONNA

I honestly hadn't expected it to get so dark when I hit the big red control button on the remote. Of course, now I'm welcoming it.

How often in the past had sex felt awkward because I was busy trying to hide my curves? That'd certainly be the case if the lights were on and Liam could see every inch of me.

Instead, I relish the anonymity, making quick work of shedding my jeans and top. When I rejoin Liam on the couch, I'm the one who gets the surprise, with him already down to his boxers.

It doesn't take me long to know he's very pleased to see me. Sure, I'd got a glimpse last night when I'd doused him with my glass of water. However, that pales when compared to his length being jammed hard against my hip.

When I graze his chest with that knuckle-duster of a fake engagement ring, his gasp stills me. "Perhaps I should take it off. I might hurt you."

In answer he kisses me like our lives depend on it, leaving me breathless and eager for more, so much more.

"No, I like the idea of you wearing it when I bury myself in you."

Wow, if I thought my panties were damp before, that's nothing compared to now. How can his words alone have my body crying out for release?

Emboldened by this, and the welcoming dark, I slide a finger inside the elastic of his boxers and run it back and forth. It would appear I'm not the only one on edge, with him finding this out for himself when he returns the favor.

My panties being smaller than his boxers means he has no trouble hitting me exactly where he wants to. My nerve endings sing their approval, while I moan mine.

"You like that, do you?"

I nod emphatically before realizing he can't see me. This makes me aware that I rarely talk during sex. Never asking for what I want, or saying what I like. At least that was how it was with Bryan, at his insistence. What a fool I'd been.

To bleach all thoughts of that loser from my brain, I say the first thing that comes to my mind. "I love it. Maybe you could..." Then I lose my nerve.

"Maybe I could what, Donna?"

Liam slides his fingers even deeper inside my panties, his hand touching me right where I didn't know I needed it. There's nothing I can do to stop my gasp of pure pleasure.

It doesn't matter that our relationship is a farce; it'll still hurt when the time comes for our charade to end. Until then, I'm making the most of it. Reality can wait.

It's with this thought in mind that I allow Liam to remove my bra and panties. When his lips close first over one nipple, and then the other, my ability to think deserts me.

Instead, I allow the senses I have left to rule me as Liam makes me his.

When he slides inside me, stretching and filling me perfectly, I'm glad of the dark. Who knew what he'd make of my tears? I don't even know what to make of them myself.

Are they tears of sorrow at all that wasted time with my ex?

Tears of joy at my being Liam's, even if only for the sake of convenience?

Or are they tears of wonder at how a man I barely know can touch my soul?

I've not decided when a gentle climax sweeps through me, making Liam my sole focus.

There's nothing gentle about the next climax, when it first rocks my world, and then his. I fall asleep tucked up in his arms, a gentle smile on my face.

I'll deal with the fall-out in the morning.

LIAM

On waking the following morning, I'm rock hard, painfully so. At least I think it's the morning. It's difficult to tell with it being pitch black.

There's nothing unusual about the erection. What is unusual is that I'm not alone as I have been for the past three months. Instead, Donna lies tight up against my side and damned if she doesn't feel as good now as she had last night.

As I run my hands over her lush form, she leans in to meet me, offering her body up as the finest banquet. When she says my name on a sigh, it's all the invitation I need.

I slide my hand into the curls at the apex of her thighs, searching for that small bundle of nerves. The one that will have her shaking with her need for me as no woman before.

We're kidding ourselves if we think this is necessary to be comfortable enough to fool the photographers. It's already more than that for me, so much more.

I'm not as relaxed as I'm making out. I've deliberately avoided getting close to a woman after dad started putting the hard word on me to settle down.

A part of me worries that if I hurry the process, I'll end up a serial divorcee, like him. Even if I don't consider myself ready for marriage just yet, I still know what I want.

I want what my parents had before mom passed when I was fifteen.

It's my refusal to settle for anything less that has me milking the playboy lifestyle for all that it's worth. I've been playing a part of sorts, with this brought home in a big way after just one night with Donna.

There'd been no pretense on my part last night, and I'm sure it had been the same for her. Unable to see her tears, I'd still felt them on my cheek when I kissed her. Hell, it was all I could do not to join her.

I don't get to think on it any further when Donna wraps her legs around me, both of us making the most of this lazy morning sex. At least that's how it starts out, but it soon transforms into something that has our antics of the night before anemic in comparison.

I hold out as long as I can, but when Donna tightens around my length, there's nothing I can do to stop from emptying myself into her.

Whilst I'd always pulled out in a timely manner last night, this morning, part of me is glad I didn't. If I'm being honest with myself, I doubt I could have if I'd tried.

Beneath me, Donna stills and her breathing hitches. "Ah, Liam, I'm not on the pill. I stopped taking it when I broke up with Bryan."

There's nothing I can do to stop my heart from speeding up. However, it's not from fear, it's from joy. Now all I need to do is convince Donna that if she falls pregnant, she'll hear no complaints from me.

I've never been surer of anything in my life.

Whereas a couple of months back, the thought of being a dad would have had me panicking. That's no longer the case.

It's something that has me laughing with delight. I'm still laughing when my hand closes over the main room remote and I turn the lights on.

Donna looks every bit as good as I've imagined since she plunged the room into darkness last night. Forget that. She looks a lot better. The only thing that doesn't sit well with me is her obvious worry.

"Donna, it'll be alright. And if you are pregnant, then I'll stand by you." A glance at her left hand and I see the engagement ring is missing. I find it soon enough, sitting in the empty popcorn bowl on the coffee table in front of us.

After retrieving it, I get down on one knee, ignoring the fact that I'm naked as the day I was born. "Donna, would you do me the honor of accepting my hand in marriage?"

As solemn as I've been, she bursts out laughing, thinking I'm pretending to lighten the atmosphere.

And yet, nothing could be further from the truth. When I was growing up, mom and dad always told of how they knew they were right for each other, even before they'd spoken.

It would seem this rotten apple doesn't fall far from the tree.

DONNA

After showering with Liam, a sudsy, fun experience, I'm once more in my bedroom, wandering back and forth. With him having disappeared off downstairs, I'm at a loss what to do with myself.

Liam emptying his seed inside me this morning has brought our carefully curated world crashing down.

What if I am pregnant? What then? A quick check of the app on my phone and I see I'm mid-cycle. If ever there was a time to slip up with protection, then this isn't it.

My steps slow until I come to a complete stop.

Would it be unwanted, though? Maybe for Liam, but I've wanted to be a mom since I held my first doll. Rather than dragging it around by one arm like most kids, I'd tuck it up safely in the bassinet I'd insisted my parents buy.

Nothing was too good for Fifi.

It's strange that the thought of an unwanted pregnancy doesn't seem to bother Liam as I'd expected. Doubtless, this is because he wouldn't be the one left holding the baby. While he's said he'll stand by me, that'll be financially.

There'll be no-one to help when the child is sick, or hurt, or simply sad that their dad isn't around.

I'm close to tears when Liam returns, carrying a large suitcase that I recognize as belonging to my dad. My clothes from home! After dropping the suitcase on the end of my bed, rather than leaving, he takes a seat in the club chair in the room's corner.

He then gestures toward the suitcase before saying, "Let's see what we've got to play with."

I stare at him, unmoving. He wants to play dress-up when my life is as good as over? Seriously?

"Donna, there's nothing we can do about it. And anyway, the chances of you falling pregnant after one slip are negligible. You know that, right?"

As practical as his words have been, my hands come to rest protectively across my tummy. Meanwhile, he holds his hands up, defensively.

"That's not what I meant, DeeDee. Whatever you decide, I'll stand by you."

My hands drop to my side, my brows knotted in confusion. "Did you just call me DeeDee?"

"Yeah, is that okay? It's what your folks put on the luggage tag. I figured if we were trying to act like we're close, that it made sense."

What follows is a fashion parade of sorts, with me becoming ever more confident at stripping off in front of Liam. He approves of all the dresses I got my mom to pack, except for one.

He leans forward in his chair after my impromptu catwalk. "Hell's teeth, there's no way you're wearing that out in public!"

I march into the bathroom to make use of the full-length mirror on the back of the door.

"What's wrong with it?" I shout through the partially closed door. "It looks okay to me!"

His head appears around the door, making me jump. I hadn't heard him walking across the carpeted room. "There's nothing wrong with it. It's more that it'd have any red-blooded man hard as rock a second after he saw you in it."

My smile fades. The shimmering silver dress is one of my favorites. The neckline plunges, while the crossover front of the skirt allows me to flash a modest amount of thigh when I walk.

I'd had it made for an awards ceremony and always felt like a million bucks in it. "I thought it would be the perfect foil for that monster ring that you're insisting I wear."

Liam closes his eyes briefly before breathing out. "Damn it, you're right. If we want people believing in *us*, then the flashier we are, the better."

Even with him agreeing to me wearing the dress on our first official date, he's not happy about it. Strange, but when Bryan had behaved that way, all I'd felt was controlled.

Whereas, with Liam, I kinda like that he doesn't want other men checking me out.

LIAM

As we walk out of the elevator and into reception, I've never felt as conspicuous as I do right now. Perhaps this is down to our *fake* date being more real to me than any of the actual dates I've been on in the past.

Could this be because Donna is more real than any of the women I've dated before?

The biggest shock had been when she'd exited her bedroom in that stunning silver dress. If I'd thought she was a knockout when she was giving her impromptu fashion parade earlier today, it's nothing compared to now.

Her makeup is flawless, her hair falls in luscious brunette waves down her back, and her skin glows. On her giving me a twirl, it had been all I could do not to scoop her up and head for my bedroom. I'd rather be spending a leisurely evening making love to her than sticking down here.

Never have I craved a woman as I crave Donna.

We've not taken half-a-dozen steps when murmured conversations spring up all over the reception area. That we're *together* is confirmed by us holding hands. On my bringing her hand up to my lips and kissing her knuckles, all hell breaks loose.

There's no missing that ring.

Half-a-dozen guys rush us, cameras flashing, and I give Donna's hand a reassuring squeeze, in hopes this will stop her from losing it.

I have to give her credit, though. Rather than step back as many women would, she holds her ground. She even stiffens her back.

Proud, confident, and all mine.

. . .

We're enjoying a romantic dessert on the restaurant's patio when I spot a photographer perched in a nearby tree. Because they'd been limited to what shots they could get of us in reception, they're getting desperate.

"Don't look now, but we've got company at three o'clock." I'm pleased I'd warned Donna this would happen, with her not tempted to check it out.

Instead, she smiles brightly, her eyes sparkling. "Let's give them a show, then."

She delicately selects a raspberry off the top of her dessert and holds the spoon out to me. That she's done so left-handed in order to flash the bling has her hand wobbling, and so I take her hand in mine.

There's nothing of the make-believe about Donna's reaction when I suck the raspberry off the end of the spoon. Her pupils dilate and her breathing catches.

If I was a betting man, I'd say her panties were damp by now.

Even thinking about this has my cock straining against my suit pants. It's time to level the playing field. After dipping my finger into the chocolate mousse I'd ordered, I hold it out for her.

There's no missing the movement coming from that tree, although I no longer give a damn about the photographer. All I'm interested in is Donna's arousal, because when we get back upstairs, I'm making the most of it.

That's if I make it that far. When Donna's lips close around the end of my finger and her tongue swirls about, supposedly searching for chocolate mousse, I come close to losing it.

A pointed cough from a nearby table says it's time to get the hell out of here. "Baby, we need to leave now. Unless you want pictures of me going down on you splattered all over the internet?"

When she makes sense of what I've said, she drops her spoon with a clatter that has everyone staring at us. She's on her feet before I've done likewise.

Luckily for both of us, there's no need to pay on the way out. The elevator doors are still closing when I claim her lips, a flash from outside barely registering.

We don't sleep late the following morning, both eager to continue exploring each other as intimately as possible.

The more I make love to this woman, the better it gets. And yet, there's something about our closeness that has me on edge. It's not supposed to be this easy, is it?

It's not even eight o'clock when my phone pings. With Donna snug up against my side, I grab my phone and hold it up so she can see as I scroll through the notifications.

Her eyes widen as she realizes just how many photos there are of the two of us. I also notice how good we look together, laughing and joking, both of us obviously so at ease.

And there was nothing make-believe about that.

Donna lays her hand on my chest, her fingers splayed wide. "Heck, so fast. I wasn't expecting it to be this fast."

"Yep, even the old man will know about it by now, and your ex, with any luck. Are you okay with this?"

She's not answered when my phone rings. It's my dad, and he's furious. He's mad as hell that I've screwed up his plans for my marriage to Madeline Olsen, and that I've shackled myself to some 'nobody' without his approval.

How dare he?!

"Dad, did you ask for my approval with wives two, three and four? No, you didn't. I'll call you back when you've cooled down." I end the call and switch my phone off before turning to Donna and kissing her softly on the forehead.

"One down, one to go."

Even as I'm saying this, my heart isn't in it. For me, our engagement is no longer about getting dad off my back. Every minute I spend with this wonderful woman has me wishing it was for real.

The only thing I don't know is whether Donna feels the same way.

It's nearly three weeks before I find out.

ELEVEN

DONNA

We're downstairs having lunch, when I receive a text from my mom about Bryan. On handing the phone over so Liam can read it for himself, my hands are shaking.

Being from an older generation, there's no text speak in my mom's message and so he has to swipe up several times before he's able to read the whole thing.

"I guess that makes us two-for-two, Liam." I'm unable to keep the disappointment out of my voice, with this last reason for our engagement now removed. "We can break up tonight if you like."

"Not so fast. Do you know if you're ah, em?" Liam stares pointedly at my tummy to confirm what he's referring to.

Notwithstanding that one slip-up, we've been careful to use protection ever since. No, the chances of my being pregnant are slim. And yet, I can't believe how much I want this with him.

It's something that has me taking my phone out of my evening purse to check my menstrual app. It's the first time I've looked at it since working out the timing of our unprotected sex.

"Ah, I might be a little late." On Liam raising an eyebrow, I'm quick to add. "Only a week," keeping the *maybe two* to myself.

We're waiting on our coffees when Liam phones Wyatt and instructs him to raid the supply cupboard on our behalf. While the pregnancy tests are available for purchase at the hotel's gift shop, there isn't a chance we're risking that. There are still too many photographers hanging around.

Sure enough, by the time we've finished lunch and made it back up to the suite, there's a small package sitting on the kitchen counter.

"I'll, ah, just be a moment." Actually, I might be more than that, as this is the first time I've ever completed one of these tests. Without another word, I grab the test and head for my bedroom and, more particularly, the bathroom.

Not ten minutes have passed when I sit on the edge of the bath, staring at the results. Devastated doesn't describe how I feel. I should be relieved, but I'm not.

It didn't matter that I'd had a little under a month to get used to the idea of being pregnant with Liam's child. The idea had taken root. And now I've got nothing, not even a reason to stick around.

I'm still wondering how I'll tell him when there's a gentle knock on the bathroom door. "Donna, are you okay?" I take solace when he asks me if I'm okay, and not what the result is.

Rather than call out, I stand, open the door and hand the test to him. There's no missing the single blue line that shows it's a negative result.

"Oh, that's..." He seems to search for the right words. If I didn't know better, I'd think he was as disappointed as I am.

It's only when he pulls me in for a tight embrace that the tears I've been holding back are free to stream down my face. I do my best to hide them from Liam, without luck.

"Hey, hey, it'll be okay." His smile as he gently strokes my back is half-hearted. "You can get back to your life now. Can't you?"

I sniffle into the tissue I've been holding onto like a lifeline before nodding. Funny, but a few months back and I'd have been well on the way to packing by now. These days my preference is to stick around.

"And you, I suppose you'll be moving back to the east coast to manage another of the family's hotels?"

Knowing this is what he wants, I'm not surprised when Liam drops the pregnancy test in the wastebasket. However, when he then reaches out to take my hand, I'm in the dark.

That is right until he slowly removes the large engagement ring.

I guess that's it then. If I thought not being pregnant was upsetting, it's nothing compared to my pretend engagement being over. A glimpse at my hand, and the shock of not seeing that huge sparkler, really hits home.

LIAM

After removing the large engagement ring, I shove it in my pocket and then drag Donna back into a tight embrace.

If I'd had any doubts about how she felt about me, those have been obliterated. The sobs wracking her body tell me this, and more.

After stepping back from our embrace, I allow my gaze to rest on her face. This is definitely one of those moments in life where I don't want to miss a thing. It's also one of the scariest, and yet I find myself at peace, as never.

"Donna," I put my hand in my other pocket, my fingers closing around the small box nestled there. I then drop to one knee before opening the lid and holding it up for her inspection. "Would you do me the honor of becoming my wife?"

And then I stop breathing. While I *think* I know what her feelings are toward me, you can never be sure. She's her own woman, and with her only impediment to returning to her previous life, now gone, nothing's assured.

She'd said often enough how much she missed city life. And yet, she'd also seemed to enjoy the quiet life at Coogan's Break. At least once, the photographers had tired of capturing the same images all the time.

"I ..."

With anything else jammed in her throat, her acceptance isn't looking likely.

However, when she holds her left hand out, I've got my answer. My hands are shaking as much as hers when I slide the smaller solitaire into place. However, on leaning forward and kissing her knuckles, my earlier nerves are gone.

I jump to my feet and sweep her into an embrace. A moment later, her feet leave the ground, and I start back for my room. The bed there is larger and more conducive to the future Mrs. Maddigan and I getting to know each other even better.

This takes a couple of days, with us living on room service and to hell with all those Instagram worthy moments. This is about us, not the publicity.

I gaze at my beautiful fiancé, glorying in her lush curves as she straddles me, my cock buried balls-deep in her slick depths.

And yet, it's still not enough

Sure enough, when she rocks back and forth, grinding her mons hard against me, I come close to losing it. "Not yet, baby. Not yet. I want us to see stars."

"I don't think ... I don't think I can wait." Donna follows this up by lifting herself almost free of my length, and sliding down again.

Her muscles clenching around my length as the climax takes her, is enough to shove me over the edge, and I fill her with my seed. These days it's bareback all the way for us. "Hell's teeth, woman, is it possible for me to love you any more than I already do?"

Donna laughs with delight. "Oh baby, I'll fight you for the right to love you more than you love me." After she flops down on the bed next to me, we roll onto our sides to face each other.

No words are necessary with us grinning at each other, our hearts bursting with love and the knowledge the future is bright.

EPILOGUE

DONNA

Next to Liam on the front steps of Maddies, the newest hotel in Coogan's Break, I marvel at how my life has changed.

I'm no longer worried about Bryan popping up. I'm engaged to be married, and Liam and I are about to celebrate our first baby.

Maddies will be our first-born, with Liam and me equal partners in the enterprise.

I've not done much more than lean into his side reassuringly when the first car comes to a stop at the bottom of the steps. It's the mayor, and our official guest of honor.

A week ago, I didn't think we'd make it. Back then, plumbers, electricians, and general contractors were still swarming over the place like ants. It's taken a lot of blood, sweat, and tears to knock one of the oldest mansions in town into shape, but it's been worth it.

These days, the old girl is as sharp as the day the original builders finished work. What had been home to one of the town's founders, and a mining magnate, is now a twelve-room boutique hotel.

Even though Liam no longer works for his dad, they are on speaking terms. Heck, the old man has even grudgingly accepted me into the family, something Liam and I thought would never happen.

I'm hoping after tonight that things will only get better. It's just a shame his father had to be out of the country tonight, of all nights.

I give Liam's hand another squeeze. "Earth to Liam."

"Hah, sorry, I was just thinking. Who'd have thought when I spotted you on that security monitor that just over a year later we'd be here?"

"And you're okay with that?" I can't help but ask. I often pinch myself, worried my life with this man is all a dream. And it is, although not in an imaginary sense.

The rest of the evening passes in a blur, with me grateful I'm not hosting the event on my own. My folks have been brilliant, about this, and everything really. No-one could have been more thrilled than they were when they found out the fake engagement had morphed into reality.

My parents having retired for the night; Liam and I are left to wave goodbye to the last guests.

"Well, Mr. Maddigan, we're on our way. I say we celebrate by christening the honeymoon suite."

I drop his hand, spin and start running before he's had time to process my words.

LIAM

My gorgeous fiancé hasn't even made it to the second floor when I'm all over her. After catching her around the waist, I press her back into the wall and claim her lips in a searing kiss.

My hands then close around her sumptuous breasts with her nipples, getting the attention they've been begging for all night.

"Liam!" she bats my hands away. "My parents!"

I guffaw loudly. "...are in a room down the back, and that has a very solid wooden door."

She, however, isn't buying it. "Come on, I don't want to make love on the staircase." She then slips out of my embrace before once again running up the stairs.

This time, I let her have her way. It isn't as if I don't know where she's heading. I therefore take my time. Each tread increases the anticipation of what waits for me. By the time I reach the top floor, my cock is like a piece of finely veined marble, ready to claim my goddess.

On entering the room, I'm brought up short, with Donna nowhere in sight. I check the bathroom, but she's not in there either. It's only when I step out onto the small balcony that fronts the room that I find her.

She's gloriously naked, leaning over the top of the balcony, her peach of an ass glowing in the moonlight. To the untrained observer, you'd think she was like that to take in the view. I'm not untrained.

In short order, I'm as naked as my girl, walking up behind her and gripping her warm cheeks. "Lean forward baby. Haven't I always said the view up here is spectacular? Let me make it even better for you."

As we lie back on the suite's Texas King, Donna's breathing still isn't under control. I'm kinda breathless myself. "I told you that view was something else."

Donna blows out through pursed lips. "You've got that right, and then some."

She then rolls away from me so she can grab something out of the nightstand on her side of the bed. After she hands it to me, I take a second to make sense of it.

"You?"

She nods tentatively, as if unsure of how I'll react. All hesitancy vanishes after I toss the pregnancy test over my shoulder and drag her into my arms with a loud whoop.

Only when we pull apart, do I rest my hand on her tummy. Never in a million years could I have believed I could be so happy after being so bereft. Until Donna stumbled into my life, it had been bleak, for all those gossip sites said otherwise.

I brush her hair back from her forehead. "We haven't set a date for the wedding, but what about in the next month? I know dad will be around then."

Donna's infectious squeal of pure joy is the answer I've been wishing for.

𝕿𝕽𝕬𝖁𝕰𝕷

If you need a break, then you can't go past Maddies by The Sea. This five star boutique hotel is the second from Liam and Donna Maddigan.

Small and intimate, it's both perfect if you're on honeymoon, or simply need a break from city life.

It isn't the only thing the couple are celebrating, with the arrival of their third child due any day now.

THANK YOU

If you've enjoyed this story, we'd be thrilled if you could take the time to give it a review on your favorite retailer. These not only give authors feedback, but they allow other readers to see if the book might appeal to them. Either way, happy reading.

ALL ABOUT HOPE

Hope believes everyone deserves love, especially curvy girls. She also likes to believe there's a welcoming town like Coogan's Break for all of us. A place where the girls are curvy and the guys hotter than hell, where opposites attract, and love is steamy and fast.

www.papersparrowsnest.com